COUNTER STRIKE

DAVID BRUNS

J.R. OLSON

SEVERN RIVER

PUBLISHING

ALSO BY BRUNS AND OLSON

The Command and Control Series

Command and Control

Counter Strike

Order of Battle

Threat Axis

Covert Action

Never miss a new release! Sign up to receive exclusive updates from authors Bruns and Olson.

severnriverbooks.com/series/command-and-control

Eternal Father, strong to save,
Whose arm hath bound the restless wave,
Who bidd'st the mighty ocean deep
Its own appointed limits keep,
O hear us when we cry to thee
For those in peril on the sea.

—The Navy Hymn

1

The White House Situation Room smelled of tense bodies and stale coffee. The sharp tang of disinfectant from the cleaning crews that came through every eight hours had long since dissipated.

Don Riley, Director of the CIA Emerging Threats Group, stood at the lectern at the head of the room watching the live feed from a high-altitude surveillance asset over the South China Sea. The weather in and around the Strait of Taiwan in February could be fickle, but they had excellent viewing conditions for the final hours of the People's Liberation Army annual war games.

The view screen showed dozens of Chinese warships. Don counted three aircraft carriers, at least fifteen escorts of various classes, amphibious landing ships, and a handful of surfaced submarines.

And they were all headed in one direction: back to port.

Just a few days ago, Riley had made the bold prediction that the world-wide attacks on the United States over the last twelve months had been nothing more than an elaborate deception by the Chinese government.

Their goal: to overextend the US military and reposition her forces away from the South China Sea.

Away from the island of Taiwan.

For most of the world, modern-day Taiwan was a jewel in the western Pacific, a place where democracy flourished and capitalism defined the very character of the people.

But for the People's Republic of China, the island was a renegade province and a burr under the saddle of the Chinese Communist Party. Over decades China had developed the military and intelligence capabilities to bring the wayward province back under Beijing's control. In recent years, the Chinese leadership had made it clear that they intended to repatriate the wayward island of Taiwan. It was not a question of if, but when.

Don gripped the side of the lectern. From this very spot, he had convinced the President of the United States that China was about to make good on their long-standing threats.

President Rick Serrano let out a sigh and sank back in his chair. Like everyone else in the room, his features showed the strain of recent events.

"Well, Mr. Riley?" he said quietly. "What do you think? Have they gotten the message?"

Don took his time answering the question. Before discovering the Chinese deception, the United States had been on the verge of launching an attack on the Russian Federation, an action that almost certainly would have sparked World War Three. At the literal last minute, Don finally put together the pieces of the Chinese deception and convinced the President to call off the attack.

But discovering the Chinese plot and stopping the Chinese plot were two very different problems.

"Take your time, Don," the President said, subtly reminding Don that he was still waiting for an answer.

Don had no intention of saying anything until he was ready. If the last few weeks had taught him anything, it was that he needed to speak his mind. Even if the President of the United States didn't exactly want to hear what he had to say.

"I think we did it, sir," said General Nikolaides, Chairman of the Joint Chiefs. "Sneaky bastards realized we were on to them."

"I agree, sir," said Secretary of Defense Howard.

The President ordered the Situation Room cleared of all but principals on the National Security Council. Don was also directed to remain, both as briefer and as a key adviser.

Don sensed the relief in the air, felt the tension bleed away minute by minute as the PLA Navy moved further from the island of Taiwan.

He tried to put himself inside the minds of the Chinese decision-makers. An invasion of another territory, especially one as desirable as Taiwan, was a risky venture. The Chinese Communist Party was a famously risk-averse body. Unless they were supremely confident in the outcome, they would not green-light the military action.

The start date of the PLA war games, an annual exercise designed to demonstrate Chinese military strength, had been shifted to just before the Lunar New Year. Today, the last day of the exercises, fell on the first day of the national holiday.

Don accepted the premise that the PLA would use the war games as a cover to mobilize troops for the invasion. He studied the screen. All the PLA ships were headed back to port. Away from Taiwan.

Maybe our plan worked after all, he thought.

The hard part about discovering the Chinese deception was not the diagnosis, it was the cure. The National Security Council had deliberated long and hard over how to prevent the Chinese invasion.

A public warning, it was decided, would only send the Taiwanese—not to mention the rest of the world—into a panic. It was feared that the ensuing chaos might cause the PLA to abandon subterfuge and launch the invasion immediately.

Likewise, a private warning to Taiwan would have the same effect. The Taiwanese government was riddled with Chinese operatives.

There was one military move that would send a clear message to Beijing. The USS *Enterprise* carrier strike force, currently on station near the Bering Sea, could be ordered back to her home port of Yokosuka, Japan. Unfortunately, the disengagement process with the Russian Eastern Military district had turned into a stalemate.

To counter the delay in the North Pacific, the President announced that the USS *Abraham Lincoln* was detaching from the strike force in the Arabian Sea and relocating to Seventh Fleet in Japan.

"If we think we're out of the woods, sir," Secretary of State Henry Hahn said, "then I recommend we talk about pulling back some of the response measures we've put in place. If any of those details got out, we'd have to deal with severe public backlash."

"I agree, sir," National Security Advisor Valentina Flores said.

Hahn and Flores formed an unlikely pair. The Secretary of State's calm, measured tones contrasted with Flores's rapid-fire Cuban-accented English, but as a team they served their president well.

Serrano's first instinct was to dispense with the long-time US policy of strategic ambiguity regarding Taiwan as a way to warn China against aggression. He reasoned that making clear the consequences of any Chinese military action would deter the aggressor. The Flores-Hahn team convinced their boss that such clarity was more likely to force a confrontation than prevent one. It helped that they had fifty years of history on their side of the argument. Serrano reluctantly agreed.

There were some obvious actions taken to enhance US readiness. An increase in the cybersecurity threat posture and prepping offensive cyber packages were go-to moves for this type of scenario. The teams at US Cyber Command and NSA were primed and ready to launch.

And then there were the outside-of-the-box options. Way outside of any box Don had ever heard of.

Don was assigned as the CIA liaison for a privateer operation run by Sentinel Holdings, a private military contractor. His contact with Sentinel had only been through secure videoconferences, but he was assured that their operation was ready to go on the President's order.

Without discussion in the full National Security Council, President Serrano ordered immediate deployment of the USS *Ohio* and *Michigan*. Both were former ballistic missile submarines, now designated as SSGNs and converted to carry special operations forces as well as over 150 Tomahawk cruise missiles.

While the President obviously had the authority to make such an order, it seemed odd to Don that he would do so without the recommendation of his Secretary of Defense.

Just another detail lost in the mix, Don thought. One of a thousand decisions. Not everything needed to be talked to death.

"The Chinese New Year celebration begins at midnight, Mr. President," Hahn said. "I think that we can safely say the Chinese have rethought any plans for hostile actions against Taiwan."

Serrano squinted at the wall screen. All of the PLA Navy forces had crossed the line on the chart that signified a return to Chinese territorial waters.

"I still don't trust those bastards," the President said. "I'll feel better when we have the *Enterprise* strike force back in Japan. Where are we with the Russians, Kathleen?"

The Secretary of Defense's face attested to her frustration. "Every time we reach a drawdown agreement, the Russians end up throwing a wrench in the works, and we're back to square one, sir. It's been a process."

Serrano scowled, then shifted his gaze to the far end of the table. "State, where are we with a list of US citizens on Taiwan?"

Hahn hesitated. "It's a tricky situation, sir. We've been able to work with the airlines, so we know who has flown to Taiwan over the past few weeks, but as far as an accurate count, that's not possible. If we press the Taiwan government for answers..." He let his voice trail off.

"I know, I know," Serrano said, with an unusual flash of annoyance in his voice. "We risk spooking the Taiwanese if we ask too many questions. Damned if we do, damned if we don't."

Don knew that thanks to the One China policy enacted in the 1970s, the United States didn't have an embassy in Taiwan. Instead, diplomatic ties with the island were maintained by a private corporation called the American Institute of Taiwan.

"Sir, I urge patience—" Hahn began.

"Enough," Serrano snapped. "We're dealing with an adversary that is responsible for the deaths of American citizens. I realize we're working for a greater good here, but do not speak to me about patience, Henry."

"Yes, sir," Hahn replied.

"What else can go wrong?" the President asked. "Anybody?"

"The weather report shows a tropical storm moving in, Mr. President,"

Don said. "That will reduce our electro-optic satellite capability for the next forty-eight hours."

"Perfect." Serrano narrowed his eyes at Don. "You never answered my question, Mr. Riley. Have the Chinese backed down?"

Don hesitated. "I'm going to offer a cautious yes, Mr. President. It appears that our actions had the desired effect."

Serrano stared at the wall screen. He caught the edge of his lip with his teeth and worried at the flesh.

"I hope you're right, Mr. Riley."

2

Port of Keelung, Taiwan

Raymond Hseih was a man who did not like change.

He had been married to the same woman for thirty-two years, during which time she had prepared him the same thing for breakfast every single day: rice congee with sweet potato and strong green tea served piping hot. He had read somewhere that American tech CEOs in Silicon Valley ate the same meal every day because they wanted to reduce the number of decisions in their lives. Raymond ate the same thing every day because he liked it.

Although he was fluent in English and liked to read American business magazines, he had never left his home island of Taiwan on a vacation—and never intended to, either.

Raymond had worked for the Port of Keelung for the last twenty-seven years. He was proud of his work history. After starting as a junior analyst in the scheduling department, Raymond had slowly climbed the promotional ladder to the lofty position of night shift manager on the outer harbor. He knew every aspect of the cargo-handling operation. From the maritime scheduling software that planned the ship arrivals to the massive gantries that removed the cargo shipping containers to the dispatch program that queued up the trucks to move the containers off-site, Raymond knew them all.

He piloted his Toyota Corolla Altis along the outskirts of the inner harbor of Keelung. A cruise ship, blazing like an enormous holiday decoration in the dusk, was getting underway with the help of a pair of tugs. The harbor on the northern tip of Taiwan had grown over the years from a ferry and cargo terminal to a massive complex that included cruise ships, ferries, two cargo terminals, and piers for Taiwanese naval ships.

Raymond had been there for every expansion. The outer harbor cargo terminal where he worked was where the huge container ships and the massive RO-ROs, roll-on/roll-off ships for cars and trucks, docked. The outer harbor had four berths for the big ships, but they were hardly ever all occupied at the same time.

He patted the leather bag on the seat beside him. Inside was a thermos of green tea, a *Fortune* magazine in English, and a book of Sudoku. Everything he desired for an uneventful night. The Friday night before the Chinese New Year holiday was bound to be boring.

He rounded the last curve before the outer harbor and nearly drove his car into the water.

All four berths in the outer harbor were full. Two RO-ROs and two container ships. Both container ships were stacked high with shipping containers, and Raymond's practiced eye could see from their draft that they were fully loaded.

His vision of a carefree Friday evening evaporated, replaced by a feeling of irritation.

Raymond's favorite saying was something he had read in an American book on management: *Poor planning on your part does not justify an emergency on my part.*

He parked his Toyota in the parking space labeled "Raymond Hseih, Night Shift Manager" and seized his leather bag.

Someone had planned poorly, and they would pay the consequences.

Douglas Tan was a new manager half Raymond's age. Whereas Raymond had gotten to his position of authority by dint of hard work and seniority, Douglas had done it the old-fashioned way: he married the boss's daughter.

Douglas wore polo shirts untucked and blue jeans. His hair flopped into his eyes all the time, requiring him to swipe his hand across his face constantly. Raymond, who wore his hair cemented in place with gel, found the kid's hairstyle most annoying.

"Sorry, Ray," Douglas said, dragging his hair out of his eyes.

Raymond grimaced. He hated being called Ray.

He pulled the day shift log sheet up on his tablet. His irritation boiled into downright anger. He reminded himself that he was on high blood pressure medicine and his doctor had advised him to reduce stress in his life. He took a deep breath. This moment was most definitely a stress-inducing event.

"How did this happen?" Raymond asked testily.

He already knew from the log sheet. All four cargo ships had shown up at the end of the shift, a last-minute schedule change caused by a perfect storm of maintenance events across all four vessels, incoming bad weather in the Pacific, and rerouting due to the PLA war games. This sort of thing did happen occasionally, although he had never seen it happen to four ships at once.

"When do the Customs inspectors arrive?" Raymond asked.

Shrug, hair swipe. "Haven't called them yet, Ray," Douglas said. "The ships just arrived, man. We haven't even moved the gangways into place yet."

"How many of your shift can stay?" Raymond asked.

"No overtime authorized," Douglas said with a hair swipe.

Raymond felt an overwhelming urge to seize a pair of scissors from the nearby desk and hack off all of Douglas's hair.

The younger man checked his watch.

"Look, I gotta go," he said. "My wife expected me in downtown Taipei half an hour ago. You got this?"

Raymond sighed. He thought about the Sudoku puzzle book in his bag and the *Fortune* magazine that he would not be reading tonight. He signed the shift change form and watched Douglas walk out of the room.

Shift staffing was determined by the shipping schedule, so Raymond only had six men scheduled for the evening, including a security guard. He checked the logs and found that two had called in sick. Not unexpected for a Friday night before the most important holiday of the year.

His dock supervisor was a competent man named Ting. Raymond called him on the radio and told him to get the gangways in position on all ships for the Customs inspectors, then position the ramps on the RO-RO ships and the gantries on the container ships.

Raymond got to work immediately on the mountain of admin needed to document a ship's arrival in port. He entered the arrivals into the Customs system to notify them to send an inspector. Since the container ships had been unexpected, there was no queue of trucks waiting to accept offloaded shipping containers, so he placed the demand request into the ground transportation computer. In the interim, they would have to store the containers in the yard, so he booted up the container tracking system so that it would be ready when they started the unloading process.

Even though Raymond had expected a peaceful evening, it felt good to be working. Solving problems, making progress.

Two hours flew by, and he hadn't even opened his thermos of tea yet. Come to think of it, he hadn't received a status report from Ting yet either.

Teacup in hand, Raymond made his way to the window overlooking the piers. The glare of overhead floodlights cast sharp shadows across the bleached concrete.

He blinked, scarcely believing his eyes.

Only one of the RO-ROs had a gangway in place. None of the ramps were down, and the overhead gantries had not moved.

What was Ting doing?

Raymond grabbed his radio and mashed down the transmit button.

"Ting, this is Raymond. Why aren't the gangways in place?"

The ensuing pause was long enough that Raymond was about to repeat his call.

"Raymond, I'm on the *Electra* in berth two," Ting replied. "I need you to come see something."

"What is it?" Raymond said.

"You need to come down here, boss," Ting said.

Boss? Ting never called him boss.

"Fine," Raymond replied. "I'm on my way."

He pulled on his dark blue windbreaker that said SHIFT MANAGER in yellow block letters across the back. Even on warm nights, the wind coming off the ocean could be chilly.

He could feel his blood pressure rising as he fumed at the delay. First, day shift saddled him with four unscheduled offloads, and now his dock supervisor was demanding he show up in person. He grabbed his hard hat and a set of keys off the rack by the door on the first level. He slammed the door of the white pickup truck and flipped on the flashing yellow lights.

He did not exceed the speed limit on the pier. Raymond would not contribute to unsafe behavior in any way.

Odd, he thought. There was no one on the pier. The crane operator cabins on the gantries were dark, and the forklifts they used to move the gangways in place were nowhere to be seen.

Only the RO-RO farthest from his office had the gangway in place. Parked next to it were three trucks, two from the shift workers and one belonging to a Customs agent.

Raymond parked his truck, clamped the hard hat on his head, and stormed up the two-story gangway connecting the ship to the pier. The main deck was deserted. Raymond whipped out his radio.

"Ting, where are you?" Raymond said. "I'm on the ship."

"Down on the first-level cargo deck," came the reply. Raymond followed the signs to a steep stairwell. He mentally rehearsed how he was going to chew out Ting and the rest of the shift. Raymond Hseih was not a man to be trifled with.

The cargo deck was brightly lit as he stepped through the hatch.

He paused, swallowed, blinked. Instead of a fleet of gleaming Lexuses and Acuras, he saw only a single row of black SUVs. The rest of the cargo bay was packed with drab green vehicles.

Like all men his age, Raymond had done his compulsory military service in the Taiwanese Army. He remembered enough to recognize armored personnel carriers and tanks as well as the newer-style four-by-four vehicles. Each vehicle flew a red flag with a yellow star and Chinese symbols for eight-one. The first of August, 1927. The day the People's Liberation Army was formed by the Communist Party of China.

"Raymond!"

He turned his head.

Seated on the deck, backs against the steel bulkhead, were Ting, the rest of the night shift, and the Customs inspector. They were guarded by two fierce-looking Chinese infantrymen in full battle gear.

Raymond's eyes slipped past the guards, past the vehicles, to see row after row of uniformed Chinese soldiers—hundreds, maybe thousands of them—standing at parade rest.

A man approached Raymond. He was dressed in a conservative suit and sported a short, fashionable haircut. If Raymond had met the man in a coffee shop, he would have assumed he was a businessman.

But there was something about the way the man held himself that caught Raymond's attention. Self-assured, he decided. Entitled. Deadly.

"Mr. Hseih," the man said, coming to a stop before Raymond. His Mandarin was crisp, like he was giving an order. "My name is Major Gao of the People's Liberation Army. I require your assistance to help me unload our forces."

Major Gao drew a tablet from inside his suit jacket and consulted the screen.

"General," Gao said. "The port is secure. We are ready to proceed."

"You may move your men into position, Major." The voice that came from the tablet was older, harsher to Raymond's hearing.

Raymond felt his pulse thundering in his ears. He was not a man who liked change, and his life had just changed. Permanently.

DAY ONE

3

PLA Navy submarine *Changzheng 12*
East China Sea, 150 miles northeast of Taipei, Taiwan

Captain Chu Jianyu stared at the digital readout of his stopwatch with a growing sense of disbelief.

Two minutes and thirty-eight seconds. This was the fourth time he'd run the simple drill to secure the ship for general quarters. How was it possible that their time was getting worse?

He glowered at Lieutenant Commander Li. "Secure from the drill, Executive Officer," he barked. "And prepare to run it again." He raised his voice. "And we will keep running it until our time is under two minutes three times in a row."

Because shipwide ventilation had been secured during the drill, the air in the control room was still and heavy with the warm funk of too many unwashed bodies packed too closely together. Chu sensed the frustration that was building in the more experienced members of his crew—the few that had been assigned to the *Changzheng*.

Good, he thought. Let them deal with the laggards in their own way.

"Aye-aye, Captain," the XO replied. He turned and began to issue orders to restore the ship to her normal state.

Chu moved to the rear of the control room, positioning himself under a newly opened air-conditioning vent. The icy air chilled the sweat on the back of his neck.

An officer stepped out of the shadows. Tall, slim, with an air of smug confidence that irritated Chu. As the ship's political officer, Commander Sun Wei was not a bad sort, but he wasn't good either.

The political officer stepped close to Captain Chu. "Captain, may I speak with you?"

Chu pretended to absorb himself in the nearest monitor. He flipped through the screens using the touchpad.

"Speak, Commander," he said.

"Perhaps a word in private?" Sun said.

"Conning Officer!" roared Chu.

"Sir!" came the shouted reply.

"Mark your depth."

A pause. "One hundred fifty-two meters, Captain."

"What is my ordered depth?"

"One hundred fifty meters, sir."

"What do my standing orders say about depth control?"

"Plus or minus one meter, Captain."

The conning officer was a lieutenant recently transferred to Chu's crew. He had promise, but this was a teachable moment, a chance to demonstrate to a young crew that their captain held everyone to the highest standards.

"What is your recommended corrective action, Conning Officer?"

The young man hesitated. Everyone in the control room knew the man on the stern planes station had drifted out of his assigned depth band. The right answer was to reprimand the young sailor.

But Chu was hoping for a different answer. He could almost see the battle raging in the young officer's eyes.

"Well, Lieutenant Wong?" Chu's tone was icy.

The young man set his chin. "The watch section is my responsibility, Captain. I respectfully request to be relieved. I will review my watch qualifications with the executive officer and submit myself for recertification."

Chu nodded. "Do so, Lieutenant."

Inside, he gave himself a mental high-five. This was one officer he could work with. Now all he had to do was train ten more, and he might have a wardroom he could be proud of.

The feeling of satisfaction evaporated when Commander Sun cleared his throat. "Captain, may we speak?"

Chu whirled on him. "Speak, Commander. I have a ship to run."

Sun lowered his voice and stepped closer. "Captain, the men are tired. I have a Party responsibility to ensure the welfare of our comrades. I suggest —respectfully, sir—that we discontinue further drills..." His voice trailed off as he saw the reaction clouding the captain's face.

Sun backpedaled. "Of course, sir, I defer to your experience—"

The XO arrived, interrupting the political officer.

"Captain, we have not cleared message traffic in over six hours. I recommend we proceed to periscope depth and allow the galley to serve the evening meal. We can restart the drills after dinner."

Chu considered the suggestion. He knew the XO was buying time to rally the crew's spirits.

For the past ten days, during the PLA war games exercises, the ship had practiced tracking and firing on Taiwanese warships. For a young crew, the operational experience was invaluable. And rare. The PLA Navy was expanding so quickly in recent years that the critical factor was not availability of submarines but the crews to man them. The sailors who reported to the *Changzheng* were trained in simulators and were not used to the hardships of life on a submarine: cramped quarters, little sleep, shift work, and never-ending drills and inspections.

To a person, the crew and her captain looked forward to spending the Chinese New Year holiday in port. But for the crew of the *Changzheng*, Chinese New Year was canceled. Just this morning, in the final day of the exercise, the ship was ordered to stay on patrol.

A busy crew is a happy crew, Chu told himself. But the XO had a point. Maybe he could ease up for a few hours.

"Very well, XO. You have permission to take the ship to periscope depth and clear message traffic. Tell the galley to serve the evening meal." He paused. "Plan to recommence drills at 2200."

Captain Chu exited through the forward door in control, took three paces and turned left into his stateroom. He closed the door behind him, sank into his armchair, and breathed a deep sigh. He felt the deck of the ship angle up as the conning officer made for shallower depth.

At forty-five years old, Commander Chu Jianyu had believed his chance to command a submarine in the PLA Navy had come and gone. Three times he had been passed over for command. Normally, that was the kiss of death in the cutthroat world of submarine promotions, a strong signal to retire.

The disappointment was not a surprise to him. He had come from a modest background in a western province. Chu had scored well in aptitude tests and earned a place in the Dalian Naval Academy. Although he had received excellent reviews from all his previous commanding officers, his lack of political connections stymied his dream of command.

Then, when he had given up hope, he was assigned to the *Changzheng* 12 as her captain. He smiled to himself. In his wildest dreams, he had imagined commanding an older diesel submarine on coastal patrols, but the *Changzheng* was the latest nuclear-powered submarine in the PLA Navy. Sleek, deadly, packed with the latest technology, she existed for only one reason—to go head-to-head with the vaunted submarine force of the United States Navy.

The smile faded. Chu never imagined being a submarine captain would be this hard. A new crew on a new ship was a daunting combination of inexperience meeting aggravation. Chinese shipyards had notorious quality control issues that only seemed to manifest themselves once the submarine left port. He stole a glance at the Out of Commission report on his desk. Freshwater evaporator operating at half-capacity, an intermittent fault on the port sonar array, a leaking hull valve on #2 seawater cooling pump—the list went on for a full page.

Using only half the issues on that list, he could have justified a return to port for the ship. Not a single member in his chain of command would have hesitated to bring the *Changzheng* home for the Chinese New Year holiday.

Instead, when the orders came in to stay at sea, Chu secretly rejoiced at his chance to prove himself and his new command.

He focused on the problem of crew readiness. Their performance in the drills this afternoon was disappointing but not unexpected. His crew was very junior. Most of them had not even completed their technical training before the *Changzheng* put to sea for the annual war games.

It did not matter, he told himself. This was what Beijing had given him, and it was up to him to make them into sailors.

He let his head roll back until he stared at the ceiling. Still, the Middle Kingdom was not built in a day. Perhaps the political officer was right. He was pushing the men too hard. He would cancel the drills after dinner.

The ship leveled out on her depth and made a series of long, slow turns as she cleared baffles, searching with her passive sonar in the blind spot directly behind the screw of the ship. The phone next to his desk buzzed. He picked it up.

"Captain," he said into the receiver.

"No close contacts, sir," the XO reported. "Request permission to take the ship to periscope depth and clear message traffic, sir."

"Permission granted," Chu replied.

The bow of the submarine angled upward again, and he felt the gentle rocking of the waves as the ship went shallow. From the monitor on his desk, he saw the indicator light for the combination periscope-communications mast change from green to red. From force of habit, he counted the seconds that the periscope was exposed above the waves. He had reached thirty-eight seconds when an unexpected call came over the intercom.

"Captain, we are receiving emergency traffic from Beijing."

Chu was on his feet and into the control room before the conning officer had released the button on the handset. He waited impatiently as the radioman brought the message traffic to him on a tablet. The political officer appeared in the doorway but waited. By protocol, he would be the second person on the ship to see the high-priority message—after the captain.

Chu unlocked the tablet. He kept his face still as he read the message. He read it a second time, more slowly, then passed the tablet to the political officer.

Commander Sun read the message and gasped. Chu held up his hand to prevent Sun from speaking. He said to the radioman, "Show me the authenticator."

The man handed him a sealed packet. All classified radio traffic was encrypted, but emergency traffic required an additional level of physical security. Each PLA Navy submarine carried a series of sealed packets containing six unique characters. The emergency traffic designated a packet and listed the six-character authentication code.

Chu broke the seal and read off the characters inside the packet. After each character, the political officer repeated the element and said, "Check." He passed the tablet back to the captain. "Message is authenticated, sir."

Captain Chu was aware that the eyes of his watch team were on him. "Conning Officer, make your depth five-zero meters."

The bow of the submarine angled downward. When the ship was steady on depth, Chu said, "Pass the word for all officers to assemble in the wardroom."

Ten minutes later, Captain Chu sat at the head of the wardroom table with his executive officer to his right and the political officer on his left. The rest of the officers sat by order of seniority all the way to the ensign at the far end of the table.

Chu fought to keep the elation from his voice as he addressed his team.

"The *Changzheng* has been ordered to attack and sink a Taiwanese destroyer."

The news electrified the room. The junior officers at the end of the table whispered with excitement while the more senior members of the wardroom stayed stoic. Chu saw the chief engineer shoot a glance at the XO.

"Captain," the political officer said, "I think I speak for the entire crew when I say what an honor it is to be chosen by the Party for this glorious task."

Chu stilled him with a look. He had heard the rumors that some of the newer subs had been outfitted with surveillance equipment to monitor the crew. Was it possible that Sun was performing for a hidden camera?

Ignoring the political officer, he projected a data packet on the wall screen. "Our target is the *Tso Ying*. We know her well because we have been tracking her for the last week." Chu rested his elbows on the table and leaned in as if he were sharing a secret. The officer cadre unconsciously mimicked his actions.

"We have run simulated attacks against this ship at least a dozen times,"

Chu said in a low voice. "This is no different. You know what to do. Your men know what to do. Trust your training."

"Do your duty," added Commander Sun.

Chu stifled the urge to snap at the political officer. Instead, he nodded. "Do your duty."

Chu sat up. His officers did the same. He indicated the wall screen with the latest coordinates for the Taiwanese ship.

"XO, set the tracking party. Load all four tubes with Yu-6 heavy torpedoes." He paused, silently hoping the political officer did not say anything.

"We attack at midnight."

"Stand by for final bearing on target one." Chu's voice cut through the tension in the quiet control room.

He raised the optical mast, switched immediately to high-magnification, infrared mode. The outline of the Taiwanese ship was crystal clear on the monitor.

"Lowering mast," Chu said.

"Five seconds, sir," the XO said, reporting the time the periscope was exposed.

The target ship was plowing along at a steady twelve knots, making for home, her crew probably eager to spend Lunar New Year with their families.

"Target angle: seven-five degrees. Angle on the bow: four-five degrees. Range six-five hundred meters."

"Fire control solution locked, Captain," the weapons officer reported. "Greater than ninety percent confidence."

"Weapon ready, Captain," the XO reported.

Chu's heart was racing, and his throat was dry. When he spoke, his voice came out as a rasp.

"Mark time," Chu said.

"One minute to midnight, Captain," came the reply.

Chu heard the rush of his pulse thundering in his ears.

"Fire."

4

Xinyi District, Taipei, Taiwan

Mission Clock: 240:00:00
Mission Status: Green

When Major Gao Yichen volunteered to lead the advance team for the invasion of the rogue province of Taiwan, he accounted for every detail, no matter how small.

Except one detail had apparently escaped his notice. The interior of the black SUV emitted a noxious odor of glue, off-gassing plastic, and singed carpet.

And it was making him nauseous.

From his seat directly behind the driver, Gao watched the nighttime scenery of the Xinyi Expressway flash by—and tried not to throw up. This road into Taipei was flanked by green space. He tried to imagine he was breathing crisp, fresh air and not this poison that coated the inside of his nostrils.

He took a surreptitious look around the silent cabin at the other five men, all seasoned operatives, hand-selected for this mission. None of their faces showed any emotion, much less car sickness.

It's just nerves, he told himself. Focus on the mission.

When he had been approached by the Minister of State Security to develop a secret plan to cripple Taiwan's infrastructure, he had wondered if the offer was a ruse. After all, his mentor was General Zhang, a well-respected senior leader in the PLA—and a relentless gadfly to the Party over the status of Taiwan. Zhang's detractors would love nothing more than to expose a high-ranking PLA officer as a rogue element in the Party.

Operational security meant he couldn't ask his mentor for advice. He couldn't ask anybody. It was his decision alone. A devil's choice: perform an action that was right for his country but was not blessed by the Party leaders or walk away.

After a sleepless night, he realized it wasn't a choice at all. Just the possibility of being involved in a pivotal moment in the history of the People's Republic was worth the risk. He could go from being a major to being—

The tablet contained in the inner pocket of his suit jacket buzzed with an incoming notification.

The device was a slim model, sized perfectly to fit in his hand. Ruggedized and waterproof, the unit was packed with cutting-edge technology that provided the invading PLA forces with a secure, fast battlefield communications network. Indeed, the network itself was named *Shandian*, or lightning, and it lived up to its name.

Gao's stomach twisted. He held the device parallel to his face, ducked his chin to look directly into the camera, and accepted the call.

"General Zhang," he said.

The leader of the Taiwan invasion had a long face and angular features. His mentor could be a kind man who loved practical jokes, but at this moment his quick gaze lanced through the screen at Gao.

"Status, Major," he said.

While the exchange was going on, Gao pulled up the pre-invasion assignments. Twenty-six teams spread across the island targeting every major communications, power, and public service function. A masterpiece of planning and all his work.

Beside every team entry was a green check mark, meaning every team leader was in position and ready to strike.

Gao tried to hold back the grin that threatened to break out. Once he executed this operation, his promotional track in the PLA would be a straight shot to the top. Someday, he might even outrank General Zhang himself.

"We are ready, General," Gao said.

"Good," Zhang said. "The mission clock begins on schedule at midnight local time."

Gao's gaze automatically ticked up to the top of the screen.

240:00:00.

Two hundred forty hours—ten days—to restore Taiwan as a province of the Chinese ancestral lands.

By the time the United States and the rest of the world reacted to the news, it would be a fait accompli.

"Remember the rules of engagement, Major," Zhang added. The subtle twist of his lip reminded Gao what his boss really thought of their invasion parameters.

Zhang was a soldier, not a politician, but there was a political element to the invasion plan. The People's Liberation Army were not invaders, they were saviors. Their mission was to pacify the island with as little bloodshed as possible. It was critical that the people of the rogue province saw the PLA not as enemies, but as brothers in arms bringing them back into the fold.

Gao and his mentor had discussed his reservations about the gentle approach to war, and the general was wholeheartedly against it. In his view, their mission should be to win the battle at all costs. Let politics sort out the blame along with the bodies.

"I understand, sir," Gao replied.

On the Shandian tablet screen, Zhang's features softened into the man that Gao knew so well. "Good luck, Major."

"And you, sir."

Gao ended the call just as the roadway entered a tunnel. He glanced around the dim cabin. No one had seemed to notice the final personal exchange. The last thing Gao wanted was to appear entitled or weak in front of his men.

The SUV emerged from the tunnel into a dazzling sea of lights that made up downtown Taipei. The driver made a left turn onto Xinyi Road, the main avenue of the district, with their second car following close behind. The Taipei 101 tower rose above the crush of commercial buildings. Massive TV screens advertised Chanel and wished the people of Taiwan good fortune in the new year.

Traffic ground to a crawl. Gao consulted his screen again. Their target was three hundred meters away on the eighth floor of the Nan Shan Plaza, an excellent vantage point from which to view the Taipei 101 fireworks show at midnight.

Minutes ticked by. The driver made the turn onto Songren Road and came to a complete stop. The road was choked with spectators waiting for the fireworks show in—Gao checked the tablet—fifteen minutes.

He cursed under his breath. These stupid people were going to wreck his timetable. He had reserved the plum assignment in this phase of the invasion for himself. How would it look if the mastermind behind the preemptive strike failed to accomplish his own mission?

The SUV moved ten meters, mostly by dint of the driver nosing the front of the vehicle into the mass of people. The driver laid on the horn. A teenager in the crowd gave him the finger in return.

"Don't draw attention to us," Gao snarled. He checked the tablet again. Twelve minutes remaining. His decision tree snapped into focus. If they waited, they were going to miss their window.

"We're going mobile," he said into his throat mic. "Both drivers stay with the vehicles, plus one man for security. Proceed to the rendezvous point. Everyone else is with me."

That left him with eight men. Not ideal, but he could make it work. The most important factor now was to acquire his target on time and get her safely back to the collection point.

Without waiting for an answer, Gao popped open the door and stepped into a raucous Chinese New Year celebration. Thumping music blasted, and the crowd danced in the street. After the oppressive smell in the car, the air was fresh and clean. A light mist of rain coated his face as he elbowed his way into the crowd.

His men followed in a loose V-formation. They looked out of place in their dark business suits that bulged in all the wrong places, but everyone around them was either too drunk or too focused on getting into position to view the upcoming fireworks to care.

They plowed their way through a small park that was absolutely packed with people. At the far end of the space, the glass tower of Nan Shan Plaza beckoned like a lighted beacon. Two uniformed policemen were stationed at the entrance.

As they drew closer, Gao gestured for all but two of his men to hang back. He hurried forward.

"Am I too late? She's expecting me," he called. "I have my invitation here somewhere." He patted his jacket, then reached inside and drew out a QSW-06, the trademark handgun of PLA commandos. "Don't do it," Gao said as the second policeman reached for his weapon. The man froze.

Two of Gao's men assumed guard duty at the door. Using the hostages as shields, Gao's team entered the sliding glass doors. The lobby was empty except for two more policemen at the elevator doors.

His men dispatched the pair at the elevator, a necessary part of the plan. Leaving two more men to guard their exit, Gao stepped inside the elevator with his four remaining men.

The time was three minutes to midnight.

The Pearl Restaurant took up the entire forty-eighth floor of the Nan Shan Plaza. The floor-to-ceiling windows offered an unobstructed view of both the brightly lit Xinyi District and the Taipei 101 tower.

When the elevator opened, everyone was gathered at the windows, their backs to Gao's entrance. The light had been dimmed to better see the upcoming fireworks display. Light dinner music played in the background. The space was arrayed with dozens of round tables littered with stemware, plates, and crumpled linen napkins.

Two of his men moved to contain the waitstaff, and a third went to turn on the lights.

Gao studied the people, looking for his target.

There. He smiled with satisfaction.

Qin Su-Wei, the President of Taiwan, was a short woman and a little stout for her age, if Gao was being honest. Her jet-black bobbed hair showed no gray. As she spoke to the man next to her, the glaring lights of

Xinyi reflected in the lenses of her glasses. A young girl dressed in a pink frock held the President's hand, her face pressed to the window.

The overhead lights in the room came on. The music stopped.

There was a hiccup in the murmur of conversation as the guests looked around to see what had happened, blinking in the bright light.

Gao stepped forward and raised his hand.

"Ladies and gentlemen, let me—"

One of the President's personal security detail moved, but Gao's men had him covered. He looked at President Qin, who nodded. The security man surrendered his weapon. The silence in the room was absolute, every eye riveted on Gao.

He smiled. "As I was saying, ladies and gentlemen. Let me be the first to wish you a happy and prosperous new year. My name is Major Gao Yichen of the People's Liberation Army, and I am here to ensure your safety in this time of crisis."

The President stepped forward. "What crisis? This is an outrage—"

"Madam President, I regret to inform you that one of your naval vessels launched an unprovoked attack on a PLA Navy submarine. We were forced to respond and sink the attacking vessel, but this act of aggression requires the People's Republic of China to take necessary steps to ensure the safety of our citizens in Taiwan."

The color drained from President Qin's face.

"When did this alleged incident take place?" she hissed.

Gao made a show of drawing the tablet from his inner pocket. The retina scan automatically logged him in. The time was 23:59:49.

"In approximately eleven seconds, Madam."

In the windows behind the President, a flash of light burst across the dark sky. The fireworks had begun.

All around the Taipei 101 tower, the glittering city started to go dark, block by block. The lights in the room went out, and a gasp ran through the party attendees.

Gao and his men pulled headlamps from their pockets and put them on. The cold light of the lamps turned the lenses of President Qin's glasses white.

Gao held out his left hand. "Madam President, it is time to leave."

A man stepped in her path. He was in his thirties, dressed in an expensive suit with a flawlessly knotted tie.

"You cannot—" he began in a loud voice.

Gao shot him in the center of the forehead. The gunshot made the room freeze into silence.

Gao felt any remaining resistance crumble. Now there was only fear.

He beckoned to President Qin. "For your own safety."

5

---

5 kilometers northwest of Taimali, Taiwan

Mike Lester made his way slowly down the dark wooded path, the smell of fresh pine needles filling his nostrils. Just a few more meters and he'd be in the clearing...

The sole of his steel-toed boot caught on a tree root, and he pitched forward. Rough tree bark scraped against his face as he arrested his fall by wrapping a free arm around the tree trunk.

He hung there for a moment, breathing in the forest smells. Maybe that fourth beer had been a mistake.

Pulling himself upright, he fumbled for his mobile phone and put it on flashlight mode. The uneven trail was illuminated in the harsh white light, and he picked his way forward.

His face warmed with embarrassment at his clumsiness. Getting old sucked.

Back in the day, a younger version of himself could have found his way down this path in the dark without making a sound while carrying sixty pounds of gear. That guy could drink all night, fight all the next day, then do it all over again. Rinse and repeat.

Now, Grandpappy Mike was tripping over his own feet after a few beers.

That's assuming he managed to stay awake past nine.

His boot caught another tree root that he'd mistaken as a shadow. He chuckled out loud.

The stories we tell ourselves. True, he'd been a damn fine Marine—still was—but he'd always been a lightweight in the drinking department.

Still, time was a cruel mistress. At fifty-eight, he was still in decent shape. At home, he maintained a rigorous workout schedule, but on volunteer field missions like this one, he rarely made time for himself. He could feel the difference in his body.

Lester reached the edge of the clearing and switched off the light to reestablish his night vision. It was a new moon tonight, the first of the lunar calendar, and the start of the Chinese New Year celebrations.

By starlight, Lester waded through knee-high grass to a flat-topped boulder in the center of the clearing. He carefully put down his phone and boosted himself up on top of the rock. On creaking knees, he lowered himself to a sitting position. He exhaled deeply, tasting the alcohol on his breath. Then slowly he lay back until he was staring at the sky.

Lester led a small humanitarian team from Phalanx, a US military veterans group that performed disaster relief all over the world. To people who asked about his calling, he joked that he'd spent twenty years as a Marine blowing shit up, so it was only fitting that he spent another twenty trying to put the pieces back together.

He wasn't fooling anyone—least of all himself. Behind that flippant answer lay a reality that he and many veterans dealt with after they retired from active duty. To his mind, the profit-driven "real world" just didn't cut it. After a few years out of uniform working for a military contractor, Lester found himself adrift. Sure, the money was great, but that wasn't enough to get him out of bed in the morning.

Something was missing in his life.

As usual, Maureen, his wife of thirty years, figured it out for him. One morning, while he was fishing, she forwarded him an email with the subject line: *Are you ready to give back?* It was a call to action from Phalanx.

The email spoke about a sense of meaning that came when a group of people worked on a mission not for their own personal gain but for a higher purpose. In uniform, he had associated that higher purpose with national defense. Now, with the benefit of a lifetime of experience, he realized he'd been thinking too narrowly. His higher purpose was simply doing right by his fellow man.

He searched for familiar constellations in the unfamiliar skies.

In the last few years with Phalanx, he'd been to the Solomons, Indonesia, Argentina, the Philippines, and now Taiwan.

He chuckled to himself. If he was being honest, he was mildly addicted to the rush of seeing a completed humanitarian project.

Phalanx had been scheduled to complete the Taiwan project three days ago, but material shortages put them behind schedule. Lester and two of his team opted to stay behind to finish the project before the Lunar New Year. Just this afternoon, the three remaining Phalanx members and their sponsors from the Taiwanese Army put the last door on hinges for the new elementary school. The local mayor joined them for the ribbon-cutting ceremony.

And now, in the words of Hardy, a sixty-year-old ex-Navy SEAL and Lester's second-in-command, it was time to party. Unlike Lester, Hardy seemed to have a natural resistance to the effects of alcohol.

The only man-made illumination Lester could see from his rocky perch was a few lights poking above the treetops downrange of his position. The town of Taimali was five kilometers to the southeast, on the shore of the Pacific Ocean. The low level of light pollution made for excellent stargazing. His eye followed a pinpoint of light as it traveled across his field of view. He wondered whose satellite he was seeing. Maybe he'd be lucky enough to see a falling star or two. Heck, maybe he'd just sleep here tonight.

The sound of rustling grass interrupted his reverie. Lester sat up as the slim form of Captain Frank Tsai loomed out of the dimness.

"You okay, Colonel?" Tsai asked. Like almost every person on the Taiwanese Army contingent assigned to Lester's project, he spoke excellent English.

"Just ducky, Frank." Lester slapped the ledge next to him. "Grab some rock. I'm just checking out the stars and trying to sober up a little."

Tsai was a sharp kid, Lester reflected, the kind he would've liked to have in his command during his active duty days. Smart, thoughtful, decisive.

"You and your team have been excellent hosts, Frank," Lester said. "We thank you for that."

"You're welcome, sir." Lester had told Tsai not to call him *sir* or *colonel*, but the young man had refused, saying it was a measure of respect.

Lester had grudgingly agreed. Truth was, he liked it.

"Know any stars, Frank?"

The shadowy shape next to Lester shook his head. "No, sir. I grew up in Taipei. You're lucky if you can see any stars there."

Lester spent the next twenty minutes pointing out what he could remember from his celestial navigation class at the Naval Academy. He caught a glimpse of the face of his wristwatch.

Midnight, he thought. A new day.

Lester hoisted himself to his feet.

"Well, Frank, it has been a pleasure, but I have a feeling I should get back and make sure Hardy gets some sleep," he said. "I have a feeling my team might be a bad influence on your young soldiers—"

Lester and Tsai looked up at the same time to see shafts of light lance through the sky. Lester counted at least ten trails, heading over the horizon to the north.

Boom! Boom! Boom!

Explosions rocked the quiet night. Flames flared on the horizon.

"Colonel?" Tsai held up his mobile phone. In the reflected light, his face was drawn tight with worry. "I don't have a mobile signal, sir."

Lester checked his own phone. Same result.

He looked to the southeast. The lights of Taimali were gone.

"How far away is Taitung Air Force Base, Frank?" Lester asked quietly.

"Six kilometers, sir." Tsai pointed in the direction of explosions. "That way."

Lester squinted at the southern and western horizons but saw nothing.

"Frank," Lester said. "Get back to base camp, shut off the beer tap, and see if you can raise anybody by radio. Go, son. Go now."

Tsai set off at a run. Lester remained on the rock, searching the horizon. His mind reeled through the possible explanations for what he'd just seen.

A terrorist attack? He discarded the idea almost immediately. There was no terrorist organization that he knew of with ten or so missiles to spare for an attack against the island of Taiwan.

No, this was an attack by a nation-state, a rich nation-state.

He heard the roar of a jet passing overhead. Taiwanese or...?

The People's Republic of China was the only entity with both the fire-power and the desire to attack the peaceful island of Taiwan.

And he was smack in the middle of it.

6

White House Situation Room
Washington, DC

What a difference a day makes, Don thought to himself as he entered the White House Situation Room.

Less than eight hours ago, the National Security Council concluded that their last-minute actions to dissuade the Chinese from invading Taiwan had succeeded. That meeting had ended on a note of hope.

How wrong they'd been.

Don paused in the doorway, looking at the controlled chaos around the long mahogany table. Staffers and deputies stood shoulder to shoulder as they frantically used the last few minutes before the President's arrival to bring their principals up to date.

"Excuse me, Mr. Riley."

Don turned to find himself face-to-face with the President of the United States. Rick Serrano's face was drawn, but his eyes burned with anger. He nodded toward the packed room as he gripped Don's arm. "This is going to get ugly, Don, and I'm going to need your experience. Don't ever be afraid to speak your mind to me. I mean that."

"I will, sir."

"Good." Serrano looked over his shoulder. "Let's get this show on the road, Irv." The President passed into the room with Chief of Staff Irving Wilkerson in tow.

His entrance was so sudden and the activity level so intense that most of the people in the room didn't realize the commander in chief had arrived. Conversations faded away one by one until only National Security Advisor Flores was still speaking, her back turned to the door. She tapped a red-painted nail on a report as she plowed on in her accented English.

Her briefer touched her arm. "Ma'am," he said, pointing to the door.

Flores whirled around, saw the President, and shot out of her chair.

"I'm sorry, Mr. President," she said. "I didn't see you come in."

Serrano waved for people to take their seats, pulled out his own chair, and sat down. He left his leather folio closed on the table.

Serrano cleared his throat, a blast of noise in the silence of the room.

"Let's start with status," he said. "Defense, you begin."

Kathleen Howard was wearing the same suit Don had seen her in that morning. The lines of her face were carved into a scowl.

"Approximately ninety minutes ago, a SBIRS Geo 5 satellite detected a series of PLA missile strikes on Taiwan. The missiles came from multiple submerged contacts as well as from the Chinese mainland. Satellite imagery confirms all of the attacks used conventional warheads and were a mix of cruise missiles and hypersonics."

At the mention of hypersonics, a murmur rippled through the room. The Chairman of the Joint Chiefs of Staff made a grunting sound.

"The missile strikes were aimed at Taiwanese air bases. Additionally, we have evidence that multiple Taiwanese naval ships were sunk or damaged by submerged hostiles. Some—a few—were able to return fire."

"Did they sink any of the PLA subs?" Serrano asked.

"No way to know for sure, sir," Howard said in her matter-of-fact delivery. "Our information is primarily satellite imagery for now. The best we can make out, the Chinese launched upwards of three hundred missiles at Taiwanese land bases. Their subs managed to sink or disable six Taiwanese warships—possibly more."

Howard grimaced and continued. "Weather patterns are changing. Over the next twenty-four hours, we're expecting heavy cloud cover to move over the entire island. That will reduce our satellite data stream. When that happens, we'll have to rely on low earth orbit SAR birds." Synthetic aperture radar used the movement of the source platform to process high-resolution images.

"How much will our capability be degraded?" Serrano asked.

Howard eyed Director of National Intelligence Zachariah Stewart.

"As much as eighty percent, sir," Stewart said. "Possibly more."

Serrano chewed his lip and looked at Secretary of State Henry Hahn. "Do we have anything from your people on the island?"

"As Kathleen noted, sir, our information is sketchy," Hahn said, his Oxford accent on full display. "In summary, at midnight local time, the entire island went dark, including all communications with AIT. Those were secure satellite and landline connections, Mr. President. For those lines to all be severed at the same time indicates a very high level of preplanning for this attack."

The American Institute of Taiwan, or AIT, was a private nonprofit company that functioned like a small diplomatic post for the United States.

With each report, Serrano's face tightened. He focused back on the DNI. "What about intelligence assets? Do we have any clarity yet?"

Stewart's dark features were grave as he nodded. "We have a video released by the Office of the President of the People's Republic of China. It's for internal use, sir. The audience appears to be armed forces. I can show it to you and translate on the fly, if you wish."

"Do it," Serrano said.

A few seconds later, Don saw the bland, doughy face of Yi Qin-lao on the wall screen. In the background was an office with the flag of the PRC featured prominently. If the President of the People's Republic of China and General Secretary of the Chinese Communist Party was actually recording this at one in the morning, he looked remarkably fresh.

The DNI translated as the man on the screen began to speak.

"He says that at the conclusion of the annual war games, radical elements of the Taiwanese military viciously attacked a PLA Navy submarine. The valiant crew of the submarine responded and sank the Taiwanese vessel."

Stewart paused to listen. "Given the circumstances, he has no choice but to declare a national emergency. China will use all her resources to bring the rogue province of Taiwan under control. Effective immediately, he is declaring a one-hundred-kilometer emergency zone around the island to ensure the safety of the Chinese people. He has ordered the PLA to put down the insurrection in the province.

"In conclusion, despite the cowardly actions of a few rogue elements, he is overjoyed to welcome the Chinese people in the province of Taiwan back into the embrace of their ancestral lands."

The screen faded to an image of the Chinese national flag.

"That's the gist of it," Stewart concluded. "I'm not a professional translator, so we'll get you a definitive transcript in short order, sir."

"What's your take, Director?" Serrano asked.

Stewart rubbed his close-cropped hair. "It's staged, probably pre-recorded. He's playing to his audience of a military that has just come off a successful wargaming exercise. They know the video will be leaked, so he's getting their justification into the world obliquely. All in all, a nice piece of political theater by a master of the craft."

"General Nikolaides," the President said, "if you were running the invasion of Taiwan, how would you handle it?"

As usual, the Chairman of the Joint Chiefs did not mince words. "They'll move to lock down the whole goddamned island, sir. Whether you're the mafia or the Commies, possession is nine-tenths of the law.

"Their opening moves have been right on the money. Cut off all forms of communications, check. Degrade Taiwan's air defenses, check. Their next move will be to establish air dominance and enforce the exclusion zone around the island while they deal with the *emergency*." He threw air quotes around the last word. "After they have those ducks in a row, they'll get as many boots on the ground as possible and crush the opposition—if there's any left."

"How long would that take, General?" Serrano asked.

"We've gamed it out, sir." The general blew out a breath. "Our best estimate is three to four weeks, maybe less. Some of it depends on their rules of engagement, which will be driven by what they think they can get away with on the world stage."

"Henry?" Serrano said to the Secretary of State. "What can you add?"

Henry Hahn steepled his fingers and considered the question.

"I agree with the general on the timeline. The PLA's top priority will be to establish physical control over the entire island as quickly as possible. That's a multi-week process. In the interim, China will do everything they can to slow down the United Nations and keep the island dark to outside eyes.

"The unknown factor is how the Chinese execute the invasion. Will they use maximum force, or will they use a gentle-giant approach? In the case of Hong Kong, the Chinese government worked for a long time to avoid direct confrontation while they insinuated themselves into the power structure. What lesson did the Chinese power elite draw from that experience? That's the question, sir."

Wilkerson leaned forward and whispered in Serrano's ear. The President nodded and directed another question at Hahn.

"What can we do politically to bolster the Taiwanese position?" he said. "Do we issue a statement in support of Taiwanese independence?"

Hahn shook his head. "I would strongly advise against that, sir. The benefit to strategic ambiguity is that it forces the Chinese to guess at our response. If we immediately call for Taiwanese independence, we might stiffen the Taiwanese resistance. But it also raises the stakes for Beijing. They will not be able to walk away from that fight. They'll have to fully commit, just to save face."

Serrano chewed his lip. He nodded thoughtfully.

"Thank you, Henry."

Serrano rested his folded hands on the leather portfolio. When he spoke, his voice was quiet and firm.

"I want to be clear: this will not stand. We will fight, and we will free the Taiwanese people—even if it's the last thing I do as President." He cracked a rueful smile. "And it might be."

Serrano allowed muted laughter to circulate through the room before he moved on.

"We have an opponent who has studied us and predicted our every move to perfection. Because of the Chinese deception over the last year, we have sacrificed American blood and treasure in search of a phantom threat. When this chapter of history is written, it will not be kind to the United

States. Not to put too fine a point on it, ladies and gentlemen, but we were played."

He shot a look at the DNI and CIA Director.

"That's on all of us, but especially me."

He placed a clenched fist on the table. Don could see the President's hand tremble, and his voice dropped to a fierce whisper.

"But that ends right now. The Chinese have studied us for decades. We are dealing with an enemy who knows us, maybe better than we know ourselves. They have exploited every weakness in our system, and I, for one, am tired of it. Today, right now, we flip the script. Where's Riley?"

Don stood up.

"Mr. Riley. I want you on the Lynx program full-time. I know we built the privateering operation to use against the Russians, but we're going live against the Chinese. Do whatever it takes to get Lynx off the ground as soon as humanly possible. And Don, I want you to make them *hurt*. Is that clear?"

Don swallowed. "Yes, sir. Make it hurt." He sat back down.

Serrano turned his attention to the Secretary of Defense and the Chairman.

"I want military options, and I want them fast. If the general's correct, we have days to respond. If the Chinese establish full control of Taiwan, that's the whole ball game. Once they are in control, they will never leave that island.

"For the last century, the US military playbook has been about over-whelming force. Well, you can throw that plan out the window, because the nearest US aircraft carriers are thousands of miles away and our forces are committed all over the globe. We have to reinvent the way we fight, use means and methods that the Chinese will not expect. Think of this as a David and Goliath story. Except for the first time in a century, we're David. Do you understand?"

Howard and Nikolaides both nodded.

Serrano stood suddenly, and the rest of the room rose in a shuffling of feet and rolling of chairs.

"Then get to work."

7

USS *Idaho* (SSN-799)
Sea of Okhotsk, 5 miles west of Urup Strait, Kuril Islands

"Steady at four hundred feet, Captain," the Officer of the Deck said. "Speed: six knots. Course: zero-three-zero. The *Orca* is in station-keeping mode, five hundred yards to starboard, sir."

Lieutenant Janet Everett pressed her back into a corner of the control room, trying to make herself as unobtrusive as possible. Captain Lannier had ignored her when she entered an hour ago.

Truth was, Janet feared she was going to lose her marbles if she didn't have something—anything—to do soon. Getting relieved of duty by the captain for breaking the rules of engagement on a mission had shown her how much she relied on work to define herself.

Save the psychobabble, she thought. Just be glad he doesn't throw you out of the control room.

Unlike on a larger Navy ship, there was no brig on a submarine. The idea of confining someone to quarters would be the equivalent of confining them to a phone booth—that they shared with two other people.

So, Janet had been allowed to roam the ship but was relieved of all other duties. She spent a lot of time in the control room, standing watch vicariously through other people. Through trial and error, she found that from this corner of the control room, she could view the nav plot, the sonar stack, and the pilot's station.

"Very well, OOD," Captain Lannier said without looking up from the electronic navigation display.

The Kuril Island chain was a volcanic archipelago that stretched across 1,300 kilometers of ocean from the northernmost tip of Japan to the Russian Kamchatka Peninsula. The island chain served as a barrier between the Pacific Ocean and the Sea of Okhotsk.

Weeks ago, when the United States was on the verge of war with the Russian Federation, the USS *Idaho* had penetrated Russian territorial waters and sailed nearly five hundred miles into the Sea of Okhotsk to tap an undersea cable. The mission was successful, but the attack on the Russians was called off at the last minute by the President.

By breaking radio silence and sending an unauthorized message to Don Riley at Emerging Threats Group, Janet had caused the war plans to change.

The question that dogged her was: changed to what? The *Idaho* had been ordered to transit out of the Sea of O into the safety of international waters, but under conditions of strict radio silence. They weren't even allowed to collect routine message traffic at their normal specified times.

Were they at war with Russia? The thought hung like a millstone around her neck. Had her frantic transmission to Don Riley prevented a war, or had it somehow made things worse?

Idaho's transit out of the Sea of Okhotsk should have taken only a few days, but that marker had long since passed. During the passage south, the *Idaho* had detected no fewer than five Russian fleet ballistic missile submarines. Each encounter required a careful retreat by the US submarine and a modified route to their destination. Stealth was their primary weapon. If they were detected, the presence of the *Idaho* in Russian waters could trigger the shooting war they had tried to avoid.

For the trip into the Sea of O, the *Idaho* passed through a northern gap in the Kuril Island chain. Their main concern had been getting on station as quickly as possible without being detected. For their exit from the Russian-held inland sea, Captain Lannier's plan had been to transit through one of the southern straits, preferably one held by the Japanese.

And that was when things got sticky for the *Idaho* and her crew.

The Russians had stepped up their anti-submarine coverage all along the Kuril Island chain. On three separate days, the *Idaho* attempted to cross into the Pacific and was forced to turn back due to increased Russian patrols.

Today, attempt number four, was on the Urup Strait, an eight-mile-wide channel between Urup Island and a pair of volcanic atolls. Janet was betting her captain was hoping that a smaller, narrower strait would be less patrolled by the Russian fleet. So far, his prediction was paying off.

"This is the captain," Lannier said quietly. "I have the conn."

"Captain has the conn, aye, sir," said the OOD.

Janet felt the tension in the room ratchet up. If the captain was taking control of the ship, that meant they were going to make a run for it.

"Sonar, report all contacts," Lannier said.

The sonar supervisor was the division chief, a short man with a round, florid face. He slipped one of the headphones off his ear.

"Captain, we have Sierra three-seven on bearing zero-three-zero. Three-seven is classified as a *Grisha*-class corvette, she is at ten thousand yards and headed away from us. On bearing one-two-zero, range twenty-five thousand yards, is Sierra three-eight. Surface contact, probably a warship, unknown classification."

"Very well, Sonar," Lannier said. "OOD, on the sound-powered phones, pass the word. Rig ship for ultraquiet."

Technically, all off-watch personnel were supposed to be in their rack, but Janet stayed where she was. What was the captain going to do? He'd already fired her.

Lannier walked back to study the nav plot again. Janet could guess what he was thinking. She had read the intel reports that said the Russians had placed underwater hydrophones along some of the straits through the Kuril Islands. What if all of the Russian naval patrols they had eluded had been a ruse to force the *Idaho* to transit this narrow alley of water? Were they driving into a trap?

They couldn't wait here forever. Lannier straightened up.

"Pilot, all ahead one-third, make turns for seven knots. Let's go home, people."

Janet felt the ship speed up slightly. She settled back against the wall. At this speed, it would take about ninety minutes to pass through the strait and get to international waters.

The first half hour passed uneventfully. As each minute slipped by, Janet felt the tension in her shoulders ease ever so slightly. If she stood on her tiptoes, she was able to see the ship's position on the nav plot. The *Idaho* was in the center of the strait.

"New sonar contact bearing two-eight-nine, range twenty-eight thousand yards. Designate Sierra three-nine."

"Do you have a classification, Chief?" Lannier asked the sonar supervisor.

"Probable warship, sir. He's hauling ass, but he'll pass behind us."

Janet studied the waterfall display. The new contact showed as a bright trace on the gray-green screen.

"Captain!" the sonar supervisor called out. "Airborne contact just flew almost directly overhead. Probably a maritime patrol craft."

Janet watched tiny white pips litter the display. She felt her breath catch.

"Sir, they're dropping sonobouys."

"Distance to international waters, Quartermaster," Lannier snapped.

"Eight miles, sir." Petty Officer Randler had a high-pitched voice that went even higher when she was under stress. Randall shot a concerned look at Janet, who held out both hands, palms down to encourage the young woman to calm down.

Lannier's jaw tightened. "Pilot, to maneuvering, makes turns for eight knots."

"Sonobouys going active, sir." The sonar chief's voice trailed off, and Janet heard him curse. She looked at the waterfall display. The bright line that signified the nearest surface contact had shifted across the screen— and split into two lines.

"Captain," the sonar supe reported, "we have a problem, sir. Sierra three-seven is *two* contacts, both *Grisha*-class corvettes. They're turning around, sir. I think they know we're here."

Janet could see over Lannier's shoulder as he studied the sonar display. What had been an uncluttered display of straight lines now looked like twisted spaghetti as the contacts changed course. Her captain was stuck in a terrible position. If he went any faster, the submersible *Manta*, which was clamped to the *Idaho*'s hull, could make noise, giving away their position. If he kept to a slower speed, the Russian corvettes might catch up.

Lannier decided. "Pilot, increase speed to ten knots."

"Captain," sonar reported, "Sierra three-eight is on an intercept course, and she's pouring on the speed. I'm estimating thirty knots, sir."

"Secure from ultraquiet," Lannier said. "Sound general quarters."

"General quarters, all hands, general quarters."

The alarm pulsed through the ship. Janet heard the sound of running feet as the ship's crew abandoned their racks and rushed to their action stations.

Janet stayed where she was. When she'd been relieved of duty, she'd lost her battle stations assignment.

The control room filled up with new faces.

"Ship is rigged for general quarters, Captain," came the crisp report.

"Weapons Officer," Lannier said quietly. "I want fire control solutions on each of the contacts closing our position. Assign one torpedo to each contact."

Janet wanted to jump out of her corner. Weapons Officer was *her* job. "One torpedo on each contact, aye, sir," her replacement said.

"Listen up, people," Lannier said. "We are not going down without a fight." His eyes searched the back of the control room until he found Janet.

"Everett, I need you on the *Orca*."

"Yes, sir." Janet stepped to the nearest free console and called up the *Orca* profile. "Standing by, Captain."

"Fire control solution ready, sir," the weapons officer called out.

"Send that data to Everett," Lannier said. "Quartermaster, distance to international waters."

"Four point eight miles, sir," Randler sang out.

"Attention in control," Lannier said. "My plan is to make a break for it. Lieutenant Everett will order the *Orca* to fall back and go active on sonar to draw their attention. If we are fired on, we will defend ourselves."

"Sir," the sonar supervisor said, "the Russian corvettes are slowing down and going active. They could be setting up for an attack, sir."

"That would be a big mistake." Lannier looked back at Janet. "On my mark, I want you to cut the *Orca* loose."

Janet's finger flew over the keyboard. "Ready, sir."

"Captain," the sonar chief called out, "Sierra three-nine is classified as a Japanese ship, probable *Maya*-class guided missile destroyer. It's a friendly, sir, and I think they're trying to come between us and the Russians."

"Well, unless they've got wings, they're not going to make it in time," Lannier said through gritted teeth. "Everett, stand by to release the *Orca*."

"The Russians are turning around, sir. They're breaking off the attack!"

Lannier stepped behind the sonar supervisor's chair and put his hand on the man's shoulder.

"If I release the *Orca*, I can't call her back," he said in a low voice. "I'm committing us to an attack on the Russians. I need you to be sure, Chief."

The front of the sonar chief's shirt was stained with sweat. He gulped as he nodded.

"I understand, sir. Here's what I'm seeing: the Japanese ship put herself between us and the Russians. The Russians are—"

He broke off as one of his team sat up straight in his chair. The chief hurriedly replaced his headphones and listened intently. He scowled as he concentrated.

"Underwater telephone transmission, Captain." His lips moved as he mouthed the words. "All...clear...*Idaho*." His eyes snapped open.

"All clear *Idaho*, sir. That's what they're saying."

Lannier took the headphones and listened. Then he went back to his station and leaned both hands on the console. Janet saw his shoulders sag.

"Secure from general quarters."

Two hours later, Janet sat at the wardroom table by herself. The ship was still abuzz with retellings of their close call with the Russian Navy, with each version drifting a little bit further from the truth.

They'd entered international waters without incident and gone to periscope depth to finally retrieve message traffic.

Janet toyed with her food. The chicken was cold, and the mashed potatoes tasted like wallpaper paste. Not that it mattered. Even if the galley had served surf and turf, she had no appetite.

Janet had taken to eating off-hours to avoid contact with her fellow officers. She couldn't fathom whether she was doing it for herself or for them, but it seemed like the right thing to do.

There was a knock at the door, then Petty Officer Randler poked her head in. She smiled at Janet. "Captain wants to see you, ma'am. In his stateroom."

Janet did her best to return Randler's chipper smile but failed. The young petty officer disappeared.

She took her time clearing her plate, then went to the head and looked at herself in the mirror.

What now? she wondered. Probably another chewing out for not leaving control during ultraquiet. She scowled at her reflection. None of it mattered now.

She made her way to the CO's stateroom, rapped on the door twice, then stepped inside.

"You wanted to see me, Captain."

Lannier turned from his desk and gestured at the chair.

"I'd rather stand, sir."

Lannier shrugged. "Have you seen the message boards?"

That was cruel, Janet thought. He knows I'm not authorized to read the boards because I've been relieved of duty.

"No, sir."

He handed her a tablet. "Have a look, Lieutenant."

Janet queued up the first message.

"Holy shit," she said and sank into the chair.

There is no war with the Russians. The Chinese have invaded Taiwan...

Lannier offered a thin smile. "I thought you might take some satisfaction in knowing that you prevented us from starting World War Three—with the wrong country, I might add."

"I don't know what to say, sir."

"Then I suggest you say nothing and listen." His tone was chilly.

Lannier squared his chair with hers and leaned forward with his elbows on his knees. His face was a scant foot from hers. His gray eyes pinned her in place.

"I don't know what to do with you, Janet. You're an excellent junior officer, maybe one of the best I've ever worked with, but you're headstrong. You decide the right course of action and nothing—nothing!—can change your mind."

Janet nodded. "I understand, sir."

"No, you don't. The military relies on a chain of command for a reason. No matter how smart you are, you will never have the full picture."

Lannier sat back in his chair.

"You were right—this time. Was that skill or luck? I don't know, and neither do you. That's the problem."

The captain shook his head.

"You're a hero, Janet. There's no way I can justify keeping you in hack for your actions, so you're back in the watch rotation, effective immediately."

Relief flooded through Janet. She felt herself tearing up.

"There's a catch, Everett. If you ever—and I mean *ever*—disobey a direct order again, I will throw you off my boat. Am I making myself clear?"

Janet stood.

"Crystal, sir."

DAY TWO

8

Beijing, China

Mission Clock: 210:41:38
Mission Status: Green

Minister of State Security Fei Zhen was not sure which thing caused him more pain. The cancer or this meeting of the People's Committee for the Reunification of Taiwan.

The pain in his gut from advanced pancreatic cancer felt like hot needles poking into his spine every time he moved—and breathing counted as movement. Although he normally only permitted himself half a pain pill at a time, he had taken a full pill before this meeting. It had done little to ease his discomfort.

Fei looked down the gleaming length of the mahogany table at the Party officials waiting to speak. Yes, he decided, the pain caused by listening to these idiots talk was worse than cancer.

Although they were in the Great Hall of the People, the secure meeting room on the third subterranean level was furnished plainly. At one end of the table sat the General Secretary of the Chinese Communist Party. At the other end was a large monitor with a secure video connection. General

Zhang, the commanding officer of Operation Tongyi, or Unification, had just finished giving an update to this cadre of senior Party officials on the status of the invasion.

His report exceeded expectations. After only thirty hours on the ground, the PLA forces were many hours, almost a day, ahead of their very aggressive plan. Yes, there were active elements of the Taiwanese military in the area of Taichung, but this was expected. Operation Tongyi called for the PLA to seize the major cities at the north and south of the island, land an overwhelming number of troops and war materiel, then crush any remaining resistance by blanketing the island with PLA assets.

General Zhang had just delivered tremendous news, the best possible news. But as soon as the general signed off the call, debate began. And for the Minister, the pain started.

He shifted in his seat, and a fresh spasm lanced up his spine. A long-winded official from the Wuhan province was winding up a meandering speech where he was doing his best to both kiss the General Secretary's ass and disparage the Minister at the same time.

"Honorable General Secretary, I would point out that since Minister Fei has not shared with us the details of this plan, it is difficult for us to weigh the probability of success. Some of us have served in the great People's Liberation Army Navy, so we may be able to improve the outcome." He smiled slyly. "I believe the Minister did not serve, if my memory is correct."

The Minister wanted to gag. The speaker's naval service consisted of two years in Beijing on a backwater staff. The closest he'd been to the ocean was a koi pond at the Forbidden Palace.

As usual, the General Secretary made no outward show of emotion. The great man himself would not weigh in on a problem until he heard all sides. His heavy-lidded eyes scanned the room before landing on the Minister. His right eyebrow ticked up a few millimeters.

The Minister sighed to himself. A response was expected. He cleared his throat.

"The honorable gentleman makes an excellent point," the Minister began. "I humbly offer my deepest apologies for not informing you about this bold stroke in advance. Security was the utmost concern."

Wuhan pounced. "Are you suggesting the patriots in this room, leaders in the Party, cannot be trusted, Minister Fei?" His eyes widened in faux surprise as he scanned the table for support. The Minister saw a few nods, but most of the room was still watching to see which way the wind blew.

Fei did not take the bait. Success had a thousand fathers, but defeat is an orphan. All he needed to do was win, and even this moron would claim paternity.

Fei shook his head, the small motion aggravating the raging pain in his gut.

"I chose my words carelessly, comrade. The situation called for the utmost discretion and swift action. The rare earth metals find in Taiwan could place the People's Republic of China at a grave economic and strategic disadvantage. If the rogue province is able to develop this find on their own, it could reduce our position in the world market. They will grow stronger economically, and much of that wealth will be channeled into their defense budget."

The Minister cut a look at the General Secretary before continuing.

"In addition, the United States has overreached yet again. Their military is overextended, and their ability to respond to an emergency in the region is at a historic low."

He left out the fact that it was due to his meticulous planning that the United States was placed at such disadvantage. They only needed to know what he was prepared to tell them.

"When I presented these facts to our President, he immediately saw the opportunity and seized the moment."

A new official spoke up from behind a cloud of cigarette smoke.

"What concerns me, Minister Fei, is that you failed to involve the Central Military Commission in your plan. You went around the military chain of command using hand-selected generals to perform your bidding. That action shows disloyalty to the Party and to the State."

The official was right, of course. Fei had circumvented the military chain of command, but the way to counter facts was not to get into an argument about the facts.

Ignoring the pain, Fei drew his thin frame up in his seat and squared his shoulders. "I owe everything to the Party," he declared. "Are you suggesting, comrade, that I do not have the best interest of the State in mind?"

It was a calculated risk. By making his response a matter of honor, he forced his opponent to put up or shut up. In a high-stakes meeting with the leader of the Party present, no politician wanted to put up, so they were content to back down in the face of a direct challenge.

The official stubbed out his cigarette, his attention on his task. "I meant no disrespect, Minister Fei."

And that was how to not answer a hard question, the Minister reflected. Of course, the downside was that he had now alienated another senior Party official. If the invasion was not as successful as he'd planned, he would need the support of the men in this room.

He dismissed the thought. In a single day, the PLA had taken over the critical infrastructure on the island and secured top political and military leaders. The population of Taiwan was in shock, the world in disarray.

No, the Minister reflected, he didn't need the support of these men. He just needed them to get out of his way.

The General Secretary stirred. "Perhaps you could share the broad outline of Operation Tongyi, Minister Fei. So that your colleagues may better understand what they will see over the next few days."

"Of course, sir," the Minister said, getting to his feet. "The three pillars of this operation are speed, technology, and brotherhood. You have already witnessed the speed with which our brave soldiers stunned the Taiwanese military and their political leaders. That is just the beginning."

The Minister reached into his jacket and withdrew a tablet. He unlocked the device with a retina scan.

"All of our military commanders carry one of these tablets. We call this battle network *Shandian*, or lightning. It allows our leaders to possess up-to-date information anywhere on the island. We activated a secure communications tunnel built into the Huawei 5G network installed on the island. For redundancy, the network can also run off a communications satellite or our military drones. Each device is personally keyed to its owner."

He positioned the screen so the assembled officials could see it. At the top of the screen, a counter showed 210:39:15.

"The complete takeover of Taiwan will take two hundred forty hours, or ten days. Every time a battlefield commander opens his Shandian tablet, the first thing he sees is the mission clock. Every milestone of Operation Tongyi has been loaded into the device so that each individual on the network knows exactly what he needs to do and when he needs to do it."

"Surely there will be issues, Minister Fei?" someone asked. "How do you compensate for setbacks?"

The Minister smiled. "We use artificial intelligence to constantly evaluate the status of the plan and make adjustments. The AI gives us an instantaneous probability of success that is represented as a color." He pointed to the screen. "The mission clock is bright green, indicating we are well ahead of plan."

The official from Wuhan stirred. "And what of this third pillar, Minister Fei? Brotherhood?"

"The great Chinese leader Sun-Tzu said: 'The best thing of all is to take the enemy's country whole and intact; to shatter and destroy it is not so good,'" the Minister replied. "All the battlefield commanders are instructed to use extreme care not to damage infrastructure and to treat their wayward Chinese cousins with great respect. If we minimize bloodshed, we can demonstrate to the people in our province of Taipei that we mean them no harm. After only ten short days, we will reclaim the island as part of greater China, and we will reopen the economy under our terms, with the full support of the former Taiwanese people. When we reestablish trade, the world will be forced to recognize the wisdom of the Chinese Communist Party in reuniting China once and for all."

He held up the tablet so they could all see the bright green mission clock. The seconds raced by. "In just over two hundred hours, we will have done what the Party has waited for generations to accomplish."

The officials craned their necks to better see the screen. The Minister expected to be inundated with requests to receive Shandian tablets of their own, but that was not going to happen. The last thing he needed was unauthorized users mucking around inside his battle network.

"Minister Fei, have you considered what this action could do to our trade with the United States in the short term?" the Chair of the Party Committee on Commerce asked.

He was a short man with thinning hair combed straight back and a weathered face. Behind thick glasses, his rheumy eyes looked worried.

The Minister noted that the General Secretary shifted in his chair. This had been his biggest objection to Operation Tongyi.

The Minister reseated himself. "I understand the concern of my esteemed colleague, but I am convinced the United States needs China more than they need Taiwan. The next few days will bear that out."

The official would not be dismissed. "But for how long?" he pressed. "Surely the United States will take some action?"

"The United States is powerless," the Minister said. "In ten days, the island of Taiwan will be under the control of the Party. There is no way the US can impact our economy in that amount of time." He looked around the room.

"You have my word on that, comrades."

9

Sterling, Virginia

Don Riley made a right turn onto Evergreen Mills Road and checked his GPS again. He'd dealt with countless government contractors over his career, and all of them maintained offices either in a high-rent district of DC or in one of the many business parks in a nearby suburb.

Sentinel Holdings was not like most government contractors, he was coming to find out. Their website did not list a physical address. When he called his main contact, a man named Manson Skelly, he'd received GPS coordinates in reply.

Since being assigned as liaison for Sentinel, Don had taken multiple conference calls with Skelly, but this was his first visit to the company site. Assuming he ever found the place.

He'd passed Dulles Airport fifteen minutes ago, driven through the bedroom community of Brambleton, and passed the town golf course. Now dusk was falling. The countryside opened up into rolling green hills dotted with thick stands of hardwood. A three-panel white fence sprang up on his right. A quarter mile off the road, a plantation-style house atop a small hill blazed with light.

Horse country, Don realized. Or at least people with a lot of money. Where the hell was his GPS taking him?

"Right turn in one hundred meters," the GPS said.

His headlights picked out a small sign on the right. Set back off the road, the sign read *Sentinel Holdings*. The *S* of *Sentinel* was integrated into what looked like a Roman shield. Don turned down a gravel road, expecting to find a security gatehouse.

He navigated the car through a stand of oaks and around the base of a small hill. Just when he'd decided he'd made a wrong turn, a building came into sight.

The two-story structure seemed to grow out of the earth organically. The exterior was glass and fieldstone, fronted by wide steps of the same stone material. Yellow light poured into the growing dark, illuminating a neatly groomed gravel parking lot. Don parked his Honda Accord and got out.

The night was still and quiet, with not a hint of road noise. Don felt as if he had driven into someone's driveway instead of the headquarters of one of the largest private military contractors in the world.

"Mr. Riley," a voice called.

Don turned quickly to find a woman standing at the top of the steps, silhouetted in light. She was tall and angular, with blond hair that spilled over her shoulders. She made a flicking motion with her hand, and exterior lights illuminated the front steps.

The woman moved down the steps, her hand extended.

"I'm Abby Cromwell," she said. "Welcome to The Ranch."

Don tried not to stare. He'd made the assumption that Aberdeen Cromwell was a man.

"The Ranch?" Don asked to cover his surprise.

Cromwell chuckled. "My husband's idea. He used to say that the CIA had The Farm and the Marines had The Basic School, so we needed a cool name of our own." She threw her arm out toward the darkness. "My family has owned this land since the country was founded. It used to be a horse ranch, so we called it The Ranch."

Don followed her up the steps. The woman had a loose-limbed way of moving that suited her rangy frame. They entered through automatic glass doors, and she flipped her hand again. The outside lights went off.

"I hate light pollution," Cromwell said. "The night sky is meant to be seen." She pointed to a glass shelf that jutted from one of the stone walls. "Leave your keys there, and Josh will park your car in the garage."

Don dropped his keys off and hurried after Cromwell.

"If you don't mind me asking," Don said, "can you fill me in on your security measures? I expected to see a front gate and a fence."

Cromwell paused in mid-stride. "I forgot, this is your first time here, Mr. Riley—"

"Call me Don."

"Okay, Don, I'll give you the nickel tour." She called out, "Josh, let Manson know that we'll be a few minutes late. I'm going to introduce Don to Mama."

"Yes, ma'am," came a voice from somewhere over Don's head.

"This way." Cromwell led Don down a wide hall paneled in knotty pine. Every few meters, framed black-and-white pictures hung on the wall. A man in what looked like a World War One US Army uniform. A woman looking up at a magnificent black stallion.

"My family," she said, not slowing down. "Like I said, we've been here a long time."

Don paused at a recent photo of two men dressed in the custom combat gear of special forces operators. Behind the full beard and the dark glasses, Don recognized Manson Skelly, the chief operating officer of Sentinel. The second man had fair skin and a scrappy beard. His piercing eyes stared directly into the camera lens.

"That's Joe, my late husband," Cromwell said. "We started this outfit together. Grew it into what you see today. He was killed on a mission two years ago."

"I'm sorry," Don said.

Cromwell smiled sadly. "He died doing what he loved, being in the field. Even as CEO, he never stopped taking missions. That was a big reason we never went public. There was no way a board of directors at a public company was ever going to let a CEO do something that dangerous." Her smile brightened. "But Joe would have wanted us to keep going. That's just how he lived his life. So we do. I handle the business side of things—mostly the labs and acquisitions—while Manson runs operations."

As Cromwell led Don to the end of the hall, a heavy steel door rolled aside. Don felt a rush of cool air flow into the hallway. Positive pressure and heavy air conditioning meant a lot of computing power was at work in the room. Inside, three operators wearing augmented reality goggles sat behind empty desks facing an interactive screen that took up the entire wall. The screen showed an aerial view of the surrounding countryside.

"We use adaptive security measures here, Don," Cromwell said in what was obviously a well-rehearsed speech. She tapped one of the operators on the shoulder. "Can you pull up Mr. Riley's arrival profile, please?"

Don saw his car passing the Brambleton Golf Course. The view zoomed in until he could see his own face.

"Whenever someone enters our security bubble, they're tagged and identified. Their vehicle is scanned for any anomalies, and any type of EM transmission is classified." She paused. "By the way, your driver's license needs to be renewed next month, and your car is overdue for an oil change."

She touched the operator's shoulder again. "Show voice recognition."

Cromwell handed Don a pair of heavy glasses. He slid them on and immediately saw a spool of data run down the side of his vision. He saw his lips move, and a voice mimicked his own as he muttered, "Where the hell is this place?"

The data spool read "Donald Riley, CIA. Voice print and facial recognition confirmed." Then it listed every electronic device in his car.

The view zoomed out again to show an aerial map.

"Primary overwatch is done by a pair of Condor drones. Secondary ID and specialty functions are conducted using smaller drones, fixed sensors, or multi-use data feeds, like traffic cams."

"I've never heard of a Condor drone," Don said.

"All of our sources are developed in-house, mostly here on The Ranch," Cromwell replied. "If we need something we don't have, we usually just buy the supplier rather than contract it out." She smiled. "We don't like to share."

"This must take an incredible amount of computing power," Don said.

"Do you hear that, Mama?" Cromwell said in a conversational voice. "Our guest just called you incredible."

"Thank you, Mr. Riley," said a new female voice. "You have a keen sense of observation."

"Mama, don't try to be funny. This is a valued client."

"Yes, Aberdeen."

Cromwell sighed. "My late husband had a warped sense of humor. He hard-coded the use of my given name into all responses because he knows I hate it. How would you like to be named after an Army facility?"

"I'd like to learn more about Mama," Don said.

Cromwell took his AR glasses back. "I'm afraid I have kept you too long, Don. Manson will be champing at the bit to show you what he's got cooking downstairs."

Walking at a pace that had Don puffing to keep up, Cromwell exited the security center and traveled back up the hallway. She took a right at the main entrance and continued to a set of elevator doors set into a wall of drystacked fieldstone.

"As you've probably guessed by now, we keep most of our operations underground. And from here forward you're operating inside a SCIF." The elevator door opened, and Cromwell ushered Don inside. There were no call buttons.

"Ops center," Cromwell said. The doors slid shut, and the elevator descended.

"Let me guess," Don said. "Mama runs the elevators, too?"

"Mama runs the whole operation. She lets us focus on what's important." The elevator door slid open. "Like Project Lynx."

Don felt his jaw slacken in disbelief. He had been in operations centers his whole career. Some were rudimentary, just whiteboards, laptops, and mobile phones. Others were state of the art, with huge wall screens and private comms networks.

None of them were like the Sentinel operations center.

"Welcome to the Planetarium," Cromwell said, enjoying his reaction.

Don immediately saw the analogy. Most ops centers were arranged as modified classrooms, with all the workstations slaved forward facing large wall screens. In the Planetarium, the workstations all faced outward. Ultra-high-definition displays projected onto the domed roof surrounding a central hub. A mix of visuals from helmet cameras, aerial views, and data streams covered the screens.

The extra space gained by using the entire ceiling allowed the working displays to be configured any way they needed it.

"This is the command cockpit," Cromwell said, mounting three steps to a raised dais in the center of the room. "You'll be working here with Manson."

Manson Skelly was a short, muscular former Navy SEAL who always looked like he needed to shave. He spotted Don emerge and raised his hand in greeting.

"Port Everglades," Skelly said into a microphone, "you're a go. Board and take custody of the cargo."

Skelly had a raspy baritone voice, and he spoke in clipped sentences. "Secure their radio room. Make sure you get the crew's mobiles and put a jammer on board. I don't want anybody phoning home. Tell the crew they're confined to the ship until Customs comes to escort them to the airport."

Skelly paused, listening.

"Yeah, well, you can tell Chairman Mao's cousin that due process applies to American citizens. We're a private outfit executing a lawful letter of marque authorized by the United States fucking Congress."

Skelly showed a flash of white teeth as he reached for Don's hand. "Don Riley, pleasure to meet you in the real world."

The man's grip was like shaking hands with a vise.

"Making friends, Manse?" Cromwell asked.

"This is the most fun you can have with your clothes on, Abby," he replied with a widening grin. "These fucking guys are shell-shocked. We walk on board and tell them we own their cargo and they just go apeshit. One of 'em even cried. A grown-ass man, ship's captain, just bawled like a middle-schooler who lost her boyfriend at the big dance."

Cromwell cleared her throat. "I'm not sure Don needs that much detail, Manse. Where are we on takedowns?"

"Anything tied up or anchored at a port has been locked down. We've taken thirteen so far, and the land-based teams are getting into a rhythm.

We've identified another sixty-seven target vessels that are currently inside the EEZ, and we're prioritizing them for seizure."

The exclusive economic zone ran for two hundred miles from the shoreline of every country out to the open ocean.

"That's excellent progress, Manse—" Cromwell began.

"There's something I want to show Don," Skelly interrupted. He spoke to one of his operators, and the screen before them displayed a visual of a Chinese-flagged ship hauling in a massive net full of fish. "This bad boy is hanging around international waters near Bangor, Washington."

Bangor was a major US submarine base for fleet ballistic missile submarines, Don knew.

"We've got them jammed using a Pelican drone," Skelly continued. He zoomed in on a boxy structure on top of the bridge of the ship. "Go to microwave scan," he ordered.

The box disappeared, and Don saw an array of high-tech antennae.

"I think we have ourselves a spy ship," Skelly said.

An idea formed in Don's mind. A spy ship would have cryptographic gear installed. If they could salvage that gear intact and quarantine the crew—even for a few days—it could give the US an edge.

"Can you seize that ship?" Don asked.

"According to the Congress of the United States, I have the authority to seize any Chinese-flagged vessel as a prize," Skelly said. His eyes gleamed. "All I need you to do is say the word, Donny-boy."

"Let's do it," Don replied, "but I have some requirements."

10

Mount Chuyun, 45 kilometers northwest of Taimali, Taiwan

Early morning light was beginning to filter through the tree canopy when Captain Tsai called a halt to their march through the mountains of Taiwan.

Mike Lester swung his pack to the ground and leaned against a handy tree trunk. His legs ached. He'd taken a few stumbles over the last few hours, and his shins bore some new bruises.

Lester sank to the ground. He hadn't done a forced march with a full pack in...well, in a lot of years. He was tired, hung over, and breathing like a wounded water buffalo.

Hardy plopped down next to him, still wearing his pack. "I truly love a brisk walk before breakfast," the former SEAL said. "Speaking of which, I'm feeling mighty peckish, skipper. When's chow?"

Lester took a drink of water from his canteen. Hardy's happy warrior act both annoyed and worried him. They were stuck in the middle of what he guessed was a PLA invasion of Taiwan, and Hardy was acting like they were on a camping trip. Lester was still struggling with how to process the recent chain of events.

He and his remaining two team members had been scheduled to fly out yesterday. At the last minute, they opted to stay for another day. The wait times on the phone to exchange their tickets had been so long that Lester hadn't cancelled their flights. Instead, he'd decided to exchange their tickets at the airport.

"When was the last time you called home, Hardy?" he asked.

"Week or so ago," Hardy replied. "Talked to my daughter."

"Did she know your travel plans?"

Hardy considered. "Yeah, I guess."

Captain Frank Tsai joined them. He'd removed the tunic of his combat uniform, and sweat stained the collar of his T-shirt. Despite having been up all night, the young man looked remarkably fresh.

"Colonel," he said, "there's a lookout point ahead. Would you join me?"

Lester held out his hand. "Only if you help me up first, Frank."

He followed the Taiwanese officer up the trail, the muscles in his thighs groaning with the new effort. After fifty meters, Tsai left the trail and scrambled up a steep wooded slope, using tree branches and roots as handholds. They broke into thinner underbrush, and Tsai led Lester onto a rocky overlook.

The view was worth the effort, Lester thought as he sank to a squat.

They faced south. To his left, the sun rose over the sharp blue line of the horizon, while gray storm clouds piled up in the west. Directly ahead, a column of thick black smoke marred the green landscape.

"Taitung Air Force Base," Tsai announced. He handed Lester a pair of field glasses.

Two jets crossed from east to west. Lester studied the aircraft, taking in the chiseled nose, delta wing configuration, and dark-gray low-visibility coating. The insignia on the tail fin sealed the identification: a horizontal bar with an inset star.

He was looking at a PLA Air Force J-20 stealth fighter jet.

"The call is coming from inside the house, Frank," he said.

"Pardon, sir?"

"Never mind," Lester replied, handing him the binoculars. "What are your plans, son?"

"We've expected this invasion for some time," Tsai said. "The military has made contingency plans. Here, in the mountains, we have rally points. You'll be safe there." He paused, then added, "For now."

Lester nodded. There was clearly more to this trip than Tsai was saying, but Lester knew one thing: he was not about to surrender to the PLA and possibly be used as a political bargaining chip against his own country. For now, his best bet was to put his faith in his Taiwanese hosts.

"I trust you, Frank," Lester said. "Lead on, son."

They climbed back down the mountain and joined the rest of the party. Lester ignored the questioning looks from Hardy and Lewis. He'd talk to them when he had something to tell them.

Another forty-five minutes of hiking brought them to a steep cliff face. Thick tree cover dotted the steep cliffs of limestone.

Tsai halted the column again, and Lester made his way forward.

"Is there a problem, Frank?" Lester asked.

Tsai shook his head. "We're here, Colonel."

Lester looked around. For the last twenty minutes, they'd left the marked hiking trails. He'd noticed three of the Taiwanese soldiers had dropped back behind the column. Lester suspected they were doing their best to erase any trace of their passing through the woods.

"We're not getting any younger, son," Lester said. They still had tree cover, but it had thinned some, and Lester was beginning to worry that the PLA might have launched drones. If there was good cover nearby, he wanted in and fast.

Tsai raised his hands to his lips, producing a series of birdcalls. He waited a few seconds, then repeated the call.

Something moved above them, and Lester spied a camouflaged form on the rock face.

"Well done, boys," Hardy muttered.

Lester agreed. The lookout's camouflage was excellent. He studied the rock face, searching for another lookout he knew would be there, but gave up. Tsai led the column forward to a narrow cleft in the rock, tall enough for Lester to stand in, but he needed to turn sideways to move forward. He traveled a few meters in darkness, then felt a draft of wind on his face flowing out of the cave.

Inside, the path widened, and Tsai halted the group. Hardy jerked his chin at a knee-high bulge on the wall. In the dim light, it took Lester a second to make out the painted wires snaking out of the rock.

"Claymores," Hardy mouthed, then he smiled.

Frank pulled aside a blackout curtain and led the group deeper into the mountain. Lester let his hand trail along the wall, feeling where the rock had been chiseled away. They were in a man-made tunnel. Dim yellow lights set at ankle height gave him just enough light to make his way forward without fear of tripping.

Finally, Captain Tsai pulled aside the final blackout curtain.

Lester estimated the base occupied a cavern about the size of a football field. Four Quonset-style huts formed a central square where Frank led his team. As they passed the opening of one of the huts, Lester got a look inside. It was a barracks with a row of three-high bunks and enough rack space for about fifty soldiers.

Inside the central square, a long row of foldable tables and chairs formed what Lester guessed was the mess hall. A group of a dozen Taiwanese, some in uniform, some in civilian clothes, watched them enter.

Tsai hurried over. "You can leave your gear here, Colonel," he said. "I need to check in with the commander."

"I'll join you," Lester said. He motioned for his team to follow.

Tsai led the way through a rudimentary ops center, where a small team huddled over laptop screens and consulted maps of the island of Taiwan. Lester spied a live feed of what looked like a port facility.

Tsai knocked on a closed door at the back of the ops center, paused, then entered.

A young Taiwanese man, dressed in civilian clothes and thick framed glasses, got up from his chair. To Lester's surprise, he came forward and embraced Captain Tsai.

"Thank God you're okay, Frank," he said. The man had longer hair than regulation, and if Lester had to guess at the man's occupation, he would have said college professor.

The two men conversed in Mandarin, never letting go of each other the entire time. Lester heard his name mentioned twice.

"Colonel Lester," Tsai said finally, "this is my brother, Major Oliver Tsai of the Taiwanese Air Force. He is our senior officer in charge."

The elder Tsai shook Lester's hand. "I left active duty three years ago, Colonel. I was the admin officer for the 3rd Tactical Fighter Wing at

Taitung," he said. "The Shadow Commander has not arrived." He shot a look at Frank. "We are concerned."

"Mind if I ask a question?" Hardy interrupted. "What's a 'shadow commander'?"

Oliver Tsai waved them to chairs. When no one sat down, he leaned against his desk. "The Chinese designs on the island of Taiwan are well known. Our military planners have long considered this invasion a matter of when, not if. With that in mind, a series of retired officers developed secret bases like this one all through the mountains of Taiwan. It's been going on for thirty years."

Lester thought the guy sounded like a professor, too.

"We have only one goal: to slow down the PLA invasion long enough for the rest of the world, led by the Americans, to come to our aid. We are trained to fight from the shadows, using guerilla tactics much like your own American Revolution against the British Empire."

Ash Lewis spoke up. She had pulled her hair back into a rough ponytail, and her face was smudged with dirt. Lester hadn't spoken to her since the previous evening, but he could tell she was getting less comfortable by the minute.

"And you're asking us to do what, exactly?" she said.

"All volunteers are welcome," Oliver Tsai said.

Lester held up a hand. "Frank, could you give me a minute to talk to my people?"

When the Tsai brothers left, Lester collapsed into one of the camp chairs. "No one is committing to anything until we get some more information about this operation," he began. "Hardy, take a walk around the camp. Look at manpower and their general level of readiness. Ash, you assess the supply situation. These guys might have the stones to go after the PLA, but see what they have in the armory and in the pantry."

Thirty minutes later, Lewis and Hardy were back.

"I'm counting thirty-five to forty men," Hardy said. He shot a look at Lewis. "And women, of fighting age and capability. We basically got ourselves a platoon here, skipper."

Lester looked at Lewis.

"I have to say, I'm impressed," she said. "They've planned for the long haul. They have enough provisions to last for three months, four if you stretch it. And the armory is solid. These guys are loaded for bear."

"Okay," Lester said. "We know they're serious, and we know they have the tools to do the job. But there's other things to consider."

"Like what?" Hardy demanded.

"Like whether or not the US will even show up, for starters," Lewis said.

"She's right," Lester said.

He hadn't bothered with politics much in recent years, but he knew the US policy of strategic ambiguity toward Taiwan's status hadn't changed since the 1970s. The problem with strategic ambiguity, he reasoned, was that it was ambiguous for everyone. The Taiwanese, the Chinese, and now the four of them. On the other hand, he'd read in *Defense News* that US special operations forces had been training with the Taiwanese Army for years, so maybe there were US military plans he didn't know about.

Still, the US military was so overwhelmed right now, Lester wasn't even sure they *could* respond to the invasion of Taiwan.

"As I see it, we have two options," Lester said. "One, we walk down the mountain, turn ourselves in to the Chinese, and take our chances. Or we stay and help this scrappy little band of misfits try to reenact the Revolutionary War in Asia."

"I'm in," Hardy said. "If the Chinese corner the market on flat-screen TVs, think of what they'll do to the prices."

Lester smiled in spite of himself, but when he turned to Lewis, he grew serious.

At barely forty, she was the youngest of the team. Ash had kids in college and a cyber security business back home. She had a lot to lose if this operation went sideways.

Lester watched the warring emotions on the younger woman's face.

"Look," Lester began, "let's take a—"

"No," Lewis said. "I'm sitting here thinking about all I could lose, but that's not the point, is it? These people need our help. Marines don't walk away from people who need help."

"Semper Fi." Lester stood. He didn't feel as tired now. "Let's go find Frank."

11

East China Sea

Lieutenant Colonel Alex "Pipper" Plechash, USMC, keyed his radio. "Exxon one-one, that'll do it for me."

"Stand by to disconnect," came the crisp reply from the massive KC-46 Pegasus tanker flying above him.

The basket end of the refueling boom drew away from the extended fueling probe of Pipper's F-35 strike fighter.

"Confirm disconnect," Pipper said. "Much obliged, Exxon."

He touched his control panel, and the refueling probe on the starboard side of his canopy folded back into the fuselage, leaving a smooth exterior coated with radar-absorbent material.

"Good hunting, sir," replied the tanker boom operator. "We'll be standing by to give you a drink on the way home."

Pipper broke left, reveling in the responsiveness of the aircraft. Although he'd come up through the ranks flying the F/A-18 Super Hornet, there was no way he'd go back now.

The foundation of the F-35 Lightning was its stealth. The smooth, RAM-covered skin of the aircraft, the low radar cross-section design, and the ability to carry ordnance inside the fuselage rather than externally on the wings, made the F-35 nearly invisible to enemy radar.

Nearly invisible, Pipper thought, but not entirely.

The E-3 Sentry AWACS that was riding herd on this section of the ocean automatically provided his navigation system with a vector to meet his advance team, which was loitering two hundred kilometers ahead.

"What the hell," he muttered to himself. "You only live once."

He hit the afterburners. The g-force pressed him back in his seat. The Pratt & Whitney F135 engine could deliver forty thousand pounds of thrust, and he tried to coax every pound out of her as he rocketed along at thirty-five thousand feet. The stressed skin of his face creased into a smile as he broke the sound barrier.

He covered 150 kilometers in a shade over five minutes, reducing speed when the datalink showed he was getting close to his wingmen. He entered a rendezvous turn, and the two other jets slowly worked themselves into a starboard echelon formation. A routine join-up, except that there was no friendly greeting. No joking banter between pilots.

In fact, Pipper was the only pilot in the formation. His wingmen were both UCAVs, unmanned combat aerial vehicles.

He was intensely proud of his eighteen years of service in the United States Marine Corps. In that time, some of his most trusted friends and confidants had been his wingmen. At times, he owed his very life to them.

Now his wingmen were a couple of frigging circuit boards, and he was flying a surveillance hop instead of blowing things up.

Times had changed. He was doing his best to keep up.

"Eagle Eye," he radioed to the AWACS, "Green One. Ready to ingress."

"Stand by, Green One."

On his helmet visor display, fed by the AWACS datalink and his UCAV wingmen, Pipper watched the pair of Chinese J-20 jets on combat air patrol make a wide turn over the north end of Taiwan, then head south.

"Green One, Eagle Eye. You're cleared for ingress at your discretion."

"Roger. Inbound." Pipper steered for the northern tip of the island of Taiwan.

The marketing material for the F-35 strike fighter made the bold claim

"You can't hit what you can't see," meaning that the aircraft's superior stealth features made it invisible to enemy radar.

That sounded great until you were sitting in the cockpit about to fly over enemy territory.

Their mission was detailed terrain mapping to unearth PLA defensive modifications made to the existing Taiwanese infrastructure. Of special interest was a grouping of truck-mounted systems parked near Taipei. Intel suspected they might be a new type of weapons system.

In a moment of geek humor, some analyst had dubbed the units as Xboxes and the name stuck.

There was a premium on figuring out what was inside the Xbox. The guesses—and that's all they were in Pipper's mind—ranged from a directed energy weapon to a new kind of radar.

So, the powers that be did what they'd done since America was established as a country: they sent in the Marines.

Not to blow up the Xboxes, but to run a low altitude sensor sweep. With two computerized wingmen.

At just under five hundred knots, Pipper's subsonic transit across the northern end of Taiwan would last a little over a minute. The sensors on the UCAVs were slaved to his own aircraft for maximum coverage on a run. The plan was to do one pass, then regroup for a second. While Pipper's team loitered over the ocean, the AWACS would analyze the upload and determine if further runs were required.

If all went according to plan, they'd be in Chinese-occupied airspace for about five minutes in all.

There was a catch. On the second pass, Pipper was supposed to hit the Xbox with his ultra-high-resolution synthetic aperture radar.

In other words, he was going to poke the dragon.

The Taiwan mainland came up on them fast. Pipper forced himself to breathe as the lights of Taipei flashed beneath his aircraft.

Then they were through, back over open water.

As he made a wide arc over the ocean, he radioed the AWACS.

"Confirm upload, Eagle Eye," Pipper said.

"Thing of beauty, Green One. Some Chi-Commie was taking a shit behind a bush, and we can see the birthmark on his ass."

"Let's keep some discipline on the net," Pipper replied, but he chuckled to himself. Maybe there was some truth to this "You can't hit what you can't see" marketing hype.

"Roger that," Eagle Eye said. "You are cleared for your next pass, Green One."

Pipper eased his throttle forward, his wingmen keeping pace via the datalink between the aircraft.

"Feet dry," Pipper muttered into his radio.

City lights blurred beneath his wings, but the skies were clear of danger. The preprogrammed sequence energized his SAR and lit up the Xbox.

Immediately, his TSD flashed an alert. Multiple alerts.

One...two...three...*four* SAM launches showed on the tactical situation display.

"Green One," Eagle Eye reported, "multiple SAM launches and incoming bogeys from the south. Bug out."

SAMs *and* a combat air patrol. In the space of a few seconds, the whole situation had gone from a sensor sweep to a fight for his life.

Pipper was already reacting. He selected burner and yanked the jet into a high-G climbing turn, his starboard UCAV exploded in the night sky. Fighting the g-forces, he grunted repeatedly, flexing his thighs and core muscles to keep the blood in his head. His brain struggled to maintain situational awareness as multiple missile plumes streaked toward him.

Don't get tunnel vision, he told himself. Don't lose the tactical picture.

He dispatched the remaining UCAV to engage the incoming Chinese combat air patrol, ordering his wingman to launch a pair of AIM-120 AMRAAMs. The air-to-air missiles would slow the bad guys down, but they'd be back.

The missile lock tone blared in his ears as the closest SAM dove in for the kill. He released two flares and pulled into an 8-G turn.

The first SAM took the bait. Another explosion.

The missiles were much faster than his supersonic jet. There was no way he'd be able to outrun them, and he still had the incoming J-20s to deal with.

Missile lock tone. The second SAM was coming at him hard and fast.

He deployed his remaining flares and chaff. He jinked hard, his body struggling against the sudden g-forces.

Seconds turned into minutes, minutes into days as time dilated. His breathing sounded raspy and strained.

The second SAM flashed behind him.

He focused on the tactical display. The J-20s were burning in from the south, the UCAV moving into position between the incoming jets and Pipper. The third SAM made a wide bend coming in behind him.

"Green One, Eagle Eye. Castle inbound from the south, ETA two minutes."

Castle was today's code word for friendly fighters. But there were not enough seconds remaining for the incoming US fighters to get there in time. They wouldn't fire missiles for fear of hitting him.

Pipper was on his own.

The F-35 was not as maneuverable as the incoming Chinese jets, and there was no way he could outrun the pursuing missile, so he did the next best—or maybe worst—thing.

He ran straight at them. Pipper put the F-35's nose on the incoming J-20s and lit the afterburner.

The search tone of the last pursuing missile blared at him. G-forces pinned him back in the Martin-Baker ejection seat. If things got any worse, he'd need that seat.

The incoming Chinese warplanes launched missiles at the UCAV, then veered off the intercept course.

"You can't hit what you can't see," he whispered. "And, dear Jesus, I *really* hope that's true."

Deploying the ALE-70 towed decoy from the rear of the aircraft, he energized the decoy to draw in the final missile.

His lips moved in a silent prayer. If he missed his timing by so much as a whisker, they'd be collecting what was left of his corpse in a test tube. The pursuing missile tone shifted to a steady tone. *Missile lock.* The tone sounded like a banshee wail in his ears.

The incoming missiles from the Chinese J-20s hit the UCAV exactly as Pipper's jet flashed past. He released the last of his flares and chaff and broke left, away from the island.

The SAM impacted the remains of the UCAV behind him. Pipper scanned his display for the Chinese J-20s.

They were vectoring away from his position, back toward Taiwan.

Two friendly blips appeared on this screen.

"We got you, skipper." The down-home twang of a genuine American voice was the sweetest sound he'd ever heard in his life.

He swallowed hard, clenching his fists to still the shaking from the adrenaline rush. Then he keyed his radio.

"What took you guys so long?"

12

Taipei, Taiwan

Mission Clock: 201:12:18
Mission Status: Green

Before the invasion, Major Gao had traveled undercover to downtown Taipei many times. He loved the crowded sidewalks, the colorful electronic billboards, the smells of restaurants and car exhaust. Like Shanghai, this Asian city felt alive with frenetic energy.

But today it was quiet. On every street corner, Gao saw a pair of armed PLA soldiers, dressed in full combat gear. The capital of Taiwan was under martial law and would remain that way until the PLA had taken the entire island.

Gao extracted his Shandian tablet from the pocket of his uniform tunic and checked the mission clock. The progress indicator was still green, but the brightness of the color had faded. The invasion was still on track and that was what mattered, but he wondered about this sudden call to General Zhang's downtown headquarters.

Good news or bad? Gao knew he had planned and executed the zero hour raid on Taiwan's infrastructure and political leadership with great success. Perhaps the general had another high-profile mission for him?

He allowed himself a smile of satisfaction. This invasion was his chance to distinguish himself in combat, set his own record of service above his many peers. The PLA was a bureaucratic organization, but with the right recognition, he might be able to leapfrog the competition.

The chauffeured vehicle stopped in front of the Taipei 101 tower. A corporal in combat gear scrambled forward to open the car door. As the enlisted man saluted, Gao stepped onto the sidewalk. The young man's back stiffened even more when he recognized Gao.

"Congratulations on your great victory, Major Gao, sir," he said.

"At ease, soldier," Gao said, secretly pleased. He crossed the wide sidewalk in a few strides. Overhead, the blood-red flag of the People's Republic of China waved in a gentle breeze.

The lobby of the iconic tower had been converted to a mobile command post for the military police. Gao enjoyed the stares as he strutted to the elevator.

General Zhang's base of operations occupied the thirty-sixth floor of the Taipei 101 tower, in the former offices of the Taiwanese Commerce Authority. The TCA would be a casualty of the coming regime change. As soon as the invasion was complete, all authority for any type of commerce would be directed from Beijing.

Gao nodded with approval. The general was a man who understood the power of symbolism. It would have been easier to set up his headquarters on the outskirts of the city, but he recognized the powerful message he was sending by occupying the most famous landmark in downtown Taipei.

General Zhang was a wise man, Gao thought. When he succeeded in returning the rogue province of Taiwan to the People's Republic, Zhang would be a household name in China. And Gao would ride his coattails to a promotion.

Gao removed his cap as he exited the elevator. A young woman manned the desk, her PLA combat uniform clashing with the gleaming chrome-and-glass reception desk. She jumped to attention.

"Major Gao," she said. "Congratulations on your great victory, sir."

Surprised, Gao glared at her with hard eyes. It would not do if he was seen as too ambitious.

"The victory belongs to the Party, Corporal."

"Yes, sir," she replied, her eyes facing front.

He softened his tone. "But thank you."

The young woman was pretty when she smiled. "You are welcome, sir," she said. "The general is expecting you, sir."

Gao rapped twice on the general's door and stepped inside the commander's office. The leader of the PLA invasion had taken the managing director's suite of the Commerce Authority. It was a corner office with space for a massive wooden desk, a sitting area, and a conference table, all separated on the white tile floor by large area rugs.

The afternoon sun slanted through floor-to-ceiling windows, glazing a stunning southern vista in golden light. Gao noted clouds building on the horizon. By nightfall, the cloud cover over Taiwan would be complete. Yet another advantage for the PLA. The overcast sky would shield their actions from the prying eyes of United States satellites.

General Zhang was not admiring the view. He was seated behind his desk, his ramrod-straight back to the glorious scenery. When Gao entered, he glanced up, gave a curt nod, and returned his attention to a videoconference call over his Shandian tablet.

"Yes, Minister," he said, "I understand your point, but what happens in the United States is not my concern."

The response was quiet and cutting. Gao recognized the voice of the Minister of State Security Fei Zhen. "General, the United States is responding more aggressively than we had anticipated, which means our timetable for the invasion is more critical than ever."

Zhang frowned at the screen. "Then I assume you will be relaxing some of the onerous restrictions you have placed on the use of force in—"

"General," Fei interrupted, "your orders remain the same. Nothing is changing, but you must stay on track."

Gao wandered to the conference table where the support staff had erected a holographic model of the island of Taiwan. The landmass, located only 160 kilometers from the Chinese mainland, was shaped like an elongated oval. The PLA forces already held both the northern capital city of

Taipei and Kaohsiung in the south, along with their associated ports and airports. Those two areas represented the major centers of population, containing three-quarters of the Taiwanese people.

The challenge lay in subjugating the rest of the island. A thick spine of mountains ran down the central part of Taiwan, including dozens of peaks over three thousand meters. The western side of the mountain range facing the Chinese mainland was flat, terraced land and thick with agriculture. On the east side, the mountains crowded close to the shoreline, leaving little room for settlement.

Gao noted red marks around the city of Taichung on the western side of the island, indicating activity by the Taiwanese Army. The invasion plan called for the PLA to take the major ports in the north and south, assemble an overwhelming land force, then drive down the flat western side of the island. Once they had secured the north-south corridor, the PLA would deal with any remaining resistance in the sparsely populated mountains and eastern coast.

The plan was simple, elegant, and they had already accomplished the most difficult part of isolating the island and seizing the major ports. Gao's part in the grand plan was over.

"Time is of the essence, General," Minister Fei's voice echoed through the speaker of Zhang's tablet. "You must stay on track."

"I understand, Minister."

Zhang ended the call and let out a low growl. He was a proud man and not used to being upbraided in public.

Gao turned as the general joined him at the table.

"You called for me, sir?" Gao said.

"The Minister is concerned." He touched the icon on the south of the island, and a data tag appeared. Gao read with him the PLA units that had already landed in Kaohsiung. "And I am troubled as well," he added.

"What is the problem, sir?" Gao asked. "Can I help?"

"The biggest problem is not with us, Major," he said. "The United States has launched a campaign to seize Chinese commercial vessels in their waters."

"But that's an act of war, sir."

"No." Zhang shook his head. "They used an ancient privateering law from two hundred years ago to award a letter of marque to a private company. The company has been authorized to seize Chinese assets at sea." He pondered the holo. "Very clever—and unforeseen by the Minister. The General Secretary is not pleased."

Zhang sighed and turned away. He walked to the sitting area and dropped onto a black leather couch. Zhang waved Gao to a seat opposite.

The general looked exhausted, Gao thought. For his part, although he had hardly slept in almost forty-eight hours, he felt no trace of fatigue.

"That's not why I called you in, Major," the general said. "You've seen the force readiness reports from General Wei's command?"

Gao pulled out his Shandian tablet and examined the database. "I've been keeping tabs on the situation, sir," he lied.

He scanned the columns of data. Troops, weapons, vehicles...what was the general getting at?

"So you've spotted the problem?" A smile teased the general's severe face, and Gao realized he was being tested.

What am I missing? Gao thought.

Then he saw it. He scrolled back a few hours to check his theory, then looked up with a grin.

"Of course, sir," Gao said. "The numbers are being manipulated. The exact same number of men and vehicles being offloaded for six hours in a row is very unlikely."

Zhang's promise of a smile was fulfilled. "Very good, Major." He picked up his own tablet and sent a field report to Gao. "What do you make of this?"

It was a traffic accident report. Six soldiers had died while escorting a munitions vehicle. Gao tapped on the address and looked at the map. It was a narrow country road with fields on either side. The truck had crashed into a bridge abutment, killing the driver, a passenger, and those inside two escorting vehicles.

Gao considered the aerial image. The bridge was an excellent place for an ambush.

"You suspect sabotage, General," he said.

"Right again, Major, and if Wei doesn't suspect it, he's an even bigger fool than I thought."

A fresh jolt of adrenaline surged into Gao's blood. "You want me to investigate, sir?"

"Can I trust you, Major?"

Gao understood the question. Lieutenant General Wei was politically connected in the Party and a close confidant of the Vice Chairman of the Central Military Commission.

Everyone wanted the invasion of Taiwan to be successful. But no one wanted to share the credit. Zhang was telling him that he doubted General Wei's loyalty.

"Well, Major?" Zhang asked again. "Can I trust in your discretion?"

Gao mouth went dry. This was his opportunity. The general was asking him for a favor. A favor fulfilled would put the very powerful General Zhang in his debt.

Gao gripped the general's proffered hand.

"Always, sir," Gao replied.

13

North Pacific Ocean, 400 miles northeast of Kadena Air Base, Okinawa, Japan

In his fifteen years in the United States Air Force, Master Sergeant Bobby Barros had dropped a lot of things out of the back of a C-17 Globemaster cargo airplane.

He'd seen the roomy cargo bay of the military transport serve as the launch point for over a hundred paratroopers on static line jumps, pallets of supplies over places like Iraq and Afghanistan, the occasional fleet of Humvees. Barros was good enough at his job that he was once detailed to work with the Secret Service to fly the President's bulletproof limo from Washington, DC, to Egypt.

Barros was pretty sure he'd seen it all. He knocked on the glass door of the squadron commander's office. Lieutenant Colonel Hanks was seated behind her desk, across from two visitors, definitely not military types.

Chet and Rita—first names only—were an older couple, maybe in their sixties. Chet was tall, lean, and really tan. He wore Teva sandals and had long, tousled gray hair. He said he was a professor and introduced the woman as his wife, Rita.

"What's your first name, Sergeant?" Chet asked.

"Bobby," Barros replied, surprised that a professor knew military ranks.

"Good, Bobby." Chet went on, "I need your help to drop some pieces of equipment out of an airplane. They get here tonight." He gestured at Hanks. "The colonel has all the details about the plane and the flight path, but I need an expert with me in the cargo area to make sure we release them the right way."

"I can do that," Barros said. "What kind of equipment are we talking about?"

Rita opened her laptop and wordlessly passed it to Chet, who ran through the details with Barros. They looked like giant surfboards.

"How many units?" Barros asked.

"Forty," Chet said.

"*Forty?*" Barros repeated. "How many trips?"

"Has to be one," Chet replied.

Barros looked at the specs again. If he stacked the units on their side, it could work. His mind was already working out the load configuration in his head.

"Okay," Barros said. "I can do it."

"One thing I almost forgot," Chet said, snapping his fingers. "We need to load them inside a hangar."

"That's a problem," the squadron commander said. "This is a fighter base. We don't have any hangars big enough for a C-17."

"Can you clear the airfield while we load the plane?" Chet asked.

Hanks's smile was like plastic. "No, I'm sorry. We can't shut down the airfield."

"What about the hot cargo pad?" Barros said. "If you're worried about someone seeing the cargo, that's about as remote as it gets."

The hot cargo pad, used for loading explosives, was surrounded by a kilometer-wide blast zone. It was located on the spec ops side of the base at the home of the 320th Special Tactics Squadron, far from prying eyes.

"That sounds perfect, Bobby," Chet said. He looked at the squadron commander. "Can you arrange that?"

"Of course."

Barros made a mental note. Chet and Silent Rita had some juice to be able to get the hot cargo pad reserved on short notice.

That evening, Barros rode the C-17 over to the hot cargo pad to find a tractor trailer waiting for them. The flight crew had been instructed that this was to be an engine-running onload. The whine of four Pratt & Whitney engines filled the air as the truck driver maneuvered the trailer close to the lowered ramp on the aircraft.

Although the driver and the passenger in the cab were in civilian clothes, Barros could tell they were definitely not civilians. Both wore sidearms and looked like they'd spent a lot of time in the gym. His suspicion was reinforced when they opened the trailer door. Inside were two more serious-looking dudes, except they had submachine guns to go along with their sidearms.

The cargo of the trailer was giant surfboards. Well, giant *pregnant* surfboards, to be more exact. The bottom of the craft had the normal slight curve of a longboard, but the top had a pod. When Barros got a closer look, he could see seams where the pod was supposed to open.

And they were black. Barros had dated an Okinawan girl a few years back, an artist. She was always talking about Vantablack, the darkest material known to man that could absorb over 99.9 percent of visible light.

These pregnant surfboards looked like they might have been painted with that Vantablack shit.

The four civilians made short work of unloading the trailer while Barros spent the next hour making sure the units were secured in the cargo hold.

Two things surprised Barros about the *Sea Skates*, as Chet referred to them. The first thing was how light they were. Chet explained that they were made entirely from carbon fiber. It would be easy enough for him and Chet to place each unit on the skid assembly that Barros had rigged along the centerline of the cargo bay. From there, the process was automated.

The parachute assembly where Barros planned to hook a static line was a first-class rigging job. It even had a seawater-activated release for the parachute after it landed in the ocean.

The loading process was complete in less than an hour. The trailer departed, the C-17 ramp was raised, and Barros was alone in the cargo hold with Chet and Silent Rita. She stowed her laptop for takeoff but immediately got it out again as soon as they leveled off at cruising altitude. She hunched over her keyboard, the light from the screen bathing her face in softness.

Chet stared at the row of *Sea Skates*. Barros switched them to a private channel on their headphones.

"Professor," he said, "what are those things?"

Chet smiled, but when he spoke, Barros noticed he wasn't looking at the *Sea Skates* anymore. He was looking at Rita.

"Those things represent ten years of my life, Sergeant," he said. "But if I told you, I'd have to kill you."

Barros chuckled and left the older man alone.

An hour later, they approached the first drop zone, and Barros got busy.

The ramp of the C-17 lowered, increasing the wind noise in the cargo hold. Barros clipped his safety harness to the static line that ran the length of the cargo bay and walked to the ramp. The Pacific Ocean was down there, but he couldn't see it. The night was black as pitch.

Barros ran the automated skid down the cargo bay and back to make sure there was no interference, then he signaled the flight crew that they were ready to begin deployment. The lumbering cargo plane descended to one thousand feet to ensure the best accuracy for the drops.

The three of them hit a rhythm. Chet and Barros loaded the skid with a Skate. Barros connected the static line and walked alongside as it ran to the back of the plane. Rita was the one who called the drop point. On her command, Barros released the Skate down a roller ramp and watched the chute deploy.

He had heard the two of them talking about linking each device to a satellite before they dropped, so Barros figured that's what was going on.

They had a few minutes between each drop to reload the skid, which made for a constant pace of loading, travel, deploy, and reload.

The first batch of *Sea Skates* went out the door, then the C-17 made a long, slow turn to reposition them for the second run.

Barros took his seat. He was surprised when Chet sat down next to him and switched their headsets to a private channel.

"The *Sea Skates* are sailboats," he said. "Really expensive unmanned sailboats." He pointed at the bulge on the board. "When the craft hits the water, the pod opens. Inside is a carbon fiber sail that extends up and a stabilizer that extends down into the water. You noticed the color?"

Barros nodded. "Vantablack."

"Very good," Chet replied with a broad smile. "The color scheme makes the Skate all but invisible on the open ocean."

"What does it do, Chet?"

"All kinds of missions. Signals intelligence, recon, mine hunting, whatever, but these are primarily configured to find submarines."

"Chinese submarines, you mean," Barros said.

Chet nodded. "A submarine is basically a big chunk of metal in the ocean, so big, in fact, that it distorts the Earth's magnetic field. The magnetic anomaly detector in the *Sea Skate* can sense that."

Barros knew some Navy guys who flew on the P-8 maritime patrol craft. They'd told him about MAD booms that were supposed to be able to detect a submarine from a few thousand feet in the air.

"But the range on those things is only like a kilometer, right?" Barros asked.

"For a detector on an airplane, that's about right, but these are much more sensitive than that and they're right in the water, much closer to the target. Besides, the Skates search in a pack. They're networked. If one gets a hit, the others vector in." Chet winked. "In no time at all, they've got a triangulated location on the target, and the submarine has no idea they've even been detected."

Chet saw Rita waving at him, and he quickly switched his headset channel. The red light of the cargo hold turned Chet's flowing gray hair the color of blood. Barros switched his own headset.

"Time to get back to work," Chet said.

Barros walked to the back of the plane to make sure the skid path was clear. He peered into the darkness.

Barros didn't follow politics and didn't give a shit about Taiwan, but he knew one thing: some Chinese submarines were about to have a really bad day.

DAY THREE

14

Mission Clock: 187:26:14
Mission Status: Green

Major Gao ducked as he moved under the spinning blades of the Harbin Z-20 helicopter toward the waiting car. Because of the ongoing fighting around the city of Taichung in central Taiwan, he'd needed to wait until first light to requisition a southbound flight. Now, he felt the time pressure of his special assignment from General Zhang even more urgently.

The rear door of the waiting black SUV opened, and a PLA captain stepped into the weak morning sunlight. Gao gritted his teeth. Captain Ren was the aide-de-camp of Lieutenant General Wei, the very man that Gao was hoping to avoid until he had done some investigation on his own.

"Good morning, Major." Captain Ren saluted with parade-ground precision. Gao let him hold the pose a second longer than was necessary before he returned the honor.

"Captain," he said. "I did not expect such personal service. Surely you have better things to do than act as my tour guide."

Ren's smile slipped. "The general wishes to see you, sir."

"As soon as I have completed my duties for General Zhang, I am at *Lieutenant* General Wei's disposal." Gao put his hand on the door handle. "Thank you for providing a vehicle for me."

Gao chuckled as Ren raced around the car and entered from the other side. He slipped his Shandian tablet from the pocket of his tunic and showed the driver the location of the ammunition truck explosion on the map.

"Take us here," Gao said.

The driver looked in the rearview mirror at Ren. The captain hesitated.

"Major, I—" Ren began.

"I gave you an order, Corporal," Gao said in a harsh voice. "Drive, or get out and I'll do it myself."

The enlisted man needed no further urging. He put the car in gear and headed across the tarmac.

Captain Ren shifted in his seat. "Major, I have orders to bring you directly to General Wei."

Gao looked out the window. He was handling this situation all wrong. Browbeating Ren was only creating an enemy when what he needed was an ally.

"General Zhang asked me to conduct a fact-finding mission on the ammunitions explosion," Gao said.

"The incident report was filed as per regulations," Ren replied. "Promptly."

Maybe too promptly, Gao thought. "Perhaps there should be an addendum to the report," he said. "We won't keep General Wei waiting long."

Gao looked out the window to forestall any further discussion.

As in Taipei, martial law was in place in Kaohsiung City. At this hour, the streets were empty and armed PLA soldiers occupied key traffic points. They passed through two checkpoints before they reached the city outskirts.

Buildings thinned as they sped out of the city. The land here was flat coastal plains that extended from the ocean to the rising foothills of the Yushan Range. The tops of distant peaks were lost in the low clouds. Green rice fields, separated by dikes, lay on either side of the elevated road.

Gao monitored their progress on his tablet. The road curved past a small outbuilding, then he saw the site of the explosion about a hundred meters ahead.

"Stop the car," Gao said.

The driver stomped on the brake, throwing his passengers against their seat belts.

Gao stepped out of the vehicle. The road was narrow and unlined with barely enough paved surface for two cars to pass without using the sandy shoulder. The ammunition hauler would have been a heavy truck with a wide wheel base. The driver would have slowed to negotiate the turn.

As Gao walked to the turn in the road, he heard the car door open and close. Captain Ren jogged to catch up with him.

"What are you looking for, sir?" he asked.

"Answers," Gao replied.

At the bend in the road, a rice paddy dike extended into the field. He walked along the grassy berm, squinting into the tall weeds.

There. His eye caught a glint of metal, and he crouched down. Gao felt in the tall grasses until he found what he was looking for.

He held up a 5.56mm casing, the kind of round used in the T91 carbine, standard-issue for the Taiwanese Army. The brass gleamed in the dull morning light. He sniffed the shell. The sharp scent of freshly discharged gunpowder was still present.

Gao got to his feet and tossed the shell to Ren.

"This is what happened," he said. "There was a vehicle parked there"— he indicated the bend in the road—"which forced the truck and the escorts to stop. The attackers fired on the convoy from both sides of the road, killing the soldiers." Gao pointed down the lane to a railroad trestle a hundred meters away. "Then they staged the accident there."

He walked in that direction. Ren followed.

"I don't see how you come to that conclusion based on a single shell casing, sir," Ren protested. As they drew closer to the scene of the accident, the ground was littered with spent shells and charred by fire. "There's all sorts of expended ammunition here."

"I agree," Gao replied. "It was a munitions truck, after all. Rounds of ammunition would have been firing in all directions. I'd say that's the perfect cover for an ambush." He turned on Ren. "Did anyone order an analysis of the slugs in the escort vehicles?"

"No, sir," Ren said. "We didn't see the point. The slugs were obviously from the explosion."

"A dangerous assumption, Captain Ren," Gao said.

As they neared the site of the explosion, Gao slowed his pace, allowing his eyes to roam over the scene. There was not much left to see, he realized. All three vehicles were gone. There were deep gouges out of the rice field where the wrecker had hauled the PLA escort vehicles out of the soft ground.

"The damage was extensive, sir," Ren said. "All three vehicles were completely destroyed. No survivors."

"Your presumption was that the driver of the truck lost control and hit the abutment?" Gao asked.

"Yes, sir," Ren replied. "It seemed the logical explanation."

Gao studied the railroad trestle. The track would need repairs, but the PLA invasion plans did not depend on the Taiwanese rail lines. He was missing something—or he was wrong and this actually was a tragic traffic accident.

"Major," Ren said, "finding one enemy shell in the grass a hundred meters away does not prove anything. An ambush would imply an organized resistance, and we have seen no evidence of that, sir."

Gao passed under the bridge, keeping his eyes on the cracked concrete that made up the rail crossing.

Ren was right, of course. Gao's sabotage theory was paper thin, and the damage from the explosion was significant. If the attackers had hijacked the truck for the cargo, they had surely lost most of it in the detonation.

Gao walked under the bridge. On the other side of the trestle, a well-used, two-lane road ran parallel to the rail line. There was a stoplight with four cars waiting for the light to change. The driver of the first car, a middle-aged Taiwanese man, saw Gao and averted his gaze.

On a normal day, Gao reflected, this would be a very busy road. Hundreds of people would pass by this intersection, maybe thousands.

The light changed. The cars pulled away, but each driver stole a glance at Gao as they sped away.

He turned around. The concrete abutment on this side of the trestle was undamaged. Graffiti covered the smooth surface with stylized balloon letters in bold colors. *LAZER*, the letters spelled. Gao wondered if that was someone's name or a gang.

The traffic light stopped traffic again. Gao noticed the drivers looking at him again.

Over the brightly colored name on the abutment, someone had spray-painted a crude black ideogram. Gao recognized the Mandarin words for *shadow* and *army*. It drew his attention because all the other stylized graffiti seemed to share the space, except for this one clumsy sign painted over the other artwork.

When the light changed again, Gao watched the drivers. They weren't looking at him, he realized. They were looking at the black sign on the wall.

The missing piece of the puzzle fell into place. The attackers didn't care about the ammunition truck; they cared about the location. They were sending a message to every Taiwanese local who drove by this place.

Shadow army, Gao thought. The black sign wasn't graffiti. It was a call to arms.

He walked briskly back to the waiting car. "I'm ready to go," he called to Ren over his shoulder.

Thirty minutes later, they arrived at General Wei's command post. Whereas General Zhang's choice of the Taipei 101 tower for his base of operations made a political statement, Wei sought comfort.

The Grand Hi-Lai Hotel in Kaohsiung City was a five-star resort. A liveried bellboy rushed to open Gao's door when the SUV stopped. It appeared that General Wei had kept on most of the local staff.

Classical music played in the lobby. The cultured atmosphere clashed with the PLA combat uniforms and armed sentries who guarded all the entrances.

"There's one more thing I need to do," Gao said to Ren as they approached the elevators.

"Sir, please," Ren said.

"It will only take a few minutes, Captain. I just need to speak with the intel unit."

Ren sighed. "Fifth floor, sir, but please be quick. The general is waiting."

The major in command of the signals intelligence unit was a short man with thinning hair and thick wire-rimmed glasses. He listened intently to Gao's request, then walked over to an interactive map.

"I can task the drone coverage to search for the same sign all over the city," he said. "My system can do facial recognition and behavioral pattern scans on anyone who comes into contact with the sign."

"That will be sufficient," Gao said. In reality, it was far better than he had hoped. Gao turned to Ren. "Now you can take me to see the general, Captain."

The look of relief was evident on Ren's face as he escorted Gao back into the elevator and used a key card to access the top floor.

When he emerged from the elevator, Gao was greeted with a stunning view of the ocean and the port city of Kaohsiung. He noticed with satisfaction the steady stream of armored vehicles coming off the nearest PLA Navy ship moored in the port.

"It's about time you showed up, Major." General Wei had the harsh voice of a smoker.

Gao saluted. "My apologies, sir. General Zhang was very clear with his orders."

On most soldiers, the long tunic of the combat uniform was loose, allowing the wearer a full range of motion. Wei was short and heavyset, and his belly strained against the material of his uniform. He waved away Gao's salute and waddled through the open sliding doors onto the balcony. Far below, Gao could hear the distant sounds of ships being unloaded.

"General Zhang sends his favorite officer into my area of responsibility. Why?" Wei had squinty eyes and a fleshy mouth. He had a habit of smacking his lips when he talked.

"Just a routine inspection of the ammunition truck explosion, sir."

"The general sent you all this way to look at a traffic accident?" Wei said in a mocking tone. "That seems excessive for a man of your talents. After all, you executed the first strike of the invasion. You are a hero, Major."

Gao felt himself flush with embarrassment. He was carrying himself with too much pride, he realized. If Wei noticed, others would have as well. He regretted his rough treatment of Ren now.

"It seemed suspicious, sir," Gao said. "To the general, I mean."

"Of course," Wei said. "And retasking my drones. Is that part of your duties as well?"

Gao cleared his throat. Wei was no fool, and his staff kept him well informed of what was going on in his command. "I was going to request your assistance with that, General," Gao began.

"Were you?"

"Of course, sir," Gao insisted. "Time is of the essence. We could be seeing a resistance movement—"

Wei waved his hand to cut off Gao's explanation. "Yes, yes, I understand, Major. Everything is a rush. Your mission is important." Wei's tone hardened. "I can run my own command without interference from you or from General Zhang. Do I make myself clear, Major?"

Gao sought to tamp down a surge of anger. It was foolish to get into an argument with a superior officer, but he couldn't help himself.

"I'll just verify your force readiness numbers and be on my way, sir," Gao said.

Wei's lips trembled as he struggled to regain his composure. Gao's veiled threat seemed to have found their mark.

"There is no need for that, Major," Wei said quietly.

Gao had him, and the general knew it. The two men eyed each other until a buzzing noise interrupted the staring contest.

General Wei extracted a mobile phone from his pocket and turned his back to Gao. All communications during the invasion were supposed to be routed through the Shandian battle network. Another violation of General Zhang's orders. Gao steeled himself for another face-off with Wei.

But when the general turned around again, his fleshy face wore a wide grin.

"You're wanted on the fifth floor, Major," he said. "It seems that your fishing expedition has yielded results."

15

Headquarters, US Space Command

Captain Nicholas Saito, US Space Force, squinted at his computer screen. The same grainy image was duplicated on the large wall screen of the top-secret mission control room.

"Standing by to open doors, ma'am," he announced on his throat mic.

Although the use of the network for all communications was standard procedure, Colonel Marjorie Lee, the mission commander, didn't require a comm link to hear his update. She was standing so close behind his workstation that Saito could hear when she cleared her throat.

"Open cargo bay doors, Captain," she said.

The top-secret mission control room had been purpose-built for the X-37B Autonomous Spaceplane program. Officially known as the Orbital Test Vehicle, the platform was essentially a mini-space shuttle.

Because the X-37 was unmanned and most of the flight functions automated, the mission control room held only six workstations—two of which were occupied today.

The man at the workstation next to Saito was definitely not a Space Force Guardian. Randy Minter was a lean man in his mid-thirties with long, brown hair and a Rasputin beard. He not only looked like a Russian mystic, he had an ego to match. His pallid complexion and stringy arms spoke of long, sedentary hours under fluorescent lights, but his brown eyes glowed with intensity.

Today, for the inventor of the Hive Unmanned Satellite Killer program, better known as HUSK, that ego was under serious strain. Randy stared unblinkingly at the wall screen and gnawed at a nonexistent thumbnail.

Saito touched his screen. "Opening cargo bay doors."

Two hundred fifty kilometers above them, in low earth orbit, the clamshell cargo doors on the X-37B began to open. From the camera extended above the vessel, all Saito could see was a shadowy black void of the open bay. Then the craft rotated, and the opening moved into full sunlight. The cargo was beautiful, like a work of art. The cylindrical satellite, which filled the entire cargo hold, was made up of a series of honeycomb-shaped structures that shone like iridescent scales in the harsh light of the sun.

Saito heard an appreciative murmur from the wall of visiting brass lining the back of the room. In addition to the brigadier who ran this section of Space Command, there were four more flag-rank officers from DC and two civilians. Due to the extreme sensitivity of the mission, all of the visitors were without aides. The lack of competing staff lowered the emphasis on rank, and the officers talked among themselves in low tones.

Randy abandoned his thumbnail and started noshing on an index finger. He had every right to be nervous. Eighteen months ago, the HUSK program had been an MIT doctoral thesis, funded by the Department of Defense. Randy had told Saito the first mockup of a killer unit was built using an empty industrial-sized can of tomato sauce and a tenpenny nail. Now, a few billion dollars later, Randy was watching his creation being inserted into orbit—all in complete secrecy.

"Cargo doors indicate open, ma'am," Saito said.

"Initiate deployment, Captain," Lee said. There was more strength in her voice now, as if she could see the light at the end of the tunnel. Once she positioned the unit in the right orbit, it was Randy's ball game from there.

"Starting deployment sequence now," Saito said. He touched his control panel.

The satellite began to rotate slowly inside the cargo bay, making the hexagonal patches on the satellite exterior wink like jewels in the sunlight.

"Rotation satisfactory," Saito reported. "Extension arms moving."

The satellite slowly emerged from the cargo bay of the X-37, held in place by extender arms on either end of the cylinder.

"Releasing in three...two...one."

The satellite floated free. A collective sigh breezed through the room.

Lee's hand fell heavily on Saito's shoulder. "Well done, Captain."

Randy abandoned his bloody fingertips and sat up in his chair. He logged in to his targeting program and then spun his chair around.

"I'm ready whenever you are, gents," he said.

"We're getting presidential release for the mission, Dr. Minter," the brigadier said in a frosty tone. "We'll let you know."

The original name for the HUSK program was LICE, which the DoD had approved for research purposes. Minter's research was funded through the Strategic Capabilities Office, an obscure branch of DARPA used to explore next-gen weapons systems.

A year ago, when the Defense Department decided to fast-track development of the technology, they insisted on a different name, one less parasitic in nature. Saito, who had been assigned to the project at that juncture, could not believe how many meetings it took to come up with an acceptable name for the nascent program. The committee compromised on HUSK as the new name because one of the DC staffers thought the hexagonal panels on the artist renderings looked like a corncob.

Nevertheless, Randy refused to bow to the military establishment. He still used the old name LICE, which meant Saito had to rewrite his reports with the DoD-approved nomenclature before they were submitted to the Pentagon.

The operation of the HUSK satellite was simple in principle but devilishly complex in reality.

The HUSK satellite consisted of 130 mini-satellites—thirteen rows of ten units each. When ordered, the mini-satellites—*lice* in Randy's terminology—would disperse from their host like flower petals in the wind.

Each louse was programmed to find and attach itself to the skin of an enemy host satellite, preferably near the central processor unit. On the execute command, the louse would drive a spike into the heart of the satellite and release an EMP pulse designed to fry the host from the inside out. Without power and control, the dead satellite host would eventually fall into Earth's gravity well and burn up. A much better kill solution than a kinetic weapon that, when it struck a satellite, added even more space debris to the twenty-thousand-plus pieces of junk already in orbit. Space junk was a collision hazard for all satellites in orbit, including those belonging to the US.

Performing that target-capture-kill evolution once on an enemy satellite was difficult enough. They were about to do it 130 times, simultaneously.

But that was only the beginning of the complexity. The original target set for the HUSK program was the Russian satellite fleet. Three days ago, their target changed to the Chinese satellites in orbit. Since then, Randy and Saito had been working around the clock to identify and track the Chinese space assets and upload them into Randy's LICE targeting program.

To be effective, the attack needed to be executed simultaneously on all targets. Once the Chinese figured out what was happening, they might change orbit on their satellites, and the killer lice would miss their targets.

This was an all-or-nothing attack. One shot. Go big or go home.

Colonel Lee drifted to the back of the room where Saito could hear her conferring with the brigadier.

"I have a green board for the HUSK satellite, ma'am," Saito said into his mic.

"Put it on the big screen, Captain," she replied over the comm link.

One hundred thirty green dots, one for each louse, populated the wall screen in neat rows. Somewhere in the middle of the screen, one of the dots blinked twice, then turned red.

"What does that mean?" one of the spectators called out.

"One of the units lost connection," Randy replied tightly. "We anticipated that."

Another dot blinked and turned red. There was muttering among the brass.

Saito shot a sideways look at Randy. They could handle a two percent loss of individual units and still complete the mission. Losing more than eight units meant they would have to choose between priority targets.

Or, rather, Randy's LICE program would make the choice for them. Over the past three days as they built up the database of Chinese targets, he had run thousands of simulations to "teach" the program how to prioritize the target list. Once he started the LICE program, Randy turned over all decisions to the targeting computer.

First on the kill list were reconnaissance satellites, then communications, then navigation, and finally, if there were enough LICE remaining, the weather satellites.

A third dot went crimson. Saito could see Randy starting to sweat now. The upload step was when they expected to lose individuals, not beforehand.

"What's going on?" Lee asked in an urgent tone.

A fourth unit died.

Randy looked like he was about to hyperventilate. "We need to upload now. If we sustained some damage during the deployment, this situation will not improve."

"The general is on the phone with the President now," she said. "It will be a few more minutes."

Another dot turned red.

"We may not have a few more minutes, Marjie," Randy said. He knew the colonel hated it when he called her that.

At that point, the brigadier strode back into the room and announced in a loud voice: "We have a go from the President, Colonel. You may proceed."

Randy was already working the keyboard. He punched a final key and sat back. He chewed the ends of both index fingers at the same time.

All the green dots on the screen turned bright yellow.

"Uploading HUSK targeting data, ma'am," Saito said into the mic.

Her heels clicked on the polished cement floor as she traveled from the pack of generals to his station. "Copy."

The model said the upload process was supposed to take three minutes. There was a digital mission counter in the corner of the wall screen.

Saito found himself holding his breath as he watched the seconds drip away from the counter. The red dots of the failed units blazed crimson in the sea of yellow, like drops of blood in a field of daisies.

The first dot turned green just as the counter showed one minute remaining. It was quickly followed by a smattering of more units turning green. By the time the counter ran down to zero, a full sixty percent of the field was green and they had lost two more units. The array looked like a Pac-Man screen.

Slowly, the field normalized to just red and green dots. "We lost six units. Four-point-six percent against a mission goal of two percent," said Saito.

"The LICE program is retargeting now to account for the losses," Randy said. Some of the green dots returned to pulsing yellow. One of them flipped to red.

"Can we stop the retargeting?" Colonel Lee asked. "We just lost another one."

"Nope," Randy said. "LICE makes the targeting calls. We're out of the loop."

Suddenly, he sat up straight in his chair as if he'd been poked by a cattle prod.

"We're ready, Colonel," he said.

Randy looked over at Saito as if he didn't quite believe it himself. Saito turned around to look at the colonel.

"Stand by," Lee said. She turned to the back of the room. "Request permission to deploy HUSK, General."

"Execute the deployment, Colonel."

Saito spun back to his screen. His hand shook as he poised his finger over the pulsing red button on his touchscreen. He realized he was holding his breath again and forced himself to breathe. Randy rolled his chair over. Saito could smell coffee on Randy's breath and feel Lee's presence behind him.

"Deploy HUSK," Lee whispered.

"Deploying HUSK." Saito touched his screen. The image of the big red button froze, then turned green.

"Put the picture on screen, Captain," Lee said.

Saito pushed the X-37B camera feed to the wall screen.

The HUSK satellite began to spin faster. The end caps of the cylinder separated from the main body and floated away. The hexagonal scales glittered as the unit reached deployment velocity, then one by one, pieces of the satellite began to fly off, vectoring into space. Over the course of a ninety-minute orbit of the Earth, the mother satellite was reduced to a naked spindle and a small control unit. The remains of the HUSK satellite would burn up in the atmosphere within twenty-four hours.

Without being ordered, Saito switched back to the dot screen that monitored individual killer units. They had turned yellow upon separation from the mother satellite. They would return to green again once they found and attached themselves to their targets.

Three hours later, they had their answer. A hundred and twenty-three of the individual HUSK units had found their targets.

Saito tried to imagine the HUSK parasite clamped to the side of a Chinese satellite. Its probe poised, ready to pierce the skin of its host and deliver a deadly burst of electromagnetic energy.

"We're ready, sir," Colonel Lee said to the brigadier. Her voice told Saito she knew they were witnessing a historic moment.

"Proceed, Colonel."

"Execute the kill command, Captain."

"Aye-aye, ma'am." Saito touched his screen for the last time.

In the outer reaches of Earth's orbit, 123 HUSK units slammed home a titanium-clad spike. Seconds later, their onboard capacitor banks delivered a jolt of fatal energy into the unsuspecting host.

"Boom-boom," whispered Colonel Lee. "Out go the lights."

16

North Pacific Ocean, 500 miles southeast of Petropavlovsk

Rear Admiral Chip Sharratt, Commander of the *Enterprise* strike force, handed the message board back to Chief of Staff Tom Zachary. He turned to face the vast expanse of Pacific Ocean on view outside the windows of the flag bridge and blew out a long breath.

Finally.

It had been three days since the Chinese invasion of Taiwan. Three long days. When the news broke, Sharratt naturally expected orders to head south and put his fighting force to work.

Instead, the *Enterprise* strike force of some thirty ships, including three aircraft carriers, had been left to steam in circles in the middle of the goddamn ocean like some civilian cruise ship regatta. His orders were to conduct flight operations and produce as much electromagnetic radiation as possible. Meanwhile, the USS *Abraham Lincoln* was sailing from the Arabian Sea into the South China Sea.

Clearly, his strike force was meant to put on a show, but for whom? Not the Russians. Although the official line was that his strike force was "tied down" by the Russian Pacific Fleet, they had steadily edged away from the reach of all but the most long-range Russian air assets coming out of Vladivostok and Petropavlovsk.

Now, finally, he knew the answer.

Chinese satellite coverage significantly degraded, the message read. *Enterprise SF proceed to Taiwan at best possible speed. Logistics plan to follow.*

From his perch in flag watch, Sharratt watched the USS *Rafael Peralta* and the USS *William Charette,* two *Arleigh Burke*-class guided missile destroyers, plow through moderate seas at a stately twelve knots. In his mind, best possible speed meant thirty knots, maybe more. Thirty knots was going to be a fun ride on a destroyer.

"What do you think, Tom?" Sharratt asked.

"We're gonna burn a lot of fuel at thirty knots, sir," Zachary replied. "Their logistics plan better be good."

Sharratt laughed for the first time in a long time. Keeping a carrier strike force afloat was a logistical problem of immense proportions, but fuel availability was a matter of life and death for an aircraft carrier. Like every admiral he knew, the first thing Sharratt checked in the morning and the last thing he checked before he went to sleep was the fuel status of his fleet. While a nuclear-powered carrier didn't need to gas up, all of the many escort ships and aircraft that protected the mighty carrier all ran on good old-fashioned fossil fuel.

A thirty-knot speed of advance for a fleet the size of the *Enterprise* strike force was unheard of. The amount of fuel that the strike force would go through as they transited—hell, as they *flew*—south was astronomical. In his quarter century of service on carriers, Sharratt had never seen an order like this one.

And that was the point, Sharratt realized. The *Enterprise* would be within striking range of the PLA naval forces east of Taiwan inside of three days, half the time the Chinese would expect the transit to take. If the Chinese satellite coverage was gone, the element of surprise would be his.

"Let's go, Tom," Sharratt said.

Sharratt took the stairs for the long trip down to Battle Watch below the flight deck. He walked to the railing of the BattleSpace display. The holographic projection gave Sharratt a three-dimensional representation of his strike force.

"Battle Watch Officer, what's the status of our new robot air wing?" Sharratt asked.

"Final units are landing now, sir," he replied. "That's seven for us, seven for the *Teddy*, and six on the *Nimitz*." He shot a look at the monitor showing the flight deck of the *Enterprise* where a MQ-25 Stingray refueling drone was landing. "That's the last Stingray landing now, sir."

Sharratt heard the distant slam of landing gear on the flight deck above them.

In a feat of engineering that Sharratt still could not quite believe, the Navy flew a full squadron of UAVs, unmanned aerial vehicles, from Hawaii to the *Enterprise* strike force in the North Pacific. In normal times, such a test would have taken years of planning and countless approvals. Instead, the Navy had executed the entire operation, from inception to completion, in less than a week.

"Necessity is the mother of invention," Sharratt muttered to himself.

The new UAVs were configurable for anti-submarine and electronic warfare missions. The thought occurred to Sharratt that with the addition of the "robot air wing," as they were called, the strike force officially had more unmanned aircraft in its arsenal than manned aircraft.

"Show me the *Zumwalts*," Sharratt ordered the BattleSpace operator. The lieutenant driving the holographic display wore VR goggles. The fingers of her gloved hand moved, and the scale of display expanded until he saw three blue arrows vectoring west across the Pacific Ocean.

All three *Zumwalt*-class destroyers would rendezvous with the *Enterprise* strike force as they were en route to Taiwan. The much-maligned DDG-1000 had once been heralded as the ship of the future. Instead, it turned into a series of technology failures and a black eye for naval procurement.

But in the last year, that began to change as the once-futuristic technologies needed to arm the ships caught up with the unique hull design.

Despite their poor reputation, Sharratt was glad to have them as part of his strike force. With their state-of-the-art SPY-3 radar and her eighty VLS launch cells, she would add both to his sensor coverage and his missile shield. But what he really valued was their newly installed directed energy weapons.

The high-power lasers were cutting-edge technology, but if they worked, it could mean the difference between life and death for his strike force. The new weapons were not like something out of a science fiction movie that disintegrated incoming missiles. The directed energy blast was designed to "burn through" the cone of the incoming missile and cause the guidance system to fail.

When a guided missile destroyer fired her last missile, she was out of the fight, but a *Zumwalt*-class ship with a laser could fire again and again.

Zachary appeared at his elbow. "The last drone is recovered. It's time, sir."

Sharratt reached for the handset over the BattleSpace display.

"All stations, this is Alpha Bravo actual." He released the transmit button to let the network chatter cease. All eyes in Battle Watch were on him. Sharratt imagined the twenty thousand sailors in his strike force hanging on to his every word.

"When the PLA invaded the island of Taiwan three days ago, we all expected to get the call to head south. I'm pleased to tell you that those orders have arrived.

"This strike force will proceed south at thirty knots. That's right, you heard me, people. Hang on to your hats, because we are all gonna be pilots for the next few days. *Antietam* and *Pinckney* will be staying behind as decoys. They're going to make enough noise so whoever is listening thinks we're still here. We owe the crews of those two ships a debt of thanks.

"I want to be up front with all of you. The People's Republic of China is a dangerous adversary, and we are fighting in their home waters. Anyone who thinks this is going to be easy is sorely mistaken. The island of Taiwan has been on China's radar screen for seventy-five years. China is prepared to fight for what they think is already theirs. You know what stands between freedom in Taiwan and Chinese aggression?

"The *Enterprise* strike force, that's who. Ladies and gentlemen, we've been given a job to do, and we will do our duty. Good luck and God bless. Alpha Bravo, out."

When Sharratt hung up the handset, he found his hand was shaking with pent-up emotion. He gripped the steel railing around the BattleSpace display. He could feel the eyes of everyone in the room on him, but he heard not a sound.

What were they thinking? he wondered. If they were smart, they'd be scared shitless. He certainly was. But that didn't matter now. The commander in chief had given him a job, and he was going to get it done to the best of his ability.

Whatever the cost.

"Battle Watch Officer." His steady tone rang in the silence.

"Sir!"

"Set EMCON condition Alpha in the strike force. Set course for Taiwan, Great Circle route, speed of thirty knots."

When the watch officer responded, the room exploded into action. Sharratt felt the mighty *Enterprise* turn. Her deck plates thrummed with power.

"Show me the South China Sea," he said to the BattleSpace operator. "I want to see the *Lincoln*."

The display reconfigured south. He picked out the blue arrows in the crowded waterways at the base of the Strait of Malacca.

"Zoom in," Sharratt said. Tom Zachary joined him at the railing.

Sharratt counted the escorts around the *Lincoln*. Two cruisers, two destroyers, and one of the new frigates. Although not on the display, there would be a submarine in support of the *Lincoln* as well.

That's not much firepower in the South China Sea, he thought. They're sailing into some dangerous waters.

"When was the last time you saw Bulldog?" Zachary asked.

Rear Admiral Seth "Bulldog" Denton was Sharratt's oldest friend, a relationship that extended from the very first day of Plebe Summer at the Naval Academy.

"Two years ago," Sharratt said finally. "I hope to hell I get to see him again."

The attack on the Chinese satellites was just part of the plan, Sharratt realized. While his strike force sped south in total electronic silence, the *Lincoln* was going to drive right up the gut of the South China Sea and raise holy hell.

A nice shiny object to occupy the Chinese while Sharratt kicked open the back door to Taiwan.

"Those poor bastards," Zachary said.

17

Mission Clock: 176:41:18
Mission Status: Green

"That makes three fish in the net." The PLA intel officer grinned at Gao from the other side of the interactive map table. "I'd say that's enough for a meal."

"I'm impressed," Gao replied.

And he was. When General Wei's intel officer described his plan to use the ideogram at the site of the ammunition truck explosion as an anchor point for a behavioral pattern recognition sweep, Gao had been skeptical.

But the officer had exceeded all expectations. By mining the data stored in the Taiwanese government files, he used facial recognition to identify the driver of each car that passed the graffiti. Focusing on males between the ages of eighteen and forty, he screened the candidates for military service, located their home and place of work, and mined the local traffic camera records to put together an individual profile for each suspect. Then he looked for behavior outside of the normal patterns.

And he found it. Of the thousands of people who had driven past the graffiti site during the day, three candidates with past military service had broken from their daily routines. All of them ended up in the same place: a campground in the mountains to their east. Although the campground was closed, a drone flyby showed six vehicles in the adjoining parking lot and ten people inside the main lodge.

"I think we should keep them under surveillance," the intelligence officer said. "See if anyone else joins."

Gao checked his Shandian tablet. The mission clock still showed pale green. He had not intended to spend the entire day tracking down a handful of young men who daydreamed about taking on the People's Liberation Army. He chuffed in frustration. He needed to be done with this nonsense and get back to General Zhang's side posthaste.

"No," Gao said. "I'll take a squad of military police and arrest them."

He studied the terrain. The campground was located in a shallow wooded valley that sloped down from east to west. The only access by vehicle was a winding road that followed a creek as it snaked into the mountains.

If this were a war game scenario, he'd put a pair of KD-10 laser guided missiles into the building and be done with it. But his rules of engagement forbid that level of direct action. Besides, taking a few of these self-styled rebels alive might provide some useful intelligence.

Gao pointed at the dirt road. "We'll block the road here and have a squad sweep down the valley using the high ground to our advantage. Secure the parking lot and surround the building. We'll have them in custody by nightfall."

"You will lead the operation, sir?" the intelligence officer asked.

Gao nodded.

"You'll need General Wei's authorization, sir," the intel officer replied. "I've been keeping him updated on our progress."

Gao recalled the smoke breaks the man had taken during the day. Every hour, on the hour, like clockwork. Perhaps he had underestimated Wei after all.

"Of course," Gao replied.

General Wei was just sitting down to a late lunch when Gao arrived in his penthouse suite. He waved a pair of chopsticks, his fleshy lips stretched into a smile.

"Join me, Major," he said. "Please."

Gao sighed inwardly. This idiot was feeding his face when there was time-critical work to be done. But as soon as he smelled the food, Gao realized he hadn't eaten a thing all day. He sat down at the open table setting across from the general.

Wei started without him, slurping and chomping his way through a bowl of noodles. Gao used his own chopsticks to put a pork dumpling in his mouth. The delicacy practically dissolved on his tongue in a riot of flavor. It might have been the finest dumpling he'd ever eaten. The reaction on his face caught Wei's attention.

"The chef here is excellent." He swilled a glass of beer. "When this is all over, I think I'll hire him."

"Why would a Taiwanese chef in a five-star hotel want to move to Beijing?" Gao asked.

"Who said anything about moving to Beijing?" Wei replied. He snatched a piece of sea cucumber from the tray in the center of the table and popped it into his mouth. His grin widened.

The second dumpling was halfway to Gao's lips when the general's words sunk in.

"You want to be the governor of Taiwan," Gao said.

Wei's rounded shoulders shrugged under his uniform. "Perhaps the General Secretary will favor me with an appointment."

General Wei was well known for his prowess as a political infighter and fierce Party loyalist, but he was a career staff officer. His appointment as field commander of the southern invasion force had been a surprise to Gao. Now he saw what he had not realized before: Wei was positioning himself for the post-reunification era.

I've been fighting this man, Gao thought, when I should be luring him in.

"Perhaps we can work together, General," Gao said. "We've located the terrorists responsible for the ammunition truck sabotage."

Wei held up his chopsticks. "Allegedly."

Gao nodded, his frustrations now securely locked behind a mask of cooperation.

"Alleged sabotage. Still, would not the capture of such a criminal be an intelligence coup, sir? I'm thinking General Zhang would consider it so. In fact, I'd ensure he viewed it in that light."

Wei considered Gao as the waitstaff cleared his place. Gao eyed the dumplings as they were taken away. No matter, he would eat later.

"If you allow me to lead a small contingent of men," Gao said, "I can take these suspects alive. The tactical situation is very favorable." Gao realized he was talking too fast and making up the details as he went, but this was his chance to finish the job and get back to Zhang.

Wei selected a toothpick from the tray and went to work on something in the back of his mouth.

"An interesting concept, Major," Wei said finally. "How many men do you need?"

"A platoon of soldiers, sir," Gao replied. "No more than that."

"My men would have to lead the assault," Wei said. "Perhaps Captain Ren would be a good choice."

Gao tried not to smile. Ren had almost no field experience. Effectively, Gao would be in charge of the mission.

"An inspired choice, sir."

From the eastern rise above the campground, Gao peered down the slope. From ground level, the terrain looked very different than it had from the air. The tree cover overhead was thick, but the floor of the forest was open, with scarcely any cover. Gao supposed that campers had used up all the lower branches for their fires. Adding to his unease, the setting sun angled into his eyes.

Next to him, his own field glasses pressed to his face, Captain Ren also scanned the forest below.

"An easy approach, sir," Ren said. "Half a kilometer, I'd say."

"We'll wait for dark," Gao said. "Make a nighttime approach."

"Sir," Ren said, "this unit is not equipped for a night raid."

"No night vision goggles?" Gao said. He'd spent his career with special operations forces units where NVGs were standard issue. In his haste to get the operation started, Gao had neglected the details.

"No, sir," Ren answered, "I didn't see it as necessary. We have at least two hours of daylight left. Plenty of time to get the job done."

Gao unlocked the screen on his Shandian tablet. The mission clock color had faded even more. The invasion was still on track but losing ground by the hour. He had worked so hard to get the invasion plan ahead of schedule, but now he could see those gains slipping away.

He cursed under his breath. The right thing to do was to pull back, maintain an aerial surveillance, and return with a properly outfitted team. But that would take hours, and he was needed at General Zhang's side.

Captain Ren was right, Gao decided. They had enough daylight to get the mission accomplished.

"Get your men ready, Captain," Gao ordered. "We move out in five minutes."

As Ren scurried away, Gao consulted the aerial view of the campground. The ten people inside the main lodge had not moved all day.

He zoomed out on the drone feed. The forest was as still as stone. Not even a squirrel stirred among the trees.

Ren arrayed his men in a line along the ridge. Gao gave one last look at the drone picture, then stood. The afternoon sun forced his eyes into a squint.

"I'm ready when you are, sir," Ren reported. The young man's face was tight with excitement, and he had a fevered smile on his face. This was probably the most action the kid had seen in his entire career, Gao reflected.

"Proceed, Captain," he said.

The line of camouflaged soldiers, weapons at the ready, started down the slope. Gao followed, his footfalls muffled by the thick carpet of pine needles.

18

Taiwu Township, Taiwan

From inside the main lodge, Lester studied the video screen. From the cameras fixed in the trees, he saw a loose line of thirty PLA soldiers advance down the forested slope. Afternoon sunlight caught the lenses of a soldier's eyeglasses.

They were kids, he realized. Regular grunts, probably just out of basic training.

A steady stream of low-key conversation came across his earpiece. Hardy's voice said, "I'm seeing a major, a captain, three noncomm squad leaders, and all the rest are grunts. Oh, the radioman is next to his captain." Lester half listened as Hardy doled out targets for his two Taiwanese sniper teams.

A pause, then Hardy's voice again. "Standing by, Colonel. We're ready to rock and roll on your mark, sir."

Lester turned to Frank Tsai. "You're sure you can do this, Frank?"

Captain Tsai's smile was a slash of white in his camouflaged face. "Absolutely, sir."

At a nod from his captain, the kid at the computer rig took control of a joystick. They all looked like kids, Lester realized. On the screen, the operator had the PLA drone, a quadcopter hovering at eight hundred meters overhead, in his sights. He punched a button on his keyboard.

"Overriding the drone, sir," he said. "Good signal." He twisted the joystick, and the drone moved to one side. "I have control." He turned to grin at Tsai. "Where do you want me to put her down?"

Christ, Lester thought, this might actually work.

"Hardy," he said into his throat mic. "You are weapons free, repeat, weapons free."

"Copy, weapons free," came the swift reply.

From their concealed position, Lester heard the snap of suppressed gunfire as the snipers did their job. Then, as soon as the PLA soldiers realized they were under attack, the firefight began.

But the fight was over before it began for the PLA. The moment the soldiers had started down the slope toward the campground, they were dead. Their leader had marched them right into an L-shaped ambush. Tactics 101, Lesson One.

"Team Alpha, cease fire," Lester said. "Team Bravo, move in."

On the video screen, Lester could just make out the prone figures of camouflaged Taiwanese soldiers squirming over the ridge behind the PLA troops. Bursts of gunfire broke out as the Taiwanese team moved down the slope.

"Bowling alley is clear, sir," Hardy announced over the net.

Lester left the hidden command post with Tsai hot on his heels. Together the pair ran through the campground and up the slope to the scene of the assault. Behind him, the hijacked PLA drone made a soft touchdown on the grass.

When the Tsai brothers had suggested they set up an ambush at the Shadow Army rally point, Lester had been skeptical. The campground was too exposed, he argued, and they had no way of knowing for sure if the PLA would even show up at the rally point.

Oliver Tsai had been adamant. "The PLA will be there, Colonel. If we don't have a plan to secure the rally point, we might as well turn our people over to the PLA and be done with it."

Lester learned that the Shadow Army used rally points as a security measure to limit the number of people who knew the exact location of the secure mountain compound.

Hardy met him as he came to the edge of the woods. "Like shooting fish in a barrel, sir. Zero casualties—on our side."

Lester ignored him. The PLA forces had been overconfident and walked right into an ambush. He had enough respect for his enemy to know they wouldn't make that same mistake twice.

He came to his first corpse. The Chinese kid was sprawled on the ground like a starfish. He looked to be no more than a teenager, and his camouflage uniform was brand new.

"Listen up," Lester called out. "Strip the corpses of anything useful. That means weapons and ammunition. No souvenirs and nothing electronic. Understand?"

Frank repeated the orders in Mandarin, and the Taiwanese team fanned out across the slope.

"I want us to be on the move in the next ten minutes, Frank," Lester said.

Before Tsai could answer, a call came over the net for Lester.

"Skipper," Hardy said, "I think you might want to see this. I'm fifty meters down from the ridge in the center."

"On my way," Lester replied.

The last rays of the day shafted through the trees as he huffed his way up the slope. Hardy crouched next to a corpse on the ground. He stood when Lester and Frank arrived.

"One of these things is not like the others," he said.

Lester saw what Hardy meant immediately. The uniformed figure bore the rank insignia of a major as well as a commando patch. His uniform was also different from the dead infantrymen down the slope.

"That's a spec ops camo pattern, sir," Hardy continued.

The man looked to be in his mid-thirties, but most of his face was covered with blood from a head wound.

Lester pointed to a device on the ground next to the soldier. "What's that?"

When Hardy reached across the body, the man moved.

"Shit," Hardy said, "this dude's alive!"

He snagged the device and tossed it to Lester. It was a computer tablet, sized to be able to hold easily in one hand. The large screen appeared to be waterproof and ruggedized for outdoor use. The device showed a lock screen.

Lester touched his throat mic. "Ash, this is Lester. I need you up the slope."

Lewis arrived and took her time examining the device.

"High-end, maybe he was using it to control the drone?" She tapped the top of the lock screen. "I'm guessing this is a retina scan." She nodded at the prone PLA soldier. "This was on him?"

Lester nodded. Lewis knelt, pried open the man's eyelid, and held the screen in front of his face. It unlocked immediately.

"Bingo," she said, passing the tablet to Lester.

Lester saw a countdown clock on the home screen that read 175:22:14. The rest of the page appeared to be text updates in Chinese characters. He changed screens and was able to view maps and what appeared to be troop numbers and placements. There were phone and video icons at the bottom of the page. He handed it back to Lewis.

"Can you change the security key?" Lewis consulted with Frank Tsai on translation of the Chinese characters, then held the device up to Lester's face. "Say cheese."

Lester tested the security lock, then handed the device back to Lewis. "We're taking it with us. Bag it in something that blocks EM signals so we don't geolocate ourselves."

The man on the ground stirred again.

"What about him?" Hardy asked.

"I'll take care of him, sir." Frank drew his sidearm and leveled it at the PLA soldier.

Lester put his hand across the barrel, pushed the muzzle down. "We don't do that, Frank."

Lester could see the muscles of Frank's jaw quiver as the man clenched his teeth. His voice was harsh with anger. "Colonel, these men invaded my country. Every one of them deserves to die."

"I can't let you do that, Frank." Out of the corner of his eye, Lester saw Hardy ease Lewis away from the PLA soldier's side. He spoke quietly to

Tsai. "I know these rules feel arbitrary, but taking out a man in battle and shooting an injured man in the head are two different things. Trust me on this, son."

He kept his hand firmly on the barrel of Tsai's weapon, keeping it pointed at the ground. Lester put his other arm around Frank's shoulders.

"Operational security has not been compromised. He hasn't seen any of us, and we've taken his only means of communication. He's no threat to us now."

The young man's shoulders trembled. The upward pressure on the gun barrel had not eased. Lester was not getting through to him.

"Frank," he said firmly, "you will not shoot an injured man. That's an order. Do you understand, Captain?"

Tsai swallowed and shrugged off Lester's arm. The Taiwanese Army captain finally holstered his weapon and stalked down the hill.

Lester let out a long sigh.

"He's not wrong, skipper," Hardy said.

Lester looked at the blood-covered face of the PLA soldier.

"He's a dead man, Hardy," Lester said. "He's no threat to us."

19

USS *Idaho* (SSN-799)
Pacific Ocean, 130 miles east of Okinawa, Japan

Foul-weather gear, orange life vests, and safety harnesses were piled by the door of the wardroom. Normally, this gear was only used for transiting in and out of port. It was not uncommon for the equipment to be stowed while still damp, which was the source of the moldy odor that permeated the small wardroom.

The team of ten, a mix of officers and senior enlisted personnel, made nervous small talk while they awaited the start of the briefing. Surfacing in the middle of the ocean and taking on a passenger were not normal evolutions for a submarine.

Captain Lannier entered and took his seat at the head of the table. "Let's get started," he said.

Chief of the Boat Henry Schumacher got to his feet. He was tall and lean with a thin face weathered by decades of sea duty. Not only was he the most senior enlisted crewmember on the sub, he was also the most experienced member of the crew. It was said that if the COB hadn't seen it done on a submarine, it didn't exist.

Schumacher described the upcoming evolution in clear terms.

"The helo will hover and drop a line," the COB said. "Harris will handle the grounding hook. Do not touch the line unless you are cleared by me. A flying helo can build up a static charge that will knock you on your ass. Understood?"

Nods all around the room.

"Good," the COB continued. "We will take on the passenger first, then the cargo. We expect three watertight Pelican cases. Harris hooks them, Peeler and Wilson put them down the hatch." The COB winked. "I don't want to see any heroes out there. If anybody or anything goes in the drink, Petty Officer Harmon will go swimming."

Unlike the others, Harmon, the ship's diver, was dressed in a wetsuit.

The COB looked around the room sternly. "We are exposed on the surface. This is a ten-minute evolution, people. We do this by the book and we get back underwater where we belong."

Despite Schumacher's promises of simplicity, Mother Nature was not in a mood to cooperate. The weather on the surface was a blustery mess. As Janet stood with the captain on the flying bridge, gusting wind chilled her cheeks and blew spray across the wet back of the *Idaho*. The horizon was a flat gray line, empty of any surface ship traffic.

"Captain," the OOD's voice crackled over the intercom. "I have an inbound helo bearing two-seven-zero."

Janet raised her binoculars, training them on the bearing. She made out a gunmetal gray SH-60 headed toward them.

Lannier put a handheld VHF radio close to his mouth. "Romeo Tango, I have you by visual. Do you copy?"

"November Mike," came the immediate response with the correct call sign. "I have you five by five. Stand by for transfer, sir."

"Roger that, Romeo Tango." Lannier keyed the intercom. "Pilot, all stop. XO, you have permission to open the hatch."

As the submarine coasted to a stop, the helo hovered on the windward side of the ship. The rotor wash flattened the spray as the hatch opened and the ship's team clambered on deck. They quickly clipped their safety harnesses onto recessed eyelets on the hull.

"Seventeen years in submarines," Lannier said. "This is one evolution I've never done."

A static line dropped from the helo. One of the sailors snagged it with a grounding hook. The COB flashed a thumbs-up sign to the helo.

"November Mike, your passenger is coming down now," the helo pilot said on the radio.

Janet used her binoculars to study the person seated in the sling. Dressed in a bulky flight suit, life vest, and visored helmet, it was impossible to tell if the passenger was a man or a woman. The message had directed the *Idaho* to a rendezvous point to take on one passenger and three cases.

Janet's gaze moved past the action on deck to the *Manta* docked on the aft hatch. The bulbous clear glass bow gave the craft a futuristic look. She glanced up at the thick cloud cover. It would also make the *Idaho* instantly recognizable to an enemy satellite.

The passenger made it safely onto the deck of the submarine and was hustled below by two of the *Idaho* sailors. One by one, the Pelican cases were lowered and manhandled by the deck crew into the hatch.

"November Mike, that's all we've got for you, sir. Good luck." The helo peeled off and sped away.

The captain waited until the deck hatch closed, then turned to Janet.

"Close out the bridge, Lieutenant." He signaled to the lookout and disappeared down the ladder.

Using the closeout checklist, Janet secured the bridge and slammed the bridge clamshell fairing shut. She closed the upper hatch and spun the wheel to dog it tight. Then she climbed down the ladder to the second hatch and repeated the procedure.

"Control, this is Lieutenant Everett, the bridge is secure," she said into the phone located at the bottom of the hatch.

A few seconds later, she heard the familiar "Dive, dive," command followed by the *ah-oo-gah* klaxon.

The deck tilted downward. The rocking of the submarine ceased. The angle steepened until she had to grab the ladder rung to stay upright. She felt a vibration under her feet as the submarine picked up speed.

Janet checked her watch. The *Idaho* had been on the surface for twelve minutes.

Anxious to satisfy her curiosity, Janet made her way to the wardroom.

She pushed the door open in time to hear the XO say, "Now, I've seen it all. We have a Zoomie on board!"

Captain Mark Westlund, US Air Force, took the jokes about his service in stride as he stood to shake her hand. "Don said to tell you that if you won't come back to Emerging Threats, then Emerging Threats will come to you." Mark smiled. "He also said to congratulate you on the Russia cable-tapping operation."

"Is that why you're here?" Janet asked.

Oddly, Mark's presence on the *Idaho* bothered her. Up until now, she had managed to keep her past with ETG and her present as a submarine officer separated by time and distance. Mark's sudden appearance made her long for the life she had left behind.

"We'll do a limited briefing after the meal," Captain Lannier said.

Janet picked at her food as she half listened to Mark talk during the meal. He was a gifted conversationalist, even managing to draw some of the quieter members of the wardroom into a dialogue. Unlike her, Mark seemed to easily adapt to what must have been very unnatural surroundings for him.

God, she thought to herself, you're jealous of this guy.

For Janet, the meal dragged on. The suspense of why Don Riley had decided to send Mark Westlund into the field was killing her. It must be about the *Manta*, she decided.

Finally, when the last of the dessert plates had been removed by the culinary specialists and coffee served, the captain indicated for the junior officers to leave. Mark retrieved his laptop, and Janet blocked the small windows on both of the wardroom entrances, standard procedure for a top-secret briefing.

Janet, Mark, Captain Lannier, and the XO gathered at the wardroom table. For this preliminary briefing, Mark had asked that the other members of the *Manta* team be excluded, and the captain reluctantly agreed.

"Now maybe you can explain to me why we risked being seen by a satellite, Mr. Westlund," Lannier began. "I trust you have some extremely urgent intel for us."

"The first question is easy, sir," Mark said. "We're not worried about

Chinese spy satellites because there are no more Chinese spy satellites."

"I don't follow," the XO said.

"As of yesterday," Mark said, "the PRC is essentially blind over this part of the world. We executed a simultaneous strike against their space-based reconnaissance assets. We took them back a few decades. They're relying on ground-based SIGINT and aerial reconnaissance by aircraft for the time being."

"I see," Lannier said. "So, the effort against the PLA is heating up?"

"It's about to get a lot hotter, sir." Mark opened his laptop. "I meant what I said about the *Idaho*'s performance in the Sea of O. Your team literally saved the country from making a very big mistake."

Lannier's gaze shifted briefly to Janet, then back to Mark.

"It was a fluid situation," Lannier said, "especially those last few hours."

Mark seemed oblivious to the sudden tension in the room.

"Well, we're going to ask you to do it again." He threw a chart to the wall screen in the wardroom. "When the PLA invaded Taiwan, they shut down all communications off the island, including satellite and undersea cables. Except for one. They kept the Taiwan Strait Express Submarine Cable in operation."

Mark highlighted the northwestern tip of Taiwan. "The TSE runs from Tanshui on Taiwan to Fuzhou on the Chinese mainland. This cable provides a direct line between the PLA forces in Taiwan and their headquarters elements on the Chinese mainland. We're asking the *Idaho* to tap into it."

The captain and XO stood next to the screen, studying the chart. The water depth for the entire length of the cable run was less than one hundred meters. Large modern-day submarines like the *Idaho* preferred to operate in waters no less than two hundred meters deep.

"Our best approach would be here." The XO indicated an area of deep water called the Okinawa Trough. "Even if we drop the *Manta* somewhere around here, that kind of transit will eat up the battery."

Janet joined them at the chart. "What about here?" she asked, pointing to a narrow finger of deeper water that extended around a tiny island twenty miles off the coast of Taiwan. She leaned closer to read the name. "Mianhua Islet," she said.

Lannier pursed his lips. "That's a pretty narrow operating area," he said. "There's no way the *Idaho* could stay on station and wait for the *Manta*. We'd have to drop you off, then leave and come back."

Janet knew what he was thinking: the navigation system on the *Manta* was not as precise as the *Idaho*'s, how would they rendezvous underwater?

"Did you bring detailed underwater surveys?" she asked Mark.

"Don said you were going to ask for that," Mark said. He loaded a bathymetric survey onto the screen.

"We need a distinctive feature on the ocean floor that the *Manta* can find," Janet said. "That'll be our rendezvous point."

"Here," Lannier said, tapping a spot on the screen.

Janet squinted at the monitor. Two pillars of rock jutted above the sea floor.

"That works," Janet replied. "We could hear the *Idaho*'s locator beacon and home in on your position."

"Even if we use that drop-off point," the XO said, "your time on station is reduced compared to the other operation."

"The more time and battery power we use in transit," Janet said to Mark's questioning look, "the less time we have on the cable."

"Time on station is really important," Mark said. "This is a different kind of operation than the Russian cable tap."

"How so?" Lannier asked.

"The Russian operation relied on capturing encrypted comms and sending them back to Washington, DC, for analysis. We're going to be doing a lot more on-site analysis." He changed screens on his laptop to show a picture of a computer with Chinese writing on the face of it.

"Thirty-six hours ago, a privateer operation took down a Chinese spy ship and seized this piece of crypto gear. We've tested it. We can read the PLA message traffic—or some of it, anyway. This isn't an intel mission, sir, this is a misinformation campaign. I'm here to get inside the PLA network and cause chaos."

"Then I think maybe you and Everett deserve each other, Westlund," the XO quipped.

Lannier frowned. "Did you say privateer operation, Captain Westlund?"

Mark smiled. "Sir, I've got some stuff to tell you."

20

Mount Chuyun, Taiwan

The mood in Shadow Base Six was festive, a much-needed shot in the arm for the embattled Taiwanese resistance.

And they had a right to be proud of their accomplishment, Lester thought. The ambush on the PLA forces had been a success by any measure. They'd not lost a single soldier. Hell, the raiding party hadn't suffered so much as a hangnail. They added ten members to their ranks and even captured the Chinese drone to boot.

On her survey of the supply rooms, Ash Lewis found a few cases of beer, which she promptly turned over to the elder Tsai brother for safekeeping. Lester suggested to Oliver Tsai that tonight might be a good time to celebrate, and the base commander allowed one can of beer per person.

Lester accepted his drink and promptly donated it to Hardy.

"You are an officer and a gentleman, Colonel," Hardy said with a mock bow as he accepted the gift. "And a damn fine human being as well."

Lester smiled but said nothing. Hardy was a fight hard, play hard kind of guy, but he knew the truth about the raid.

They'd gotten lucky. The PLA major leading the raid on the campground had been overconfident to the point of stupidity. He'd made the biggest possible error one could make on the battlefield: underestimating his enemy.

The PLA would not make that mistake again.

Dance music rang out from a set of speakers someone had jury-rigged together. Teams moved the picnic tables out of the way to form a makeshift dance floor in the open space between the Quonset huts.

Lester sat on the picnic table and watched the impromptu dance party, his mood waffling between being proud of these resistance fighters and morose at their murky future.

Ash Lewis arrived and perched on the table next to him.

"Well, sir, we most definitely poked the dragon today," she said.

Lester nodded. "Where's your beer?"

"I have standards, Colonel," Lewis said. "I don't drink anything but microbrews, preferably pilsners. I'll drink when this is over. Besides, I think he needs it more than I do."

She pointed to Hardy. The tall SEAL was on the dance floor. Beer raised high, eyes closed, gray head bobbing to the music, he danced with a young woman easily half his age.

"He misses it." Lewis jerked her chin at Hardy.

Lester nodded again but said nothing.

"What about you, sir?" Lewis asked. "Do you miss the military?"

Two years ago, his answer would have been *hell yes*. Mike Lester was a miserable son of a bitch in the civilian world. Phalanx made him realize that it wasn't the military he missed. He missed the mission.

With Phalanx, instead of shooting people, he helped them. Now he was right back in the shit. What's more, the Taiwanese soldiers and his own people deferred to him as their commander. He didn't ask for it and hadn't expected it. It just happened.

And he liked it.

They even gave him a nickname: Gong-gong.

Lester had felt pretty good about the new name until he found out it meant *grandpa* in Chinese. By then, it was too late. The name stuck.

"Those days are behind me," he said finally, "but I'll do what I need to do, Ash."

"Amen," she replied.

Oliver Tsai approached the pair, his glasses glinting in the light. "Gong-gong, I wonder if I might make an assessment of the tablet that you brought back."

Lester jumped to the ground, feeling the day's activity in his muscles.

"That's a fine idea, Oliver." He shot a look at Lewis. "You game?"

Ash Lewis was already on her feet.

In the base commander's office, the three of them considered the PLA tablet. The device was still encased in a protective foil bag to block electromagnetic signals.

Lewis unsealed the EM-proof bag. "I'm confident that we're shielded from any signals this deep inside the mountain, so let's see what we've got here."

Gingerly, she withdrew the tablet and handed it to Lester. He unlocked the device using his retina scan and handed it to Oliver. He and Lewis crowded next to the Taiwanese intel officer as he scanned the home screen.

"This looks like a mission clock countdown," Major Tsai said. "The clock started with two hundred forty hours."

"Ten days," Lester said. "That's an aggressive schedule."

Tsai nodded. "The color bar below the clock looks like a dashboard progress assessment. It's green, so I assume that means they're ahead of schedule..." He mumbled to himself as he flipped through screens. Lester saw interactive maps, what looked like troop dispositions, and ship landing schedules. Tsai flipped through more pages, followed links, and scanned information written in Chinese characters, moving too fast for Lester to follow.

Finally, Tsai set the tablet on the desk carefully and swallowed. When he spoke, his voice was taut with emotion.

"This is an intelligence gold mine, sir," he said. "The PLA established a battle network that links all of their field commanders to a database that contains their entire invasion plan. This is everything, literally everything, they intend to do, scheduled and updated down to the minute..."

He looked up at Lester. "If this is accurate, our situation is even worse than I thought. We don't have weeks to get this information off the island. We have days, maybe less. Anyone coming to help us will need this. It contains everything they need to know to plan an attack."

Tsai's shoulders sagged, and he sank back in his chair. "Except, there's no way to do that. All communications off the island are blocked. The mobile phone networks are offline, and our satellite comms are jammed or have been destroyed. We're holding the keys to the kingdom, and we're screwed."

"What about a landline?" Lewis said. "If we could break into a PLA command post and access their network, we could send an email, right?"

Tsai shook his head. "They've taken all of the submarine cable stations offline."

"But they didn't destroy them?" Lester asked.

"No," Tsai said. "According to the battle network tablet, the rules of engagement are very clear. Do not damage infrastructure. They want to be able to turn everything on again as soon as they've established control over the island."

"Then that's what we have to do," Lester said.

"I don't follow, sir," Lewis said.

"If the submarine cable station isn't damaged, then we break in and phone home." Lester went to the map of Taiwan pinned to the wall. "Where's the nearest cable landing point?"

Oliver Tsai picked up the PLA tablet and scrolled through screens. "Fangshan," he announced. He pointed out the location on the map, a tiny town on the western side of southern Taiwan.

At least it was in the south of Taiwan, Lester thought. He eyeballed the straight-line distance of fifty kilometers, which would be more like sixty since they'd have to hike down using mountain trails. His mind worked ahead. A hard day's march to get a team into position. There would be PLA patrols and drones to contend with.

"You're sure the cable station is not damaged?" he asked Tsai.

Oliver focused on the tablet. "It has a software lock, but the hardware is available. The station is guarded by a security detail. Looks like three soldiers, changing every four hours, and an hourly check-in from a coastal patrol vehicle."

"That's workable," Lester said. "A small team could handle three guys." He looked at Lewis. "If we get you inside, can you get us online long enough to send the contents of this tablet back to the US?"

"I do this for a living, Gong-gong," Lewis said. "If you get me in, I'll figure out a way to phone home."

"Party's over, Oliver," Lester said to Major Tsai. "Tell Frank to pick two teams of his best people, squad size. And tell him to bring that PLA drone we stole."

"What are you thinking, sir?" Lewis asked after Tsai had departed.

Lester had a strange feeling growing in his belly, something he hadn't felt since the start of the PLA invasion.

Hope? No, he decided, a mission. If the US was coming, they needed the best possible intelligence, and his team had it. All he had to do was lead a team fifty kilometers into enemy territory, stage an assault on a piece of critical infrastructure, hack into a secure Chinese installation, and get away safely.

Impossible, he thought, unless...

"We're going to need a diversion," Lester said. "A big one."

DAY FOUR

21

Da-Tung Hospital
Kaohsiung City, Taiwan

Mission Clock: 163:15:19
Mission Status: Green

Gao surfaced from sleep slowly. He tried to blink his eyes open and experienced a wave of panic when his right eye stayed black. Through the ringing in his ears, he heard his own ragged breathing.

With shaking fingers, he explored his facial features. Bandages covered the right side of his face and the crown of his head. There was a smooth patch over his right eye.

The events of the raid flashed back in full color.

Blinding afternoon sunlight silhouetted the figure of Captain Ren walking a few paces ahead of him. The body jerked like a puppet, then collapsed. The *pop* of small arms fire. A blaze of pain on the right side of his head, then his face hit the dirt. He smelled pine needles.

Then, nothing.

The few seconds of memory stretched out as he considered what had happened. An ambush. They'd walked right into an ambush, and a well-executed one at that.

But he was alive.

His fingers explored the rest of his body. He was naked underneath a thin gown and blankets. An IV protruded from his forearm, and there were plastic leads attached to his chest.

A hospital. He was in hospital, but where? His good eye made out a hanging curtain all around his bed, like a cocoon. His hand closed on a plastic control panel, and he focused on the keypad.

Touching the up arrow, he raised his body to a sitting position, then pressed on the call button. When nothing happened after a few seconds, he pressed the button again and held it down.

A nurse entered the room and drew aside the curtain. By the light of the hallway, he could see she was dressed in blue scrubs and wore a mask, safety goggles, and latex gloves.

"Yes, sir," she said, her voice muffled by the mask.

Gao opened his mouth to speak, but nothing came out. His throat was too dry.

"Water," he managed finally.

The young woman filled a paper cup and held it to his lips. Gao felt his hands shake as he took a sip. The moisture flooded across his tongue. He swallowed and cleared his throat.

"Where am I?" he asked.

"Kaohsiung Municipal Da-Tung Hospital," the nurse informed him. "They bring all the Chinese officers here." From her accent, Gao knew she was Taiwanese. He could sense the resentment in her tone.

"I'll get the doctor," she said and left quickly. The door banged shut behind her.

Gao sat back against the pillow, sipping water from the cup and taking stock of his situation. His thoughts processed slowly.

The last thing he remembered was being on the ridge. That was late afternoon. What time was it now? How long had he been asleep?

He found the control panel again and pushed the button for the light. Gao clenched his good eye shut at the sudden illumination. He scanned the space enclosed by the curtains, but apart from a rolling table containing the pitcher of water, the area was empty. He needed to find his Shandian tablet and report to General Zhang.

He swung his right leg out of bed and tried to lever his body off the pillow. A wave of vertigo passed over him. Gao breathed through the nausea.

The door opened again, and a man in a white lab coat entered with the nurse in tow. He was younger than Gao and also Taiwanese. He rushed to the bedside, gripped Gao's ankle, and placed his leg firmly back in bed. Then he pressed Gao back against the pillow.

"Major," he said. "You should not be up yet. You have a serious head wound. Very likely a concussion."

Gao blinked his one good eye. That explained the fuzzy thoughts and the raging headache.

"Where." His mouth seemed to be taking a long time to form words. "Where are my things?"

"Your uniform?" the doctor asked. "It was covered in blood. We had to cut it off you, and we threw it away. Your sidearm and anything else will be in property control. We don't allow weapons on the hospital floor."

As he spoke, the doctor took out a penlight. He shined it in Gao's left eye. Then he uncovered Gao's right eye, pinned the eyelid open with his finger, and shined the light. To Gao, it felt like he was poking a hot needle into his brain.

"Your pupils are not dilated," he said. "You're a lucky man, Major. If the bullet had been a centimeter to the left, you'd be dead. As it stands, you'll probably come out of this with no more than a wicked scar. You're all stitched up, but I'll need to keep you for another twenty-four hours for observation—"

"Where are my things?" Gao demanded. "I was carrying classified material. I need to make sure it was secured properly by the assault team."

"You were the only survivor, Major," the doctor said quietly. "Anything on your person, except for your bloody uniform, was taken by the PLA military police." His tone took on a brittle quality. "If you're worried about someone stealing from you, I can assure you that no Taiwanese people touched anything you were carrying."

"I want my belongings brought to me now," Gao said. "Immediately."

"Of course, sir," the doctor said. The nurse opened the curtains and refilled Gao's water, then followed the doctor out of the room.

As the minutes ticked by, Gao looked out the window. His room faced east, toward the mountains, and the sky was growing pale. Dawn in this part of the world was about 0630, so Gao now knew he'd been out for almost twelve hours. He wondered if someone had informed General Zhang. How had the general taken the news?

His mind wandered. He was the only survivor, but he'd come out of the engagement with a spectacular wound...that meant at least a Meritorious Service Medal, which could only enhance his promotion chances. This whole thing might be a blessing in disguise if he played it right.

The PLA MP arrived just as weak sunlight made an appearance over the mountain range. He was a hulking young corporal from northern China, with heavy broad shoulders and a blank expression. Gao waited anxiously as the military policeman cut the box open. He seized the carton, hauled it into his lap, and pawed through his belongings. Boots, dirty socks and underwear, trousers, belt, his QSZ-92G semi-automatic pistol, and his combat knife.

For the first time, Gao felt a twinge of fear. Where was his Shandian tablet?

"This is everything?" Gao demanded. "You're sure?"

"Yes, sir. I was on duty last night and took custody of all your belongings in the emergency room. I sealed the box myself." He pointed to the signature on the seals that he had just cut open. "This is everything, sir. I swear it."

"Was there a computer tablet?" Gao held his fingers to show the size of the object.

The MP shook his head.

Gao forced his thoughts to slow down as he thought back to the moment of the ambush. The Shandian tablet had been in his hand. He was sure of that. But it wasn't here. It must have fallen away, Gao reasoned, been covered by leaves. It must still be in the woods...

A new memory came back to him unbidden, like a fragment of a dream. Voices floated around in his mind. Voices that were speaking in English.

"Help me get dressed," Gao said. He sat up in bed, fighting back the dizziness. He stripped the leads off his chest and pulled the IV out of his arm. The enlisted man gaped at him.

"Don't just stand there," Gao yelled. "Put on my damn socks."

His head wound throbbed when he looked down for too long. When the corporal had gotten his socks on his feet, Gao said, "Now my trousers."

The young man obeyed. Once Gao felt the material move over his ankles, he put his hand on the kneeling corporal's shoulder and pushed himself to a standing position. Gao hauled the pants over his hips and buckled the belt by touch. He pulled off the hospital gown and realized that he had no uniform shirt to put on.

"Give me your T-shirt," Gao ordered.

"I don't understand, sir," the MP said.

"Take off your T-shirt and give it to me," Gao snapped. The young man took off his uniform tunic and pulled his T-shirt over his head. Gao put it on. It smelled of sweat and hung on him like a loose dress, but it would have to do. He stuffed the excess material into his pants.

Gao reached for the corporal's arm. "Now help me get out of here."

The nurse met them at the door. "Sir, you can't—"

Gao pushed past her. "I'm checking myself out."

By the time they reached the street, Gao had the dizziness under control. Moving helped, as did the cool morning air. Gao could see the hotel housing General Wei's command post only a few blocks away. If he kept his head up, he would be fine on his own.

"You can go," Gao said to the MP. The young man looked like he might ask for his T-shirt back, but then he turned and practically ran back inside. Gao set off slowly, allowing the chilly air to cool his overheated senses.

When he got to the entrance of the hotel, he ordered one of the guards to find him a fresh uniform. Then he took the elevator up to the fifth floor where the intel office was located.

The intel officer had been warned of Gao's arrival. He met Gao at the elevator and helped him into the office, where Gao collapsed into a chair. The man's face held a worried frown.

"Major Gao," he said. "You should be in the hospital, sir."

Gao pulled off the eye patch. His right eye was sensitive to light, but he was able to see fine. A tray of tea arrived. When he accepted a cup, Gao's hand trembled slightly.

"I need your help, Major," Gao said. "My Shandian tablet was destroyed in the attack. I need a new one. Immediately."

The intel officer beckoned a captain over. "Captain Ro is our communications officer. He handles all the cryptological gear, sir. Major Gao requires a new tablet," he said to the officer.

"Of course, sir," Ro said. "If you can give me the remnants of the original tablet, anything with an identifying mark on it, I will mark the tablet as lost and issue a new one."

Gao shook his head. Bad idea. The room spun, and he took a deep breath to still the nausea. "I'm sorry," he said. "I left the damaged pieces back at the hospital. Please, I need to log in immediately. General Zhang is expecting an update from me."

Why am I lying? Gao wondered to himself. Just tell them that the device was lost in the attack.

The two officers exchanged glances. The intel officer gave a slight nod.

"I can issue you a replacement tablet, Major," the captain said, "as long as you can bring in the nonfunctional unit this morning."

Gao looked the communications officer straight in the eye. "Of course," he lied.

A few moments later, Gao held a new tablet to his eye for a retina scan. The device did not respond.

"I think my login will need to be reset," Gao said.

The captain shook his head. "It shouldn't matter, sir."

Gao tried to log in again and failed. He felt sweat break out under his armpits. The fragment of a dream with voices speaking English flashed back to him.

"Perhaps the head injury has thrown off the retina scan," the intel officer suggested. "Please reset the major's account login, Captain."

"Yes, sir." The captain made a series of keystrokes on his laptop and handed the tablet back to Gao. "Scan in, sir."

The tablet opened. Gao saw the familiar mission clock, but the green was faded. The invasion had lost even more progress overnight.

The captain looked at his screen. "You said the tablet was destroyed, sir. There was considerable network activity last night."

Gao's breath caught. He did not look up.

"My tablet was damaged in the firefight," he lied, "but I was able to use it until the battery failed."

"Of course, sir," the captain replied. "You'll bring me the damaged unit this morning? It's a controlled device."

Gao smiled. He hauled himself to his feet.

"You'll get it as soon as I can lay my hands on it."

22

The Ranch
Sterling, Virginia

Abby Cromwell lifted a flute of champagne and rapped on the rim of the glass with a Mont Blanc pen. The crystal tone echoed through the domed underground chamber of the Sentinel Holdings operations center. She stood on a chair in the command cockpit in the center of the room.

"May I have your attention, please," Abby said in a clear voice. "Raise your glasses, Team Sentinel, because we have reached a milestone: one hundred billion dollars in prize money from Operation Lynx."

In the enclosed space, the roar of the hundred or so Sentinel employees was deafening. Although not a member of Team Sentinel, Abby had insisted Don stay for the celebration. Now he wasn't so sure he'd made the right call. Don held his glass by the stem, raised it with everyone else, and took a sip.

The alcohol burned on his tongue. He knew the champagne was Dom Perignon, but the expensive drink was wasted on his palate—and on his mood. While the private military contractors celebrated their financial windfall, things were not going so well outside the Sentinel bubble.

Although the United States had taken out the Chinese spy satellite coverage and made clear military overtures by moving the *Lincoln* into the South China Sea, the PLA showed no signs of slowing down or even negotiating on the subject of Taiwan.

Back at the White House, where Don was headed next, the President was making decisions about further use of force. This wasn't over yet.

The political speculation inside the Beltway was that Serrano would back down to preserve his legacy and run for a second term. Don had seen the look in Serrano's eyes, and he was pretty sure all the talking heads on TV were going to be proven wrong. The President was not going to back down.

Manson Skelly approached holding an open bottle of champagne. "Drink up, Donny-boy, this is the good stuff."

All around the ops center floor, people chattered and laughed. They'd all pulled long shifts, fueled by coffee and Red Bull, and the alcoholic buzz that hit their collective systems released all that caffeinated energy.

For Don, it was too much. "I'm good, Manse," he said. "I need to drive back to DC."

"Suit yourself, buddy." Skelly drank from the bottle, chugging the last of the expensive champagne. He wiped his mouth with his forearm and winked at Don.

Abby held up a manicured hand and waited for silence. She was a striking woman who could look boyish or regal depending on her mood and the lighting.

Right now, she looked like royalty. Head held high, fierce eyes, squared shoulders. She dropped her hand and slowly looked around the circular room, as if she wanted to look each person in the eye. In his peripheral vision, Don saw Skelly grab another open bottle of champagne.

"When my husband and I established this company," Abby began, "the only employee we had was Manson Skelly. We used to call ourselves the Three Musketeers."

She beamed at Skelly, who returned the smile. As soon as Abby turned away, the smile fell from Skelly's face. He took a slug from the fresh bottle in his grip and grimaced.

"It was tough going in those early years. We put together a platoon of ex-special forces operators and took any job that came our way, no matter how dangerous. All of us did our time in the field."

She shook her head. "Joe decided that there had to be a better way to grow our company. We started a string of mergers and acquisitions of private military contractors all over the world." She smiled at Skelly again, and the man mirrored the gesture.

"That was five years ago. Not long after that, I lost Joe." The room hushed into stillness. Don heard the soft *whoosh* of the air-conditioning unit pumping chilled air into the computer space.

"When we lost my husband," Abby continued quietly, "I knew it was a sign that we needed to change. I needed a new mission." She looked back at Skelly. "*We* needed a new mission. One that honored Joe's sacrifice.

"Our motto is 'peace through strength,' and I give my word to you that we will use that strength for good. Our mission, our reason for being, is to spread democracy to the darkest corners of this planet. With the infusion of cash from Operation Lynx, we are well on our way to doing that. Thanks to all of you for your hard work. You will share in the rewards."

Applause and cheers erupted in the room. Abby, a broad smile still on her face, drained her flute of champagne. Then she raised it up and smashed it on the floor. The room filled with the sound of smashing glass as everyone followed her lead.

Don drained his glass and set it back on the tray.

Skelly stepped up on the vacated speaker's chair, his arms raised in a V-for-victory gesture. A chant sprang up in the crowd: "U-S-A, U-S-A, U-S-A." Skelly pumped his arms in time with the chant, urging the crowd on for a full minute.

Skelly closed his hands into fists and drew them apart. The shouting stopped. His eyes sparkled at his control over the audience. He dropped his hands.

"All right, you lazy bastards, get back to work and make me even richer than I already am."

The celebration ended with roars of laughter. There was a sound of crunching glass as everyone moved back to their workstations.

Still grinning, Skelly hopped to the floor of the command center to face Abby.

"Make me richer than I already am?" Abby hissed. "Really? What would Joe think?"

"Joe isn't here anymore, Abby," Skelly shot back in a low tone. "It's just you and me now. Get used to it."

Skelly realized Don was within earshot. He turned his back on Abby and slipped on a headset. "Team Bravo, what's the status on that ship off Long Beach? When do we move in?"

Don watched Abby's reflection in his computer monitor. Her face was flushed, her shoulders set. Just when it looked as if she was about to reengage with Skelly, a technician carrying a laptop came into the control cockpit. "Ms. Cromwell, I have an update on cicada."

Don feigned a deep interest in his computer screen, but he recognized the name from the National Security Council meeting minutes. What was the connection between Sentinel and Project Cicada? He strained to hear what was said next.

"Yes," Abby snapped. "What is it?"

"I have the new pattern recognition features programmed and modeled. Mr. Skelly asked me to look at three different patterns and adjust the lethality quotient."

Abby took the laptop from the young woman, and Don heard her fingernails clicking on the keyboard. "This can't be right," she muttered.

"It's what Mr. Skelly told me to model, ma'am," the tech said.

"Manson," Abby said, "can you come over here, please?"

Don heard the rhythmic clump of Skelly's feet on the cockpit floor, then his gruff tone. "What is it, Abby? I'm busy."

"Did you change the pattern rec function on Cicada?" Abby asked in a low voice.

"I *improved* the pattern rec feature on Cicada," Skelly countered.

"But these lethality quotients are too high," Abby said. "The collateral damage potential is—"

"This is not an experiment, Abby," Skelly said. "If we get the green light on this thing, it has to work out of the box. There won't be a second chance.

So what if we take out a few civilians? The alternative is failure on the battlefield. Not an option in my book."

"I'm just worried about the political fallout if something like this ever got out," Abby snapped in voice laced with fury.

"And I'm worried about it not working right the first time," Skelly growled. "You stick to Wall Street. I'll stick to operations. How's that sound?"

Without waiting for an answer, Skelly clumped back to his post.

Don got up and moved quickly to Abby's side. He caught a glimpse of a chart before the CEO shut the laptop.

"Don," she said. "Quite a day, isn't it?" She still had spots of color on her cheeks.

Don tried to keep his voice low. "Did I hear you mention Project Cicada? I didn't know Sentinel was involved in that program."

"Above your pay grade, Riley," Skelly called over his shoulder. "We take operational security very seriously here at Sentinel."

"Of course," Don said. "I just want to be ready if we have to deploy it."

He deliberately used the term *deploy* to see if he'd get a rise out of either Abby or Skelly, but he got no reaction.

"Don," Abby said, "Sentinel developed Project Cicada. I promise you that when you are cleared, I'll brief you myself."

Abby took Don's arm and led him to the edge of the command cockpit, away from Skelly.

"How are your people?" she asked. "I've been told that you have ETG folks on the *Idaho*."

How does she know about that? Don wondered. He offered her a faint smile. "I can't discuss it. Operational security."

Abby laughed. "Touché."

Janet Everett and Mark Westlund had not been far from Don's thoughts all day. There had been no word since the update that Mark had arrived safely on board the submarine. Now, the USS *Idaho* was on a mission to penetrate deep into the Chinese exclusion zone and drop off the *Manta*. The sub was out of radio contact for the next day.

The champagne left a sour aftertaste in his mouth. While he was helping a military contractor get filthy rich, Janet and Mark were sailing into the teeth of the Chinese threat.

"Well," Abby said, "I hope the crypto gear we salvaged from the Chinese spy ship works."

"So do I," Don replied.

23

PLA Navy submarine *Changzheng 12*
East China Sea, 150 miles north of Taipei, Taiwan

Mission Clock: 157:03:12
Mission Status: Green

"Conning Officer, come left to course two-zero-zero," Captain Chu ordered.

While the submarine made a slow turn, Chu turned his attention from the sonar display to a bathymetric chart detailing the underwater geography of the East China Sea.

Like navies around the world, the PLA Navy used a system of water-space management to avoid contact between their own submarines. Put simply, each sub was assigned a patrol area. If you detected an unidentified submerged contact in your patrol area, you could be certain it was not a friendly.

The *Changzheng*'s sector extended out from the northeast tip of Taiwan. Bracketed by the Ryukyu Islands in the south and the East China Sea shelf in the north, this area encompassed thousands of square kilometers of ocean. Contained in his hunting ground was an underwater feature known as the Okinawa Trough, a valley thousands of meters deep that ran from the Japanese island chain all the way down to the tip of Taiwan.

To his north and west, the Strait of Taiwan and East China Sea were too shallow to safely operate large, nuclear-powered submarines like the United States *Virginia*-class ships. Besides, PLA Navy diesel-electric subs heavily patrolled those areas, making it even less enticing for an approach.

Chu knew that if the Americans sent their submarines to attack the northern end of Taiwan, he would find them in these deep waters. And he could hunt them in the deep ocean, too. The *Changzheng* was a *Shang*-class nuclear-powered submarine, the latest in the PLA Navy fleet. She was every bit as quiet and deadly as her American counterparts.

"Steady on new course two-zero-zero, Captain," the OOD reported. "Depth one-one-zero meters."

"Very well." Chu clenched his eyes shut, counted to ten, then opened them again to focus on the sonar display.

For the past twenty-four hours, he had painstakingly searched his patrol area for intruders. Passive sonar searches were a three-dimensional game of chess. Layers of varying temperature and salinity bent sound waves in strange ways. Sometimes layers might block an enemy's noise signature, allowing an adversary to hide. But other times, the layers could work for him by forming a sound channel, a conduit of acoustic information that might extend for hundreds of kilometers.

Less than two hours ago, the *Changzheng* had found a possible enemy target. It was not much, a single frequency, or tonal, in submarine terms, but Chu was determined to run the lead to ground.

"Towed array is stable, Captain," the sonar supervisor reported. "Commencing search."

Chu acknowledged the report but kept watch on the sonar team using his own monitor on the opposite side of the control room. He knew he made the sonar chief nervous, and nervous men did not listen well, a key quality in a good sonar operator.

Patience, he told himself as he waited for the screen to update. Searches like this one took time.

The towed array was a string of hydrophones streamed out for a kilometer behind the submarine. By processing data from each sensor along the array, the sonar computer generated a bearing to the target.

"Regained contact Sierra one-seven!" the sonar supervisor reported. "One hundred ninety-eight hertz, bearing three-zero-zero."

Chu felt a rush of energy surge in his tired body. "Excellent, Sonar. Now calculate a range for me."

He held his breath. This was the moment of truth. A single bearing on a contact only told part of the story. Given the variabilities of the undersea environment, the contact could be one kilometer away or one hundred kilometers distant. In order to complete the underwater picture, they needed to know the distance to their target, the range.

Using only passive data, a submarine needed to triangulate the target's position to determine range. By changing their own course, the *Changzheng* got a different bearing on the target. By accumulating data from multiple "legs," or course changes, they would eventually be able to pinpoint the location of the enemy submarine. The whole process was painstaking, sometimes taking an hour or more to refine their solution.

The single frequency they tracked was a tenuous thread of information. Every time they changed course and disrupted the stability of the towed array, they risked losing their target. Also, if their target changed their course and speed, Chu's tracking team needed to start all over.

Behind the captain, a man cleared his throat. Chu sighed. He knew that distinctive bodily function belonged to Commander Sun, his political officer.

"Captain," Sun said, "may I have a word?"

"What is it, Commander?" When Chu turned, he saw that the political officer had a young sailor with him. "We are tracking a possible enemy submarine, Commander. You cannot be serious about doing this now."

"Is there a better time for patriotism than before taking the fight to the enemy of our country?" Sun replied smoothly.

"What's the status on the range estimate?" Chu demanded from the sonar supervisor. The enlisted man quailed under the captain's transferred anger, and Chu immediately regretted his action.

"The data is unstable, sir," the sonar man said. "I recommend we stay on this course until we can sort it out."

Chu turned back to Commander Sun, who wore an expectant smile.

As usual, the political officer was not wrong, but his timing was impeccably poor.

Killing the Taiwanese destroyer on the eve of the invasion had electrified the crew of the *Changzheng*. As a way to ride the tide of patriotism in the ranks, Sun had come up with the idea to sing the national anthem each evening before the evening meal. At first, it was a shipwide singalong, but then Sun decided to add a new dimension. Each night, a new sailor would lead the anthem using the shipwide intercom. The new concept was an instant hit with the crew. It turned into a singing contest with informal votes and repeat performances by favorite singers.

Chu thought the idea was beyond ridiculous, but he also recognized the boost to morale among the crew. Whatever he thought of the privileged Commander Sun as a person, the man knew how to do his job as the Party representative.

"Captain," the sonar supe called out, "estimated range to Sierra one-seven is thirty-five thousand meters. Tentative classification is a *Virginia*-class submarine."

Chu smacked his clenched fist into an open palm. "Excellent work, Sonar."

"Captain," Sun said, "I suggest we send this information to Beijing and let them conduct a full ASW exercise."

Chu shook his head. The target had breached the emergency zone and was within his ship's area of operation. The *Changzheng* had found this intruder, and the *Changzheng* would have the honor to kill her.

A picture emerged in his mind of his adversary. The US nuclear submarine was transiting down the western edge of the Okinawa Trough, using the shallow waters of the East China Sea Shelf to mask their signature.

The plot showed a contact running a steady six knots on course 200, directly toward the port of Keelung.

"They've been on the same course for hours," he said. "We will go deep and run west. We'll catch them here"—he pointed to a tiny dot of an island —"and kill them." He expanded the scale of the electronic chart. The place was called Mianhua Islet.

Sun's eyes glittered. "It's a brilliant plan, Captain. I approve."

Chu bit back a reprimand. He did not require the approval of the political officer to run his ship.

"Conning Officer, make your depth two hundred meters, new course two-seven-zero. Come to twenty knots."

He waited for the repeat back of his orders as he studied the monitor. It was a calculated risk. Traveling that fast, his sonar sensors would be useless. When he slowed again, he would have to reacquire the target, possibly in different water conditions.

The ship angled downward. The deck thrummed with power as they increased speed. Chu turned to Commander Sun.

"Political Officer, you may use the shipwide intercom to sing the national anthem."

Ninety minutes later, a frustrated Captain Chu studied a very different sonar picture. The magnificent sound channel that had enabled them to track the US sub from thousands of kilometers away had vanished. In its place was a cacophony of ocean noise: everything from whale calls to shipping lane traffic to the active sonar of the PLA Navy warships patrolling the nearby shallower waters.

A more experienced sonar team might have been able to suss out the mysterious tonal they had found before, but his sonar team lacked that level of expertise.

Chu dragged in a breath of the humid air, rank with the smell of body odor. He had called the ship to general quarters before the *Changzheng* slowed, so the control room was now packed with men at their action stations. As time wore on, the energy in the crew ebbed.

I've lost the American, Chu realized. The US sub should be here, but something had happened to change the equation. A course change, a change in aspect to the enemy sub, the poor sonar environment—whatever it was, it meant failure for the *Changzheng*.

One more towed array search on a new heading, Chu decided, then he would call it off.

The sonar supervisor bolted upright in his chair, his eyes wide.

"Transients, bearing two-four-zero!" he shouted. "They're close!"

"Fire control," Chu said, "match bearing and—"

"Wait!" the sonar supe's voice slid up the register. "New contact, designate Sierra one-eight, same bearing. Captain, it's a diesel!"

"Check fire," Chu rapped out. "Tube one to standby."

"Check fire, aye, sir. Tube one is in standby."

Chu pushed in behind the sonar supervisor. "What the hell is going on?" he hissed.

"I-I don't know, sir." Sweat poured down the sonar chief's face, and the front of his uniform was soaked. "It's a diesel. I'm sure of it."

Chu dragged his fingernails across his scalp. The United States didn't have any diesel submarines. Was this a PLA sub in his waterspace? A Russian?

"Where is the American sub?" he demanded.

"We've lost them, Captain."

Whatever had happened, Chu's tactical advantage was gone. With an unknown diesel submarine in the mix, all that remained for the *Changzheng* was risk. He made his decision.

"Conning Officer, new course one-one-zero."

"One-one-zero, aye, sir." The sub banked gently into the turn toward deeper water.

The *Changzheng* ran away bravely to fight another day.

24

USS *Idaho* (SSN-799)
East China Sea, 5 miles southeast of Mianhua Islet

"*Idaho*, this is *Manta*," Janet said into her microphone, "standing by to launch—"

BANG!

The metallic clang rang like a rifle shot in the enclosed space of the *Manta* submersible that was still attached to the back of the USS *Idaho*. Janet even felt it in the soles of her feet.

"*Manta*," the voice in her ear shouted, "you just created a loud transient. What's going on?"

Janet twisted in the copilot's chair. "What the hell was that?"

Mark Westlund stuck his head through the open door of the lockout chamber. "Sorry," he said. "The hatch slipped—"

"Dog that hatch and get in here now, Mark."

Janet faced forward, her heart racing. Through the bulbous front window, the work lights of the *Manta* illuminated the hull of the *Idaho*. In the right conditions, a sound like that could travel for miles in the ocean. If there was a PLA sub nearby...

"*Manta*, this is *Idaho*." The voice was Captain Lannier's. "We have detected a possible submerged contact, bearing one-one-zero."

"Request emergency launch, Captain," Janet said. Without the *Manta* on her back, the *Idaho* was a much more maneuverable fighting platform—if it came to that.

"Granted. *Idaho*, out."

Janet turned to her pilot. "Get us out of here, Tony. Now."

Tony, who had been the *Manta's* pilot since the Sea of Okhotsk operation, was already way ahead of her.

"Launching now," Tony replied. He punched his display panel, releasing the magnetic lock that held the submersible in place. Janet felt the familiar feeling of weightlessness as the craft floated away from the hull of the moving submarine. Then she was anchored back to her seat as Tony pumped the thrusters and moved them to starboard. The dark hull of the *Idaho* disappeared from view.

"*Idaho*, *Manta* is clear."

"Roger that, *Manta*. Good hunting."

"Same to you, sir."

Janet hunched over the copilot's station, where she controlled the *Orca*, their unmanned submersible escort. Janet typed instructions.

"What are you doing?" Mark asked from the cabin behind her. He sounded stressed, and Janet wondered if he'd really understood what he was getting himself into before he volunteered for undersea duty.

"Putting the *Orca* between us and whoever is out there. Maybe we can throw them off the *Idaho's* scent. I'm programming her to run a search pattern and catch up with us later."

Tony, who was busy driving, ignored the conversation. He put the submersible on a course to take them around the northern tip of Taiwan. The sooner they got away from the scene of the crime, the better.

Janet sat back in her seat, taking deep breaths to calm herself. She cut a look at Tony. His face was rigid with concentration, but there was an angry red flush on his neck. She unbuckled her three-point harness and twisted in her seat to face her passengers.

The cabin of the *Manta* was designed to hold six combat-loaded SEALs, but for this mission it held two racks of computer equipment with a narrow central aisle that ran back to the lockout chamber used for underwater entry and exit of the submersible. The amount of computer equipment reduced the crew of the *Manta* to three, and even that was a squeeze.

Today they carried four. Desperate times called for desperate measures.

Mark Westlund sat on the deck in the central aisle, his knees drawn up to his chest. Their other passenger, Dr. Hector Delgado, was an expert in submarine cables. He was bundled into a parka with the hood pulled up and strapped into the only other available seat.

Hector pulled back the hood. The tint of his black skin was ashen. When he spoke, Janet detected a quiver in his normally calm voice.

"Janet," he said, "just how close a call was that?"

She considered her answer. The truth was she didn't know for sure, but if a submarine's greatest weapon was stealth, they had deprived the *Idaho* of that weapon. With each passing minute, the *Idaho* got closer to the safety of deep water outside of the PLA's exclusion zone around Taiwan.

"Too close for comfort," Janet said finally. Hector nodded and pulled his hood back up, like a turtle retreating into its shell.

"I'm sorry," Mark said from between the computer stacks. "I didn't realize the hydraulic assist on the hatch was broken."

"It's not your fault," Janet said. "It's mine. I knew about the hatch. I should've warned you."

The *Manta* was a prototype. It had never been designed for the operating conditions the craft had endured over the last three months. Hasty internal and external modifications, a high-speed transit across the Pacific Ocean on the back of a submarine, daily excursions in the Sea of Okhotsk for a cable-tapping operation, and now a second, more dangerous cable-tapping mission.

The hatch hydraulics was not the only system on the *Manta* showing wear and tear. The electrical system had been patched and repatched to accommodate more and changing computer equipment, and one of the external mechanical arms was starting to stick. There were few spare parts on the *Idaho* for this type of submersible, so submariners did what they do best: they improvised. But it was only a matter of time before the *Manta* encountered a failure that they could not overcome.

"Let's get back on mission," Tony said from the pilot's chair. "What's done is done."

Janet called up the detailed bathymetric survey of coastal Taiwan that she had requested from Don Riley. One of the key lessons learned from the Sea of O operation was that just finding the underwater cable was difficult, especially in areas with strong underwater currents.

For the Taiwan operation, Janet hoped to follow the underwater geography like a topographic map using the depth of the *Manta* instead of altitude. Janet used the last locational fix from the *Idaho* as their starting point and began to track their progress by dead reckoning, a measure of course and speed with an offset for currents.

Janet recovered the *Orca* and put their escort into station-keeping mode five hundred yards to starboard. She gathered enough data from their progress to get a match on the bathymetric survey and synched their position on the chart. Waypoints for their journey to the submerged cable appeared on the screen.

"I've got us here." Janet pointed to the screen. "Next turn in an hour."

Time moved slowly. Most of the *Manta*'s systems were automated and did not usually require a copilot. While Tony drove, she watched the ocean floor pass by in a hypnotic blur.

Their mission clock was set at twenty hours. After the three-hour transit, they expended another three hours to find the buried cable using magnetic sensors, then more time to locate a repeater and uncover it using the *Manta*'s thrusters. By the time Tony jockeyed the *Manta* into position perpendicular to the cable-tap site, they had consumed almost half of the mission clock.

For the cable-tapping operation, they reconfigured personnel in the confined space. Janet shifted over to the pilot's chair, and Hector took the copilot's seat for the delicate operation.

The repeater was a one-meter-long steel capsule, shaped like a lozenge with flexible tapered tails that merged into the cable. The device gleamed in the work lights of the *Manta*.

Hector, stripped down to a T-shirt, worked the mechanical arms to position a watertight "coffin" around the repeater. Another hour went to evacuating any moisture from the box so that Hector could commence with the taps. Using remote tools located inside the coffin, he drilled two holes into the repeater and placed MEMS devices onto the eight fiber optic lines inside the cable. Janet knew from prior experience that this was the most delicate part of the operation.

Hector sat back in his seat. "Man, I have a splitting headache." His body was bathed in sweat.

"Me, too," Mark said.

Janet realized her own head ached as well. She reached over Hector and tapped the monitor. She muttered a curse.

"What?" Tony asked.

"Our CO2 levels are elevated," Janet replied.

"That sounds bad," Mark said.

"It's not good," Janet said. "Tony, can you check the scrubber? Hector, do you feel well enough to continue?"

Hector nodded.

"Let's do it now, then," Janet said. "Mark, power up the signal processing computer."

Hector hunched over the monitor. When he reached out to touch the joystick, his hand shook.

"Standing by," Mark reported.

Janet leaned over to Hector. "Do you want me to do this part?" she asked.

The man leaned back in his seat. "I think that might be best."

Janet switched places with Hector and gripped the joystick lightly between her thumb and index finger. She dialed in the focus on the camera and positioned the micro-auger over the hair-thin fiber optic line. Janet worked deliberately. If she screwed this up, the mission was a bust.

"That's good," Hector said.

Janet touched the display. The tiny drill bit disappeared into the line.

"That's it?" Janet asked.

"All that's left to do is position the mirror to split the signal and Mark should see it," Hector said. Janet noticed the s sounds in his words were slurring slightly.

"Stand by for the signal, Mark." Janet adjusted the mirror.

"I've got it!" Mark said, excitement creeping into his voice.

Janet, knowing her own motor functions might be impaired, took her time with the seven remaining fiber optic lines. Finally, she leaned back in her chair and let out an exhausted sigh. Tony crouched next to her.

"The CO_2 scrubber is on," he said. "It looks like it's working."

"It's not." Janet pulled up the life support screen on the display. "We're at three-point-seven percent CO_2 and rising. That's about eight times the normal level."

"Can we do anything?" Tony asked.

Janet cut a look at Hector. His skin had a mottled undertone, but he was asleep. CO_2 poisoning affected every person differently. In his fifties, Hector was older than the rest of them by twenty years, and Janet wondered if the scientist had any underlying medical conditions.

"The carbon dioxide will keep building up because we're adding to it every time we breathe out. The CO_2 scrubber is a sealed unit, so there's nothing I can do there." She racked her brain. "I can buy us some time by using oxygen to raise the pressure in the *Manta*, then we'll bleed off the excess atmosphere. Hopefully, that will dilute the effect of the CO_2, at least for a while."

"Good plan," Tony said.

Janet cycled through the menu on her display until she found the reserve oxygen tanks. She tapped on the screen to activate the pressure regulator. Her ears popped with the increase in pressure.

Tony looked at Hector. "He doesn't look so good."

Janet checked the mission clock. They had three hours before they had to head back to rendezvous with the *Idaho*. It would do them no good for them to arrive early to the pickup point because the *Idaho* would not be there.

"Mark," she called, "how's it going back there?"

Mark looked up from his laptop screen. Like the rest of them, his features were haggard and sweaty.

"Working like a champ. Let the mayhem commence." He cracked his knuckles for effect. "I'm gonna start small. Let's reroute blood plasma shipments from Taipei to Hainan."

25

Seven hundred miles in only twenty-four hours, Sharratt mused as he checked the daily progress reports.

It was amazing how much ocean you could cover when you opened up the throttles on a nuclear-powered aircraft carrier. In a normal transit speed of twelve knots or so, they'd be lucky to make that distance in three days.

The deck of the *Enterprise* thrummed with energy. With each passing hour, Sharratt could feel the tension ratcheting up in the people around him. The incoming reports were crisper. Orders were executed with an extra energy and attention to detail as if every single sailor in the strike force believed that their job, no matter how small, was essential to their mission. Maybe even the difference between coming home alive and not.

Focus, he realized, was a good thing. Whatever the future held for the strike force, his sailors were ready.

There had been issues to iron out, of course. The sailing configuration of the strike force was a headache. In EMCON condition Alpha, use of radar was prohibited and the fleet sailed without running lights. At thirty

knots, things happened fast. The last thing his armada needed was a collision, so he'd relaxed the sailing formation.

The three carriers sailed in a diamond formation with *Enterprise* in
the lead and *Nimitz* and *Teddy Roosevelt* 2,500 yards off her port and starboard quarters. The escorts were arrayed in a loose circle around the
carriers at distances ranging from five thousand to twenty thousand
yards. Unlike the nuclear-powered carriers, most of the escorts needed to
break off from the strike force to slow down and conduct underway
refueling.

Meanwhile, the carriers charged forward, never slowing their forward
progress. In practical terms that meant that there was always a string of
escorts either peeling off to refuel or running at a flank bell to catch up
with the rest of the strike force.

It wasn't the prettiest formation, and it was most definitely not taught at
command school, but it got the job done.

Chief of Staff Zachary appeared on the opposite side of the BattleSpace
display. Drops of rain spattered his uniform.

"What's the weather topside, Tom?" Sharratt asked.

"Shitty, sir." He broke into a grin. "Just what we ordered. Cloud ceiling
at fifteen hundred feet, visibility less than two miles. I'm told this'll last at
least another day, maybe two."

"Your lips to God's ear, my friend," Sharratt replied.

Even with the Chinese spy satellite fleet degraded, Sharratt welcomed
the thick cloud cover as added insurance against a chance sighting by a
PLA air patrol or surface ship.

Each carrier kept a combat air patrol aloft at all times with another
team on the catapults in an Alert-five status. The CAPs, directed by an Air
Force AWACS platform on overwatch duty, ranged three hundred miles
ahead of the strike force. If there were any Chinese aircraft out there, Sharratt wanted to intercept them well before they got a sniff of the strike force.

In fact, all of their sensor data came from the AWACS platform. The
strike force remained in an EMCON-Alpha status, and he directed the air
assets to operate passively as well. Sharratt was taking no chances about
giving away their presence until he was ready.

If their luck held, the *Enterprise* strike force would be within striking range of Taiwan in another day, a full three days earlier than the PLA probably expected them.

Sharratt nodded to the BattleSpace operator to expand the range of the holographic display. Sharratt had spent so much time at the plot that by now the operators knew what the admiral wanted to see without receiving a verbal order. Sometimes they adjusted the plot before he even knew himself what he wanted to see next.

He studied the display. One hundred fifty miles in advance of the strike force was his secret weapon, a vanguard of unmanned seaborne assets. With Chinese satellites out of commission and strike force CAPs in place to intercept enemy air and surface assets, that left subsurface threats as his main concern.

Sharratt was of mixed mind about his robot flotilla. There was so much new technology packed into these platforms that his people were still discovering new features and struggling to integrate the remote sensors into the decision-making process. The US Navy had put to sea a fleet of R&D platforms for a live fire test in combat conditions.

On the other hand, he was grateful for anything that might offer an edge, any advantage at all, in the upcoming battle. There would be a battle, Sharratt was sure of that. He'd not been a fan of the new president, but Serrano showed no signs of backing down. The move to drive the *Lincoln* up the South China Sea as a feint for the *Enterprise* strike force's southwesterly sprint was breathtakingly bold.

Assuming Sharratt's strike force wasn't detected first.

As he stared at the BattleSpace display, a red dot appeared on the line of their future track.

"We have a possible submerged contact on our track, Admiral." The Battle Watch Officer was a lieutenant commander, recently promoted from BattleSpace operator to watch officer. He strode to the plot, full of nervous energy, and pointed to the red dot.

"If it's a sub, it's not one of ours, sir," he said. "We're conducting a localization sweep to confirm and identify the contact."

The BattleSpace display zoomed in on the vanguard unmanned fleet. Sharratt saw a string of blue tracks. "Talk me through this, Tim," Sharratt said.

"The two advance lines are *Sea Skates*, sir. Those are the sailboat things. We got a hit from the magnetic anomaly detector on one of the Skates. They're programmed to converge on a possible contact and run cross-hatching search patterns to isolate and confirm the target."

A second red dot appeared on the holographic display. Then a third.

"Three submerged contacts, Admiral," the watch officer said. "We're vectoring in an MQ-4E Triton drone to drop sonobuoys. ETA in three minutes."

Three minutes passed very slowly when you watched the clock. Sharratt's mind raced ahead to the next decision point.

"What are you thinking, sir?" Zachary asked.

"I think we just found a wolfpack," Sharratt replied, referring to German U-boat tactics in World War Two. "The question is, who's the alpha? Russia or the PLA?"

"Admiral!" the watch officer announced. "We have an ID on one of the contacts. Confirmed as a *Kilo*-class submarine."

"Very well." Sharratt cut a glance at Zachary. That identification of the submarine did not help matters. The Russians had sold *Kilo*-class diesel electric submarines to many countries around the world, including China.

"Watch Officer," Sharratt called out, "how many Stingray drones do we have on Alert-five that are armed with torpedoes?"

The officer consulted his status board. "Three, sir."

"Launch 'em. All three."

"Launch drones, aye, sir."

Sharratt caught Zachary's look. "Options, Tom. I want to have options." He nodded at the BattleSpace display. "What are the odds that we're showing up on the submarine sensors?"

His chief of staff had far more experience in submarines than Sharratt.

"It's possible, sir," Zachary said. "In deep water like this, we're two, maybe three convergence zones away. Even if they can hear us, they'll have no idea on range yet."

"Drones are in the air, sir," the watch officer reported. "Time to intercept is one-five minutes."

The military maxim of "hurry up and wait" applied equally well to battle operations as well as military life. As the minutes dragged by, he was treated to an inside look at how the unmanned naval assets operated.

The *Sea Skates* acted as advance sensors, silently crisscrossing the ocean ahead of the strike force. The sailboats, patterned after America's Cup vessels, could reach speeds of over forty knots under ideal weather conditions, all controlled by computers. They operated as a pack. If one unit registered a detection, they collaborated to triangulate and identify the target.

The picture that emerged from their search pattern was of three submarines running on parallel tracks at eight knots.

"Sir, we have IDs on the last two subs." The watch officer approached the BattleSpace display just as the data tags on the submerged contacts updated with the new information.

Two *Kilo*-class and one *Yuan*-class boat. Three People's Liberation Army Navy submarines were in the path of his strike force. Did the Chinese already know the location of the American fleet, or were these submarines advance pickets?

"Sir," the watch officer said, "the torpedo drones will be on station in three minutes."

Decision time, Sharratt thought. Battle Watch had gone quiet. He could sense that all eyes were on him, waiting for his orders.

"Thank you, Tim," Sharratt replied without looking up from the holographic display.

He deliberately relaxed his grip on the steel railing, took a deep breath, and raised his head.

"Battle Watch Officer, position the incoming drones behind the submarines' track. I intend to launch a simultaneous torpedo attack on all three targets as soon as they are in position."

The watch officer's eyes were wide. "Understood, sir. Repositioning the drones now."

Zachary sidled up to Sharratt. "You sure about this, sir? It might be a hard sell to say that a submarine a hundred fifty miles away represents an imminent threat. That's what the ROE calls for."

"The rules of engagement allow for command discretion," Sharratt said. "We're about to sail into harm's way against an enemy with superior numbers and very short supply lines. This is not the time to be timid." He smiled. "Besides, the only way they can court-martial me is if we live through this."

The blue arrows representing the ASW drones with their deadly torpedo payloads were now lined up behind the PLA submarines.

"Battle Watch Officer," Sharratt said.

"Sir!"

"Weapons free. Put those subs on the bottom of the ocean."

26

Mission Clock: 156:15:59
Mission Status: Green

"Minister Fei, my concern deserves an answer." The speaker was the Chair of the Party Committee on Commerce, a short, stout man with thinning hair and soft, weathered features. But today, his grandfatherly face was red with passion, and from behind thick glasses, his flinty gaze bored into the Minister.

He pounded the table and shouted. No one flinched. The People's Committee for the Reunification of Taiwan was meeting in a subterranean chamber beneath the Great Hall of the People. The room was sound-proofed, and the Minister had ensured the cameras were turned off.

"You told us the United States was powerless," the Commerce Chair continued. "You said our commercial relationships would not be impacted." He snatched a sheet of paper off the table and shook it in the air. "As of this morning, the United States has seized two hundred and seventeen of our commercial ships, including some that were hundreds of kilometers from shore. We are powerless to respond. How do you explain that, comrade?"

The Minister could not explain it. In all his planning scenarios, he had not foreseen this maneuver by the United States. Not only had President Serrano found a pressure point in the seemingly invincible Chinese armor, but he had the balls to put that plan into motion. No hesitation, no dithering, no political backchanneling. Just clear, direct action.

Impressive, Fei thought. Brilliant. Perhaps some of the old men in this room could learn a lesson from the American leader.

Using something called letters of marque to place a bounty on Chinese ships was a master stroke. The perpetrators of the crimes against China were not United States government assets but private companies. Breathtakingly simple, yet highly effective.

"I am waiting for an answer, Minister Fei!" thundered the Commerce Chair. He balled the paper he'd been brandishing, and for a second, Fei thought the man might throw it at him.

The Minister wanted to sigh but held it in. Yes, this move by Serrano was unexpected, but it did not change anything, not really. The pain of lost trade would be temporary. It was only money. China would negotiate for the "lost" ships, trade would flow again, and they would make more money.

A lot more money. With the commerce from the province of Taiwan added into the mainland Chinese economy, they would make more money than any country in the history of humanity.

But these idiots failed to see the big picture. They were no more than a gaggle of old men, ever anxious to protect their cherished Party status.

The Minister got to his feet, an expression of solemn contrition on his face. He was acutely aware that the full attention of the room was on him, including the General Secretary of the Communist Party. He still had the leader's confidence, but the man's patience was not infinite. The Minister needed to make this performance worthwhile.

"Comrades," Fei began, "for decades the People's Republic of China has sought to reunify the rogue province of Taiwan with greater China. It has been a goal of our generation, our fathers' generation, and even our grandfathers'. Today, we have the power to achieve that goal."

He reached into his breast pocket and extracted his Shandian tablet.

"We will land nearly one hundred thousand troops on the island of Taiwan. There is no way the United States or any other power is going to dislodge us. We need to stay the course, comrades." He sat down, wincing as his backside touched the chair seat.

The pain in his body had changed over the last few days. He had almost gotten used to the fickle pain that came and went. It changed depending on his level of activity or his diet, moving and gnawing at his insides like a parasite seeking sustenance. What remained now was a dull, throbbing ache that ran through his body like waves hitting the shore. Washing in, washing out, never stopping, this new pain was a constant companion.

Before, he limited himself to doses of half a pain pill. As of yesterday, he now took a full pill every few hours. His doctor told him he could take up to three at a time, multiple times a day, but the Minister resisted. Narcotics would only dull his senses, and he wanted—no, he needed—to remain sharp.

In addition to the added pain burden, the Minister began to experience twinges of worry about the invasion progress. He told himself that was only because the initial invasion had been so successful. After all, by the end of the first day, the PLA was nearly a full day ahead of schedule. But as the hours turned into days, the momentum appeared to be fading. According to the Shandian tablet, their success of the first few days had regressed back to the original timeline. Barely.

The lost satellite coverage had always been a contingency, albeit an unlikely one. But that also did not matter in the grand scheme of the invasion. The PLA had control of 75 percent of the island population. Soon, they would begin their drive down the western side of Taiwan to crush the remaining remnants of the Taiwanese military and complete the job.

Even at best speed, the *Enterprise* strike force was still far to the north of Taiwan. The United States had only a single aircraft carrier, the USS *Abraham Lincoln*, entering the South China Sea. A few Marine air squadrons on Okinawa and US Air Force assets on Guam were mere pinpricks against the PLA airpower occupying Taiwanese airspace.

No, Fei decided, the American president was holding a losing hand. But that did not mean Serrano wasn't playing his hand well.

The Minister turned his attention to the large television screen dominating the end of the table.

"Play the video again," the General Secretary rumbled.

President of the United States Ricardo Serrano stood tall at the lectern in the United Nations General Assembly. With all the setbacks and humiliations his country had suffered in the past year, Fei would have expected the American president to look haggard and worn, but the man on the screen appeared vigorous and vital. His showy hairstyle glinted in the soft light, and his eyes glowed with intensity. Typical American politician, Fei thought. All flash and no substance.

Serrano rested his clenched fist on the podium. "The invasion by the People's Republic of China against the people of Taiwan cannot go unanswered. I call on China to leave the island of Taiwan and restore the status quo to the region that has lasted for over eight decades."

He paused, gazing over the assembly. "I do not expect China to simply heed my words. Action is required to show the resolve of the international community against this senseless aggression, and America will lead the way.

"Effective immediately, the United States is creating a one-hundred-mile exclusion zone around the island of Taiwan. The PLA forces have twenty-four hours to depart the exclusion zone, after which time those forces will be considered hostile and will be removed using whatever means necessary. This will not be a US-only action. Already a dozen nations have agreed to participate, including the AUKUS alliance. Today, I call on the ASEAN members to join my country in freeing the people of Taiwan from the yoke of Chinese aggression."

Every seat in the General Assembly was filled, and people lined the walls two and three deep. With a collective roar, the entire assembly rose, and the room echoed with applause. The camera focused on the Chinese delegation. They remained seated, staring impassively into space, lips pursed in sour grimaces.

The Minister scanned the crowd. Even the Russians were on their feet, clapping politely.

Disgusting, Fei thought. After their invasion of Crimea he would have thought the Russians would offer some diplomatic cover. But no, they were looking to see which way the wind was blowing before they took a stand.

Of course, Fei mused, the way we framed the Russians for everything we did to the Americans over the past year might account for their lack of support for China on the UN floor.

The video ended.

"Honorable General Secretary." The Vice Chairman of the Central Military Commission got to his feet. As he waited for an acknowledgment, he fiddled with an unlit cigarette. "Comrade, I could not help but notice that the United States president left us an opening for compromise."

The Minister couldn't believe what he was hearing. He started to get to his feet, but the General Secretary stayed him with a hand gesture. The leader nodded for the speaker to continue.

In his agitation, the Vice Chairman managed to shred the cigarette wrapping. Tobacco flakes littered the table. "For all their bluster, the United States did not insist on Taiwan independence. If we reconsidered our action, we still preserve our right to absorb the province of Taiwan at a future date. I only mention this because the invasion seems to have stalled—"

The Minister couldn't contain himself any longer. He shot to his feet. "That is a lie! We are exactly on schedule with our plans."

"Do you deny we have lost momentum, Minister Fei?" the General Secretary asked in a mild tone.

Too late, Fei realized that his overreaction displayed a lack of confidence in his own plan. It was the damn pain pills. They dulled his senses.

He struggled to get his emotions under control. After bowing to the Vice Chairman, he said, "Apologies for my outburst, comrades. These are stressful times. The Vice Chairman is correct. The United States is a cunning adversary. They offer a way for us to pull our forces back, but why? I submit to you that the United States is bluffing. It is because we are so close to our goal that they are making these bold claims of exclusion zones and diplomatic off-ramps."

The Minister could see his words were landing with some of the men in the room. He pressed his advantage.

"These are empty threats, comrades. The US will not risk a global war over the island of Taiwan! They are weak, their forces are scattered, and this posturing is no more than the piteous cries of a once great nation." Fei thumped the table, feeling the pain shoot up his arm in protest.

"But we are a rising power, and we will claim our destiny. Not at some future time, but now. Today. This is the opportunity of a lifetime, of multiple lifetimes, within our grasp. We must not lose faith now."

The Minister trembled with excitement at his own speech. Even the pain seemed to recede for a few moments. He dropped into his chair, exhausted.

He half listened as the meeting wound to a close. As he stood, the General Secretary placed a heavy hand on Fei's arm.

"We will stay the course, but there can be no more delays, Minister Fei," he said calmly. "The invasion must proceed on schedule."

"It shall be done, sir," Fei said, putting as much confidence into his tone as he could muster. "It shall be done."

27

Mission Clock: 153:39:43
Mission Status: Green

Major Gao managed to convince himself that his injuries didn't look that bad. When he stepped off the elevator on the thirty-sixth floor of the Taipei 101 building, he got the first unfiltered reaction to his appearance.

It was not good.

The young female soldier behind the reception desk jumped to attention, but she stared at him with a look of undisguised horror.

After a summons from General Zhang to return to Taipei, Gao had gotten a medic at the airport to rewrap the bandage across the right side of his head into a smaller profile. He also discarded the eye patch. The light and airflow irritated his injured eye, but if he was going to convince General Zhang to send him back to the southern front in Taiwan, he must appear capable.

He needed to get back to Kaohsiung City as soon as possible. He needed to find that missing tablet.

Gao started across the foyer toward the general's office.

"Sir," the soldier called.

"What?" Gao snapped.

"You're injured—"

"Don't you think I know that, soldier?" Gao said.

She placed her index finger on her cheek below her right eye. "You're bleeding, sir. Your injured eye is weeping blood."

Gao swiped his hand across his face and came back with blood-smeared fingers. He cursed to himself.

The receptionist approached with a handkerchief. "May I?"

Gao stood still as she dabbed at his face. Her delicate fingers were cool against his hot, bruised skin. She held the cloth against the corner of his eye.

"That should do it," she said.

Gao's head throbbed. He wanted nothing more than to let this young woman with the tender hands caress his face all day, but the lost tablet nagged at his conscience like an itchy scab. If the tablet had fallen into the wrong hands, the entire Shandian battle network might be exposed to the enemy. And he had already lied once to cover up the loss...

Anger and shame welled up in Gao. He caught the young woman's hand as she pulled the cloth away from his face.

"What's your name?" he asked.

"Private Su, Fourth Battalion—"

Gao cut her off. "No, what's your name?"

She blushed. "Mei Lin."

Gao squeezed her hand, then let it go. "Thank you, Mei Lin."

"The general is expecting you, sir," she said.

Gao strode across the marble tiles to Zhang's office, each step like a jackhammer in his head. He rapped twice on the door, then entered. He marched to the general's desk and saluted.

"Reporting as ordered, sir."

At the general's back, the view through the windows showed a gray pall of low clouds hanging over the city of Taipei. The dirty weather outside matched the scowl on Zhang's face. He spun his laptop around so Gao could view the screen.

"Have you seen this?" he asked.

Gao recognized United States President Serrano. The chyron on the bottom of the screen gave the location as the UN General Assembly. Zhang tapped a button on his laptop so Gao could listen. He stepped from behind his desk and paced his office, his face lined with worry.

Gao tapped the laptop keyboard when the recording was finished. The image froze on the Chinese delegation seated in a roomful of cheering diplomats.

"A one-hundred-mile exclusion zone," Zhang said. "Clever. Their exclusion zone encompasses our emergency zone."

"Surely he's bluffing, General," Gao said.

Zhang stopped pacing. When he turned, his face was ruddy with emotion. "There is no greater danger than underestimating your opponent. And a desperate opponent is a dangerous one. Did we foresee their attack on our satellites?"

"No, sir," Gao said.

"Did we anticipate their attack on our commercial shipping?"

"No, sir."

"Then I ask you this, Major Gao: What else are we not seeing?"

Zhang did not wait for an answer. He strode across the room to the holographic display of Taiwan. "Until this entire island is under our control, we are vulnerable, Major. There must not be a single place where American forces can gain a foothold."

Gao followed the general to the map table. "I understand, sir."

The general studied him, and Gao fervently hoped his eye was not bleeding again. He must return to the southern command, whatever it took to make that happen. Gao felt sweat break out under his arms just thinking about the urgency of the situation. He had to find that missing tablet.

"Will your injuries prevent you from further service?" Zhang asked finally.

"Absolutely not, sir," Gao said with as much gusto as he could manage.

"Tell me what happened," Zhang said.

Gao ran through his investigation of the ammunition truck explosion and his conclusion that it had been sabotage. Zhang nodded with approval when Gao described how he had used intelligence resources in General Wei's command to find the rebels in the mountain campground.

"And that is where you were injured?" the general asked.

"We were ambushed, sir," Gao said. "I tried to convince General Wei to use a larger force, but my advice was ignored."

Another lie, thought Gao.

Zhang pursed his lips. "Anything else, Major?"

Gao swallowed. He'd omitted the part about his missing Shandian tablet. If he was going to be honest with Zhang, he needed to come clean now. The communications officer in Wei's command had already tried to call Gao once this morning. It was only a matter of time before the young officer reported the discrepancy.

"There is one more thing, sir," Gao said.

"What is it?" Zhang looked up sharply. "Out with it, Major."

Gao made a show of hesitating. He needed to play this exactly right. He cleared his throat.

"When you sent me to the southern command, sir, you stressed the need for discretion."

"Yes," Zhang said.

"General Wei knew I was coming, sir," Gao said. "He had someone meet me at the airport. He tried to cover up the investigation. That's my opinion, sir," Gao added hastily.

General Zhang did not reply. Instead, he focused on the holographic map and paced around the table as if Gao weren't even there. Fresh sweat bathed Gao's body, and he suddenly felt dizzy. He put a hand on the edge of the table to steady himself.

Zhang looked up. "Continue, Major."

Gao's heart rate ramped up. The stitches in his scalp throbbed with the added pressure.

"General Wei," Gao began. His mouth was dry as sand, and he had trouble forming words. "I don't know how to put this, sir, but General Wei offered me a bribe. He says he will be the next governor of Taiwan province, and he said he would help me if I spied on you."

Zhang showed no reaction. He continued to pace as if lost in contemplation about the geography of Taiwan.

Gao felt his knees loosening. Had he gone too far? If General Zhang confronted Wei, it would be Gao's word against a politically connected senior officer. There was only one way that match-up ended.

Confess now, Gao thought. He tried to open his mouth, but his jaw seemed locked shut.

"I need you to return to the south of Taiwan," the general said. "You will be my eyes and ears in General Wei's command." Zhang hesitated, then smiled as he continued, "Can I trust you, *Lieutenant Colonel* Gao?"

General Zhang held out his hand, and Gao gripped it as much to stay upright as to accept the congratulations.

The feeling of relief that washed over Gao left him giddy. He was headed south again. He had been granted a chance to fix this problem. And he had received a promotion! It was all working out in his favor.

"Hold still, Gao," Zhang said, gripping his forearm. He pulled a handkerchief from his hip pocket and pressed it to Gao's right eye. "Your eye is weeping blood."

"It's nothing, sir."

The general's face was only a few centimeters away. The older man's breath painted Gao's cheek.

"I want you to accept General Wei's generous offer," Zhang continued in a low voice. "When the time comes, we will trap the traitor in his own lies."

28

East China Sea, 200 miles northeast of Taiwan

Marine All-Weather Fighter Attack Squadron 121, based in Okinawa, Japan, was formed in 1941. In their storied history, the proud men and women of the Green Knights had flown every major fighter aircraft platform for their country in every conflict since World War Two.

On the transparent visor of his helmet, Lieutenant Colonel Alex "Pipper" Plechash, CO of VMFA-121, could see all twelve F-35B Lightning II strike fighters flying in formation around him. The Distributed Aperture System took inputs from six infrared cameras on the body of his aircraft and displayed a 360-degree view of the space around him onto the interior of his visor. The helmet he wore cost as much as a single-family home in a decent neighborhood back in his hometown of Minneapolis, but at moments like this one, it was worth every blessed penny. When he turned his head, it was as if he were looking through the fuselage of his own aircraft.

His wingman was Captain Roger "Sally" Salisbury, joined tightly on Pipper in right echelon formation. He studied Sally's F-35 in the visor display. The normal profile of the F-35 was smooth and futuristic, with all the ordnance contained inside the twin sealed bomb bay doors on the underside of the aircraft.

Not so for this mission. Tonight, the Green Knights were in "Beast Mode," carrying ordnance mounted on wing hardpoints in addition to their internal bomb bays. The external load ruined the F-35's famous stealthy advantage, but it nearly quadrupled ordnance capacity to twenty-two thousand pounds. His payload tonight was four air-to-air missiles and six GBU-31 JDAMs. The two-thousand-pound Joint Direct Attack Munitions were all-weather precision guided bombs. Once released, these fire-and-forget units were guided by GPS to their target.

Stealth was not important for this mission. Once the Air Force B-2 stealth bombers out of Guam struck their PLA targets in Taiwan, the Chinese would be expecting them.

ATO incoming. The message alert popped up on the LCD display in his cockpit.

The Air Tasking Order was generated by Eagle Eye, the AWACS flying high above them. Taking into account the damage assessment from the B-2 bombing run, the orders designated a primary and secondary target for each pilot of the VMFA-121 strike package. Pipper was pleased to see he and Sally had been assigned the PLA command bunker on the outskirts of Taiwan. The same area he had performed a surveillance run on only a few days ago.

Pipper consulted the panoramic touchscreen to verify targeting coordinates had been updated during the ATO download. From the datalink update, he could see each member of the squadron had received and acknowledged their tasking.

He keyed his radio: "Green Knights, Green One. Targets assigned. Heads up for SAMs and J-20s. Good hunting."

He received datalink acknowledgments from ten of his pilots, the eleventh was Salisbury, the youngest and newest member of the squadron.

"Ooh-rah, Colonel," Sally said.

Pipper smiled in spite of himself. The kid was a good pilot, just had a lot of energy. Not unlike himself at that age.

The formation broke apart. The aircraft nav system automatically calculated an intercept for Pipper to reach his UCAV wingman. The unmanned aircraft were slower than the manned jets. They had been launched in advance of the main squadron, refueled in flight and stationed along the route to their destination.

When Pipper's UCAV was in range, the datalinks between the manned and unmanned aircraft merged. The X-47D was capable of carrying nearly the same amount of ordnance as the F-35 in stealth mode. Its weapons load for this mission was two AIM 260 Joint Advanced Attack Missiles for air-to-air combat and a pair of two-thousand-pound Mark 84 precision guided bombs for land-based targets.

Pipper piloted to his assigned vector from Eagle Eye. Using the datalink, the UCAV automatically matched his heading and speed.

The Chinese were waiting for them. Pipper's breath hitched as his screen populated with a slew of inbound PLA air contacts. The closing speed between the two opposing air forces was over a thousand miles per hour. At that speed, they would cover the fifty miles between them in less than three minutes.

"Green Knights, Eagle Eye. Stand by for target assignments." The voice of the AWACS operator was rock steady.

Pipper drew in a deep breath and let it out slowly. Show time.

At thirty miles off the coast of northern Taiwan, Pipper's visor display highlighted an incoming air contact, his first assigned target, a PLA Air Force J-20 fighter.

"Copy assignment contact Alpha-two-one," he said, allowing the voice recognition to send his acknowledgment. He popped off an AIM-120 AMRAAM. From the furthest hardpoint on his starboard wing, the missile dropped, flared to life, and sped off into the darkness.

"Fox three," Pipper said, indicating he had launched an air-to-air radar homing missile.

He slammed the throttle forward and selected the afterburner, the UCAV keeping pace. He wanted to close the distance as rapidly as possible to deprive the incoming Chinese pilot the chance to launch a standoff missile.

The J-20, which had been built partly based on stolen F-35 design specs, was a worthy aircraft; Pipper knew that. But his opening maneuver was not designed to test the plane. He wanted to test the opposing pilot's skill.

The Chinese pilot broke off to avoid the incoming missile. Pipper flashed by, their positions on his screen merging for a split second. He released a Sidewinder, the AIM-9X Block II design, a lethal short-range infrared-seeking missile. The freed weapon looped over Pipper's aircraft to pursue the Chinese warplane that was now behind them.

"Fox two," he called on the radio, using the brevity code for an IR-guided missile launch.

He swung his head to the side so the visor showed him a view behind his aircraft. A blossom of white appeared in the IR display.

"That's a confirmed kill, Green One," Eagle Eye said.

"Roger," he replied. He checked the rest of his squadron. Ten aircraft were still engaged in dogfights with their Chinese counterparts. One had lost a UCAV wingman, but the pilot was still in the hunt.

Only Sally, designated Green Six, had not been assigned an air threat contact. Instead, he started the first attack run.

"Green One," Eagle Eye said. "Follow Green Six and conduct a Wild Weasel run."

"Green One. Roger."

Wild Weasel was the Air Force term for Suppression of Enemy Air Defenses, or SEAD. Pipper maneuvered into position ten miles behind Sally. The B-2 should have taken out most of the SAM batteries, but he would target any remaining sites that were still a threat.

"I got your six, Sally," Pipper said.

"Roger, Pipper," came the swift reply. The kid sounded confident, solid.

"Feet dry," Pipper reported as he flashed over the Taiwanese coast. His display registered heat signatures from several SAM sites where the B-2 had dropped bombs earlier. It looked like the Air Force had done a thorough job.

A warning flashed on screen. A surface-to-air missile radar had illuminated the lead aircraft.

"Spike at nine o'clock!" Pipper called.

"Got it," Sally replied. His voice was tight.

A SAM launch flared on Pipper's visor. Then a second from the same site.

"Incoming SAMs at your nine o'clock!" Pipper called. "Break right, break right!"

Pipper launched a pair of AGM-88E HARM missiles to destroy the SAM launch site. He saw a satisfying explosion on his visor a few seconds later.

Meanwhile, Sally, in the lead aircraft dealt with the incoming SAMs. He broke hard to the right, leaving an IR decoy in his wake. The first missile got suckered by the decoy, but the second stayed on Sally's tail. He broke left and deployed his "Little Buddy," an ALE-50 towed decoy designed to foil RF-guided missiles.

The entire engagement took less than fifteen seconds.

Sally was breathing heavily when he came back on the comms circuit, but his voice was calm. "Green Six, commencing attack run."

Pipper turned his attention to the coordinates of the command center. The square shapes of the unidentified Xbox mystery weapon showed on his screen. Two of the boxes opened, but nothing registered on Pipper's sensors.

"Sally," he said, "keep an eye on those Xbox systems."

"Roger," Sally replied. "What the—"

"Sally, get out of there!" Pipper shouted.

What emerged from the Chinese weapon was not a missile, it was more like a cloud of projectiles.

Ahead, Sally pickled off his bomb load, and Pipper's display updated as six JDAMs went into guided flight.

The cloud enveloped the incoming ordnance. Pipper saw the bombs explode in midair.

And it kept coming. The silvery cloud enveloped Sally's aircraft. The warplane went into an uncontrolled spinning descent.

"Sally!" Pipper shouted.

No answer.

Pipper broke hard right and accelerated, leaving the silvery cloud in his wake. His jaw muscles popped as he gritted his teeth.

Behind him, he traced the arc of his wingman's shattered jet as it slammed into the ground. The explosion flared in his visor display.

"Eagle Eye, Green Six down. No parachute."

"Copy, Green One. We're seeing an anomalous reading on the target."

Pipper swallowed hard, trying to pull his emotions into check. Trying to reconcile what he'd just seen.

Plenty of time for that later. First he had to get back on the ground in one piece.

He turned hard back toward the target.

"Eagle Eye, Green One, I'm starting my attack run now. Be advised, we're gonna need a lot more iron on target."

DAY FIVE

29

Wutai Township, Taiwan

Mission Clock: 143:12:39
Mission Status: Green

The shower room at the campground smelled of mold. A line of four dripping shower heads lined one wall. The walls and floor were covered with yellow tiles, but in the light of the single fluorescent bulb, the sunny color took on a garish orange hue.

The night air was cool this high in the mountains, making Gao thankful for his thick uniform tunic. The stitches in his scalp throbbed every time his heart beat, and the vision in his right eye was still fuzzy. He took a packet of Tylenol from his pocket, ripped open the packaging with his teeth, and dry-swallowed the pills.

Then he considered the naked man on the floor in front of him. The Shandian tablet in Gao's right hand told him all he needed to know about the prisoner.

The young man who stared back at him from the screen had a stylish haircut and a rakish smile. The picture looked like it was taken from a social media site, one of the many sources for the data-scraping program that fed the PLA facial recognition program.

Lucas Han was twenty-eight years old and single. Father deceased, mother still living, an only child. He worked for a design firm in Kaohsiung City, and there was no girlfriend listed. Lucas Han had also served three years in the Taiwanese Army as an intel officer.

He was also Gao's only tenuous link to what had happened to his lost Shandian tablet.

The fact that they had managed to capture young Mr. Han was a stroke of good luck. Upon arriving back in Kaohsiung City in the afternoon, Gao immediately took a squad of soldiers to the site of the ambush. He ordered them to comb the area for any personal belongings of their fallen comrades, but that was just a cover to search for the missing tablet.

Gao had not found the tablet, but he did find Lucas Han.

He reasoned that the Taiwanese terrorists must have left a lookout in case any more locals saw the graffiti call to action and drove to the campground. Instead of warning away civilians, the terrorists had given Gao a prisoner.

Lucas would have been fine if he had just stayed in his hideout. From the cleft between two rocks, Lucas had an excellent view of the area and was shielded from any drones overhead. Using the cover of the falling darkness, Lucas had tried to sneak away, but an aerial drone using IR imaging had picked him up.

Gao gave himself a mental pat on the back for remembering to make sure his men had come equipped with night vision goggles this time. Once detected, his trained soldiers had run Lucas down inside of thirty minutes.

But what to do with his prisoner once he had him in custody?

Gao considered the problem. If he took the prisoner back to General Wei's headquarters, he would be subject to the rules of engagement for the invasion. Any interrogation would be conducted after the prisoner received medical treatment for the bullet wound in his thigh. In Gao's mind, that was wasted time. Also, he didn't dare risk letting any information about the missing tablet get out.

Finally, he selected the two biggest soldiers to stay and sent the rest back to Kaohsiung City. He ordered the men to take the prisoner into the showers, strip him, and put him in a mood to answer questions. Then he left them alone.

Gao stood outside, watching the lights of the distant city reflect off the low clouds of the night sky. He half listened to the sound of the two soldiers beating the young Taiwanese man. The sounds went from shouts to cries to screams to whimpers before Gao went back inside.

That was two hours ago, and Lucas had given Gao exactly zero useful information.

Gao nodded at the two soldiers. They had stripped off their tunics, and Lucas's blood dotted their tan undershirts. One of the men had bloody knuckles.

"Get him up," Gao ordered. "Get him under the water."

When they lifted Lucas Han's naked body, he was shaking with cold. They held his upturned face under the cold water until he started to choke.

"Okay," Gao said, gesturing for them to bring him away from the shower stream.

Colorful bruises blossomed under his bare skin, prickled with goose-flesh. Gao put his index finger under the young man's chin and lifted his face so he could see his eyes. Lucas blinked. His head lolled, but Gao gripped his chin.

"Tell me where the base is," he said in a quiet voice.

Lucas pursed his lips. "I d-d-d-don't know." His teeth chattered with cold.

The two soldiers were holding Lucas with one hand under his armpit and the second on his wrist so his arms were stretched out. On the inside of the prisoner's right forearm, a strange tattoo stood out on his ashen flesh. It looked like a high-tech sword, but there was no blade, just the hilt. Gao felt like the image was familiar to him, but he couldn't place how he knew it.

He turned away in frustration. If he kept this up much longer, the kid might die, and then he'd be useless as a source of information. He needed to make a choice: continue and risk killing him, or take him back to Wei's command post and lose time.

Gao decided to try again. "Lucas, this can all be over if you just tell me what I need to know." He talked to the young man like he was just there to help. After all, Gao wasn't hurting him, it was the two apes holding him up.

"Wouldn't you like a warm blanket and some tea?" Gao said.

Lucas's head lolled down, and one of the soldiers whipped his skull against the tiled wall. "Answer him," he barked.

"The Americans are here," Lucas whispered.

Gao froze. He gripped Lucas's jaw with both hands and wrenched his face up. He moved in close until their noses nearly touched. Gao peered into the young man's eyes.

"What did you say?" Gao demanded.

To his surprise, Lucas smiled.

"Get out," Gao ordered the two soldiers. They let the young Taiwanese man go, and he collapsed onto the wet tiled floor. Gao waited until the door closed behind them before he crouched down next to Lucas.

He tried to keep his mind calm, but his thoughts ricocheted into endless possibilities. Americans? Was it possible the United States had already landed special forces on the island? Gao knew the US Army Green Berets had been training for these kinds of missions for years.

It was entirely possible, Gao decided. A HALO jump during an airstrike or a submarine insertion, these were all real possibilities—and something his superiors would want to know.

But first, he needed to know if the Taiwanese terrorists had his missing tablet.

Gao knelt next to Lucas, feeling the puddled water soak into his trousers. He pulled the young man's head into his lap. His skin was clammy and chilled.

"Tell me what you know, Lucas," Gao said in a soothing voice. "Tell me about the Americans."

Lucas didn't respond.

Gao felt a wave of panic grip his guts. If the Americans penetrated the Shandian battle network using his tablet...

He slapped Lucas across the face.

"Answer me, you stupid son of a bitch," he said. "Where is the tablet?"

Lucas opened his eyes.

"Tablet?" His voice was weak, and he slurred the word.

Gao put the prisoner's head on the floor and stood up. The young man was too weak to continue. He'd warm him up, feed him, then question him again later. Perhaps knowing he'd go through this same treatment all over again would finally break the kid.

Gao was about to call for help when Lucas spoke again.

"Gong-gong has the tablet."

Gao fell to his knees. "What?" He put his face close to Lucas's. "What did you say?"

Lucas wasn't breathing anymore. Gao put two fingers on his carotid artery. No pulse. Gao rolled Lucas onto his back. He started CPR, yelling for the two guards. They stumbled in.

"Help me revive him," Gao ordered.

The two men looked at each other but did nothing.

Gao tried to recall how to do CPR. Was it fast reps or slow? Lucas's chest was like cold meat under his fingers. Gao pushed harder, and he felt ribs crack. He screamed in frustration, then rocked back on his heels.

Lucas Han was dead.

Gao put his face in his hands, feeling the clammy dampness of Lucas's flesh on his own skin. What had the kid said?

Gong-gong has the tablet.

Gong-gong...grandfather. Grandfather has the tablet? What the fuck did that mean?

Gao's head pounded with fatigue. The kid was hallucinating, Gao told himself. The last words of a dying man. He slowly got to his feet.

"Get him out of here," Gao ordered.

"What do we do with him, sir?" one of the soldiers asked.

In frustration, Gao kicked the corpse. "Bury him in the woods with all his gear. And you do not talk to anyone about this, do you understand? That's an order."

The soldiers nodded and mumbled, "Yes, sir" as they clumped across the tile floor. One seized Lucas's wrists, the other gripped his ankles.

"Nice *Star Wars* tattoo," one soldier said.

Gao looked up. "What did you say?"

The soldier nodded his head at the tattoo on Lucas's forearm. "It's a *Star Wars* tattoo, sir. That's Luke Skywalker's lightsaber."

The foggy memory that had dogged Gao all night came into clear focus.

Growing up, the kid who lived next door was a *Star Wars* nerd. That's why he recognized the tattoo on Lucas's arm.

Gao held the door for the two men carrying the corpse of Lucas Han. They paused outside to pile his gear on the dead body, then marched into the night.

Gao leaned against the cinder block wall and breathed in. The night air was cool and damp. It smelled like it might rain.

His mouth tasted sour from the events of the shower room. He had been so close to some answers, and now all he was left with were the words of a dying man rambling on about his grandfather.

Gao took a stick of gum from his pocket and unwrapped it. As the minty sweetness washed over his tongue, his thoughts shifted to the tattoo. If the Shadow Army of Taiwan identified with Luke Skywalker's rebel alliance, then that made the People's Republic of China the Empire.

He grinned. It had been a long time since he'd seen the movie, but he seemed to recall that the Empire won.

30

Fangshan, Taiwan

Mike Lester looked at his wristwatch: 0249.

Using binoculars, he peered through the weave of the chain link fence at the Fangshan cable relay station. The one-story cinder block building served as the terminus for three undersea cables. Lester's team had done their homework. They wanted to access the Southeast Asia-Japan Cable 2. The ten-thousand-kilometer long cable connected Japan with Singapore and beyond. It was not only the newest of the three cables, it was also the only one that did not touch mainland China. The last thing Lester wanted was to expose his team to a dangerous mission only to have their communications intercepted by the Chinese Ministry of State Security.

The yellow glare of the sodium lights showed an empty gravel parking lot fronting the terminal building and an emergency diesel generator. The compound was surrounded on three sides by mango orchards, which provided excellent cover for Lester's team as they transited from the rugged mountain paths into the flat farmland along the coast. The fence was topped with razor wire, but the owners of the building, Chunghwa Telecom, had let the thick green vegetation bordering the station to grow right up to the fence.

Lester smelled the salt of the ocean and heard the distant surf. Palm trees waved in the breeze. A peaceful night in the tropics, he thought, but not for long.

He focused the optics on the open gate of the compound. A green PLA utility vehicle idled in the gravel yard. His team had been watching the yard for six hours, and the patrol vehicle stopped by fifteen minutes before the hour, every hour. Through the early evening, the patrol car had an officer riding in back, but with the midnight shift change, he disappeared. One of the three guards crowded next to the vehicle shouted something, and they all laughed.

Lester checked his watch again: 0255.

"C'mon," he muttered. They could not risk using radio communications, even encrypted ones, so his plan depended on timing. And these jokers were messing up his timetable.

Finally, the senior enlisted soldier in charge of the station security detail slapped the roof of the SUV. The vehicle exited the compound, turned right onto the adjoining highway, and drove north.

Lester breathed a sigh of relief. He turned to Ash Lewis nestled in her own cocoon of tall weeds. She had camouflage paint smeared on her face, and her sandy-blond hair was tucked into a cap. "You ready, Marine?"

Lewis's smile was a slash in the dark. "Semper Fi, sir."

Another glance at his watch: 0259. Any second now.

As if in answer to his thoughts, he heard a distant boom like a rumble of thunder. On the dark northern horizon, a fireball erupted into the sky.

"Looks like they might've overdone it just a bit," Lester muttered.

Better too big than too small, he reasoned. His major concern about the raid was drones. One high-flying overwatch UAV had the ability to ruin his whole day. Lester figured the best way to make sure that a drone wasn't watching them was to give it something else to look at. Like a massive explosion in a railyard.

Lester waited until the distant explosion had captured the attention of the three guards. He pressed his throat mic. "Snipers, take the shot."

He barely heard the suppressed shots over the sound of the surf. Three PLA bodies hit the gravel.

"All teams, move in," Lester said.

A squad of four Taiwanese soldiers rushed the gate. Three of them picked up the corpses, slung them over their shoulders, and hustled out of the compound. The PLA soldiers would get a quick burial deep in the mango orchards. The fourth man, dressed in a PLA combat infantry uniform, assumed guard duty.

Lester and Lewis made the gate a few seconds later and trotted across the compound yard, gravel crunching under their boots. Lester was breathing hard by the time they entered the building.

He wasn't sure what he had expected for his very first visit to a cable relay station, but he was underwhelmed all the same. The single room had a row of power distribution cabinets along the back wall, followed by a bank of blinking computer racks, then a small office for the station manager. The air was ice-cold, and the room was silent save for an electronic hum like an undercurrent of sound.

Lewis seated herself behind the desk in the office and started working the keyboard. Lester watched her.

She cocked an eye at him. "This might go faster if you don't stare at me, sir."

He paced the room. There was nothing for him to do but wait—and worry.

The door opened, and Frank Tsai entered.

"Problem, sir." He shot a glance at Lewis, clearly interested in her progress.

"Tell me," Lester replied, directing Tsai's attention away from Lewis.

"One of the scouts missed his last two check-ins," Tsai said. "Lucas Han. Good man, conscientious."

"The guy with the hair?" Lester asked. "The one with the Star Wars tat?"

Tsai grinned and nodded.

Lester absorbed the information. During their march south, they had left sentries on mountain ridges to serve as lookouts for what Lester anticipated would be a forced-march return trip. The lookouts had line-of-sight handsets and had memorized a table of check-in times and frequencies. They were instructed to use only clicks of the transmit button—no voice comms. He could picture the kid's face and his elaborately styled dark hair.

"He was posted near the campground where we ambushed the PLA, right?" Lester asked.

Tsai nodded.

"Equipment trouble?"

"I hope so," Tsai replied.

"One problem at a time, Frank," Lester said. "But let's change our route back home to avoid the area. Just to be safe."

"Yes, sir." Tsai left.

Lester looked at Lewis, then at his watch: 0312. The plan called for them to be out of here by 0330.

"I know what time it is, sir," Lewis said, without looking up. "It's right here on my screen."

To distract himself, Lester made coffee at a small brew station. The smell filled the room. With his back to Lewis, he checked his watch: 0317. He could feel the tension building in his shoulders.

"I'll take some of that if you're offering," Lewis called.

Lester poured a cup and delivered it to Lewis's desk. "Cream and sugar?"

"Black and bitter, sir," came the reply. "Just like my attitude."

Lester forced a laugh and returned to his pacing.

He tried not to look at his watch and failed: 0323. Their window was closing, Lester realized. He poked his head out of the office door and spoke to Tsai in a low tone. "Get the team ready to roll in five."

When he closed the door and turned, Lewis pushed back from the keyboard.

"I'm in."

Lester was at her side in three strides. She had the Dropbox website pulled up on the screen. He dictated his login information. She opened a new folder in his account.

"What do I call it?" she asked. "Chinese secret battle plan?"

"Call it Texas," Lester replied.

"Texas, it is." Lewis plugged the thumb drive containing the information taken from the PLA battle network into the station computer.

"Moment of truth." She tapped the keyboard to start the download. A progress bar showed six minutes to complete the download.

Lewis switched screens and stood up.

"I'll let you do this part," she said.

Lester took the chair and logged in to his email account. He started a new email and addressed it to his wife.

He and Lewis had discussed this part of the plan at length. If they tried to send a blind email to the FBI or CIA or anyone in government, it would almost certainly end up in a spam folder. They needed to send a note to someone they trusted with coded instructions on how to find the data and what to do with it.

I'm fine, Lester typed in the subject line of the email. He blew out a breath, then continued with the rest of the message:

Honey —

I'm okay and staying with friends. I need you to pick up a package at our dropbox and take it to Liz Soroush. She needs it for a very important meeting at work.

We'll always have Paris,
  Mike

Lewis read over his shoulder. "We'll always have Paris?" she asked.

"That's how she'll know it's me," Lester replied. "It's an inside joke about our honeymoon. We went to Paris, Texas." Lester fought back a sudden wave of nostalgia. "It's a long story."

"I'd like to hear it sometime," Lewis said.

Lester checked his watch: 0331.

"And I'd like to tell you, but it's gonna have to wait." He snatched the thumb drive from the computer's USB socket and stood up. "Do your computer thing, Ash."

While Lester cleaned up their coffee cups, Lewis erased all the logs containing evidence of their activity and restored the software lock the Chinese engineers had installed on the system.

At 0333, Lester shut the door to the cable relay station and followed the last of his men out of the compound. They entered the shelter of the mango groves and jogged toward the mountains.

31

USS *Enterprise* strike force
North Pacific Ocean, 800 miles east of Taipei, Taiwan

Rear Admiral Sharratt watched the BattleSpace display with unseeing eyes, his thoughts lost in a memory.

Thirty years ago, on the first day of Plebe Summer at the Naval Academy, he'd met Seth "Bulldog" Denton. Short, stout, with jet-black hair and a five o'clock shadow that lasted all day, Denton had dumped the contents of his seabag on the floor of their shared room. When Sharratt arrived, he was trying to stow the piles of uniforms, underwear, socks, gym gear, shoes, and books into his assigned shelf space.

Sharratt smiled at the thought of his closest friend. It was impossible not to. Denton had earned the nickname Bulldog from his time on the rugby team, but not for his tenacious play. Whatever the circumstances, Denton always had a crooked smile on his face.

Since they were both commissioned, Sharratt and Denton had leapfrogged one another in the milestones that made up a Navy career. Both made rear admiral in the same promotion cycle. But it was Sharratt who had become an aircraft carrier strike force commander first.

"Congrats, Bulldog," he muttered to himself. "Be careful what you wish for. It might just come true."

The *Lincoln* single-carrier strike group had stopped in Singapore to reinforce its ranks with United States allies. In addition to the Royal Navy's flagship, the aircraft carrier HMS *Queen Elizabeth*, they'd also plussed up with destroyers and frigates from the German Navy, the Royal Australian Navy, and the Canadians. Also in the mix, but not directly part of combat operations, were ships from the Japanese Maritime Self-Defense Force, the Indian Navy, and the French.

You can't surge trust, thought Sharratt. Building this coalition was years in the making. All the combined exercises, naval exchanges, and partnered training programs US Indo-Pacific Command had initiated years ago were paying off right now.

The BattleSpace avatars of the USS *Abraham Lincoln* coalition strike force, under the command of Rear Admiral Seth "Bulldog" Denton, sailed across the holographic display.

Although pressured by President Serrano, the Association of Southeast Asian Nations had declined to contribute combatants. Instead, they offered logistical support, such as air and sea refueling capabilities.

Better than nothing, Sharratt reflected. Not that he blamed them. No country in ASEAN wanted to get sideways with the PLA in the South China Sea.

Sharratt did his best to tamp down his bitterness. His orders were to stand by while his best friend in the world sailed into harm's way. That's what passed for diplomacy these days.

Serrano was playing a weak hand, and playing it pretty well, in Sharratt's view. Although the President—and everyone else—had been fooled by the Chinese, Serrano hadn't tried to shirk his duty. He gave as good as he got in this matchup with the PLA. Taking out Chinese satellites was a bold move, and from what Sharratt knew about the privateer operation on Chinese commercial shipping, the President had put the Chi-Commies on notice that he wasn't taking this lying down.

But neither of those tactics were going to remove the PLA from Taiwan. That was going to take sacrifice. Real sacrifices of blood and treasure.

Today was the first real test of how far the Chinese were willing to go. There would be shots fired in anger, but not from the *Enterprise* strike force.

"They're launching aircraft, sir," CAG said. "Mongoose" Collins would have looked at home on the back of a horse in the middle of a Montana prairie, but he was also one of the finest pilots Sharratt had ever flown with. "Won't be long now," CAG concluded.

"No reaction from the Chinese yet," Chief of Staff Tom Zachary added.

The three men each took a side of the BattleSpace table, their attention riveted on the display. The Spratly Island chain lay four hundred miles to the northeast of the *Lincoln* coalition strike force. In historical terms, calling them islands was overly generous. For centuries, the dots of land were more accurately bits of reefs poking out of the waves of the South China Sea.

More than two decades ago, the Chinese claimed a few of the reefs and began a dredging and building operation. The reefs became islands, and the islands grew into fortified military bases complete with sheltered harbors, piers, and runways capable of handling military aircraft. The manmade islands bristled with the latest PLA sensors and weapons.

There were protests, of course, but no one actually did anything about it. The United States, distracted by the Middle East and the war on terror, managed to run regular FONOPS, but not much else.

Meanwhile, the People's Republic of China announced the First Island Chain policy, which essentially annexed the South China Sea, one of the most trafficked sea lanes in the world. The Hague Tribunal ruled against China in the territorial dispute, and China had completely ignored the ruling. No nation had done anything about it for fear of sparking a shooting war.

Until now, Sharratt thought. That false Chinese claim on the Spratly Islands was now the political fig leaf being used to justify an allied attack on the PLA in the South China Sea.

The blue arrows, signifying friendly contacts, grew thick over the *Lincoln* strike force as the US and UK carriers launched their warplanes. The escorts made a protective ring around the valuable aircraft carriers. Beyond the cluster of ships, four friendly submarines, a six-pack of maritime patrol craft, and a horde of ASW helicopters searched the waters for PLA Navy subs.

"Here we go," Zachary said. The chief of staff's face was an unreadable mask, and Sharratt wondered if Zachary had friends in the *Lincoln* strike force. Probably, he decided. The Navy was a small family.

Instructions from the INDOPACOM command center at Camp Smith in Hawaii scrolled down one side of the BattleSpace display. For this attack, there were no voice comms, just text messages.

"Last aircraft is off the cat," CAG said.

The cursor on the INDOPACOM link blinked.

Weapons free. Missile launch authorized.

Within seconds, the holographic display bloomed with hundreds of blue arrows as the strike force launched missiles. The first wave of missiles, mostly Tomahawks traveling at subsonic speeds, moved like a wall of blue toward the Spratlys. Within minutes, Sharratt started to see separation as the missiles peeled off to attack their designated targets. The bulk of the missiles were allotted to the largest PLA strongholds of Fiery Cross Reef, Subi Reef, and Mischief Reef. For each island, the missiles were targeted at SAM sites, radar installations, fuel depots, command bunkers, and runways.

Although launched first, these missiles would not impact the targets first. The coordinated strike package had three waves, each timed for maximum effectiveness. Subsonic missiles would take over a half hour to reach their destination. Once they were on their way, the strike force would launch hypersonic missiles. Due to their speed, the superfast weapons would overtake their subsonic cousins and strike the Spratlys first. Hypersonics were also much more difficult to shoot down, so the PLA would be forced to waste valuable defensive weapons to protect themselves.

The last wave was aircraft. They followed right in the smoke of the Tomahawk missile attacks, but their mission changed midflight as satellites assessed bomb damage and retasked individual aircraft. Once the multirole F-35s released their GPS-guided ordnance, their mission changed from bomber to fighter as they engaged the PLA Air Force planes that would surely come out to meet them.

"Here they come," CAG said.

"Multiple missile launches from Fiery Cross and Subi, Admiral," the watch officer reported.

The holographic space over the Spratly Island targets began to fill with red arrows as the PLA responded by launching aircraft and missiles.

The minutes ticked by. It was a surreal feeling, Sharratt realized, to watch a battle being fought in real time 1,600 miles away. It felt like he was playing some kind of computer game. No, he decided, a computer game would have sped up the attacks to hold the viewer's interest. This battle progressed in real time. Second by painful second.

The red and blue wall of missiles met on the BattleSpace table. Some of the colored arrows disappeared as the red defensive missiles found their blue marks. The blue arrows continued on to their island targets. The red arrows, missiles and PLA fighters, traveled toward the carrier strike force.

Sharratt's sense of helplessness increased.

Minutes later, the first US hypersonic missiles struck their targets. The number of PLA defensive missiles being launched from the Spratlys slackened considerably.

Damage reports began to flow in. Dozens of incoming Tomahawks were knocked out of the air before they reached their targets. Sharratt tried to do the math in his head and gave up.

"Two F-35s out of contact, sir," the Battle Watch Officer reported. A euphemism for "shot down." Sharratt offered a quick prayer for the pilots.

"Three more," the watch officer reported a moment later.

The missile waves had passed each other, leaving a melee of dogfights. The incoming data tracks sputtered and glitched under the sheer volume of information. Sharratt saw two more F-35s wink off the screen, and the pit of his stomach hardened into a knot of tension.

"The HMS *Richmond* has been hit, sir," the watch officer said. "The Chinese missiles are getting through the air defense screen."

There was nothing they could do. Sharratt, Zachary, and CAG stood helplessly at the BattleSpace display, gripping the steel railing and grinding their teeth in frustration. Watching their friends and comrades come under fire.

The Battle of Fiery Cross Reef lasted for an hour and twelve minutes. Sharratt unclenched his fingers from the railing and unlocked his knees. His arms and legs trembled from the strain, and he felt sore all over.

The *Lincoln* strike force turned west. The PLA did not pursue them.

Sharratt ticked through the list of ships and aircraft lost or damaged in the battle.

HMS *Defender*, one of the Royal Navy's newer destroyers, had been damaged but was still mission-capable. Not true of HMS *Richmond*. She was on fire, taking on water fast and listing. Her commanding officer gave the order to abandon ship.

Lincoln had taken a missile hit, damaging her port side, but she was still in the fight. The news for the US carrier escorts was not as promising.

An even dozen of the US escorts had suffered some sort of damage in the battle. The USS *Leyte Gulf*, an old *Ticonderoga*-class guided missile cruiser, was savaged. She'd been in the shotgun position along the threat axis covering both *Lincoln* and the HMS *Queen Elizabeth*. After unloading her entire inventory of missiles to blunt the Chinese attacks, she'd absorbed three missile hits. Still afloat, she was on fire, and her crew was losing the battle to save their ship.

The strike force had lost thirteen F-35s in total, eight US planes, and five from the Royal Navy.

It could have been worse, Sharratt thought as he surveyed the initial missile inventory reports for Denton's strike force, but if the Chinese chose to pursue the attack, the strike force would be in danger.

And what would the Chinese do now? he wondered.

The PLA bases were hammered. No signals emanated from any of the islands, according to SIGINT. Initial bomb damage assessments showed the SAM batteries, radars, buildings, and airfields were either destroyed or required major repairs. The *Lincoln* strike force would make sure the PLA Navy couldn't send any resources forward to effect those repairs.

A draw, then, Sharratt decided, but not really. It could have been—should have been—much worse for the attacking forces.

"What do you think, Tom?" Sharratt asked.

"No hypersonics, sir. No Dong Feng 'carrier killer' missiles." Zachary's eyes were red from the strain of staring at the display. "I think the Chinese held back."

From his post at the end of the BattleSpace table, CAG nodded agreement.

"And what is your considered opinion of that strategy, Captain Zachary?" Sharratt continued.

"If I were a diplomat," Zachary said, "I'd say that's a signal that the Chinese don't want to escalate this thing."

"And your non-diplomatic assessment?" Sharratt asked.

"I'd say they're saving their missiles for us."

32

White House
Washington, DC

Don Riley followed Secretary of Defense Kathleen Howard and Secretary of State Henry Hahn into the Oval Office.

What the hell am I doing here? he thought. He'd been summoned to the Oval Office by text. Howard and Hahn were there when he arrived. To Don's mind, they didn't seem surprised to see him.

President Serrano sat behind the Resolute desk. Chief of Staff Wilkerson leaned against the desk, arms folded as he spoke to the President. He looked up as Don entered with the two cabinet secretaries.

"Good, you made it," he said, then went back to his conversation. It seemed to Don that the comment was directed at him, but he couldn't be sure.

Through the bulletproof windows behind the President, dusk was falling on the nation's capital. Having just come from the Situation Room, Don's thoughts were half a world away.

It was dawn in Taiwan. The battle between the PLA and the alliance carrier strike force was over. Both sides had taken a beating, but neither was out of the fight.

Mischief Reef, Fiery Cross Reef, and Subi Reef, the three Chinese islands targeted in the attack, were in ruins. From a military standpoint, the bases were not a serious threat now.

The *Lincoln* strike force had not emerged unscathed. *Lincoln* herself was damaged, and the USS *Leyte Gulf* was beyond saving. The HMS *Queen Elizabeth*'s escorts had also sustained damages. Don hadn't seen the casualty numbers yet, but he was bracing himself to see hundreds.

Despite the apparent tactical victory, the President's military advisers believed the Chinese had held back, choosing to engage the allied forces only with assets that were already deployed in the South China Sea. The PLA had not sortied any additional ships from Hainan, nor had they launched any Dong Feng missiles from batteries based on the mainland.

The Dong Feng anti-ship missiles were the crown jewel of the PLA strategy against the US aircraft carriers, the so-called "carrier killer" missile. The latest model, the DF-26, was capable of hypersonic flight with maneuverable terminal warheads.

Most of the President's advisers were briefing reporters at the Pentagon and in the White House. More were fanned out across the evening news programs to push the message that the United States would not stand by while the island of Taiwan was invaded by the Chinese. The President was scheduled to speak to the nation in just a few hours.

Internally, the President's advisers were split. A faction believed that the combination of commercial pressures and bold military response by the US and her allies had given the Chinese leadership cold feet. The Chinese were afraid to escalate the conflict and were looking for a way out of an increasingly bad situation.

An opposing view had it that the Chinese were biding their time. Sure, they took some hits in the South China Sea, but those islands weren't going anywhere and could be rebuilt in the future. By not attacking the allied carriers with the full force of their military capabilities—despite ample provocation—the Chinese were trying to reinforce the idea that they were being reasonable.

For his part, Serrano listened to both sides but kept his options open. He had already increased pressure on the Chinese more than any US president in modern times. If he quit now, Don reasoned, the history books would say he made a stand when it counted, but the world had changed. President Serrano had accepted the new world order with grace and dignity.

Their opportunity to gain some clarity about the Chinese mind-set arrived that afternoon when the Chinese ambassador asked for an emergency audience with the President of the United States.

"This will be a short meeting, so don't get comfortable," Serrano said. "Stand behind me, next to Irv." Don found a spot next to the Chief of Staff. The Obi-wan of the White House, as Irving Wilkerson was called, had a grim set to his grandfatherly features.

Serrano appeared energized. He'd shaved since Don had last seen him in the Situation Room and donned a fresh suit. The President gave one last look behind him, then touched a button on his phone.

"Send him in."

Don knew the Chinese ambassador by sight but had never met him. He was medium height, with a receding hairline and a dignified carriage. His eyes took in the small group arrayed around the Resolute desk, and the trace of a frown crossed his features. He stopped in front of the desk, gave a half-bow, then extended his hand.

"Mr. President, thank you for seeing me." The ambassador's voice was pure Midwest America, where he had been educated from high school through post-grad.

Serrano stayed seated. He dismissed the offer of a handshake with a glance. After a few beats, the ambassador withdrew his hand. He cleared his throat.

"You have a message for me, Mr. Ambassador?" Serrano said, his tone icy.

"I do, sir," the ambassador replied with equal chill in his tone. "My country wishes to protest the ruthless attack on our sovereign territory in the South China Sea." He paused, as if expecting to be interrupted.

"Despite the unprovoked attack," he continued, "I hope you will agree that the People's Liberation Army exercised extreme discretion in our response."

That got a rise from Serrano. His right eyebrow ticked up. "Discretion?"

A thin smile graced the ambassador's lips. "It is an established fact that the Chinese Dong Feng class of missiles are impervious to American air defenses. I believe your own analysts call the missile the 'carrier killer.'" His expression hardened. "We could have destroyed every single ship in your strike force, but we wished to demonstrate military restraint in the face of your unprovoked aggression. We have shown the world that we do not wish to escalate this conflict, Mr. President."

As he spoke, the sun had set, leaving the Oval Office in dimness. No one moved to turn on a light.

The silence lengthened. Then the ambassador spoke again. "I have a proposal, sir."

Serrano offered a barely perceptible nod.

"The People's Republic of China will withdraw from our rightful holdings in the South China Sea," he said. "In exchange, the United States will cease all retaliation against our effort to secure the safety of the rogue province of Taiwan. We will expect all our commercial ships to be restored to—"

"Your invasion, you mean," the President said.

"Mr. President," the ambassador did his best to look shocked, "my country was responding to a legitimate national emergency on the island of Taiwan. We put security forces in place to guarantee the safety of our people."

The soundproofing in the Oval Office was so complete that when the Chinese ambassador stopped speaking, the only sound Don heard was the breathing of Wilkerson next to him.

"Do you have an answer to our proposal, Mr. President?" The ambassador narrowed his eyes as he tried to make out Serrano's shadowed features.

The President stood. As his chair rolled back from the desk, Wilkerson caught it.

"I believe there is already a proposal on the table concerning the island of Taiwan, Mr. Ambassador."

The diplomat looked puzzled.

"Yesterday, at the United Nations," the President continued, "my country and more than twenty allied nations announced a one-hundred-mile exclusion zone around Taiwan. The People's Liberation Army was given twenty-four hours to move their forces out of the exclusion zone and turn the island over to an international peace-keeping force."

Serrano looked over his shoulder. "Henry, how long has it been since we made that declaration?"

"Twenty-four hours, sir," the Secretary of State said.

"Kathleen," the President continued, "what is the status of the PLA forces on and around Taiwan?"

"Still there, sir."

"Mr. Ambassador, I realize that you've had some issues with your satellites, but ours work just fine. Before I give you an answer to your proposal, I believe the United States of America has the right to hear *your* response to *our* proposal. Doesn't that seem fair to you?"

The ambassador's face darkened. "Mr. President, we have shown great patience. You have destroyed billions of dollars of sovereign Chinese satellites and launched an unprovoked attack on our holdings in the South China Sea. The issue of the rogue province of Taiwan is an internal matter within the Chinese state—"

"What is your answer, sir?" Serrano's harsh tone interrupted the Chinese diplomat.

"I am unable to address your concern without first consulting with Beijing, Mr. President. Thank you for your time, sir."

The Chinese ambassador gave another curt bow, turned on his heel, and walked out of the room.

Serrano clicked on a desk lamp. He turned, leaned against the desk, and crossed his arms. A cozy circle of light formed in the tight ring of five people.

"That could've gone better," Wilkerson said.

Serrano grunted. He looked at Hahn.

"I do not believe we have deterred them, sir," the Secretary of State said. "If you wish to pursue this matter, additional force will be required."

Serrano's gaze swiveled to Howard. "Defense?"

"He was telling the truth about one thing, sir," Howard said. "They were holding back in the South China Sea. I don't think they want this, but the PLA is not going to back down. If we're serious about freeing Taiwan, we're going to have to take it from them."

Serrano looked at Don. "You're probably wondering why I asked you to this meeting, Mr. Riley."

"Yes, sir." Don's throat was dry, and his voice sounded raspy. "I am wondering."

"You were the only one among all of us who figured out what the Chinese were up to," the President said. "If it weren't for you, we'd be in a death match with the Russians and the Chinese would have already taken Taiwan. You have more insight into this problem than anybody in the Situation Room. What do you think we should do, Mr. Riley?"

Don felt trapped. The answer was obvious, but that answer also meant the deaths of hundreds, maybe thousands, of Americans. That answer might lead to World War Three, even nuclear weapons. Don's mind reeled with disaster scenarios.

But there was only one right answer. Don drew in a deep breath.

"Mr. President, I am an intelligence officer. My job is to provide you with the finished intelligence products you need to make national security decisions. It would be out of my lane to comment on policy decisions."

"Answer the question, Don," Serrano said quietly.

"They won't stop, Mr. President," Don said. "Not unless we give them a reason to stop."

"That's my conclusion as well." Serrano hung his head. The vital energy Don had felt only a few moments before seemed to have left his body.

"Henry," Serrano said, "should we wait for an answer from Beijing?"

"Mr. President, diplomacy is my life's work," Hahn said, his cadence even more deliberate than usual, "but in this instance, I have to say we would just be wasting valuable time."

Serrano stood up straight, his eyes bright again. He checked his watch.

"I go on the air in an hour." The President looked at his Secretary of Defense. "Order the *Enterprise* strike force to attack Taiwan."

DAY SIX

33

USS *Enterprise* strike force
750 miles east of Taiwan

Sharratt stood on the flight deck of the USS *Enterprise.*

When the strike force had been running at thirty knots into the westerly winds, being topside was like stepping into a hurricane.

It was quieter now. Sharratt had slowed the strike force to a more typical twelve knots and turned south. He wanted to get within striking range of the waters around Taiwan, but no closer than necessary. After days of running at flank speed, the change felt like they were moving in slow motion.

The calm before the storm, Sharratt thought.

Their long-awaited orders had come through overnight. *Prepare to attack the PLA forces on and around Taiwan.* Simple words that would have grave implications for the twenty thousand men and women under his command.

His first move was to tighten the layered defenses around the carriers. The race from the North Pacific to Taiwan allowed the strike force to spread out both for reasons of safety and to allow the conventionally powered ships to refuel.

Sharratt squinted into the darkness. The strike force was running dark, but he knew they were out there.

The defensive strategy of protecting an aircraft carrier looked like a picture of an atom in a textbook. The carriers were the nucleus, the center of the atom. The first shell of electrons was the ring of guided missile cruisers some two thousand yards distant. During an air attack, they would protect the carriers with a shield of interceptor missiles.

The next shell were the pickets, frigates and destroyers ranging between five thousand and ten thousand yards from the carrier nucleus. In addition to their own missile capabilities, the pickets were also charged with anti-submarine warfare, mostly using ASW helicopters. Three fast attack submarines had also been assigned to the strike force, and Sharratt had positioned them to the north, south, and east to patrol for submerged PLA Navy submarine threats.

Sharratt had thought long and hard about how best to use his robot flotilla. The unmanned surface vessels had more than proven their worth to Sharratt. He placed the *Sea Hunters* in a loose ring fifty miles in advance of the strike force, positioned along the eastern threat axis.

After seeing what the *Sea Skates* could do as ASW assets, he'd asked for a full briefing on the capabilities of the platform. The vessel was nothing more than an oversized surfboard with a sail, not unlike a Sunfish dinghy he'd sailed on a Minnesota lake as a kid. But looks were deceiving. Constructed almost entirely from carbon fiber, the ship was nearly invisible to radar or any other kind of enemy sensor.

And it was fast. He'd had a hard time believing that the unique hydro-foil hull design could make fifty knots, but he'd seen the video.

After the briefing, Sharratt had promptly peeled off six of the *Sea Skates* and sailed them toward the PLA Navy fleet as embedded intel platforms. He wasn't entirely sure how he'd use them, but in the coming battle, more options were not a bad thing.

The last addition to the strike force had joined them only a few hours ago. Three *Zumwalt*-class destroyers, sailing directly from San Diego at top speed. Sharratt had positioned them between the inner ring of cruisers and the pickets.

The coming battle was a math problem for Sharratt, and he recognized he was on the losing side of the equation. When the PLA launched a missile at him, Sharratt would use a missile to shoot it down which meant he now had one less missile.

The PLA had a lot more missiles than Sharratt. Eventually, when he ran out, he either absorbed the incoming missiles or ran away.

But lasers never ran out of ammunition. The prototype directed-energy weapon was the longest of long shots, but he would use whatever advantage he could find.

Sharratt sighed into the cool night breeze. Who was he fooling? He was headed into a major battle against a superior enemy in their home waters, and he was relying on untested technology to give him an edge.

His final move before calling the strike force to battle stations was to order a feast. Across the fleet, the culinary teams broke out the best of whatever they had left and served it to their crews. Who knew when they were going to eat well again—or at all.

Ironically, the order created a festive atmosphere on board the *Enterprise*. Sharratt received reports of singing and dancing on the mess decks. He'd instructed commanders to let it go on. He was surrounded by thousands of twenty-somethings who had made a commitment to fight for their country. Who was he to deprive these sailors of a celebration of life in the hours before they stared death in the face?

While the celebration went on, Sharratt had come topside to get some fresh air and clear his head. He thought about his wife and daughters back in Yokosuka. He wished he could say goodbye to them, hold them one last time.

That was not going to happen. They knew it. He knew it. He just hoped his girls understood why he'd chosen this life.

Sharratt walked to the railing and leaned into the wind. The cold air numbed his cheeks, dried his eyes, roared in his ears.

This could be it, he thought. By this time tomorrow, I might be fish food.

He opened his mouth and howled his frustration into the wind. When he was done, Sharratt's chest heaved, and his skin felt clammy with sweat.

Then he turned and walked back across the flight deck.

It was time.

"Ready to commence flight operations, Admiral," the Battle Watch Officer said. "CAG is in Strike Ops. He requests permission to launch the Stingrays, sir."

"Tell CAG he has permission to launch the refueling assets," Sharratt replied.

With Tom Zachary at his side, the two men studied the BattleSpace display. The United States had three bases from which to launch air strikes against the PLA.

Guam, 1,700 miles southeast of Taipei, was the most distant. The US Air Force maintained a daily stream of bombing runs from there using the B-2 stealth bombers. The next farthest was Okinawa, four hundred miles northeast of Taiwan, where the Marine Corps had done a solid job of harassing the crap out of the PLA.

In contrast, the PLA warplanes flew from mainland China, airfields in north and south Taiwan, as well as the three PLA Navy's aircraft carriers patrolling the Strait of Taiwan, protecting the invasion forces. The enemy had hundreds of aircraft at their disposal and nearly unlimited refueling options.

Classic David and Goliath, Sharratt thought, except the US found themselves in the unusual position of playing the underdog. Any attempt by the US at establishing air superiority over Taiwan had been easily rebuffed by the PLA.

The addition of the *Enterprise* strike force's three carrier air wings to the equation would go a long way toward evening the odds. They'd still be outnumbered, Sharratt knew, but they might just slow down the PLA war machine long enough for the US to bring stateside forces to bear.

Like the best plans, this one was simple. Their goal was to make mince-meat of the eastern flank of the Chinese emergency zone around Taiwan. That meant wiping out the PLA warships in the eastern waters and establishing air superiority on the eastern side of the island.

The Chinese would not expect to see the *Enterprise* for another two days at the earliest. By mixing the *Enterprise* air assets in with the attacks from

Okinawa and Guam, they hoped to conceal the presence of the strike force from the PLA.

It might work for a while, Sharratt knew, but once the Chinese realized they were dealing with carrier-launched warplanes, they would come looking for the *Enterprise* strike force.

The Chinese lacked satellite coverage. By staying on the move far out to sea and launching long-range strikes, the *Enterprise* could hide for now.

But anyone with half a brain looking at the BattleSpace display could spot the flaw in the plan.

"They can't reach us, and we can't reach them," Zachary said.

"Exactly what I was thinking," Sharratt said.

The PLA Navy ships on the eastern flank of Taiwan were older vessels, smaller and less capable than the ships sheltering inside the Strait of Taiwan. In the Strait, the high-value targets were plentiful. Type 075 helicopter landing ships, *Jiangkai*-class frigates, *Luhu*-class destroyers, and the three aircraft carriers. As long as the *Enterprise* stayed far away from the Taiwanese coast, they could not touch the valuable PLA Navy ships inside the Strait of Taiwan.

"Even if we complete the mission perfectly," Zachary said. "We're screwed. All the PLA has to do is sail a new set of warships out of the Strait, and we're right back to where we started. It's whack-a-mole."

"I don't think so," Sharratt said. "Once they realize we're out here, they're going to have to make a decision about how to deal with us."

"You think they'll try to take us out?" Zachary said. "You think they'll use hypersonics? They held back with the *Lincoln*."

"If they find us," Sharratt said grimly, "they'll try to kill us. That's what I'd do, at least."

It could be a defining moment for China, Sharratt thought. If the PLA eliminated four aircraft carriers from the United States arsenal, that would set back the US Navy for a generation. Maybe permanently.

On the other hand, if he got a shot at those PLA carriers, he'd show them what the finest Navy in the history of the world was made of.

"I guess we'd better stay hidden, then," Zachary said.

"Admiral," the watch officer said. "CAG requests permission to launch fighters."

"Tell CAG to release the hounds," Sharratt replied.

"Aye-aye, sir."

As he watched the BattleSpace display fill with blue arrows indicating launched aircraft, Sharratt reflected that he was lighting a beacon fire for the PLA.

That's right, he thought. I'm out here. Catch me if you can.

34

Taipei, Taiwan

Mission Clock: 116:34:28
Mission Status: Red

Lieutenant Colonel Gao drove himself from the downtown airport to the Taipei 101 tower in the early morning hours on the sixth day of the invasion. The rain-slicked streets were deserted. The PLA military police posted at major intersections had retreated into their vehicles.

He parked at the curb and stepped out the car. When he looked up, the top of the glass-and-steel structure was shrouded in fog.

His phone rang. "Gao," he answered.

"Sir," a male voice said, "this is Captain Ro, the communications officer at southern command, sir. I was calling about your defunct Shandian tablet. I still haven't received it, sir." He struck an apologetic tone. "I'm sorry about the hour. I expected to leave a message."

"I'm very busy, Captain," Gao snapped. "I will get you the tablet when I have a moment."

"Sir," the officer pressed, "I should have reported the asset missing yesterday. Any further delay—"

"Are you accusing me of something, Captain?"

"No, sir, but the rules around controlled assets are very strict. I thought maybe I could retrieve the damaged device from the hospital for you."

"That will not be possible," Gao lied. "I am in Taipei. I have the device with me."

"I see, sir," the captain said. "When will you be back?"

"Today," Gao said. "I will bring it to you."

"But, sir—"

Gao hung up.

His Shandian battle network tablet had been stolen by the Taiwanese terrorists. He felt sure of that now. Possibly the Americans were involved, but Gao wanted to believe that was just nonsense from a dying man. Like the comment about his grandfather.

Did it matter? he wondered. The Shandian tablet was keyed to his retina scan, and surely the Minister had used the best possible encryption for the battle network. Even if the enemy had the tablet, it was useless to them.

His thoughts went back to his time in the hospital. There was that annoying fragment of a dream, the one with voices speaking in English.

Say cheese, he remembered a voice in his dream saying. What did that even mean? He used his mobile phone to look it up and found it was an English term used when taking a photograph.

A sudden thought made Gao stop. Standing on the empty, rainy Taipei street, he drew out his new Shandian tablet. He opened the device and navigated to the settings menu. Under the tab labeled "advanced settings," he found what he was looking for.

Assign this tablet to a new user.

When the captain had assigned the new tablet to Gao, he'd had to rescan Gao's retina. At the time, Gao had passed it off as a side effect of his head injury, but what if it was because his tablet had been assigned to a new user. An unauthorized user.

What had the kid said? Gong-gong? Grandfather. Gao had dismissed the term as a hallucination, but what if it was more than that. In his dream, he remembered English voices. Native speakers of American English.

Calm down, he told himself. The old tablet was not active, which meant that even if an unauthorized user had the tablet, he wasn't using it.

The air was damp with a chill that seeped through his uniform tunic. His head ached, and Gao was bone tired. Apart from a nap on the helo ride up from the south, he hadn't slept since his stay in the hospital.

But the summons from General Zhang had been unequivocal: get your ass back to Taipei. Now.

The lobby of the Taipei 101 tower was clouded with cigarette smoke and abuzz with activity. Odd for this hour of the morning, Gao thought.

"What's going on?" he asked the watch officer.

"Two of our ships on the east coast came under attack an hour ago," he said in a rush. "One of them is sinking fast. We're trying to organize a rescue effort."

As he pushed the elevator call button, Gao wondered if the rescue operation would delay his return trip south.

Whatever Zhang wants with me, Gao decided, I need to find these Taiwanese terrorists and get my old tablet back before someone discovers the truth. He had stalled General Wei's communications officer for as long as he could.

He was still holding his unlocked tablet. The mission clock was an angry red color, an indicator that the invasion was officially behind schedule. Not by much, only a few hours, but any schedule contingency they had built up on the successful front end of the operation was gone.

When the elevator opened on the thirty-sixth floor, Gao felt a small pang of disappointment to see that the young enlisted woman was not on duty. Mei Lin, that was her name. He recalled her soft touch on his bruised flesh when she had so gently wiped the blood from his injured eye.

Gao shook off the sentimental feelings. He needed to be on his game for the general. The man on duty had a round, flat face and a Wuhan accent.

"The general is expecting you, sir."

Gao nodded curtly and made his way to the hardwood double doors of the general's office. He knocked and stepped inside.

A pool of light illuminated the general's desk, but the rest of the room was in shadow. The air smelled of morning breath and dirty socks. Gao spied a rumpled blanket on the leather couch and realized the man must be sleeping in his office.

The general looked up from his desk, and Gao could see he was scrolling through newsfeed updates on his Shandian tablet. A flash of annoyance crossed his face.

Gao played his entrance by the book. He marched to Zhang's desk, came to attention, and saluted.

"Lieutenant Colonel Gao, reporting as ordered, sir." He held the salute.

A full beat passed before the general spoke in a voice that was clogged with sleep.

"At ease, Colonel."

Zhang's face looked drawn, and the skin below his jaw sagged. But his mouth was pressed in a firm line.

"Tell me about your progress," the general said. He had a cup of tea on his desk but did not offer any refreshment to Gao.

"We captured one of the Taiwanese terrorists," Gao began, "but he was not able to provide any useful intel. Unfortunately, he died of his injuries."

For the briefest moment, Gao considered telling the general about the claim of Americans and *Gong-gong*. He rejected the idea.

"You have been gone for more than an entire day," the general said in a voice clipped with anger. "What did you find out about General Wei?"

For the first time, Gao realized why Zhang had insisted on an in-person visit. He wanted to know if Gao had pressed the bribery angle with Wei. And Gao had not even met with General Wei.

"The capture of the Taiwanese spy was very time-consuming, sir."

"You did the interrogation yourself?" Zhang seemed surprised. "Are you a trained interrogator?"

"No, sir," Gao said. "The circumstances required prompt action." The answer sounded lame even to his own ears.

"Was the prisoner able to tell you anything about how they managed to pull off the railyard bombing?"

"No, sir." Gao picked a spot on the window and stared at it. He could predict where this conversation was headed, and it was not good for him.

The general looked at his tablet, then back to Gao. "I didn't realize there was a prisoner from the railyard bombing."

"There wasn't, sir." Gao hesitated. "The questioning happened before the railyard bombing."

"How did you manage that?" Zhang asked.

Gao realized he had boxed himself in. The only way out was to plunge ahead.

"We received a confidential tip that a Taiwanese soldier was seen at the site of the ambush." He touched his bandaged head. "Where I was injured, sir."

"So, you captured this rebel soldier, questioned him, and received no useful information," Zhang said. "This is how you have spent your time, Colonel?"

"I met with General Wei, sir," Gao said. It was a complete lie, and more importantly, one that could be easily disproved if Zhang chose to investigate.

What am I doing? he thought. Sweat broke out under his arms.

But the effect on Zhang was worth it. He leaned forward, his lips parted.

"Tell me," he said.

"I accepted his offer to come work for him after the invasion is complete," Gao said, words rushing out of his mouth as if saying the lies faster would make them less untrue.

"And then what?" Zhang said. "Is he the one behind the supply chain issues?"

"It's possible, sir," Gao said cautiously. "I'm not sure. Yet."

Zhang sprang up from behind his desk. "It's got to be him. There's too many issues for it to be a coincidence." He snatched up his Shandian tablet and read aloud. "Blood plasma was rerouted to Tibet. Loads of ammunition for the ZTZ 99 main battle tanks in Taipei and spare parts for our PCL-161s have been canceled. An oil tanker out of Hainan was sent back to port. There's at least a dozen more instances. All of them designed to make my operation in Taipei look bad."

The Shandian battle network employed newsfeed-style updates curated for the user's rank and job description. Gao would not see a supply chain update unless it impacted him directly. Zhang, on the other hand, had access to all updates.

"I didn't know about those issues, sir," Gao said.

"But is Wei behind it?" Zhang said. "That's what I need to know, Colonel."

"I understand, sir," Gao said, "but I need more time."

Zhang's face tightened in anger. "You've seen the mission clock?" He thrust the tablet screen at Gao where the numbers counted down on a bloodred background. "I cannot fight a war on two fronts, Gao. The Americans have increased their air raids, and we have fallen behind on our schedule. I don't care about these petty terrorist attacks. What difference does it make if they break into a cable relay station? That's not your mission."

"What did you say, sir?" Gao's stomach clenched with anxiety. "What cable relay station?"

"Colonel!" Zhang snapped. "Stay focused on what is important. I need you to expose General Wei's treachery and help me get this invasion back on track. Do you understand?"

Zhang's eyes were puffy with sleep, and his breath was foul.

"I will need to go back to the southern command, sir," Gao said.

"Of course," Zhang shouted. "How can you catch that treasonous bastard if you're up here in Taipei?"

"I'll leave at once, sir."

He exited the office in a rush, without saluting. In the elevator, he opened his Shandian tablet and searched for an attack on a cable relay station.

The elevator door opened. He ignored it as he scanned the report. Three soldiers guarding the Fangshan facility had deserted. Nothing was damaged, and the computer logs showed no unusual activity. The software lock was still in place to prevent communications traffic from moving on or off the island.

But there was an addendum to the report, only a few hours old. Gao clicked on it, and a digital picture filled the screen. The three PLA guards had not deserted. Their bodies had been found in a shallow grave in a nearby mango grove.

Gao used two fingers to enlarge the photo. The report added that all three men had been shot through the heart twice with armor-piercing rounds. Sniper rounds.

The elevator door opened again. Gao stumbled through the lobby and onto the empty street. Outside, he gulped in great gasps of damp air, trying to stop the stampede of his racing heart.

That could not be a coincidence, Gao knew. The Taiwanese terrorists had his tablet and they had broken into a submarine cable relay station. He could draw only one conclusion from that sequence of events. They had sent the contents of his stolen tablet off the island. They had given the PLA battle plan to the enemy.

And it was Gao's fault.

Meanwhile, he had just convinced a senior PLA officer that his direct subordinate was a traitor to his country.

If there is a traitor in the ranks, it is me, Gao thought.

No, he told himself just as quickly, this is not over yet.

I. Can. Fix. This.

35

PLA Navy submarine *Changzheng 12*
East China Sea, 50 miles northeast of Taipei, Taiwan

Mission Clock: 112:46:38
Mission Status: Red

"Captain," the sonar supervisor said, "new contact bearing three-one-zero."

Chu, dozing at one of the fire control consoles, snapped awake at the new information. As he stepped behind the sonar chief, he saw the man's shoulders tense.

Chu was edgy, his nerves stretched. Although he tried to project outward calm and confidence, inside he boiled with emotion. His attitude was taking a toll on his crew's performance.

"Report," Chu said. He modulated his tone to be less aggressive.

"Three hundred hertz, sir," the supervisor reported. "Tenuous signal. It looks like we're on the edge of the detection range."

Three hundred hertz. Chu tried to hide his disappointment. It was not the American sub, then. And why would it be, he chided himself. Why would an enemy sub risk coming back into PLA-controlled waters?

Chu had convinced himself their contact from the previous day was an

American *Virginia*-class nuclear-powered submarine. In his mind, it was the only possible answer.

But he had come up with no explanation for the second submarine, the mysterious diesel-electric. He reviewed the sonar records and reluctantly arrived at the same conclusion as his resident sonar expert.

They had encountered two submarines, one nuclear, one diesel-electric. His report to Beijing had been met with stony silence, which to him equated to scorn. He could imagine the analyst reports:

New submarine captain with inexperienced crew reports two enemy submarines in operating area near Taiwan. Analysis: Low probability.

Everyone knew the Americans had no diesel boats in their submarine fleet, so what country owned the second submarine?

"We lost them again, sir," the sonar supervisor said. He scowled in frustration. "Last good bearing was three-one-three. Low probability track puts him at course zero-two-zero, speed seven knots. Range in excess of fifteen thousand meters."

"Good job, Chief," Chu said.

"Thank you, sir." The sonar supervisor smiled.

When they had reviewed the sonar logs together, Chu had been impressed with the man's knowledge. It was the chief who had first identified the second diesel submarine. A lesser operator would have missed it. Chu needed this man to be at the top of his game.

The political officer appeared at the door to the control room. "Permission to enter, Captain," Commander Sun said.

Technically, Sun didn't have to ask permission to enter the control room. He and Chu were the same rank, and Sun knew there were no restrictions on where he could go on the ship. Everything on the *Changzheng* was open to the Party's representative.

But Commander Sun was careful to observe naval traditions and not undercut Chu's command authority. Of course, that did not make his presence any less annoying, Chu thought as he gave a curt assent to Sun's request.

Sun joined the captain at the sonar screen. Whereas Chu felt tired and on edge, the political officer appeared relaxed and well rested. The twinge of annoyance in Chu's mind flared.

"Do you think it's the same submarine, Captain?" Sun asked.

"It's a different tonal," Chu said.

It bothered him that Sun had not expressed an opinion about the encounter the day before. As per PLA regulations, Chu had written up the contact report for Beijing and offered it to Sun for approval. The political officer had not changed so much as a word, and his reaction to the report was unreadable to Chu.

Chu considered the encounter a complete failure. He had rushed in with an assumption about the tactical situation and been blindsided by the presence of the mystery diesel submarine. Chu could blame his inexperienced crew and the operational challenges of a new submarine just out of the shipyards, but it was a poor craftsman who blamed his tools.

He was lucky he hadn't gotten his entire crew killed by his rash actions.

Commander Sun had been nothing but gracious. Chu had been copied on the message sent to Beijing where Sun lavishly praised the bravery of the crew and her captain.

Not for the first time, Chu wondered if Sun knew something about PLA Navy operations in the area that he was not sharing.

He shook his head to clear the wayward thoughts. He was seeing conspiracies where there were none. What he needed was a few hours of uninterrupted sleep. Tired captains made poor decisions.

"You think the contact was traveling away from Taiwan?" Sun said, studying the fire control monitor.

"Yes," Chu said, "but that's based on very little data."

"Hmm," Sun mused. "I'm not trained in these matters, Captain, but if you were commanding a submarine, how would you use your environment? For my own information, sir."

Chu moved to the nav table where the underwater features of the area were displayed. The Okinawa Trough was a rough rectangle oriented to the northeast, abutting the East China Sea Shelf at the top of the box. He ran his finger along the northern edge of the box.

"The US Navy submarines love deep water, where they have room to maneuver and hide. The water depth changes very rapidly here, going from a thousand meters to less than two hundred meters in only a few miles. If I were the captain of an enemy submarine, I would run along the edge of the changing depth zone where my very quiet submarine could hide amidst all the noise—"

Chu stopped suddenly. Why had he not seen this before? If this was really a US submarine, they would not venture into shallow water. He already had a rough idea of course and speed. Using the obvious geographical constraints, he could guess how far away the submarine was.

"Captain?" Sun asked.

Chu held up his hand for silence. He sketched a two-thousand-meter-wide corridor based on the projected course and speed of the target.

"Conning Officer," Chu ordered, "make your depth two-one-zero meters, increase speed to twenty knots, steer new course two-eight-zero."

"What are you doing, Captain?" Sun said.

Chu motioned for the sonar chief to join them. Using his finger, he drew a line across the projected track of the contact.

"I think he's here, Chief. I'm going to take us across his stern to see if we can get a different aspect ratio on the target," Chu said.

"I don't understand," Sun said.

But the sonar chief saw Chu's plan immediately.

"The tonal map of a submarine is like a fingerprint, sir," he said, his voice alive with excitement. "Each one is unique. We try to be very quiet, but every submarine emits sonic information. There might be a pump that is starting to fail or a sound mount that was compressed on installation. Little things. These tiny faults put sound into the water as discrete frequencies in a specific direction. We have a whole database of sound signatures of enemy submarines."

Sun's eyes shone with understanding. "So, if you hear the same frequency from the same direction, that means it's the same submarine as yesterday?"

"Exactly," Chu said, "but we will have an issue."

"Why?" Sun said.

Chu tapped the nav plot. "Our assigned waterspace runs out here. We can't follow him past this point." He sighed. "I think our best course of action is to go to periscope depth and report the contact. Let another ship try to find him."

"I disagree, Captain," Sun said. "I believe it is in the best interest of the Party for you to pursue this contact as aggressively as possible."

"Thank you, Political Officer," Chu said. "I will do as you recommend."

"I simply wish to make the greatest possible contribution to the State, Captain," Sun replied smoothly. "The operational decision is yours, of course."

Chu paced the control room until fifteen minutes had expired.

"Conning Officer, slow to seven knots, make your depth one hundred meters."

The deck angled up as they climbed to the new depth. Chu waited impatiently for the towed array to stabilize. On this course, they were driving almost straight toward the edge of their waterspace. He had twenty minutes on this course until he would be forced to turn.

Time seemed to stand still in the close confines of the control room. Chu stared at the sonar screen as if he could will the contact into existence.

"Anything, Chief?" Chu asked.

The sonar chief shook his head.

Inside Chu's mind, he immediately began to question his actions. Just like yesterday, he had made questionable decisions. Going deep and running to a new position to intercept a contact was a risky move when they had a good track. He had done it on the flimsiest of fire control solutions.

"Conning Officer," he began.

"One-nine-eight hertz, bearing zero-one-zero." The sonar chief stood up out of his chair, fist raised. "It's him, Captain. I'm sure of it."

Chu cursed. He had to maneuver to stay within his assigned waterspace.

"I'm sorry, Chief," Chu said, "but I have to turn."

"It's a weak signal, sir, but it's him. I know it."

"I believe you, Chief." Chu ordered the conning officer to take the ship to periscope depth, then returned to the nav plot. Commander Sun appeared on the opposite side of the table.

"Congratulations, Captain," Sun said.

Chu grunted a noncommittal response.

"You have doubts that this is the same submarine, sir?" Sun asked.

"No, but I don't understand why he would come back," Chu replied. He called to the sonar supervisor. "Chief, cue up the recording of the transients from yesterday."

As the conning officer took the ship to periscope depth, Chu listened to the recording over and over again.

A sharp metallic clang, then a softer scraping sound. A slammed hatch? A stuck torpedo tube door?

Chu tried to imagine why a US Navy submarine would come that close to an enemy shoreline. They were too far away from the port of Keelung to be laying mines. If the sound was a torpedo tube, why hadn't the American fired?

Maybe the US sub was also surprised by the diesel submarine, he thought. Maybe the diesel sub was Russian and both of them had been surprised. He pinched the bridge of his nose in frustration. His thoughts were jumbled. He needed sleep.

"Question," he said to Sun. "Why would the same submarine come back the next day?"

"To meet someone," Sun replied.

Chu's head snapped up. Of course, he thought. He readjusted the nav plot until he had the coordinates of the encounter from the previous day.

The answer was staring him in the face. The Mianhua Islet was a tiny speck of rock poking out of the Pacific Ocean fifteen miles off the northernmost tip of the island of Taiwan. Just below the island, a tiny finger of deep water pointed to the mainland.

Chu touched the speck of green in a sea of blue.

"It's a rendezvous point," he said.

"What are you going to do, Captain?" Sun asked.

"First, I'm going to take a nap." Chu smiled. "Then we set a trap."

36

The Ranch
Sterling, Virginia

The domed underground operations center of Sentinel Holdings no longer felt to Don like a high-tech arcade anymore. Now, it felt more like a prison.

He was tired of hearing how many ships they had taken down, how stupid the Chinese were, and most of all, how much money they were making. If he saw one more picture of a red Lamborghini on someone's workstation, he was going to throw up.

With each takedown of a Chinese vessel, the celebrations got less exuberant and more routine. Operation Lynx was a job to these people now. They were bored with it.

Don sat at his assigned desk in the central command hub and liaised, whatever that meant. Mostly, he spent his time worrying. He worried about what was going on back at ETG, he worried about his career, he worried about Janet and Mark. Hell, he worried that he was worrying too much for his own health.

On this seventh day of the operation, he had yet to see Abby Cromwell, which he found a little surprising.

Twelve hours ago, Sentinel Holdings had been authorized to expand their privateer operations beyond the Exclusive Economic Zone of the United States and into international waters. Naturally, they sought out the target-rich environment—those were Skelly's words—of the Panama Canal.

The Chinese made a critical decision in the days leading up to the invasion that Don wished he had keyed on earlier. Almost all Chinese commercial maritime traffic destined for the European market was normally routed west, through the South China Sea, the Strait of Malacca, and the Suez Canal. In the weeks before the invasion, the Chinese quietly began moving commercial traffic east. It was a longer, but safer, route.

Or not. The most direct route from China to Europe from the east was via the Panama Canal. Mistake. Big mistake.

Sentinel had already taken down two merchant ships as they exited the Canal. A live drone feed from the third target was displayed on the domed ops center ceiling of the Planetarium.

The ship was massive. According to the specs Don pulled up, *Ever Blossom* was fifty-one meters wide and nearly two football fields in length. The Neopanamax freighter was the largest container vessel that could fit through the canal and carried fifteen thousand TEUs, a measure of shipping container capacity.

"Come to papa," Skelly said, "you big, beautiful container bitch."

Down on the operations floor, Don heard a ripple of laughter. He realized that Skelly had said the last on the open comms circuit.

The man's soldier of fortune persona was wearing on Don, and he wondered if he should say something. Not that it would make a difference.

"Sterling, this is Black Widow," came a female voice over the network. "Standing by to board the *Blossom*."

Don winced. The Sentinel strike teams were all named after superheroes. There was even a friendly rivalry between DC and Marvel characters.

"Black Widow," Skelly replied, "you are clear to rock and roll. Show me the money, people."

One of the side effects of Sentinel's success was that they had begun to run short of equipment and strike teams. Rather than reduce the number of takedowns, Skelly decided to do more with less. Single strike teams that had been staffed with ten members were divided into two teams of five.

It was a calculated risk. The only resistance to any of the boarding parties so far had been one captain who waved a handgun before reconsidering his position.

In this instance, the Black Widow team had another handicap. Takedowns at sea were always done by air, fast-roping down from a UH-60 helo. A last-minute maintenance issue had grounded their chopper, so the team was boarding via the small boat that was coming out to pick up the pilot.

Don listened to the exchange between the ship and the pilot's ride. He watched as the boat came alongside the extended stairs and the Sentinel team raced up to the deck of the freighter.

Two women and three men reached the freighter's main deck and spread out. They wore paramilitary gear favored by special forces operators, a mix of standard military issue and sportswear from companies like Patagonia and Columbia. Their armament varied as well according to personal taste, but they all carried an assault weapon, a handgun, and wore body armor.

As he might have guessed from the call sign, the team leader was a woman with a thick braid of blond hair that ran down her back like a rope.

They were an experienced crew. Two of the team gathered crew members together on deck. While one stood guard, the other searched the captives. He tossed mobile phones and knives overboard, then zip-tied his prisoners. The other three Black Widow team members raced into the superstructure of the ship.

"Sterling, we are en route to the bridge."

"Roger that, Black Widow," Skelly said. He leaned against a console and sipped coffee from a mug that read "World's Greatest Boss" in bold letters.

The sound of heavy breathing came over the circuit, then shouted instructions: "Get down! On your knees!"

There was a single pop, like a distant firecracker.

Skelly put down his coffee cup. "Black Widow, what is your status?"

The comms circuit erupted in a cacophony of gunfire, then went silent.

Skelly cursed, and Don saw he was looking at the drone feed.

At the sound of gunfire, the two men on deck looked up. One of them started to raise his weapon, then he pitched backward into a spread-eagle position.

"Snipers!" Skelly yelled. "Black Widow, abort! Abort!"

The second man on deck dove for cover behind a shipping container. The door to the superstructure opened, and soldiers in PLA uniforms rushed out. Don counted eight men.

"Where's my air cover?" Skelly roared.

"Still down, sir," came the reply.

Helplessly, they watched on the drone feed as the PLA soldiers hunted down the lone Sentinel operator on the deck of the freighter.

"Make a break for it," Skelly whispered.

As if the man had heard him, he sprinted across the deck and vaulted over the railing.

"Get eyes on him!" Skelly shouted.

"Manson," someone called. "Look at the bridge."

Don shifted his gaze from the deck upward to the bridge wing. Without asking, the drone operator refocused the camera.

The door to the bridge wing was open. Two men dragged a body into the bright sun and propped the form up on the railing. A thick blond braid swung in the breeze. The men flipped the body over the railing. It took a long time for the inert form to hit the water.

The Sentinel ops center was as still as ice, everyone shocked into silence. Manson Skelly's jaw was slack; his expression looked as if he had just been slapped.

"Those motherfuckers," he exploded. "They will pay for this. Get that helo in the air now and make sure it is armed with Hellfires. We are going to—"

Don stood up. "No, you're not," he said quietly. "Stand down. We will not escalate this, Manson."

"You just watched my people get butchered." Skelly bore down on Don. "And you're telling me I can't retaliate?"

"That's exactly what I'm telling you. This will already be an international incident, so let's not make it worse. Let them go."

Skelly turned away, still seething. "They can run, but they can't hide. I can wait."

"You need to get ahead of this," Don said. "It will be on the news. Talk to

Abby now and tell her what happened. You need to do damage control on this."

The party's over, Don thought. The Chinese figured that the US would never allow a paramilitary force to fire on uniformed soldiers. Even Serrano wouldn't go that far.

Skelly was right about one thing. There was nowhere a commercial freighter could hide on the open ocean. It was a long way to Europe.

Don headed for the elevator. He needed to call this in to the NSC and make sure that Abby got involved.

As soon as he emerged from the elevator, his phone lit up like a Christmas tree. Seven missed calls and an equal number of texts from Liz Soroush.

He walked onto the front steps of the Sentinel headquarters building. It was a beautiful February afternoon. Golden sunlight slanted through the evergreens around the parking lot. The peaceful scene was a jarring contrast to the violence he had just witnessed in the underground bunker.

I need a vacation, he thought as he dialed Liz's number.

She answered on the first ring. "Where have you been?" she demanded.

"I've been assigned to—" he started. "Never mind, talk to me."

"Not on this line," she said. "Get to my office ASAP. It's important. "

"Liz," Don began, "I'm really wrapped up in—"

"I know what you're wrapped up in, Don," Liz snapped, "and what I have for you directly relates to that. Trust me."

Forty-five minutes later, Don peered over Liz's shoulder at an email from a guy named Mike Lester to his wife.

"He's in Taiwan now," Liz explained. "She just got this email from him last night."

"You're sure it's the real deal?" Don asked.

"The line about Paris is an inside joke between them," she replied. "Maureen says there's no way anybody could have known about it but Mike."

"What's in the Dropbox?" he asked.

Liz clicked on the computer icon and opened the first file.

"Ho-lee shit," Don said.

37

Guantian District, Taiwan

From the back seat of the stolen PLA utility vehicle, Lester watched the headlights cut through the misty night. The big car skidded on the rain-slicked road as the driver took the turn too fast.

I never should have agreed to this, Lester thought.

"Slow down!" Lester commanded. "You're driving like you're guilty."

"Sorry, Gong-gong." The driver was one of the younger Shadow soldiers, dressed in a PLA military police uniform.

"It's okay," Lester said. "Just drive like you're supposed to be here, and we'll get through this just fine.

Which was a total lie, Lester knew. They'd be lucky if they didn't get picked up.

On the seat next to him, Frank Tsai moaned. He checked the field dressing on Frank's thigh.

"Hang in there, kid," Lester said to him.

When Frank and Oliver Tsai had brought their plan to Lester, his first answer was no. Hell, no. Too big, too audacious, too dangerous, he told them. You'll get yourselves killed.

But when they left his office, Frank left the map on the desk. He'd known that Lester would look at it when they were gone and he'd see what they had already figured out.

The Zengwen River ran for 138 kilometers from the central mountain range of Taiwan west to the ocean. This time of year, it rained in the mountains, and the river ran at its peak.

The People's Liberation Army in the south of Taiwan had landed in the port of Kaohsiung City. To start their drive north to Taipei, the bulk of the PLA forces would have to cross the Zengwen River on one of three major bridges. Big bridges. Four-lane highways spanning a kilometer-wide river.

The Tsai brothers proposed to blow all three of the bridges. At the same time.

When they came back to him a second time, Lester said no again. "You can't blow a bridge that big," he said. "We don't have the firepower do it right."

Oliver spoke, "We don't need to destroy the bridge, Colonel. We just need to damage it. Of course, the PLA will fix it, but it will take them hours, maybe a whole day. We don't need to stop them. We just need to slow them down until the Americans arrive."

And that, thought Lester, is what was *really* bothering him. Lester had heard the reports of American air strikes in the north, but he had also seen the size of the PLA forces landing on the shores of Taiwan. Air strikes were not going to win the day. This was a boots-on-the-ground problem if he'd ever seen one.

The Taiwanese were almost childlike in their faith that the Americans were coming. They had no doubt, but Lester...he had doubts.

He wondered what had happened to the information he'd sent to his wife. If the email went to her spam folder, would she even see it? Even if she found the files and got them to Liz Soroush at the FBI, how long would it take for someone to realize what they had?

And then the Big Question: Would it even matter? If a political decision was made to abandon Taiwan, then having all the top-secret PLA plans in the world would not make a whit of difference.

In the end, he could boil the problem down to a simple question: Did he believe that delaying the PLA's drive north by a day would make a difference? Or was he just sending people on a fool's errand?

He talked it over with Lewis and Hardy.

"They're right, sir," Hardy said in his typical laconic way. "It's their country and their fight. If the PLA crosses the Zengwen River, they're not gonna stop until they hit Taipei."

"It's not up to us, sir," Lewis said. "If they want to risk it, who are we to tell them no?"

But if he had said no, then Frank Tsai would never have done the op. Now the younger Tsai had an extra hole in his body.

Lester agreed, albeit reluctantly. Like everything else, the operation played out on a hyper-accelerated time schedule.

Dressed in stolen PLA uniforms, Frank and two of his fellow soldiers entered a PLA motor pool outside of Tainan City and stole two heavy trucks and an SUV.

Lester watched from a safe distance. The amount of equipment that the PLA had brought into Taiwan was mind-blowing. The Shadow Army team had raided an overflow staging area that had outgrown the allotted space, forcing the motor pool to park vehicles along the road. The detachment of three soldiers assigned to nighttime security detail seemed less than enthusiastic about guarding trucks that were parked down the block and around the corner.

The vehicles were all push-button start, no keys required. The vehicle acquisition went off without a hitch, raising Lester's spirits. So did the trip to the farm supply store owned by the family of one of the Shadow Army team members. There they loaded the trucks with urea nitrate, a fertilizer used on the local rice fields. The irony was not lost on Lester that he was making an IED, the same type of explosives he had feared during his time in the Sandbox.

Things got more difficult after that.

The plan had a lot of moving parts. Hardy led a small team with explosives to take out the most distant bridge. In the confusion following Hardy's attack, Frank and the other driver would place their truck bombs on the riverbank under the remaining two bridges and abandon them. Lester, following in the SUV, would trigger the detonations using a mobile phone.

The convoy departed the farm supply store on time and headed west. From the back seat of the SUV, Lester could make out Frank's face behind the windshield of the following truck. The last truck in their column peeled off at the Route 19 bridge with instructions to park and return to the road on foot. They would pick him up on the way back and detonate the bomb.

The convoy had gone less than a kilometer when a massive explosion tore into the night sky. Somehow, the truck they had just left behind exploded prematurely.

Lester's driver slowed. "What should I do?" he asked.

Lester looked back at Frank driving the truck behind them. He waved his hand forward. "Keep going," Lester said.

A second explosion, this one more distant, bloomed up in the night sky. That would be Hardy.

What a cock-up, Lester thought. Two bridge bombings would surely alert their intended target.

They rounded the next bend, and the third bridge came into sight. The long span ran over glistening dark water and wide riverbanks. Lester leaned forward to study the tactical situation. Whoever was in charge of the security for this detail was on alert. The PLA military police contingent had parked their vehicles lengthwise across the four-lane highway.

They had to abort. There was no way that Frank was going to be able to access the riverbank without attracting attention.

"Slow down," Lester said. "Pull over."

Frank had other ideas. When Lester's SUV slowed, he swerved around them and turned onto the access road for the bridge.

"Frank, what are you doing?" Lester muttered. "Follow him," he ordered the driver.

Frank slowed the truck as he approached the security detail, then punched the accelerator and surged forward. He clipped the front bumper of an SUV but made it onto the bridge.

"Go!" Lester shouted. His own car shot past the security team as they followed Frank onto the bridge.

A kilometer never felt so long to Lester. The two vehicles were incredibly exposed to a drone strike or an airborne attack. To make matters worse, their planned escape route was behind them, on the south side of the bridge.

There was no security detail on the north end of the bridge. Frank slowed the truck and drove it down the bank.

"Follow him," Lester ordered.

The truck stopped underneath a bridge span between two concrete pylons. The SUV skidded to a halt, and Lester told the driver to turn around.

Frank did not emerge from the truck cab.

Lester couldn't take it anymore. He bolted out of the back seat and ran to the truck. When he wrenched open the door, Frank fell into his arms.

He dragged Tsai into the back of the SUV and told the driver to move. Lester watched the bridge through the rear window. When they made the paved road and picked up speed, he triggered the bomb.

He felt the blast shake the car and watched the fireball shoot skyward. Bits of concrete and macadam rained down on them. The driver's eyes in the rearview mirror were wide with fear.

"Keep driving," Lester said.

He assessed Frank's wound. A shot through his thigh muscle. He was lucky. The leg wasn't broken, and the bullet hadn't hit an artery.

He dressed the wound, treated Frank for shock, and then pulled out the map to figure out their next move.

"Here," he pointed to a small town on the map. There was a trailhead where they could hike into the mountains.

It took them nearly an hour to navigate to the town of Liukuei tucked into the foothills of the mountains. The light rain turned into a downpour, for which Lester was thankful. Drones would have a hard time finding them in this weather.

He spied the sign for the town and told the driver to slow down even more. Houses crowded next to the road, their doors opening directly onto the street. Lester saw curtains on a window stir. He supposed these people didn't get much traffic in the middle of the night out here.

It took them two passes down the narrow road to find the turnoff for the trailhead. Lester fretted when he saw another window curtain move on their second drive through. They were too exposed. All it took was one phone call...

The driver stopped the car in a muddy parking lot, and Lester got out.

He was soaked in seconds. He grabbed the waterproof map and checked to make sure he had his compass. It was an eight-kilometer hike as the crow flies, more like ten accounting for switchbacks and terrain. A long night by any measure.

All I have to do is get close enough to Mount Chuyun base, he told himself. One of the lookouts will see me.

"Take the car north," he said to the driver. "Go at least an hour, then hide it and hike back to base. Understand?"

"Yes, Gong-gong."

The driver looked terrified, and Lester didn't blame him. He gripped the kid's shoulder through the open window.

"You did good."

Lester looked at the two houses that backed onto the trailhead, hoping that their occupants were asleep.

He reached into the back seat and hauled Frank's body toward him. Carefully, he slung the kid onto his shoulder in a fireman's carry.

Then he headed into the darkness.

DAY SEVEN

38

Don Riley's body was a study in contrasts.

His leg muscles felt like lead and ached all the way down to the bones. His stomach was a bundle of jittery nerves, as if he'd swallowed a handful of bees.

Too much coffee and not enough sleep, he thought.

He gripped the edges of the lectern and shifted his weight on his aching feet. In the silence that followed the end of his briefing, Don realized he'd forgotten to shower this morning. From the ragged look of some of the attendees at this early morning meeting, he wasn't the only one.

They're shocked, Don thought. Not that he blamed them. He'd just informed the President of the United States and his closest advisers that they were totally, utterly, and completely screwed.

Don and his team at ETG had spent the night analyzing the data from what they now referred to as the Lester File. It outlined the PLA's invasion plan in excruciating detail. The first half of the night they'd spent absorbing the information. Like good analysts, they spent the rest of the night trying to disprove what they'd learned.

His people were good, Don knew. If the file was a fake, they would have figured it out.

They failed. The Lester File was the real deal.

"You're certain of the authenticity of the source?" the National Security Advisor asked Don's boss.

"A former Marine colonel named Mike Lester was on Taiwan at the time of the invasion," Director Blank said. "We can verify that. The email to his wife contained language that only she would recognize. We know that, too. How he managed to access this level of detail is beyond us."

The President cleared this throat. "Can they do it in ten days, General?" he asked the Chairman of the Joint Chiefs. "Is that possible?"

Nikolaides shrugged. He jerked his head toward Don at the head of the room.

"*Can* they do it in ten days, sir? Hell, they *are* doing it. Riley's people confirmed that this plan matches with all the intelligence we've collected on the PLA advances. SIGINT, imagery, even acoustic intelligence on the shipping traffic between the mainland and Taiwan. It all tallies up. They're a day behind in the south, but they could make up that time. Not to put too fine a point on it, sir: we're screwed."

Serrano shifted his attention to the Secretary of Defense. "Kathleen? You agree?"

Howard nodded.

Serrano sat back in his chair. He looked shell-shocked. "But the *Enterprise* strike force," he said, "surely we can slow them down?"

Nikolaides's silver crew cut caught the light as he disagreed with the commander in chief.

"Sir, all due respect, we're outmatched. We can clear out the eastern side of the island, maybe even establish some level of air superiority, but on the other side of the central mountain range, we can't touch the Chi-Commies. Not in any meaningful way. They have three aircraft carriers in the Strait, and they're only a hundred miles from the mainland. There's too many of them and not enough of us."

"What about the Marines?" National Security Advisor Flores asked. "They're already in transit, right?"

"Yes, ma'am," Nikolaides said, "but they won't arrive on scene until day fourteen. That's too late. If this plan is the real McCoy, that's four days after the PLA owns the whole island."

Nikolaides exchanged glances with the Secretary of Defense.

"There is an option," Howard said, "but it's a long shot. Very high risk profile."

"Let's hear it," Chief of Staff Wilkerson said.

The Secretary of Defense seemed thrown off by the fact that the President had not answered.

"Well?" Serrano said.

"We've already repositioned elements of the 18th Airborne Corps from Venezuela to Joint Base Pearl Harbor-Hickam," the Chairman said. "We have the ability to airlift paratroopers from the 82nd and the 101st into Taiwan. I want to emphasize this is truly a last-ditch effort, sir."

"I'm listening," the President said.

"Mr. Riley," the Chairman said, "put up the map of Taiwan, will you, please?" While Don found the correct image, Nikolaides strode to the front of the room. He borrowed Don's laser pointer.

"The PLA has pretty much ignored the less-populated eastern side of the island. Riley's confirmed that," the Chairman said. He put a red dot on a small town on the eastern side of Taiwan about fifty miles south of Taipei. "This is Hualien. Small town, but it has a commercial airstrip that's long enough to land cargo aircraft."

Nikolaides continued speaking to a rapt audience. "It's four thousand miles one way from Hawaii to Taiwan. Eight hours, give or take. If we employed every bit of military transport we have available, we could airlift half a division from Pearl to Taiwan. Between the *Enterprise*, the Marines at Okinawa, and the Air Force out of Guam, we might—*might*—be able to safely airdrop paratroopers into Hualien. If they can take that airstrip, we could land transport planes all day long."

"What's your probability of success?" Serrano said.

The Chairman snorted, and Howard spoke. "I'd put this in the Hail Mary category, sir," she said. "I hesitate to even bring it up. We're talking about dropping thousands of soldiers on an enemy-held island and hoping —and I emphasize, *hoping*—that our airpower is strong enough to keep them alive. Apart from what we can fly into that captured airfield, those soldiers are on their own."

"It's worse than that, Mr. President," Nikolaides said.

Serrano managed to smile. "Worse, General? How so?"

"This is day seven in Taiwan, sir," the Chairman said. "If you give the go order right now, I mean, this very second, we can have US troops on the ground by the end of day eight. By that time, the PLA will be well on their way to having the western side of the island locked down. You literally cannot delay this decision for a minute."

Nikolaides's challenge—that's what it was in Don's mind—hung in the air. Most of the people around the table looked at their notes. Anything to avoid eye contact with the men on either end of the room.

President Serrano drew in a deep breath and let it out slowly. He'd shaken off the shock of Don's presentation, and his complexion had more color now. When he spoke, his voice was quiet, almost contemplative.

"I could ask for a vote on this," the President said, "but I won't. This is my decision. I need to decide between forcing the battle and losing the war."

"When this started"—he barked out a laugh—"less than a week ago, I made a promise to you and to my country. What the Chinese have done will not stand, I said, not while I have strength to resist. We are poised on the precipice of a new world order, one where the values of the United States are second-class. I cannot, I will not, allow that to happen."

Serrano stood, and the rest of the room followed.

"General, send in the 18th Airborne Corps."

39

USS *Idaho* (SSN-799)
50 miles northeast of Taipei

The carbon dioxide scrubber removed from the *Manta* lay on the wardroom table like a piece of art. From the outside, it was a stainless steel pipe about four inches in diameter and two feet long, with screens on both ends and electrical leads protruding from the end closest to Janet. According to the tech manual, inside the sealed pipe was a zeolite matrix impregnated with a nanomaterial that absorbed CO_2.

The specifications for the *Manta* claimed the CO_2 scrubber was rated for fifteen thousand hours of continuous operation. It had failed in a fraction of that time.

"I can't believe they don't have a backup built into the system," the XO said. He tugged at his mustache in frustration. "That's just shitty engineering."

Backup systems among submariners were an article of faith. When you spent your life in a steel tube underwater and living next to a nuclear reactor, you tended to see life as a series of accidents that had not yet happened.

"The submersible is a prototype," Captain Lannier said. "It was never designed for the kind of service we're putting it through."

"Still," the XO countered, "it's a crappy design, sir."

The captain looked around the table at Janet, Tony, the ship's Damage Control Assistant, and the division chief. The DCA was responsible for all of the non-nuclear systems on board the submarine, including atmosphere control.

"What are our options?" Lannier said.

The DCA was a junior officer who knew enough to defer to his chief, a twenty-year submarine veteran.

"Well, sir," the chief began, "it's not designed to be serviced, only replaced. We tried to heat it, hoping to get it to release some of the CO_2, but no dice. I could cut it open, but..." He let his voice trail off.

Lannier shook his head. "I'm not interested in a science experiment, and I'm not coming off station. How do we keep our people safe to make another run at the cable tap?"

"The only short-term fix we have is to put a canister of lithium hydroxide in the mini-sub and increase airflow," the chief said. "Space is tight, but we could fit one canister and a fan."

"How much time does that give them for each mission?" the XO asked.

"Ten to twelve hours, sir," the chief said. "Maybe less."

Janet watched Lannier's face as he did the calculations. For the *Idaho*, each trip from open water through the Okinawa Trough to the *Manta*'s launch point at Mianhua Islet was a risk. Start to finish, the whole evolution took a little over eight hours. Reducing *Manta* mission length from twenty hours to ten meant that the *Idaho* would need to remain on station in PLA-patrolled waters.

"What if we reduce the number of people in the *Manta* from three to two," Janet asked, "and add in another canister of lithium hydroxide?"

"What are you thinking, Lieutenant?" Lannier asked.

"Mark and I can handle the mission, sir," she replied. "I've got enough stick time on the *Manta* to be a competent pilot, and I can back up Mark on computers. Mark and I are smaller people, so we breathe out less CO_2. If we only have two people, we can use the third seat for another CO_2 absorber canister. What does that do for our mission profile, Chief?"

The chief scratched out some figures on a napkin. "Lieutenant Everett's math is right on target, sir. A second canister and one less person"—he shot a look at Tony—"especially one less larger person, means we can get the *Manta* back to a twenty-hour mission."

Lannier shook his head. "What about *Orca*?" he asked. "Who's going to run the drone?"

"The *Orca* runs itself, sir," Janet said. "I've written preprogrammed search patterns, so most of the time I'm twiddling my thumbs in the second seat." She looked at Tony for agreement, but his face was stony. The only reason why the SEAL was on board the *Idaho* and not with his unit was to be the pilot of the *Manta*. His expression told her he was not happy about being cut out of the job.

"Well, Lieutenant," Lannier said, "is Everett right?"

"Piloting the *Manta* doesn't have to be a two-person job, sir," Tony finally admitted. "But if something goes wrong, then you'll be glad there's someone in that second seat."

"By reducing the crew of the *Manta*," Janet said, "we reduce the risk to the *Idaho*, Captain. Two people versus a hundred and twenty. It's math."

A brief scowl flitted across the captain's features. Too late, Janet realized she was pushing too hard.

"Mr. Westlund," Lannier said. "What do you think? You're on the mission either way."

"I trust Janet, sir," Mark said. "If she says she can do both jobs, I believe her."

The room was silent. Lannier steepled his fingers.

"The mission will go with three people," the captain said. "Pilot, copilot, and Mr. Westlund. We'll have to live with the increased risk profile of twelve-hour missions."

Janet started to speak, but the XO cut her off with a glare.

"That said," Lannier continued, "I am concerned about the PLA patrols, so I want to take precautions."

———

The *Idaho* glided through the dark waters along the northern edge of the East China Sea Shelf toward the rendezvous point at Mianhua Islet. An hour before, Captain Lannier had set a modified general quarters, flooded torpedo tubes one and two, and opened the torpedo tube outer doors. The ship ran silently at seven knots, two hundred fifty feet below the surface of the ocean.

Sitting at her GQ station at the fire control system, Janet stewed at the inaction.

The captain had also decided to keep the *Manta* unmanned and sealed off from the *Idaho* until they were on station.

"Coming up on the next turn in one thousand yards, sir," the navigator said.

"Very well," the captain replied. "What's the status of the fathometer matching?"

"We're receiving good data, but no match yet, sir."

The *Idaho* was equipped with a high-frequency sonar array mounted on the "chin" of the submarine bow. Used for shallow water operations, the HF sonar array allowed the *Idaho* to paint a three-dimensional map of the bottom contour ahead of the ship. When combined with a precision bathymetric survey, the HF array could be used for underwater navigation.

"I have a match!" the navigator called out. "We are seven hundred fifty yards right of base course, sir."

"Countdown the turn, Nav," the captain said, never taking his eyes off the sonar display.

"Come left to new course one-nine-three in five...four..." When the navigator completed the count, the captain gave the order to turn.

"On final approach to launch point for the *Manta*, Captain," the navigator said. "Two thousand yards. We should see the Twin Towers in another three minutes."

The underwater pair of rocky spires on the bathymetric survey had been dubbed the Twin Towers by the ship's company. Since neither the *Idaho* nor the *Manta* could get a GPS fix while submerged, the feature served as a distinct landmark for their rendezvous point.

"Sonar," the captain said, "report all contacts."

Lannier nodded as the sonar chief ran through all his contacts, starting with the closest ones and working outward, delivering target classification, course, speed, and range. Of the six contacts in sensor range, the closest was a PLA warship ten thousand yards away and crossing into the shadow of the Mianhua Islet.

"Pilot," Lannier said, "all ahead one-third. Make turns for five knots." He looked at Janet. "Lieutenant Everett, man the submersible."

"Man the submersible, aye, sir." Janet had already breathed her relief. She unclipped her seat belt and shifted her chair back.

"Captain," the sonar chief called out, "possible submerged contact bearing one-seven-eight. I'm getting a weak tonal at one-two-seven hertz."

Janet pulled her seat back in and heard the clamp that locked the chair to the deck click in place.

"Transient!" The sonar chief came out of his chair. "He's close, sir!"

"Snapshot tube one, bearing one-seven-eight," Lannier said.

"Tube one ready!" Janet replied.

"Shoot!"

Janet mashed down the button to launch the weapon. Her ears popped as the water ram ejected the torpedo and pressure bled back into the ship.

"Left full rudder, all ahead full," the captain rapped out. "Make your depth four hundred feet."

The submarine banked to the left and down. Janet felt the deck tremble under her feet.

"Cut the wire on tube one," Lannier said. "Standby tube two."

"Wire cut on one, sir," Janet reported. "Standing by on two."

"Report, Sonar."

"Torpedo running normally, Captain," sonar reported. "No return fire. He's cavitating like crazy, sir. He's running away."

"You're sure there's no return fire?" Lannier asked.

"Nothing, sir."

Lannier blew out a breath. "All ahead two-thirds."

Janet watched the warring emotions on her commanding officer's face. If they ran now, they would waste hours of careful planning to get the *Idaho* into position to launch the *Manta*.

"Everett," Lannier said. "Join me at the nav plot, please." He nodded at the navigation team to step away.

"All right," he said, "we'll go with a two-man team on the *Manta*. That'll give you extended time on station with Westlund."

"Yes, sir." Janet tried to hold back the rising surge of excitement that threatened to break out into a smile.

"Sonar," Lannier called, "what's our PLA friend doing?"

"Running like a bat out of hell, sir."

"Pilot," Lannier said, "reverse course."

Janet started to move away, but Lannier reached across the plot table and clamped a hand on her arm. "Everett, don't do anything stupid out there."

40

PLA Navy submarine *Changzheng 12*
8 miles south of Mianhua Islet, Taiwan

Mission Clock: 83:23:13
Mission Status: Red

"We must have frightened them away," Captain Chu muttered to himself as he stared at the navigation plot.

The plot showed two red Xs, the sites of the prior encounters with the American submarine. Chu had debated with his XO and navigator about how to position the *Changzheng* to best advantage. In deeper water, his sensors were more effective, but he was also more likely to be detected by the US submarine. He finally opted to use the same tactics as the American submarine captain. He placed the *Changzheng* in shallower water to the south and ran a long racetrack pattern with the submarine's towed array streaming perpendicular to the expected incoming target.

Then he waited.

And waited some more.

In his excitement at the possible attack, Chu had called his ship to action stations. In hindsight, it was a mistake to keep his crew at general quarters for an extended period.

After four hours and no sign of their quarry, the control room smelled more like a locker room than a military space. Moisture from their collective exhalations dripped from the overhead. Chu ordered the shipwide ventilation system restored to normal lineup.

Four more hours dragged by. After multiple entreaties by the political officer, Chu allowed an evening meal to be served. Two hours later, he moved to a normal watch rotation. There was still no sign of the American submarine.

After twelve hours, Chu was exhausted. He went to his cabin and lay down on his bunk fully clothed. As always, the intercom in his cabin broadcast what was happening in the control room. The rhythm of the control room was soothing to him.

The American is not coming back, Chu thought. I had my shot at success, and I missed.

There was a soft knock, and his door opened a few inches. "Request permission to enter, Captain."

Without turning on the light, Chu sat up in his bunk. "Enter."

The messenger was outlined by the dim light of the hallway. "The chief engineer sends his respects and requests permission to switch the seawater cooling pump lineup. He says the maintenance is long overdue."

Chu recalled how the engineer had been pestering him about taking the starboard pump offline for maintenance. He thought about the long Out of Commission list on his desk. If they added a failed seawater pump to the list, it could mean the end of their deployment.

"Tell the chief engineer he has permission to change the seawater pump lineup for maintenance," he said. "Coordinate with the Officer of the Deck."

The messenger repeated the order and left. Chu lay back into the cool darkness and closed his eyes again. He wondered what his wife was doing right now.

What day was it? he wondered. Without natural light, time had lost all meaning. Back at home, they would still be celebrating Lunar New Year.

His wife would make the spicy pork dumplings, her mother's recipe that she only made on special occasions.

In the background, the soothing sounds of the control room played like a soundtrack to his daydream. The control room was only a few meters from where he lay, but it might as well have been a thousand kilometers distant.

The submarine changed course, and his bunk angled slightly as the ship turned. He heard the OOD on the phone with the engine room, giving orders for the new seawater pump configuration. Chu felt himself slipping more deeply into the comfort of sleep.

"Conning Officer, we are radiating noise from the port side of the engine room," the voice of the sonar supervisor penetrated Chu's dream. "Sir, it's loud! You need to switch the pumps back, sir."

The words tugged at Chu's mind, but his need for sleep was too great.

"Maneuvering, Conn, return pumps to normal configuration."

A second passed.

"The noise is gone, sir," sonar reported.

Chu relaxed again. His crew had found the problem and handled it. That's what his officers were supposed to do...

"*Torpedo in the water!*"

Words from every submariner's nightmare.

Still fully clothed, Chu was vertical in an instant, wrenching open the door to his cabin. Stepping into the control room, he raced to the fire control station.

"Make tube one ready!" Chu shouted. "Sonar, what's the bearing to the target?"

"Tube one ready in all respects, Captain," the fire control tech yelled back.

"Best bearing zero-one-three," sonar said.

"Match bearing and shoot," Chu said. He had his hand on the fire control tech's shoulder, and he could feel the kid trembling.

"Match bearing and shoot, aye, sir," the tech repeated. The launch button flashed green. He flipped the plastic cover off and pushed the launch button.

Chu waited for the familiar feel of the water ram ejecting a torpedo from the tube.

Nothing happened. The tech's panel lit up with red lights.

"Weapons fault." The petty officer's voice cracked.

"Pilot," Chu shouted, "come right to one-eight-zero. All ahead flank."

The sonar supervisor was levitating out of his chair with anxiety. "Mark 48 torpedo is in search mode!"

Chu turned to the nav plot. The torpedo had a crazy speed advantage over the *Changzheng*. If he tried to outrun it, he would die. All he could do was try to fool the torpedo's sensors.

He traced out the ship's track on the plot. To his right was shallow water, to his left deep water.

"Active homing, Captain," the sonar supervisor shouted. "The torpedo is in active homing."

Chu made his choice.

"Launch countermeasures," he ordered.

The order was repeated, but Chu waited until he heard the soft *punk-punk* sound of the two seawater-activated devices being launched from the deck below them.

"Right full rudder," he ordered.

Chu gripped the edge of the nav plot as the submarine heeled over at the sudden change in direction. The maneuver was designed to leave a pocket of disturbed water in their wake which, when combined with the countermeasure decoys, would provide a ghost target for the incoming torpedo.

The ship was headed toward shore and shallower water. Chu monitored the depth readings on the nav plot. They passed the two-hundred-meter mark and were hurtling toward the line marked 150 meters.

"Pilot, make your depth one hundred meters," Chu ordered.

"One hundred meters, aye, sir."

The control room had gone silent. Chu could hear the heavy breathing of the fire control technician a meter away from him.

"Captain," the conning officer said. "Our speed, sir."

He was right, Chu knew. They were barreling into shallower water. If there was an underwater knoll not marked on the chart, or a small rise in the sea floor, it could be catastrophic for the *Changzheng*.

"Noted," Chu snapped. Before he let off the speed, he needed to know whether they had fooled the American torpedo.

As a teenager, Captain Chu loved to watch submarine movies. In films, the action happened in quick succession. Shoot a torpedo, a few seconds later, a ship explodes. In reality, a torpedo attack was a slow-motion event, consuming minute after minute.

A real torpedo attack would be a boring movie, he decided.

"Captain, the torpedo is still active," the sonar supervisor reported. His voice had gone hoarse from all the shouting. "The torpedo is range gating."

"Tell me when the torpedo is within five hundred meters, Sonar," Chu said, not taking his eyes off the nav plot. "Reload countermeasures. Stand by to launch."

The *Changzheng* passed the 150-meter mark on the chart. At this speed, they would reach the one-hundred-meter line in minutes. Chu was literally betting his life on the accuracy of the chart and the ship's navigation system.

Captain Chu breathed in. He smelled the acrid scent of fear, heard the rush of the air conditioning blasting down from the vent overhead, felt the throb of the main engines in the hull—

"Five hundred meters, Captain," the sonar supervisor said, his voice cracking with defeat.

"Very well, Sonar." Chu stood straight and gripped the edge of the nav plot. "Sound the collision alarm. Launch countermeasures. Conning Officer, emergency blow, full rise on the stern planes."

"Aye-aye, sir!"

The deck rose to a steep angle as the *Changzheng* shot toward the surface. Chu felt a lift as the massive submarine crested out of the water, then crashed back down.

41

Liukuei, Taiwan

Mission Clock: 82:13:47
Mission Status: Red

Gao gnawed his thumbnail. He had broken himself of the practice as a teenager, and now decades later, the bad habit was back.

He slipped his thumb inside a clenched fist and stared out the window of the moving SUV. The rain had finally stopped, leaving a sodden green landscape in its wake. The road they were following wound along the western edge of the foothills. The elevation increased rapidly until at some points, Gao had to crane his neck to look up the mountainside.

"How much longer?" Gao snapped at his PLA driver.

"Ten minutes, sir."

Gao's half-chewed thumbnail was in his mouth before he knew what he was doing. To occupy his time, he took out his Shandian tablet. When he unlocked the screen, the red background lettering of the mission clock glared at him.

The PLA invasion plan was officially behind schedule. There was no denying it anymore. The bridge bombings delayed General Wei's drive north, but the situation in the northern command was not much better.

Supply chain issues continued to crop up all over the system, throwing the carefully calibrated PLA war machine out of alignment. Individually, the shipment issues were easily explained—a double order here, a mistyped stock number there, especially in the chaos of war operations— but, collectively, the issues were a disaster.

The PLA ground forces were massive. Maybe too massive. Tanks, armored personnel carriers, heavy artillery, and thousands upon thousands of soldiers. Thanks to the success of Gao's preinvasion operations, Taiwanese military resistance in the north and south of the island was much less than expected. The only real pocket of organized resistance was in the city of Taichung on the central western coast.

Yet, the invasion plan logistics had not changed. The PLA continued their buildup of enormous resources in Taipei and Kaohsiung in preparation for the drive through western Taiwan.

We are victims of our own success, Gao thought as he considered the mission clock. We're wasting time.

And then there was the increasingly intense American response. The United States had managed to triple their airpower over the eastern side of the island virtually overnight. They had fought the PLA Air Force to a standstill and sunk a half-dozen PLA Navy ships on the Pacific side of Taiwan.

It won't matter in the end, Gao reflected. Even if the PLA temporarily lost air superiority in the east and sacrificed a few older ships, the invasion would proceed anyway.

But, in the back of his mind, the doubts gnawed at his conscience the same way his teeth chewed on his ragged thumbnail.

The missing Shandian tablet, *his* missing Shandian tablet. Was it linked to the stiffened American response? Gao had convinced himself there was no way a missing tablet had anything to do with the slowed invasion, but the possibility was never far from his mind.

At the start of the invasion, he'd been ambitious, hungry for an opportunity to shine. His hard work paid off. He'd already netted one promotion out of this conflict.

But if the missing tablet surfaced, it would be a devastating blow for Gao's future. Shame, demotion, perhaps even prison.

Enough, he chastised himself. Focus on the job in front of your nose.

Gao reasoned the problem out. If the Taiwanese terrorists had his tablet, then he needed to find and destroy them. The best lead he had was the bridge bombings.

The bombings were a fine bit of guerilla warfare. He had to admit that. The bombers had stolen PLA vehicles right out of a motor pool. Two heavy trucks and an SUV like the one he rode in now.

Of course, it had taken the Chinese military police hours to piece together enough of one of the truck bombs to realize what the terrorists had done. Then more precious time wasted to conduct a physical audit of every motor pool to find out which vehicles were missing.

At that point, the military police investigation made some real progress. The stolen SUV was equipped with a GPS tracker. They were able to follow the track of the vehicle from the time it was stolen until when it was abandoned.

And finally—*finally*—Gao caught a break.

"We have a prisoner," the MP captain in charge of the investigation told Gao over the phone.

"This is it, sir," the driver said, interrupting Gao's cascading thoughts. "The town of Liukuei."

Calling this place a town was generous, Gao thought. Two-story stone and concrete houses crowded close to the edge of the road. The driver turned at a side street, and Gao spied the PLA captain waiting for him outside one of the homes. The paved road ended, and the dirt extension continued on for another fifty meters to a muddy parking lot.

Gao opened his own door and stepped outside. The air smelled of damp leaves and chickens.

"Where is the prisoner?" he demanded.

The captain led Gao into the house. The front door opened into a tiny sitting room. Gao took it in at a glance. Worn furniture, family pictures on the wall, swept floors. The door to a small kitchen was open, and Gao could see the dirt parking lot from the window over the sink.

An old woman occupied an armchair. Her gray hair was like straw, and she wore thick glasses.

"Where is the prisoner?" Gao asked.

"Here, sir." The captain motioned at the woman. Gao felt the heat of anger rising up his neck. He expected to find a terrorist, not someone's grandmother. His disappointment must have shown on his face.

"She saw something last night," the captain said. "Listen to her, sir. Please."

Gao sat down on the adjoining couch and leaned forward, elbows on his knees.

"What did you see?" Unconsciously, he spoke in a loud voice, assuming she was hard of hearing.

The old lady's head swiveled to focus on his face, slowly, as if she had all the time in the world. Gao guessed she might be ninety years old. Her skin was the color and consistency of crinkled parchment paper, and she blinked her eyes like an owl. Gao bit back his frustration at her languid movements.

"I have a hard time sleeping," she said.

Gao sighed. This was taking too long. More time wasted.

"I saw something last night," she continued.

"What did you see?" Gao's voice was near the level of a shout.

"It was late," the woman said, then added, "No need to shout. I can hear you just fine."

"What did you see?" Gao asked again, more quietly this time.

"A car," the woman said slowly. "I saw a car out there." She pointed toward the wall at the back of the house.

Gao stood up, walked through the kitchen, and peered through the back window. The dirt parking lot was empty, but he could see a wooden sign on the edge of the clearing.

"Captain," Gao called. "What is that back there? What does that sign say?"

"It's a hiking trail," the captain said. "It leads into the mountains."

Gao returned to the woman and sat down. "Tell me what you saw."

"I can't sleep," the woman said. Gao drew in a calming breath.

"There were men in the car, right, auntie?" the captain prompted her. The woman's head swiveled like a turtle at the new voice.

She blinked at the captain. "Yes."

"And what did the men do?" the captain asked.

"There were three men," the woman said. "One driver and two men in the back seat."

She spoke as if she were forming each word in her head before she released it to her mouth. He tried again.

"Please, auntie," Gao said, taking a cue from the captain. "What did the men look like?"

"They wore uniforms," she said.

"Did they all get out here?" Gao asked.

"Two got out," the woman said. "One man carried the other one. Over his shoulder, like a fireman. My grandson is a fireman."

Gao looked at the captain, unsure of what to ask next. To his surprise, the captain was smiling. "Was there anything unusual about the man?" he asked.

"Oh, yes," the woman said. "One of them was a white man."

Gao sat back in his seat as if he'd been slapped. "A white man, you're sure?"

"Oh, yes. I saw his face clearly in the headlights. He had a gray beard, and he was carrying the other man. They went up the trail."

The rumors were true, Gao thought. There was an American helping the Taiwanese terrorists. And a gray beard. Was he the mysterious Gong-gong?

"What did the other man do?" Gao asked.

"He drove off," the woman said. "He went that way." She pointed to the opposite wall.

"What time did this happen?" Gao asked.

"About 0200, sir," the captain answered for her.

Gao's mind worked overtime. Why had they stopped here? If the old man was carrying someone, that meant the terrorist base must be close.

"I sent some men up the trail," the captain said, "but the rain washed out any footprints."

Gao started to pull out his Shandian tablet but then stopped. He did not want his actions recorded on the network. Not yet, at least.

"A map," Gao demanded. "Get me a map."

He followed the captain outside and waited impatiently as the man spread out a topographical map on the hood of Gao's SUV. The trailhead fed into a network of hiking paths across three mountains. Mount Peinanchu, Mount Chuyun, and Mount Huanshi. Even if he restricted the search just to this side of the mountains, it was a vast, tree-covered area. Gao would need dedicated drone coverage and at least a company of soldiers to comb the forest.

"How many men can you have here in the next two hours?" Gao demanded of the captain. "We need to search these mountains."

The captain shook his head. "Sir, I don't have that kind of authority."

"I need at least a company," Gao said. "Soldiers with combat experience. How do I get that many men?"

"You'll have to talk to General Wei, sir."

Of course, thought Gao.

General Wei was eating when Gao arrived at his penthouse command post in the Grand Hi-Lai Hotel. He looked up when Gao emerged from the elevator.

"I saved you some dim sum, Major Gao," Wei said, his mouth full. He looked over Gao's uniform. "Or, should I say, Lieutenant Colonel Gao. Congratulations on your unexpected promotion, sir."

"Thank you, General," Gao replied. "I'm short on time. I am here to request—"

"Nonsense." The general waved to an empty place across from him. "I've been expecting you. Sit, eat. Let us celebrate your promotion."

Gao was famished. Apart from chewing on his fingernails, he could not remember the last time he'd had a hot meal. He sat and plucked a dumpling from a steam basket with chopsticks. He put the morsel in his mouth and chewed. The dumpling was prepared to absolute perfection, practically melting on his tongue. Gao closed his eyes in sheer pleasure.

"Good, huh?" Wei asked, snapping Gao back to reality.

"General, I came to ask—"

"Eat first, then we talk."

Gao gave in to his hunger, snatching dim sum bites from every basket and eating greedily. Finally, he sat back in his chair to find Wei grinning at him with his fleshy smile.

"General Zhang must think very highly of you to give you a field promotion, Colonel Gao," he said. "What can I do for you?"

"I have located the Taiwanese terrorist base," Gao said. "I need a company of soldiers to take them down."

"You have an obsession with these people," Wei replied. "Why do you care? Focus on the invasion and bypass the Taiwanese resistance. Deal with them later."

Gao felt a flutter of panic. Wei was right, of course. Even the bridge bombings were more of an inconvenience than a serious concern to the PLA. Then he hit on the answer.

"What if I told you the Americans were involved, General?"

Wei blinked at him. "Why do you think that?"

Mentioning nothing of his lost tablet, Gao outlined the information he had gleaned from the old woman.

"And what does General Zhang think of this?" Wei asked.

"He doesn't know," Gao said. "Yet," he added with a slight shrug of his shoulders.

Wei stroked his jowls. "I can imagine the man who captures an American spy inside Taiwan would be famous."

"The general who singlehandedly dealt a death blow to the Taiwanese resistance would go down in history as a great man," Gao replied.

"Why would you keep this information from General Zhang?" Wei asked. "He has just promoted you, Lieutenant Colonel Gao."

Gao watched Wei's face. This was a dangerous game he was playing.

"Perhaps I see my real future in politics, General Wei," Gao said carefully. "I would like to count the new governor of the Taiwan province as a friend and ally."

The grin that spread across Wei's fleshy face told Gao his words had found their mark.

"Tell me exactly what you need, Colonel Gao," said Wei.

DAY EIGHT

42

USS *Enterprise* strike force
510 miles southwest of Okinawa

Launch aircraft, recover aircraft, arm aircraft, repeat.

Thirty-six hours into their air campaign over Taiwan, and monotony had set in.

Sharratt found it hard to believe, but war had become tedious.

He stared at the BattleSpace display, listening with half an ear to the chatter from Pri-Fly, where flight deck activities were handled.

The flight crews in the three carriers of the *Enterprise* strike force were seasoned by months of daily flight ops. They, too, had settled into a routine. One-third of the aircrews were engaging with the enemy in the skies over Taiwan, one-third were on their way home, and the final third were off-duty for rest.

The unmanned UCAVs did not need rest, of course, so they flew as long as they had ordnance on board, often changing duty between the inbound and outbound strike teams. The unmanned Stingray refueling drones formed the backbone of the support aircraft in the sky.

Sharratt's reliance on unmanned assets did not end in the sky. The *Sea Skates* and *Sea Hunter* USVs had proven to be a formidable screen against

PLA submarine threats. Three times in the last twenty-four hours, the strike force had detected and prosecuted attacks against subsurface targets. Unlike the three PLA submarines they had sunk on the transit to Taiwan, these new targets were on their guard against enemy attacks.

The dirty little secret of this war, Sharratt thought, is that without the robots, there would be no war.

He brooded, unconsciously swilling coffee from the cup at hand.

War was not the right word, he thought. Not for what they were doing. *Holding action* might be a better name for it. After thirty-six hours of tangling with the Chinese, it looked to Sharratt like both sides had agreed to retire to their corners, stepping out only to throw a jab now and again.

Sharratt's strike force had lost eight aircraft and taken at least twice that many PLA fighters off the board. In addition, the US forces had cleared the Pacific Ocean of PLA surface threats on the eastern side of the island. If he wanted to be kind to their progress, he could even say that as long as his war planes stayed on this side of the Taiwan central mountain range, the US had established air superiority.

But for what? Sharratt thought. The US wasn't able to parlay those fragile gains into real progress. They'd barely touched the PLA ground forces that were now slowly making their way south.

Meanwhile, the PLA Navy refused to engage. They kept their valuable aircraft carriers tucked safely inside the Strait of Taiwan, putting the island between them and the American forces. The SAM batteries at the north and south ends of the island remained active, cutting off any attempt at an end run around the landmass.

The Chinese were playing the long game. They played defense to run out the clock and avoided escalating the conflict.

Chief of Staff Tom Zachary appeared on the other side of the Battle-Space display.

"Here to relieve you, sir," Zachary said. He still had sleep in his eyes, and Sharratt could see creases from his bedsheets across his face.

"You look like hell, Tom."

"Right back at you, sir."

Sharratt did a quick self-assessment. His mouth tasted like the inside of a garbage disposal, and he needed to pee, but other than that he felt good. "If you need a few more hours, Tom, I can handle it."

Zachary shook his head. "Take some downtime, sir. You need it. We all do." He nodded at the BattleSpace display. "Anything new?"

Sharratt snorted. "No, they come out of their corner and punch us in the nose. We punch back, and everybody calls it a day. Helluva way to run a war, if you ask me. "

"We need to change the rules of the game," Zachary said.

They'd had this conversation any number of times over the last few days. The *Enterprise* strike force operated at least five hundred miles off the coast of Taiwan and stayed on the move to prevent the PLA from pinpointing their location.

If the Chinese wanted to take the confrontation to the next level, they had two options. If they moved an aircraft carrier out of the Strait of Taiwan and into the open Pacific, they could put a lot of planes in the air. It would not take them long to find the *Enterprise*.

A long-range missile strike would follow. Even this far out at sea, the US strike force was vulnerable to Chinese missiles. If the PLA threw everything they had at the *Enterprise* strike force, his odds of survival were not good. Just the thought of it made Sharratt break into a cold sweat.

So, they stayed far out to sea—out of reach of PLA airpower—and on the move to complicate a long-range missile strike.

But in the long run, their current "run and hide" model of warfare was a losing strategy. Unless the dynamics of the battlefield changed dramatically and soon, then those eight F-35 pilots had died for nothing more than a participation trophy.

Sharratt yawned. It seemed he was tired after all. He reached for his empty coffee cup.

"Well, Captain Zachary, I had it, you got it. I stand relieved. See you in six hours. Call me if you need me." Sharratt started toward the door.

"Admiral!" the watch officer said. "Incoming flash traffic from INDOPACOM."

Sharratt put down his coffee cup and took the proffered tablet. His eyes widened as he read the message. Zachary, reading from his own tablet, let out a low whistle.

"No rest for the wicked, sir," Zachary said.

Sharratt felt a fresh surge of adrenaline course through his body. He stepped back to the BattleSpace display and read off the coordinates to the display operator. The tabletop zoomed out, then back in as it focused on the eastern edge of Taiwan.

"Open a data tag on Hualien City," he said. He read through the details of population, geography, and local landmarks. Hualien City was on a narrow plain sandwiched between the mountains and the Pacific Ocean. Located fifty miles south of Taipei, he noted there was only one road into the city from the north and a large airfield.

His eyes dropped back to the message:

Elements of 18th Airborne Corps en route from Hawaii for airdrop on Hualien City, Taiwan. Enterprise *directed to maneuver strike force as needed to clear air corridor and maintain air superiority over drop zone.*

Sharratt met Zachary's eyes across the BattleSpace table.

"Be careful what you wish for, Admiral."

43

Liukuei, Taiwan

Mission Clock: 52:16:22
Mission Status: Red

Gao surveyed the company of PLA soldiers mustered at the trailhead. The company wore rain gear, making them look like slick, faceless blobs in the reflected light of the car headlights.

Heavy rain drummed on the raised hatchback of the SUV that Gao sheltered under with his three platoon commanders. The downpour, which had begun two hours ago and showed no signs of letting up, only added to his problems. Even with General Wei's approval, breaking a company of soldiers away from the pending PLA drive north had proven difficult. He ended up with platoons from three different units, and as far as he could tell, they were all raw recruits, just out of basic training.

Because of the Taiwanese terrorist bridge bombings, much of the north-bound traffic was routed to smaller local bridges, which clogged the narrow secondary roads. Then the weather rolled in. The rain fell straight down, as if someone had turned on a shower overhead. There was flash flooding everywhere, snarling traffic and slowing Gao's planned search even further.

His feet were soaked. The trailhead was churned into ankle-deep mud from the boots of the mustering forces.

Gao needed to make a decision. He was hours behind schedule, about to start a search for a dangerous enemy in the dark in suboptimal weather conditions. There were three peaks considered possible locations for the Taiwanese terrorist base. If he split his men into three search parties, he would cover more ground. On the other hand, a platoon of green PLA troops against an experienced resistance force fighting from a defensive position was a recipe for a bloodbath.

Gao unlocked his Shandian tablet, bypassing the home screen with the glaring red mission clock. The PLA invasion progress had fallen behind even more over the afternoon. The Taiwanese regular army forces, dug into a defensive posture around the city of Taichung, had rallied and driven back PLA probing attacks.

He established a video connection with General Wei's intel officer. As soon as Wei had approved the operation, the very capable intel officer had been Gao's first stop. While Gao was mired in kilometers of traffic, the intel officer used drones to survey the search area for clues to the terrorist hideout.

"What do you have for me, Captain?" Gao asked.

"It's difficult to say, sir." There were bags under his red-rimmed eyes.

"Then give me your best guess," Gao snapped. "Please," he added. "I value your opinion."

"Before the rain started, we caught some flashes of thermal activity in this area." The intel officer circled the summit of Mount Chuyun on the screen. Gao touched the screen to open the data tag and saw the peak was 2,800 meters.

"The area is littered with caves," the intel officer continued. "Some of them might be large enough to shelter a small group of soldiers. That's the best I can do. In this weather, the drones are useless, sir."

Gao ended the call. He stabbed a finger at the map on Mount Chuyun.

"This is our objective, gentlemen." He traced three tracks around the peak using his finger and issued orders for each platoon commander. The young men, all second lieutenants who looked barely old enough to have graduated secondary school, acknowledged his orders with gusto.

Maybe what they lack in experience, they'll make up for in enthusiasm, Gao thought.

The next two hours was a miserable climb through the dark forest. The boots of the men ahead of him churned the dirt trail to a trough of flowing mud. The heavy rain sluiced off the tree branches in sheets and formed little cascades that ran down the slope. As they climbed, the temperature dropped, leaving Gao with a chill that permeated his wet clothes.

Their approach to the summit of Mount Chuyun was not subtle. A shipment of thirty thousand night vision goggles that was supposed to arrive in Kaohsiung City never arrived, which meant his soldiers were handicapped in the night fight.

It might be easier if we sang marching songs to announce our arrival, Gao thought.

When all three platoons were in place, Gao ordered his troops to spread out and sent two recon squads forward.

An hour passed. Gao sat with his back to a tree and tried to will away the gnawing cold. While he had little confidence in the skill of his recon teams, it didn't matter. Even if his soldiers stumbled into the enemy, that was success. Gao would know where the enemy was hiding. He had more men. Once the weather cleared, he would have aerial support. Hell, in the worst case, he could just drop bombs on the mountain. Whatever he needed to do, the Taiwanese terrorists would not escape this time.

With these thoughts running through his head, Gao was surprised when the leader of the first recon team radioed back that he had found a concealed entrance to a cave.

Gao made his way up the slope with the platoon commander in tow to find the five-man recon squad grinning with pride. A camouflage blanket was pulled aside to reveal a cleft between two rocks.

"We found it by accident, sir," the corporal in charge of the team said, his words in a rush. "We were staying close to the rocks and just ran into the cover."

"Good work, Corporal," he said. The grin got wider.

Gao shined a light into the opening, which was wide enough for one man to pass at a time, if he turned sideways. The dirt floor inside was dry, and it looked as if the opening widened after a few meters.

"Bring your men up here," he said to the platoon commander.

Gao formulated a plan in his head. If the terrorists had abandoned the base, then he needed to know that as soon as possible. If they were still in there, they were dug in and ready for an assault. His instincts told him to proceed with caution, but he needed answers fast.

Speed won out. He would lead the infiltration himself.

His Shandian tablet buzzed with an incoming call. Gao opened the tablet, using his hood to shield the glare of the screen. The intel officer was calling. Maybe he had picked up new information from the drones. Gao accepted the call.

"Colonel Gao," the intel officer said, "there is something you need to see immediately."

Before Gao could respond, the intel officer handed the tablet to another person. It was the communications officer, Captain Ro.

"I don't have time for your—" Gao began.

"Listen, Colonel," the officer responded. His chin was thrust out, his jaw set. "It's important."

The urgency in the young officer's tone silenced Gao.

"Your tablet," he continued, "your *old* tablet—the one you said was destroyed—is active."

Gao leaned back against the rock, letting rain stream across the screen. He willed his face not to show any emotion, but he was failing.

"You lied to me, sir."

An idea, a ray of hope glimmered in Gao's consciousness.

"You said it's active?" he asked. "Right now?"

"Yes, sir, but—"

"Can you track it?" Gao interrupted.

The mask of anger on the young man's face cracked. "Yes, sir."

"Send me the tracking information," Gao ordered. "Do it now."

He waited impatiently for his screen to update. The topographical map showed his location on the southwestern edge of the mountain peak. A red dot blinked, moving slowly in a northwesterly direction. Goa found the scale of the map.

It was less than a kilometer away.

Gao switched back to the communication screen. "I'll get back to you, Captain." He ended the call before the other man could object.

Gao turned to the platoon leader. "There's something I need to do, Lieutenant," Gao said. "You are in charge. You remember your urban warfare training?"

The young officer swallowed hard. "Yes, sir, but our course was shortened due to the war games exercise. We only did the classroom part."

Gao cursed under his breath. He glanced at the screen of his tablet. Every second he waited, the missing device got further away. This was his chance.

He put his hand on the second lieutenant's shoulder and gave him a reassuring squeeze. "Inside there"—he pointed at the mouth of the cave—"is a kill zone. If it moves, you shoot it. Go slow, watch for booby traps. Got it?"

"Y-yes, sir, but the rules of engagement—"

"The rules are suspended for this operation, Lieutenant," Gao said. "On my authority. Do you understand?"

The officer straightened up. "I understand, sir."

44

Mount Chuyun, Taiwan

If he was ever given the chance to debrief on his experience with the Taiwan Shadow Army, Lester thought, his only comment would be that they had prepared for every contingency.

Including evacuation.

The scouts had reported in about the PLA company of soldiers moving up the same trail Lester had used to carry Frank Tsai to safety. When the trail split, the company stayed on course for Mount Chuyun. At that point, Lester knew the game was over.

"Major Tsai," Lester said to Oliver, "I recommend you evacuate your people."

Within thirty minutes of Oliver's order, four squads departed. They traveled north by separate routes, bound for other Shadow Army bases. A fifth squad was dispatched to cover their trail.

A small detachment changed into civilian clothes and made for various small towns on the eastern side of Taiwan. A few carried sidearms, but most went unarmed. Blending in with the local population, they would serve as the eyes and ears of the resistance.

Lester, Hardy, Lewis, and Oliver Tsai stayed behind to prepare the base for the inevitable infiltration by the PLA.

Hardy traipsed out from the armory with Claymore mines under each arm. He carefully added his load to the growing pile of explosives in the open space between the Quonset huts.

"That's the last of it, sir," Hardy said. "I'll finish the rigging." He picked up a spool of detonator cord and walked toward the main entrance of the base carrying blocks of C4 explosives.

Oliver Tsai emerged from the nearest building and joined Lester. "The last team is gone. Thankfully, it's still raining very hard outside. That gives us a fighting chance."

Lester nodded. The weather was about the only thing that was going in their favor tonight. He could not shake the thought that by carrying Frank Tsai back to the base, he had led the PLA to their doorstep.

"How's Frank doing?" he asked.

"As well as can be expected, sir," the elder Tsai answered. "He's able to walk, but slowly. We have arranged for him to stay in a safe house in Taimali."

They'd come full circle, Lester reflected. The town of Taimali was where he had first met Captain Frank Tsai. The dark feeling that he had failed his Taiwanese friend chafed at his conscience.

The rain won't last forever, Lester thought. When it ends, the PLA drones will own the skies again. They were outnumbered and outgunned. In a firefight, his people would lose. He had to do something, change the rules of the game.

Hardy reappeared. "We're all set, boss. Charges spaced around the perimeter and up the tunnel leading in. The trigger is at the door. Once they cross the threshold, it sets off a two-minute timer. Then it's lights out in here."

Lester looked around the place they'd called home for the last week. The damage would be horrific. It might even collapse the whole cavern. When he'd joined Phalanx, Lester believed his days of blowing things up were over. Old habits die hard.

"Lewis," he called out.

"Here, sir," came the reply from inside the supply tent.

"Let's roll." Lester hoisted his pack.

Headlamps on, Oliver Tsai led the way, followed by Lewis, then Hardy, and Lester bringing up the rear.

In addition to the main entrance, which was now booby-trapped, the base had two other emergency exits. Oliver had described the alternate ways out of the mountain as challenging. His description was painfully accurate.

After a hundred feet, Lester had to stoop to walk. He removed his pack and dragged it behind him. Then the path got more restrictive. Lester got on his hands and knees and crawled, pushing his pack ahead of him. The air was damp and close. The rocky ceiling slick with moisture.

If I was claustrophobic, Lester thought, this would be my worst nightmare.

"Stop looking at my ass, sir," Hardy said. "I can feel your eyes all over me."

"You're such a child," Lewis said from ahead of them.

Their forward progress stopped. Lester bumped into Hardy.

"I know that was deliberate, Colonel," Hardy said, "and if you do it again, I'm lodging a formal complaint at the head office."

"What's going on up there?" Lester called. He had no idea how far they had traveled. His knees ached from the crawling.

"Oliver's digging," Lewis said.

"He's *digging*?" Lester replied.

A burst of fresh air streamed past Lester's face, sweet and heavy with moisture. Hardy moved forward, Lester followed, pushing his pack ahead of him. A few paces later, he was able to stand up straight.

His three companions stood under a rocky overhang. Outside their dry enclave, heavy rain pelted the trees, raising a soft roar of white noise. At any other time, it might have been relaxing.

"Rain gear on, people," Lester said. "Miles to go before we sleep."

He knelt next to Lewis as she opened her pack. "I want you to give me the PLA tablet."

"Sure, sir." Lewis pulled the slim tablet from her pack. It was still wrapped in EM-shielded plastic.

"Thanks." Lester stood. He nodded at Hardy. "You know where you're going?"

"That I do," Hardy replied. He pointed north. "Heading for them thar hills."

"Good." Lester unwrapped the tablet. "Get going. I'll give you a ten-minute head start."

"Sir," Lewis said, "if you turn that on, it will register on the PLA network. They'll know where you are."

Lester grinned. "That's the plan, Ash. A little game of fox and hounds."

"Sir," Hardy said, his tone uncharacteristically serious, "with all due respect, I can run you into the ground. If you really wanna give those bastards a run for their money, I'm your guy."

Lester held out a hand. "Maybe next time, Hardy. I got this one."

Hardy shook his hand, then spun around. "All right, people, you heard the man. Move out!"

"Oliver," Lester said.

"Sir."

"Tell Frank I said goodbye and I'm glad I got to know him. He's a helluva officer and a good man."

Oliver's glasses glinted as he nodded. He gripped Lester's hand. "I'll tell him, Gong-gong. Be safe."

Lester smiled to himself as the night swallowed his companions. Being safe was not the plan.

He closed his eyes, letting the soothing sound of the rain calm his mind. He thought of his wife. He wondered if she had received his email and gotten the information to Liz Soroush. Maureen was a smart girl. She'd figure it out.

He chuckled to himself. If she were here, she'd call him a fucking idiot for what he was about to do. She was probably right.

Gong-gong. Lester laughed. He'd gotten to be a grandpa after all. Just not the way he'd planned.

He pulled the tablet from the EM-shielding and scanned his retina.

The home screen lit up. He saw the icon at the top of the page register a connection to the battle network. The mission clock on the home page was fire-engine red, he noted with some satisfaction.

I guess we did make a difference, he thought.

The time was one minute after midnight. A new day.

He flipped up the hood of his rain poncho, stepped into the rain, and turned south.

Catch me if you can, assholes.

DAY NINE

45

Mount Chuyun, Taiwan

Mission Clock: 47:02:13
Mission Status: Red

After half a kilometer, Gao shed his pack and rain gear. His injuries forgotten, he raced pell-mell down the mountain trail, slipping in the mud, falling, but always moving forward.

Closer to the stolen tablet.

He reached for a tree branch, missed, and landed on his ass in the mud. Gao caught his breath. He pulled out his Shandian tablet to check his progress.

The red dot was only half a kilometer away, still heading down the mountain. Gao was gaining on him.

He pulled himself to his feet and plunged ahead.

Ten minutes later, Gao reached a fork in the trail and checked his progress again. His quarry had taken the left turn, continuing south.

The rain stopped suddenly, as if someone had turned off the shower. The rushing sound of raindrops on the leaves ceased, and an eerie quiet settled over the forest. Gao heard his own breathing over the soft plops of water running off the leafy canopy.

His hands and legs trembled from the fierce race down the slope. Steam rose from his wet uniform. He slowed his breathing until the sound was no more than the background forest noises.

Gao checked the tablet. The red dot was stationary, a mere three hundred meters away.

He pulled his pistol from his holster. Tablet in one hand, weapon in the other, he stepped off the muddy trail and made his way silently through the forest.

Gao took his time. A few careful steps forward. Stop. Listen.

He had turned down the brightness of the tablet to the lowest setting, but he kept the face of the device pressed against his chest all the same. The only sound was the irregular *drip-drip-drip* of the forest canopy.

Step, step, step, pause.

The lost tablet was close by, within ten meters according to his screen.

Gao surveyed the forest around him for anything out of the ordinary but found nothing.

Maybe they had dropped the tablet or thrown it away, he decided. Maybe it was just lying on the forest floor, waiting to be picked up.

Don't be a wishful fool, he told himself.

Step, step, step, pause.

Then he remembered. Had he not been in a tactical situation, he might have slapped himself on the forehead.

The tablet had a locator feature. He could turn on the screen, make it play a noise.

With shaking fingers, Gao navigated to the screen and activated both light and sound. He looked up, then tapped the button.

The sudden *ding-ding-ding* startled Lester. In the crotch of a pine tree a few meters away, the screen of the tablet lit up like a beacon.

Lester froze.

When the rain stopped suddenly, Lester thought about ditching the tablet and making a run for it.

He discarded the idea. Instead, he looked for a place to stage an ambush.

The rational side of Lester's brain told him he had already done everything possible to give his friends a good head start. But his guilt would not let his mind rest easy.

Guilt that he had led the PLA to the Taiwanese Shadow Army base. Guilt about not being able to do more for these brave people. Guilt about whether his country was going to be able to help the people of Taiwan.

Guilt is not a cause worth fighting for, he thought. And yet, here I am.

He selected a tree with a clearing around it so he could see someone coming from any direction. He tucked in next to a boulder and waited.

The locator chime on the tablet sounded like a fire alarm in the silent forest. The screen blazed at full brightness like a beacon.

If he'd been carrying the device, he'd probably be dead.

For a long time, nothing happened. Then Lester thought he saw a shadow move. A man dressed in a PLA combat uniform crept into the clearing.

Water dripped off Lester's nose, and he took shallow, silent breaths. He tightened his grip on the T75 handgun as the PLA soldier surveyed the area. His gaze passed over Lester's hiding place.

Was he alone? Lester wondered. I could take him out now with one shot.

The man circled the tree warily as if looking for a booby trap, then he sidled up to the trunk. The hiding place of the tablet was a good three feet above his outstretched hand. The man would have to climb to get the tablet.

When the PLA soldier holstered his weapon, Lester saw his chance.

While the man was busy dealing with the slippery tree trunk, Lester holstered his own weapon and drew his combat knife. It was a carbon fiber model, all black, light and razor sharp.

He stalked into the clearing, the damp forest floor muffling any sounds. He closed the distance until only a few meters separated them.

Suddenly, on the mountain behind him, a massive explosion ripped through the night.

The man spun around at the sound. Their eyes met, and Lester recognized him as the wounded soldier from the campground.

I should have let them kill you, he thought.

Lester rushed, his knife sweeping in from the right. The blade tip landed exactly where he wanted it. Just above the point of the hip, where there was a gap in the body armor. Once the knife entered the flesh, Lester could rip upward, gutting the man.

The knife connected with something solid. The blade would go no further.

Lester's momentum carried him forward. He smashed the soldier against the tree trunk, feeling the man's breath blast out of his body.

But the PLA soldier was fast. Even as he hit the solid tree, he pivoted his hips, turning Lester's momentum against him.

Lester felt his feet leave the ground. He was falling. He slashed out with the knife, felt the blade bite into flesh. Then he hit the forest floor, and his own breath left his body.

He rolled, his hand reaching for his sidearm, but it was too late.

The PLA soldier's weapon was out by the time Lester hit the ground. The muzzle moved in an arc, bearing down on him.

The flash of the gunshot lit the soldier's face. Lester's last image was of his feral grin, his bandaged head, and a red slash across his cheek where Lester's blade had found its mark.

The roar of the gunshot numbed his eardrums.

He felt the heavy dampness of the soil, the splash of fresh rain on his cheek.

A searing pain. Then nothing.

46

From his perch on the flag bridge, Rear Admiral Chip Sharratt surveyed the action on the flight deck.

An F-35 rolled into position on number one catapult. A sailor connected the jet wheels to the catapult block. Another crewmember checked his work, then both retreated from underneath the fighter.

As the F-35's engine was brought to full power, the "shooter" cleared the deck one final time, then she dropped to her knee, arm outstretched, to signal the catapult to be fired. The jet rocketed forward.

Within seconds, the warplane was out over the ocean, climbing, headed for open skies and the fight ahead.

Sharratt's body experienced the muscle memory of a catapult launch. As a backseater in an EA-18G Growler, he'd performed the evolution hundreds of times. Going from zero to 130 knots in two seconds flat was a thrill. Even better was the moment of near weightlessness when the thrust of the catapult faded but before the plane's own power took over.

He walked along the windows scanning the deck. A queue of four

Growlers waited for their orders to launch. Sharratt checked his watch: 0230 local.

Not long now, ladies, he thought as he watched the idling aircraft. You're going to have your work cut out for you today.

Although he could not remember the last time he'd slept, Sharratt was not tired in the least. In fact, he felt energized, as if he'd tapped some inner well of energy. Or maybe it was just a looming sense of his own mortality.

That was a real possibility today. More than a possibility, a likelihood. Yet somehow, it didn't matter. Sharratt had made his peace with the situation. If today was his time, then he'd meet his Maker with a grin.

Apart from his own state of mind, he was very aware that every soul in his twenty-thousand-person strike force was going to take their lead from how he handled himself. It might be only a rumor, but everyone was going to hear something. If he had anything to say about it—and he did—they were going to hear that the Old Man was ready for the fight and confident that there would be a tomorrow.

There was *zero* room for error. Sharratt accepted that challenge—hell, he welcomed that challenge. In these last few days, he even started to believe that he'd been put on this earth just to be that guy for this moment in history. He felt a sense of purpose all around him, as if every single thing that had happened to him in his life was all in preparation for this moment.

The phone under the railing buzzed. Sharratt looped a finger around the heavy black plastic receiver and hoisted it to his ear. "Sharratt."

"Admiral," Tom Zachary said, "we have them on radar, sir."

And so it begins, he thought. "On my way," he said.

Sharratt descended from the flag bridge down to Battle Watch on the O-2 level beneath the flight deck. He entered the room at a brisk clip and joined Zachary at the BattleSpace holographic display.

Despite their high-tech surroundings, the fact that he was on an aircraft carrier conducting continuous flight operations was never in doubt. It was a background soundtrack that Sharratt barely heard anymore—launch, recovery, launch, recovery.

Jet engines racing to full power just before the catapult fired. The resounding *boom!* the catapult made as it hit the end of the run. The *wham!*

of a jet slamming down on the flight deck as the pilot caught the three-wire. The whine of the arresting gear spooling out to catch the aircraft.

"There they are, sir." Zachary pointed to the eastern edge of the display where a crowd of fifty C-17 military transport planes flew in trailing formation.

"Jesus," Sharratt said. At nearly two hundred feet long, each four-engine C-17 Globemaster was a massive aircraft on its own. Sharratt could not imagine what it looked like to see fifty of them gathered together in one chunk of airspace.

The incoming airlift was transporting nearly five thousand para-troopers and their equipment from Hawaii, some five thousand miles away from Taiwan. Not only was this the longest-range airborne assault in history, Sharratt thought, it was also the ballsiest move he'd ever seen.

Fly five thousand miles and drop half a division on the doorstep of a hundred thousand PLA troops. The guy who hatched that plan was either going to get a medal or a firing squad.

The number of ways this could go sideways were too many to count, but Sharratt was only concerned with one part of that long list. His strike force needed to own the skies over the landing site to give the airborne forces a fighting chance.

Everyone else felt the same pressure, Sharratt realized. With the incoming airborne assault in radar range, the tension in Battle Watch boiled into a fever pitch. He could feel it in the way orders were given and responses lodged. Crisp, clear, and by the book. If there was ever a time to bring your A-game to your job, today was that time.

Sharratt's plan was simple. He was not going to hang around five hundred miles away from Taiwan. The best place for his carriers to be was close to the action. Close enough that he could deal with the PLA aircraft carriers if the Chinese decided to move them out of the Strait of Taiwan. Close enough that he could extend his umbrella of air defenses over the airfield at Hualien.

For the last twenty-four hours, the *Enterprise* strike force had steamed directly for Hualien. Combined with the Air Force assets out of Guam and the Marines out of Okinawa, they conducted SEAD missions, one after another. Normally, suppression of enemy air defense missions targeted SAM batteries, tracking and fire control radars, and anti-aircraft artillery, but Sharratt's main goal was to take out any long-range radar or command function on the eastern side of the island. He wanted to blind the Chinese to the incoming US Army airborne assault. Every minute he bought the Army was one minute closer to success.

Of course, every mile closer to Taiwan he sailed meant he was giving the Chinese a more accurate targeting solution—if they chose to press the attack. It was a calculated risk, but worth it, in his opinion.

Move and countermove. Action and reaction.

He was heartened by the fact that the PLA mostly ignored the renewed air attacks. To Sharratt's mind, they had ceded the eastern side of Taiwan, at least for now, as they focused on their ground-based drive to secure the heavily populated western side of the island.

"We are officially dancing with the dragon, sir," Zachary said. His attempted joke fell flat in the amped-up tension of Battle Watch.

Sharratt studied the display. The strike force had officially crossed the PLA-declared one-hundred-kilometer emergency zone. In the planning stages of this operation, they had called crossing the boundary "dancing with the dragon."

The move would give the Chinese an excuse to attack, but Sharratt weighed that risk against the need to provide air cover for the incoming airborne assault. Besides, if the PLA decided to fight back, he wanted to make sure the *Enterprise* strike force was seen as a bigger threat than the troops landing on Hualien.

"Watch Officer, how long before the Army reaches their drop zone," Sharratt called out.

"ETA 0400, sir," came the prompt reply.

Less than an hour.

"CAG reports all ECM assets are ready, sir," the watch officer said.

Sharratt nodded. "Watch Officer, inform CAG he has permission to launch."

Sharratt's final move to protect the incoming C-17s was to put all of his electronic countermeasures aircraft in the vanguard of the assault. Their job was to flood the airspace with a wall of electronic noise. If there were any Chinese sensors still remaining, he wanted to keep them blind for as long as possible.

The final piece of the plan was in play. Now came the hard part:

Waiting.

47

35,000 feet over the Western Pacific Ocean

Lieutenant Colonel Kevin Merriman, US Army, bit into the hose on his CamelBak hydration pack and sucked down a swallow of water. He was wedged in between two soldiers, both asleep. He closed his eyes and let his head drop back against the webbing of the jump seat.

On an eight-hour flight with more than a hundred soldiers packed into the back of a C-17 military transport, staying hydrated was a balancing act. Proper hydration was essential for mental clarity and physical stamina, especially in the dry atmosphere of the aircraft. On the other hand, if he drank too much, he'd be in the long line waiting to pee.

He'd done the math. He needed to consume about 1.5 liters of water over the course of the flight from Joint Base Pearl Harbor-Hickam to the drop zone over Hualien, Taiwan. With four hundred milliliters to go and just over two hours left in their flight, he was right on schedule.

Merriman took comfort in the details. All the details.

As commander of 1st Battalion, 502nd Infantry of the 101st Airborne Division, he'd jumped out of an airplane hundreds of times. But he'd never done a for-real combat jump. Not a single person on this entire operation had.

The last time the US Army executed a combat jump was in the early days of the twenty-year Afghanistan War. The Army had possessed overwhelming odds of success in that jump. But this? This was completely different. In Afghanistan, paratroopers dropped into a combat situation where the US owned the skies and the Taliban forces they were fighting were guerilla militias. Tough soldiers, for sure, but lacking the firepower and training of a modern army.

Taiwan was nothing like that. At Hualien, he and his soldiers were dropping on a zone where the fight for air superiority was still an ongoing battle. Just fifty miles to the west, over the coastal mountains, were one hundred thousand Chinese soldiers. The PLA was no joke. It was a twenty-first-century army with twenty-first-century hardware. Go another hundred miles west and you'd hit the Chinese mainland with 1.4 billion people, all the supplies in the world, and overwhelming combat power.

On the US side of the equation, the 101st was tasked with securing a foothold on the island of Taiwan with half a division—roughly five thousand combat soldiers—spread out across fifty-plus aircraft. Even assuming they got every soldier on the ground in fighting condition, a near impossibility, they entered the fight with only the weapons they brought with them, plus whatever they could scavenge on the ground.

Over the course of the flight, they'd been in spotty contact with a company of regular Taiwanese Army and some sort of local militia who claimed they held the Hualien airfield. The combined airpower of the US Navy, Marines, and Air Force were supposed to clear the air over the drop zone in preparation for their arrival.

Merriman was deeply thankful for both pieces of intel but also skeptical. The larger strategic picture told a different story. The PLA was ignoring the eastern side of the island, including Hualien, while they focused on capturing the more populated western side of Taiwan and crushing the last remnants of the Taiwanese military. The United States was taking advantage of the PLA indifference to gain a foothold on the island.

But *gaining* a foothold and *keeping* a foothold were two entirely different things.

Once we kick that dragon in the balls, Merriman thought, we're gonna find out that Mr. Dragon has some really big teeth.

Four days. Ninety-six hours.

That's how long they needed to hold Hualien. Long enough for the Marines who were sailing from San Diego to land in force.

Four days was a long time. Their survival depended on being able to land military transport planes on the Hualien airfield for resupply. If the PLA woke up and decided to retake Hualien, either from the ground or in the air—or both—it was going to be one hairy situation.

Merriman bit down on the CamelBak tube again and swallowed another mouthful of water. He pulled himself to his feet and pushed through the narrow aisle of seated paratroopers to the front of the C-17 cargo bay where a cluster of soldiers huddled over laptops.

Colonel Anne Pratchett, the 18th Airborne Corps G3, or Chief of Staff for Operations, led the discussion. By her side was Captain Margaret "Peg" Corcoran, Merriman's S2 intel officer. Corcoran had gotten her nickname not from her given name but from her ability to "peg" the target in the drop zone during accuracy contests. Rounding out the meeting were Major Sam Turner, the battalion exec, and Sergeant Major Royal "Eight Ball" Jackson, the senior enlisted man in the battalion.

Merriman raised an eyebrow at Jackson to ask if there was anything new since he'd left. Jackson's dark bald scalp gleamed as he shook his head no.

Pratchett ran a tight operation. The team had been at it since they'd departed Pearl, fleshing out the battle plan as new intel came in from INDOPACOM's J2.

The clock was ticking. Whatever information they had now was as good as it was going to get.

Merriman joined the circle. He got a nod from Pratchett that she wanted Captain Corcoran to do the briefing.

"All right, Peg," Merriman spoke over the engine noise in the cargo bay. "Tell me what we've got."

Corcoran had a mop of cropped brown curls and a square jaw. She flipped her ruggedized tablet around to show the team and ran through the briefing material. Merriman listened carefully to the details of their drop zone, rally point, and an overview of what they expected on the ground.

Merriman cut a glance at Pratchett for her seal of approval and got the nod. He jerked his head to the back of the plane. "Good job, Peg," he said. "You lead the briefing. I'll be along in a minute."

When Merriman was alone with Pratchett, he leaned closer. "What do you think, ma'am?"

Merriman had a lot of respect for Pratchett. She could have remained back at Hickam and taken the second lift into Taiwan with the Corps commander. Not only had she volunteered for the first jump, but she insisted on being in the lead aircraft.

Pratchett grinned at him. "It's as good a plan as we're going to get with the intel we have, Kevin. It'll change a thousand times once we hit the ground."

Merriman appreciated her attempt at humor, but he knew her well enough to see past the bravado. This entire operation was a seat-of-the-pants, Hail Mary operation, and they both knew it.

The plane hit a pocket of air turbulence, jostling them together.

"I appreciate you being here, ma'am," Merriman said.

Pratchett chose to evade the compliment. "Corcoran's solid," she replied. "We'll both be working for her one day."

"Ten minutes!"

The order from the lead jumpmaster rang out. All the seated soldiers in the cargo bay, including Merriman, echoed the call. His heart ran like a triphammer—it always did before a jump. He controlled his breathing.

"Stand up!"

The young men and women of the 1st Battalion, 502nd Infantry, each wearing one hundred pounds of combat gear, were helped to their feet by members of the aircrew. Merriman gripped the outstretched hands of two soldiers and heaved them upright. A few paces away, Eight Ball did the same thing.

The energy in the air was like a living organism, an insane mixture of fear, excitement, dread, joy.

He saw fear in the eyes of his soldiers—that was healthy. Fear focused the mind and raised the adrenaline.

"You ready, soldier?" he shouted in the face of the next man.

"Ready, sir!" the man yelled back.

Merriman laughed out loud and moved on to the next soldier until they were all on their feet.

He heard the C-17's engines change tune and felt the floor tilt as the transport began an aggressive descent to drop altitude. From his place at the front of the cargo bay, four lines of paratroopers faced him.

"Hook up!" came the next order from the lead jumpmaster.

In unison, the four lines of paratroopers unclipped their yellow static lines and attached the hook to overhead cables strung the length of the cargo bay. They inserted a small cotter pin into the hook and bent it to ensure it stayed in place.

"Check equipment!"

Merriman watched as every soldier ran their hands across their gear one last time, feeling for sharp edges, checking the cotter pin on their own gear. Then they checked the gear of the soldier in front of them.

"Sound off for equipment check!"

The paratroopers at the back of each line slapped the soldier in front of them on the backside.

"One, OK!"

"Two, OK!"

The equipment check calls at Merriman's position.

Merriman signaled the jumpmaster. Crewmen on both sides of the cargo bay cracked the doors open, and he felt the pressure change in his ears. The jet engines screamed and wind noise roared into the cargo bay as the doors rolled upward.

Merriman felt his stomach drop. The open doorway was a black hole in the red-lighted cargo bay.

"Stand in the door!"

Merriman stepped forward and gripped both sides of the door frame. His breath came in short huffs. To his right, at eye level, a red light glared at him.

Five hundred feet beneath them, Merriman thought he detected a change in the texture of the ground below. They left the flat glimmer of the ocean for the darkness of land. He saw distant lights on the ground.

The red light shifted to green.

"Go!" the jumpmaster yelled at Merriman.

Merriman stepped forward and leaped into the darkness.

Silence surrounded him. The noisy rush of air was gone. He was falling.

Muscle memory took over. He clamped his feet and knees together and counted out loud.

"One one-thousand, two one-thousand, three one-thousand, four one—"

His parachute snapped open, jerking him upright. He hauled on a riser to take a quick glance over his shoulder. Hundreds of US Army paratroopers hung in the night sky, soldiers swinging gently back and forth like so many pendulums.

Feet and knees together! The command was drilled into the brain of every airborne candidate.

He sensed the ground was near, but it wasn't clearly visible in the darkness. The line with his pack dangled ten feet below him. The line went slack, and a split second later he hit the ground at thirteen miles per hour. His training took over, executing a PLF—parachute landing fall—his feet hit first, then calves, thighs, butt before he executed a shoulder roll to bleed off the last momentum of his impact.

Merriman popped one of his risers, releasing the chute. The adrenaline rush and muscle memory had him on his feet and out of his harness before he processed a single thought.

All around him, hundreds of parachutes drifted to the ground. He could hear no enemy gunfire.

Merriman got his bearings. In the east, over the ocean, the sky was beginning to lighten.

He pulled his rifle, shouldered his pack, and headed for the rally point.

48

Hsinchu City, Taiwan

Mission Clock: 40:10:49
Mission Status: Red

Lieutenant Colonel Gao's driver navigated the clogged highways surrounding the industrial metropolis of Hsinchu City. The roads were choked not by the Taiwanese natives but by PLA ground force vehicles headed south to crush what remained of the Taiwanese Army.

Early morning sun touched the massive factories lining both sides of the highway. They were giant buildings, most with floor plans larger than a football pitch and soaring ten stories or more in the air. Here was the economic engine of Taiwan. Hsinchu manufactured flat-screen televisions, LED billboards, semiconductor computer chips, and other expensive electronics. They competed with the People's Republic of China all over the world.

No longer, Gao thought. In another day, when Zhang's forces from Taipei connected with General Wei's forces from the south, Taiwan would once again be part of the PRC.

That is assuming they managed to clear this epic traffic jam.

Gao's driver braked behind a seven-and-a-half-ton heavy transport loaded with boxes of ammunition. He laid on the horn and cursed. The six-by-six vehicle belched diesel smoke and inched away from the concrete barrier on the elevated highway. The driver nosed into the narrow opening, then punched the accelerator.

The sudden shift in speed jolted Gao from his thoughts. It hurt, too. His right arm was in a sling, a going-away present from the old man he had killed on Mount Chuyun. Gao started to smile, then remembered the stitches along his right jawline.

Gao was among the walking wounded now, but he wore his injuries with pride. No one would be able to say Lieutenant Colonel Gao had not given his all in the invasion of Taiwan.

His report to General Zhang was not required, strictly speaking. His injuries could have, should have, kept him confined to his hospital bed, but Gao was not about to miss this victory lap with his boss.

He had gambled and won. In one fell swoop, he had recovered the missing Shandian tablet, destroyed the Taiwanese terrorist base, and executed an American agent on Taiwanese soil.

Not a bad day's work. Using his left hand, he pulled out his tablet.

This was now his third Shandian tablet in a week. The last one had saved his life. Had the tablet not been in his hip pocket, the American's combat knife would have gutted Gao like a fish. Still, the American was good. Although the tablet had stopped the killing blow, the man had still managed to slice into Gao's right arm and up the side of his face.

I was lucky, Gao thought. Maybe more than lucky. Blessed.

On the face of the battle network tablet, the mission clock was still red, but the invasion was gathering speed toward a satisfactory conclusion. Nothing could stop the PLA now. Taiwan was within their grasp.

He closed his eyes and rested his head against the back of the seat. The painkillers they had given him at the hospital were wearing off, but Gao was determined to be present when Zhang's and Wei's forces met in the city of Taichung.

The Taiwanese President, her cabinet, and top military leaders would be on hand to sign the Taichung Accord, the document that dissolved the

Taiwanese government and returned the province to its historical place as part of the People's Republic of China.

Technically, the PLA still had not dealt with the eastern side of the island, but the political decision had been made to stage the signing early, before the Americans could cause any more trouble.

The driver swung the vehicle into the parking lot of the Taiwan Semiconductor Manufacturing Corporation. The manicured lawns in front of the gleaming high-tech building were in need of cutting, and the parking lot was empty save for General Zhang's mobile command operations center.

Gao waited for the driver to park and open his door. The driver fussed as he draped Gao's camouflage uniform tunic over his slinged arm. After his release from the hospital, Gao changed into more comfortable civilian clothes that did not put stress on his injuries, but he wanted to wear at least a semblance of a uniform for his report to General Zhang. Besides, the awkward dress drew extra attention to his battle wounds.

Zhang's mobile command post was an expandable van with an assortment of host vehicles and generators clustered around it. Gao climbed the three steps, waited for the driver to open the door for him, and entered the heavily air-conditioned space.

General Zhang stood in the center of the room, studying a holographic display of the island of Taiwan. Banks of computer screens manned by PLA soldiers with headsets flanked him on either side.

When Zhang looked up, he smiled. "Colonel Gao," he said, "you returned to witness our final drive to conquer Taiwan."

Zhang held out his hand, and Gao gave him a left-handed return grip.

"It is my honor to be present for such a great day, General." Gao lowered his head modestly, sending a wave of pain across the stitches on his chin. The local anesthetic they'd given him was definitely wearing off.

Zhang led him to his private office at the front of the command post. The small room housed a desk, one chair, and a neatly made-up cot folded down from the wall. Gao stood awkwardly as the general made tea.

Gao was amazed at Zhang's change in demeanor. Gone was the angry, frustrated leader from the thirty-sixth floor of the Taipei 101 tower. This man was happy, excited. He hummed to himself as he worked.

General Zhang was a true soldier, Gao realized. He loved being in the field with his troops. Zhang poured tea into two cups and passed one to Gao.

"To your second Medal of Loyalty and Integrity," the general said. "When this day is done and we have linked north and south Taiwan in victory, we will share a more appropriate beverage."

Zhang settled into the only chair and gestured for Gao to sit on the bunk. "Tell me of your operations in the south of Taiwan," Zhang said.

"I am pleased to report that the Taiwanese terrorist operation has been crushed, sir," Gao began. He outlined a heavily redacted version of how he had located and destroyed the secret terrorist base on Mount Chuyun.

Gao made no mention of the lost tablet or of the American he had killed. He also made no mention of the twelve PLA soldiers who had died in the blast when the terrorist base was destroyed.

"You have done well, Colonel," Zhang said. "I chose well when I promoted you."

"Thank you, sir," Gao said. "For your trust in my discretion."

"And were you able to exercise that discretion in the other matter?" Zhang asked quietly.

For a brief moment, Gao wondered if it was possible this conversation was being recorded. He felt the sudden tremor of fear. He chose his next words carefully.

"I was able to spend much time with General Wei, sir," he said. "The general is giving you his full support. I found no evidence of any corruption or back-dealing in his operation."

Zhang leaned forward on his desk. "You're sure?"

The words were exactly what Gao and Wei had agreed on. His job was to set Zhang's mind at ease until the invasion was complete. Then Wei would swoop in and capture the governorship. Gao was offered a career choice: a second promotion to full colonel or a career in politics.

"I see," Zhang said. "And the supply chain interruptions?"

"A ghost in the bureaucracy, General," Gao said. "In an operation of this size and speed, supply chain problems are inevitable."

Zhang's happy mood seemed to evaporate, but before he could say anything else, the intercom on his desk buzzed.

"Are we ready to move?" he said in answer.

"No, sir," came the reply. "We have new information coming in. Priority message from Beijing."

"Well, what is it?"

"I think it best if you see for yourself, sir."

Gao followed Zhang into the main command center, where a captain wearing the insignia of the intel corps waited next to the holographic display.

"General," the captain said, "we're experiencing a disturbance on the eastern side of the island."

"What does that mean?" Zhang demanded. "Disturbance?"

The captain used his tablet like a shield between him and the general. He pointed to the display. Whereas the rest of the interactive map bristled with integrated data readings, the area around Hualien was blank.

"We don't have any drone coverage in that area. The United States forces have launched aggressive electronic countermeasures," the intel officer said. He hesitated. "What should I do?"

"Redirect air resources and get me some answers, Captain!" roared Zhang.

"Yes, sir." The officer scurried away, leaving Zhang and Gao at the display.

Gao felt the truck that the command post was built on rumble to life. Zhang's face clouded with irritation.

"I don't have time for this," Zhang said. "I need to get to Taichung immediately."

Gao saw the real problem. The general did not want Wei to reach Taichung before he did, and he certainly did not want Wei to sign the Taichung Accord without him.

The display updated just as the captain hurried back.

"Sir, new information." Gao thought the young man might hyperventilate. "We have a report of three American aircraft carriers only eighty kilometers east of Hualien."

Gao felt a prickling sensation run up his back. The Americans had breached the emergency zone? Was it possible the Americans were launching a counterattack? His chest tightened. What if his lost tablet had given them the needed intel to attack?

"Sir," Gao said, "it might be prudent to move forces from Taipei down the eastern coast. As a precaution."

"I agree," Zhang said. "Order General Ho to move one of his two divisions down the coast road and capture the city of Hualien," he ordered his aide. "I'm going to recommend to Beijing that we attack the American carriers."

"General," Gao said. "I wish to be useful, sir. Useful to you, to the success of the invasion."

"There is one thing." Zhang looked thoughtful.

"Anything, sir. No matter how small."

Zhang moved closer and lowered his voice. "I need someone I can trust. I want you to be my eyes and ears at Hualien."

49

Mission Clock: 39:55:12
Mission Status: Red

Minister of State Security Fei Zhen despised tardiness. He hated it when people failed to arrive on time for a meeting with him. Lack of punctuality showed a gross lack of self-discipline. Which was why, as his chauffeured vehicle entered the parking garage under the Great Hall of the People, Fei was furious with himself.

He should have been happy. Last night was the first time he had gotten a good night's sleep in months. The miraculous new pain meds had kept at bay the never-ending ache of his cancerous guts for the entire night.

True, he had overslept, but not more than a few moments, and not enough to impact his driving time.

What made him late was what he saw on his drive to the Great Hall: a demonstration taking place in Tiananmen Square.

Fei had ordered his driver to stop the car. He stepped out into the chill morning air. It was barely dawn in downtown Beijing, and yet there were hundreds of people in the Square. And they were protesting against the government.

Free Taiwan, read one sign. *Stop imperialism*, read another.

Fei thought he might be hallucinating from the new medicine. This level of dissent had not been seen in the city since 1989, long before most of the young people before him were even born.

He got back into the limo. One crisis at a time, he thought. Taiwan first, demonstrations later. Let the local police deal with this for now. His office would ferret out the instigators. There was nowhere to run in China that could not be reached by the umbrella of the Ministry of State Security.

Inside the parking garage, Fei scarcely waited for the car to stop before he opened his own door and got out. Although the garage was icy and damp, he did not bother to put on his overcoat. He just hurried past the plainclothes guard. The elevator to the subterranean secure conference room was operated by a dull-eyed functionary who did not seem to understand the meaning of time. He reached the meeting room, only to be stopped by another security man who inspected his ID and compared it to a list before he cleared him for entry.

Finally, Fei snatched back his ID and opened the heavy door on his own. He could smell it as soon as he stepped inside.

Fear.

The conversation in progress stopped suddenly. The door shut behind him with a heavy *thunk*, punctuation to the ensuing silence.

He sighed to himself. Fearful men made poor decisions. They looked to distance themselves from the crisis and shift the blame elsewhere, anywhere but on themselves.

Fei had his work cut out for him. He was not worried. Forty years in service of the State had prepared him for moments like this one.

Fei bowed to the General Secretary, then to the room at large. "I apologize for my lateness, gentlemen. My rudeness is unforgivable."

"Your absence gave us a chance to bring the committee up to date on recent events," the General Secretary said, his tone laden with meaning.

Fei had seen the update on the Shandian battle network. The American carrier strike force was less than a hundred kilometers from the shores of Taiwan.

For the life of him, Fei could not fathom the American strategy. Three aircraft carriers within striking range of Chinese weapons, inside the declared emergency zone around the province of Taiwan. It was as if the United States was begging to be destroyed.

But any action taken would depend on the opinions of the men in this room. And a decision of that magnitude would require strength of spirit.

Maybe the Americans weren't so stupid after all, Fei thought. He let his face betray none of these colliding emotions.

"And what is the opinion of the esteemed committee?" Fei asked.

Instead of answering, the General Secretary directed his gaze to the Vice Chairman of the Central Military Commission. As usual, the Vice Chairman was fingering an unlit cigarette.

"Would you like a light, comrade?" Fei asked the man.

"I'm trying to quit smoking," he said.

A gentle laugh filtered through the room.

Encouraging, Fei thought. Where there is humor, there is hope.

"Surely you see this turn of events as an opportunity, Mr. Chairman," Fei said.

"I hardly think three United States aircraft carriers off the coast of Taiwan and another in the South China Sea as cause for celebration," the Vice Chairman said acidly, his face growing red.

"I did not say celebration, sir," Fei replied, "I said opportunity."

Fei had not yet seated himself. He took his time draping his overcoat on the back of his chair. He stayed on his feet.

"The United States possesses eleven aircraft carriers. China has only three," Fei said. "It takes the US Navy more than a decade to build a single ship and make it fully operational. But when they are completed, they are fearsome platforms, able to project the might of the United States anywhere in the world."

Fei paced now. He did not rush. If he pressed them too hard, they would resist. If he did not press them hard enough, they would not be bold.

"But now, at this very moment, four of the United States Navy's carrier fleet is within range of our forces." Fei cut a look at the General Secretary. As usual, it was pointless. The man's features might as well have been carved out of wood.

"We have declared a national emergency in Taiwan—as is our right. We made it clear to the world that one hundred kilometers from the coast of Taiwan was an exclusion zone, controlled only by the People's Liberation Army Navy."

Fei reached the end of the table opposite the General Secretary. He braced his knuckles on the dark wood. "The United States has violated that policy with impunity. They have disregarded, and disrespected, our lawful orders. Their action demands a response."

Silence. Fei watched as the men at the table traded glances. They were not there yet.

"Comrades," the Minister continued, "by this time tomorrow morning, the former Taiwanese government will have signed the Taichung Accord. The province of Taiwan will once again be ours. We will have achieved the goal we set out to accomplish."

Fei's pacing brought him back to his chair. He rested his hands on the carved wooden back.

"But now we have been given a new opportunity," the Minister said. "If we destroy the American carriers, we not only teach the United States a much-needed lesson. We can change the balance of power in the world. Right here, right now."

Fei spread his arms wide. "Think of it. The United States Navy goes from eleven carriers to seven. Meanwhile, the PLA Navy will add three more carriers to our fleet in the next two years. We will be at parity with the United States Navy!" He clapped his hands together. The sound echoed in the meeting room.

"But only if we seize the initiative."

Fei had them. He could see it in their eyes. What had been fear was now confidence.

"Sail the fleet out of the Strait of Taiwan," the Minister shouted. "Meet the American forces at sea. Engage the carriers with our superior numbers in the air, then crush them under a hail of missiles!"

The Vice Chairman stood again. "Honorable General Secretary, I move that we order the Navy to engage the United States carrier strike force immediately."

The man trembled with patriotic passion. The unlit cigarette was a pile of shredded tobacco and paper.

The vote carried unanimously. The Minister had done it. If only for a moment, he'd turned this flock of sheep into warrior wolves.

But a moment was all it took to bend the arc of history to the will of the State.

As the meeting ended, the General Secretary laid a heavy hand on Fei's arm.

"I am told there were protesters in the Square this morning, Minister," he said.

"A small crowd, sir," Fei replied quickly. "I'm dealing with it."

"See that you do."

50

PLA Navy submarine *Changzheng 12*
8 miles south of Mianhua Islet, Taiwan

Mission Clock: 36:47:12
Mission Status: Red

Captain Chu wanted to shout at the political officer, but he contained his frustration. A petty display of emotion would not help the situation. Besides, the rumor that surveillance equipment was installed on board his submarine was never far from his mind.

Commander Sun is only doing his job, Chu thought to himself, but that doesn't make him any less wrong.

They were alone in the wardroom. After the evening meal, which was abnormally quiet, Sun asked the other officers to clear the room. He poured tea for his captain, placed an electronic tablet on the table between them, and said, "We need to talk, sir."

The conversation quickly went sideways.

While Chu was managing his emotions, Sun was decidedly less so. Normally easygoing and genial, the political officer's style was a rarity in his profession. In Chu's experience, Commander Sun never dictated the Party's decisions. He always used his considerable powers of persuasion to convince the people around him of the wisdom and generosity of the Party.

But now, his lean features were stern with his resentment, and he scowled darkly at the captain.

"You are making a mistake, Captain," Sun said in a hot tone. He must have heard himself because he stopped, took a deep breath, and exhaled. "I am telling you this for your own good, sir."

Chu dropped his gaze to the tablet containing recent message traffic, the source of their argument. Less than an hour ago, the *Changzheng* had received new orders to support the movement of the fleet. The PLA Navy was mobilizing to meet the United States aircraft carrier strike force.

Fair enough, Chu thought. There was nothing he would like better than to add an American warship to his record as the first PLA submarine to kill a Taiwanese destroyer.

Well, there was one thing: killing an American nuclear submarine.

Managing submarine movements was a bureaucratic process. Unlike surface ships or airplanes, the exact location of a submarine was never known by their superior officers. Submarines were assigned vast tracts of water to patrol. Where in that space a submarine commander chose to operate was his prerogative, in consultation with his political officer.

And that was the root of their argument.

Beijing had expanded the waterspace of the *Changzheng* outward into the Pacific but left their current operating space close to shore in place. Sun wanted to drive the *Changzheng* eastward into the Pacific Ocean to support the PLA Navy movement. Captain Chu wanted to stay close to shore on the chance that his ship might find—and kill—the elusive enemy submarine.

"The American submarine will come back," Chu said. "I know it."

"The American fleet is out there now," Sun snapped back, pointing toward the wall.

He's pointing west, toward China, Chu thought wryly.

"Your Party needs you to do your duty, promptly and without question," Sun continued. "Your country requires it."

In the two days the *Changzheng* had waited for the American to return, they had not gotten even a hint of her presence. It was possible the US sub had come and gone. Hunting for submerged contacts using passive sensors was never an easy task. The recent storms and incessant PLA Navy surface fleet movements only made a challenging problem more difficult.

But the American would be back, Chu could feel it. Whatever they were doing that required them to make multiple trips this close to shore was not over.

And this time, he was ready for them.

With Sun's help, Chu had convinced Beijing to give him three *Kilo*-class diesel-electric submarines to set up a screen for the American's next visit to the Mianhua Islet. Sun had been more than helpful. He threw his full support behind the request, and Beijing had responded. Now, the political officer expected the same consideration from the captain—and he was not getting it.

What's the point of this argument? Chu thought. In less than six hours, their assignment to this operating area expired, and the *Changzheng* would be forced to depart. He was within his right to stay on station to hunt for the American sub.

Sun pinched the bridge of his nose between his thumb and index finger and clenched his eyes shut.

"Then at least release the other subs," he said. "Let them support our Navy comrades. There is no need for them to suffer for your foolish pride."

Chu started to get up.

"I apologize, Captain," Sun said quickly. "That was uncalled for. But I ask you to consider what you are doing. In the context of the greater good, sir. In the context of your *career*."

And there it was, Chu thought. The knife behind the veil. If you do not do what I say, I have the power to destroy you. This wasn't about the greater good at all. This was about getting close to the glory. It wasn't about doing what was right, because Chu knew he was right. It was about doing what was politically expedient.

On paper, Commander Sun had the ability to order the *Changzheng* to leave the area for a different mission, but Sun would not be that foolish. Political officers did not dictate orders to captains of naval vessels. They cajoled, they persuaded, they threatened, but they did not order. That would be career suicide for Commander Sun, and he knew it.

The only way the *Changzheng* was leaving the leeward side of the Mianhua Islet was if Captain Chu gave the order.

And he was not going to do that. At least not yet. Still, maybe there was a way to give the political officer a partial win.

"I will release two of the *Kilo*-class submarines," Chu said. "Will that be sufficient, Commander?"

Sun nodded. He knew he was beaten. "Thank you, Captain. For your consideration of my concerns."

He started to get up, then paused.

"You only have six hours left in this operating area," he said. "What do you propose to do?"

Chu changed screens on the tablet, calling up an underwater bathymetric survey of the area south of the Mianhua Islet. He enlarged the screen until they were looking at two spikes of rock surrounded by a kilometer-wide open plain. In the jumble of underwater features, the two rocky towers stood out clearly on the screen.

"Submarine captains call this feature The Twins," Chu said. "We will place the remaining *Kilo* here"—he pointed to a spot on the screen—"and we will be here." Chu pointed to the open area.

Sun studied the screen. "You're that sure the American will come?" he asked. "Why?"

"Because that is what I would do."

51

5 miles east of Mianhua Islet

Janet squinted through the bow window of the *Manta*. The work lights carved a cone of illumination on the sea floor. Seven hundred yards to seaward, the *Orca* was in station-keeping mode at a matching six knots.

Janet's eyes burned from the chemicals in the jury-rigged CO_2 removal system. To add to her discomfort, the mini-sub smelled like a public toilet thanks to an unfortunate spill of the bucket that had served as their makeshift sanitary facilities.

The shitty smell of failure, she thought. All of their work, all the risk to the *Manta* and to the *Idaho* had made little difference that she could see.

The PLA invasion down the western side of Taiwan was in progress. Maybe their efforts at misinformation had delayed the start of the final drive, but it was too little too late. According to the message traffic Mark had intercepted, in a matter of hours the ground forces driving from the PLA strongholds in the north and south of Taiwan would meet in a city called Taichung. There, the former independent government of Taiwan would sign the Taichung Accord, formally turning over the island to the People's Republic of China.

The invasion of Taiwan was all over but the shouting, she thought.

And their mission was over, which was not a bad thing. Janet was beyond exhausted. The stress of being the *Manta's* pilot, copilot, and operator of the *Orca* combined with the extended mission length left her with no reserves.

A boulder the size of a minivan loomed out of the dark, and Janet veered to the right.

Focus, she told herself. She returned the *Manta* to base course with some difficulty. The underwater current here was strong, which meant she was constantly fighting against the push of the ocean. Once they made the next turn, the Mianhua Islet would shield the *Manta* from the fierce currents and she could relax.

After the turn, it was less than an hour to the rendezvous point of the Twin Towers and the safety of the *Idaho*.

They were almost home.

Mark napped in the copilot's seat. He looked as bad as she felt. His skin was pasty, and he'd spilled something on the front of his uniform. She wasn't sure if she was smelling herself or Mark, but both of them were in desperate need of a shower.

And all for what? Janet grimaced at her distorted reflection in the convex window. After their stunning success in the Sea of Okhotsk cable tap against the Russians, perhaps she had expected too much.

Save the world once? Why not go for two times? She laughed at her own inflated ego. Captain Lannier was right. She had a savior complex. She took too many chances because deep down she believed she was the only one who could perform the mission.

The navigation computer chimed softly, indicating their waypoint. She turned to a new base course, their final leg of the journey. The current slackened as the *Manta* entered the leeward side of the Mianhua Islet.

She leaned back in her seat. Almost home. The external hydrophone was patched into the intercom, and the sounds of their ocean environment filled the cabin like a meditation.

Janet found it soothing. The crackle of tiny shrimp, the suss of waves, the occasional whale song echoing through the ocean depths. It was mysterious and beautiful, like a sound puzzle.

Now she heard something else, a distant warble. She increased the volume of the speaker. A background hiss filled the cabin.

Nothing. Seconds passed, then she heard the noise again. It had rhythm, like music, pacing. It sounded like a warbling kazoo or—

An underwater telephone.

Of course, it was rhythmic, it was someone speaking. In Mandarin.

She slowed the *Manta* and slapped Mark on the shoulder.

"Wake up," she said, "and listen to this. Can you understand it?"

Mark startled awake. The whites of his eyes were bloodshot pink.

"What?" he said.

Janet shifted the input on the hydrophone and tossed him a pair of headphones. "Listen. Can you make out what they're saying?"

Mark pressed the headphones against his ears and closed his eyes.

Janet's mind raced. An underwater telephone meant a PLA submarine was communicating with another ship. Their rendezvous point was compromised. She needed to warn the *Idaho*.

"I don't hear anything," Mark said.

"Keep listening," Janet replied. She drove along the bearing of the last transmission. There was little chance of an underwater collision. The *Manta*'s depth gauge read 310 feet, and she was only a few meters off the bottom. In this water depth, no submarine captain in his right mind would take his ship any lower than two hundred feet.

Janet increased her speed and checked her position on the chart. The last bearing to the PLA sub was close to the Twin Towers. Too close.

"What is that?" Mark asked, pointing at the broadband display. Steady white pips marched down the screen.

"That is a high-frequency submarine fathometer," Janet replied. She angled the submersible upward.

"Fathometers measure depth, right?" Mark asked. "So, they're located on the bottom of the sub."

"Yup," Janet replied. "They're above us."

"You're going up," Mark said. "Is that a good idea?"

Janet didn't answer. She didn't have to. The steel skin of a submerged submarine filled the bow window. She immediately dove underneath it.

"Jesus Christ." Mark gripped the armrest of his chair. "Won't they see the lights?"

"Nope," Janet said with a gasp. She realized she was holding her breath and let it out in an explosive rush. When she had safely passed beneath the PLA submarine, she turned to parallel its course.

"Well, won't they hear us?" Mark asked.

"I don't think so," Janet said.

"You don't *think* so?" Mark shot back. "What if you're wrong?"

"Quiet," Janet hissed. "I'm trying to think."

Judging by the size and configuration, she was looking at a nuclear PLA sub. The ship traveled on an east-west course, which put its towed array perpendicular to the path of the incoming *Idaho*.

This submarine had been talking to someone, so there was at least one more ship out there. The sonar display showed no sign of a PLA surface ship, so the other ship must be a submarine.

The *Idaho* was driving into a trap—and there was nothing she could do about it.

Janet called up the *Orca* control screen and ordered up a search pattern to the south. She kept the underwater drone within range of the laser comms system.

"What are we going to do?" Mark asked.

"I don't know," she said.

Her control screen flashed a message. Janet cursed.

"What?" Mark said.

"It's the *Idaho*'s homing beacon," Janet said. "They're close."

A new sound radiated from the hydrophone speaker. Metallic scraping, then a noise like a plunger that showed up on the broadband display as a heavy blotch. A second later, a whining noise.

"That's a torpedo!" Janet said. "Somebody shot at the *Idaho*!"

But it wasn't the submarine they were trailing, Janet realized, and the Chinese plan crystallized in her brain. This sub was waiting for the *Idaho* to fire a return shot. When the *Idaho* revealed her position, the PLA submarine would shoot to kill.

Janet acted on instinct. She drove directly at the PLA submarine.

"What are you doing?" Mark shouted. "You're going to hit it."

"That's the point," Janet said.

She aimed for the area just behind the sail. When the *Manta* scraped along the hull, she energized the powerful electromagnet that was used to lock the submersible to the *Idaho*'s steel hull. Only this time she was locking onto the back of an enemy submarine.

She called up the *Orca*'s command screen and energized the active sonar.

A blast of sonic energy rang through the hull of the *Manta*. The data from the *Orca*'s fire control system appeared on Janet's monitor.

There was only one target: a massive steel PLA submarine a mere thousand yards off the *Orca*'s bow. And the *Manta* was clamped on top of the target.

"Janet?" Mark said.

"I'm sorry, Mark," she replied.

Then she launched the *Orca*'s torpedo.

PLA submarine *Changzheng 12*
5 miles south of Mianhua Islet, Taiwan

"New submerged contact bearing two-seven-six, Captain," the sonar supervisor shouted. "We have the hundred-ninety-eight hertz tonal, sir. It's the American! It's him!"

The announcement rang in the control room like a rifle shot. Captain Chu smiled triumphantly at Commander Sun.

"What's his range, Sonar?" Chu said.

"Working on it, sir," the sonar supervisor said. "We'll need another leg on him before I can give you an accurate estimate."

Chu took a steadying breath. Of course, they needed more data to refine their firing solution. He knew that. He must not rush his people. This time there could be no mistakes.

"Torpedo launch, bearing zero-three-zero, Captain!" the sonar supe said. "It's ours. It's the *Kilo* firing on the American!"

Chu cursed. He had earned the right to kill the American, but if the other submarine commander had the shot, it was his duty to strike first.

I can use this to my advantage, Chu thought. If the American fires back, the *Changzheng* will have him. There was no way the American sub could outrun two torpedoes.

The sonar chief had his eyes clenched shut, hands clamped over his headphones. His eyes flew open.

"Launch transients, bearing two-nine-eight, range five thousand yards. The American is firing back."

I have you, Chu thought.

"Firing point procedures," Chu said. "Tube one—"

Above his head, Chu heard a screech of metal on metal, then a *ka-CHUNG* rang through the hull.

"What the hell was that?" Commander Sun shouted. His voice pitched up in fear.

"Sound the collision alarm," Chu shouted.

We must have run into something, Chu thought. Something metal—

The broadband sonar display in front of him went white with sonic energy. Then a pure tone rang through the hull.

PANG!

"Active sonar off our beam, Captain! It's close!' The sonar chief's voice rose a full octave. "Torpedo in the water!"

"Pilot, all ahead flank!" Chu roared. The engine room responded almost instantly. Chu felt the ship tremble as the throttle opened on the main engines.

"Active homing!"

It's not too late, Chu thought, it's not too late.

"Range gating!"

His eyes locked onto the sonar chief's gaze. There was a pleading quality in the man's eyes.

It was too late.

Chu gripped the nearest stanchion. With his free hand, he snatched up the shipwide intercom microphone.

"All hands, brace for—"

The torpedo exploded.

52

USS *Enterprise* strike force
50 miles east of Hualien, Taiwan

Sharratt had been standing in the same place for so long that his feet felt numb. His fingers clenched the steel rail bordering the BattleSpace tabletop display. His forearms ached from the strain of gripping the metal bar, his thigh muscles quivered.

He glanced up at the clock. The battle to take back Taiwan was less than three hours old.

The Battle Watch staff worked in tight precision, the air filled with a constant flow of orders, responses, and updates. The adrenaline rush was long gone, replaced by the muscle memory of how to do your job.

Still, the room held an undercurrent of tension. They knew their ship— their home—was in enemy waters.

Paratroopers of the 101st Airborne Division had landed safely in Hualien. That is, Sharratt reflected, if you considered the act of jumping out of a perfectly good airplane onto an enemy-held island a "safe" activity. He might talk smack about Army on the football field, but those soldiers knew their business on the battlefield.

The *Enterprise* strike force's air dominance missions created just enough space to get the US Army on the ground. The 1st and 3rd Brigade Combat Teams had taken the Hualien airfield within an hour of landing on Taiwanese soil.

Mission accomplished, Sharratt told himself. Good job. Now all he had to do was make sure his Army comrades-in-arms didn't get slaughtered on that same ground.

The threat was twofold. The PLA had finally woken up. The air over Hualien was a hornet's nest of red and blue tracks as the Chinese fought back with their superior numbers of aircraft. The strike force had lost another six F-35s and twelve UCAVs.

The Chinese had lost more planes—a lot more—but they were starting with an enormous surplus. In a war of attrition, the US lost every time.

"Admiral, we've got another supply plane trying to land at Hualien," the Battle Watch Officer reported. "I've got video."

Sharratt turned his head to view the flat-screen off to the right. The footage getting beamed in from the high-flying overwatch drones was sharp and clear.

The C-17 Globemaster approached from the southeast. The massive four-engine craft dwarfed the fighter escorts, a six-pack of Air Force F-35s. A second C-17 hung in the air miles behind the lead aircraft.

The strike force CAG had been coordinating this approach for the last thirty minutes, trying to clear an air corridor for supply runs to the Army forces on the ground. The 18th Airborne Corps advance elements had dropped with the essential equipment to take the airfield and establish control of the area. The few thousand soldiers were just a beachhead on an island with over one hundred thousand PLA troops. Resupply was essential to their success.

Sharratt watched the lead C-17 make what looked like a painfully slow descent. The friendly fighters moved like bees around the airborne beast.

The Globemaster touched down. The picture was so good that Sharratt could see a puff of smoke when the wheels hit the tarmac. A cheer went up in Battle Watch. High fives, fist pumps.

"Bogeys inbound!" Sharratt heard the call on the open net. His eyes snapped back to the BattleSpace screen.

Three separate pairs of PLA fighters converged on the second C-17 lined up for an approach into Hualien. He watched as the F-35 escorts vectored for an intercept, but not before the Chinese pilots released their air-to-air missiles.

"Tracking four...eight...twelve missiles inbound," the watch officer called. "ETA one minute."

The C-17 pilot broke off his approach, turning south, leaving a series of flares in his wake. Sharratt saw a flash as one of the missiles connected in midair. A UCAV signal on the BattleSpace display winked out.

A zip of light flashed across the video screen, and the fleeing C-17 exploded.

Battle Watch went silent, numb.

"Back to your stations, people," Zachary roared. "We need to do better."

They did need to do better. Unless they were able to support the soldiers already landed, it was entirely possible that the US forces might win the air war and lose the ground battle.

"What's the ETA on those PLA troops coming down from Taipei?" Sharratt asked the watch officer.

"An hour, sir," the watch officer replied. "One point five, if we're lucky."

The BattleSpace shifted the display to give Sharratt and Zachary a close-in view of the area north of Hualien. He could see now why the Army had chosen this place to land.

Four miles north of the city, the coastal mountain range ran down to within a few hundred yards of the Pacific Ocean. That was where the bulk of the US Army forces would dig in.

"What's the name of that place?" Sharratt asked.

"Manbo Beach," came the reply.

A pleasant name for what was shaping up to be an unpleasant battle. Neither side was going to win through airpower alone, and both knew it.

If the Chinese intended to retake Hualien, they needed to pass through Manbo Beach. If the US forces wanted to keep Hualien, they needed to stop the Chinese there.

But the Army was not content to wait for the PLA to come to them; they had other plans. At the moment, the battle for Hualien was being fought by vanguard elements even further north.

The highway from Taipei to Hualien ran through a series of tunnels, natural choke points from which to ambush the oncoming PLA forces. First Battalion, 502nd Infantry had been assigned the task of bottling up the PLA inside the tunnels. The overwatch drone feed showed the scene as a haze of smoke through which Sharratt could make out the burning hulks of three PLA tanks.

The US Army forces were dug into the wooded hillside overlooking the tunnel entrance. The leader of the halted PLA ground forces was undoubtedly screaming for air support to take out the US Army elements impeding his progress.

Sharratt's forces were doing everything they could to protect their Army comrades. But for every hour that passed, he had fewer aircraft to do the same job. He was locked in a battle of attrition. A *losing* battle.

On the video screen, another C-17 landed successfully, but the next one was waved off.

Two successful supply flights out of four, Sharratt thought. With that math, we don't win.

"They're on the move, sir," Zachary said from the other side of the table. "The PLA carriers."

The BattleSpace display expanded again. The *Liaoning* and *Shandong*, surrounded by a flock of top-of-the-line escort combatants, were coming around the north end of Taiwan.

"Well," Sharratt said, "look who's come out to play."

"Admiral," the watch officer reported, "the PLA carriers are launching everything they have."

"They're looking for us," Sharratt said. "When they find us, it's gonna get hot in here."

This was the opportunity he'd been waiting for. A crack at the PLA carrier fleet. The only remaining question was how far the Chinese were going to take this war.

"Admiral," the watch officer called. "The *Lincoln* reports they have incoming missiles from the Chinese mainland."

Question asked, questions answered.

Sharratt snatched the microphone off the hook over his head.

"All stations, this is Alpha Bravo actual," he said. "Execute Strike Package Zulu."

The order triggered a flurry of activity in Battle Watch. All over the strike force, waves of missiles launched. In Strike Ops, CAG vectored aircraft toward the PLA carriers.

"Well," Zachary said, "if they wanted to know where we are, we just sent up a flare."

The BattleSpace display flooded red with enemy missile tracks.

"Missile Defense Agency alert, Admiral," the Battle Watch Officer said. "The first wave contains hypersonics."

"Acknowledged, Watch Officer," Sharratt said. He'd been wearing his flash hood around his neck, and now he pulled it up over his head and rolled down the sleeves of his uniform.

Poke the dragon hard enough, Sharratt thought, the dragon pokes back.

"We knew it was too good to last, Tom," Sharratt said

To his credit, Zachary did his best to smile.

"ETA two minutes, ten seconds," the watch officer called out.

Sharratt felt a sense of calm settle over the room. In a way, they'd been expecting this deadly scenario for so long that when it actually happened, it was somehow anticlimactic.

The background noise changed too. The constant percussion of the catapults launching planes and the arresting gear capturing landing planes went eerily silent.

"CAG reports emergency sortie complete."

They wanted to salvage every possible aircraft for the upcoming fight. If a plane was flyable, it was launched. All recoveries were stopped.

The already crowded BattleSpace display updated. A tsunami of red incoming missiles flooded the tabletop, inching closer to the *Enterprise*, *Theodore Roosevelt*, and *Nimitz* with each update.

"One minute to impact," the watch officer said.

In the background, Alpha Whiskey, the air and missile defense coordinator, issued a steady stream of orders on the open battle circuit.

"All stations, Alpha Whiskey, incoming attack exceeds saturation levels. Shift to automatic control of air defenses."

Exceeding saturation levels was a nice way of saying that there were too many missiles to target and some—maybe a lot—were bound to slip through their air defenses.

In other words, they were screwed.

"Thirty seconds to first impact," the watch officer called out.

Sharratt turned to the video monitor.

The guided missile destroyer *William P. Lawrence* steamed only one thousand yards east of the *Enterprise*. Smoke billowed from her forecastle area as the last few missiles of her ripple fire lanced away into the sky. On the horizon, another warship was also launching, her forward area clouded in smoke and fire.

Thanks to technology, he was going to be able to watch the destruction of his own strike force live on TV. Sharratt didn't know whether to throw up or laugh at the absurdity of the moment.

"Show me the *Zumwalt*," he said.

The incoming ballistic missiles showed up as distant contrails in the sky. Accelerating at speeds in excess of Mach 5, the hypersonics were not only fast but maneuverable. The strike force missile defenses were almost useless against them.

But not lasers, Sharratt thought. The new directed-energy weapons on the three *Zumwalt*-class destroyers had the ability to take out incoming hypersonic missiles.

In theory, at least.

"Ten seconds."

As the USS *Zumwalt* cut through the waves, Sharratt watched bolt after bolt of red energy lance up from her bow. In the sky, a puff of smoke appeared, then another as her laser took out incoming missiles.

A distant boom pulsed through the hull as if someone had dropped a heavy box in the next room.

"*Dewey* is hit, sir."

Another boom. Closer this time.

Sharratt kept his eyes on the video feed. The *Zumwalt* was magnificent, firing again and again, like something out of a science fiction movie.

This could make the difference, Sharratt thought. The difference between life and—

The screen saturated to pure white. When the picture returned, Sharratt almost wished it hadn't. The *Zumwalt* was in two pieces. As he watched, the bow slipped under the water.

The room gave a collective gasp as if they'd all been punched in the gut at the same time. Sharratt heard a new noise, a muttered chant. He looked over to see a young sailor hunched over her computer screen, talking to herself.

Praying, he realized.

The BattleSpace display glitched. Information on the screen disappeared as their inputs stopped transmitting.

Sharratt swallowed hard.

He felt the SeaRAM missile batteries on the starboard side of the *Enterprise* light off, a rhythmic *pop-whoosh* sound of the close-in weapons system.

The shipwide intercom blared out.

"All hands brace for impact!"

53

6 kilometers north of Hualien, Taiwan

Lieutenant Colonel Kevin Merriman rode into battle in a canary-yellow Buick Enclave SUV. The vehicle showed only 1,200 kilometers on the odometer, and it was a sweet ride. White leather seats, now marked and muddied from their combat gear, a panoramic sun roof, and a smoking-hot Bose stereo system.

The drop on Hualien prioritized men and munitions over machinery. While the US Army had managed to get nearly five thousand paratroopers on the ground, they had not landed enough Army vehicles to move even a fraction of that number.

So they made do. The Taiwanese Army regulars who met them on the ground had requisitioned anything with wheels from the nearby town.

Now, Merriman, Radio Operator Sergeant Sanchez, and Sergeant Major "Eight Ball" Jackson rocketed up a curvy mountain road in the luxury vehicle to inspect the defensive positions of Charlie Company.

There were two ways to approach the Hualien airfield over land. Merriman's soldiers, 1st Battalion, 502nd Infantry, had both of them covered.

As they took another hairpin turn, Merriman spotted Captain Davis, Charlie Company commander, on the embankment.

"Pull over," he said to the driver.

Highway 8 wound its way over the rugged coastal range. It was a twisting, turning, narrow road that provided Merriman's soldiers with ample opportunities for ambush. The nature of the road also limited the speed of any PLA advance, which meant they'd have plenty of warning from overwatch drones. Merriman had decided a single company was sufficient to guard this flank.

He and Jackson listened as Davis briefed his defenses. The captain knew his business. Jackson gave a slight nod to his boss to indicate he approved.

"Good job, Captain." Merriman clapped Davis on the shoulder. "If things get really hairy on the other side of the mountain, I'm going to call on you as reinforcements for Alpha Company. Keep some vehicles handy."

"Yes, sir."

Merriman's crew piled into the Buick to head back down the mountain.

Survival at Hualien depended on being able to land resupply planes with more troops and equipment. There was nothing Merriman could do about the battle in the air. His concern was making sure those planes had a place to land.

The defense of the Hualien airfield was built in layers. The innermost layer was the forces digging in around the perimeter of the airfield itself. A few kilometers to the north, at Manbo Beach, where the ocean squeezed up against the mountains, the bulk of the 101st were setting up defenses. The US forces evacuated the civilians from the town and cleared the highways so that any munitions, heavy weapons, or soldiers that arrived by air transport could be rushed immediately to the front.

After Manbo Beach, the next defensive layer was the Liwu River, which was crossed by two bridges. The Buick passed by the smaller of the two, the Jingwen Bridge, where a team of combat engineers was placing charges on the supporting columns. If Merriman's companies failed to stop the advancing forces, they'd blow this bridge to slow the PLA.

They approached the larger Taroko Bridge and turned north onto Highway 9. A concrete-and-steel bridge of this size would require close air support to destroy it. But that was a last resort to stop the enemy, Merriman told himself.

The Buick sped across the bridge, heading north. After less than a kilometer, Merriman spied elements of Alpha Company digging in on the wooded slopes over the entrance to a tunnel. This black semicircle at the base of the mountain was their next layer of defense. He motioned for the driver to pull over.

Captain Chris Bentley scrambled down the slope to meet him. "Talk to me, Chris," Merriman said by way of greeting.

Bentley outlined where he had placed his fire teams on the hillside. He pointed out the M2A1 .50-caliber machine guns, the Mark 19 belt-fed grenade launchers, and M240 machine guns with interlocking fields of fire.

"The Javelins are up on the ridge," he said, referring to the anti-tank weapon. "They have a clear view of the tunnel entrance. If they get this far, we'll bottle them up inside."

Merriman nodded his approval and took note of the command post location on the ridge.

"If they break through Bravo Company's defenses on the first tunnel," Merriman said, "I'm going to have Charlie Company send down a platoon of reinforcements. Think about how you want to use them."

"You got it, Colonel," Bentley said. "Tell Harder good luck up there in the Pit."

Merriman climbed back into the Buick.

The vehicle entered the dark tunnel. Up ahead, a half-circle of light grew larger until the Buick broke into bright sunlight.

The Pit, Merriman thought. This is where we break the PLA's advance. Everything after the Pit—Alpha Company at the second tunnel, blowing the bridges, the forces massed at Manbo Beach—were just holding actions compared to this spot.

The open road ran for a half kilometer until it entered the next tunnel. The sign next to the tunnel entrance read 1,460 meters. To his left, a steep, boulder-strewn hillside rose three hundred feet to a ridge. The other side of the road was a narrow gravel shoulder, a metal guardrail, then a steep drop down to the sea.

The morning sun was already baking the rocks, making Merriman glad he had paid attention to drinking enough water on the plane. Although it felt like a lifetime ago, it had only been about six hours.

Captain Mike Harder was his best company commander, hands down. The man poked his head up from behind a rocky outcropping halfway up the slope, then worked his way down the hill using a rope. "Eight Ball" Jackson walked down the road, his eyes on the hillside emplacements.

Harder was a prior-enlisted Marine. After tours in Iraq and Afghanistan, he'd mustered out of the Corps, earned a bachelor's degree, then restarted his military career as an Army infantry officer. He was the right man for this assignment.

Harder dropped to the ground. "We're ready for 'em, sir." Without being asked, he started to brief Merriman about the defenses.

Radio Operator Sanchez, never more than a few paces away, passed Merriman a handset. "Major Turner, sir."

Merriman keyed the transmit button. "Go ahead."

"Sir, the S2 has a live feed from the eye in the sky. PLA tanks and armored personnel carriers are headed south and moving fast." He named a recreation area. Merriman traced the thin line that represented Highway 9 on the map until he found the spot. "They're one-five mikes out from Bravo."

"Acknowledged," Merriman said. "I'll be at—"

"You've got incoming!" Turner shouted. "Two jets inbound from the north."

Merriman's head snapped around, but Jackson was faster. The sergeant major's outstretched arm pointed at two dots low on the horizon.

"Take cover!" Merriman yelled. He dove behind a pair of boulders next to the road. Sanchez hit the deck next to him.

The jets rapidly grew larger. Pips of fire appeared on their wings, then there was a deafening roar as the jets passed overhead. Merriman put his face in the dirt as a barrage of rocket fire smashed into the rocky hillside, sending deadly shards of stone in every direction.

Rockets, Merriman thought. Of course—they don't want to destroy the road with bombs.

Somewhere up the hillside, someone shouted in pain, calling for a medic.

Merriman hauled himself to his feet. His ears rang from the explosion. "Harder!" His own voice sounded very far away.

"Sir." Sanchez gripped his arm, pointing further up the road.

The area above Captain Harder's cover had taken a direct hit from one of the rockets, creating a small landslide. The dust-covered corpse of the Bravo Company commander was pulverized almost beyond recognition.

There was no time to curse or grieve or even think. Merriman seized the nearest rope and used it to climb up the slope. He reached the first fire team location, a .50-caliber machine gun team.

"Where's the CP?" he shouted.

They pointed up and to the right. Merriman climbed higher until he reached the ridge and scrambled into a wide cleft between two rocks. As always, Sanchez was right on his heels.

From this vantage point, Merriman had a clear view of both tunnel entrances. Halfway up the slope, he saw Sergeant Major Jackson drop into a small depression where the Javelin team had set up their gear. Merriman grunted with satisfaction. Jackson had instinctively placed himself where he could do the most damage to the enemy.

A pair of People's Liberation Army Type 99A main battle tanks emerged from the tunnel, side by side, closely followed by six APCs. The Javelin team launched a missile, scoring a direct hit on the nearest enemy tank. The sound of the explosion ricocheted around the confines of the Pit.

The second tank did not slow down. The armored personnel carriers also navigated around the burning hulk and continued on. One of the APCs disgorged a dozen PLA troops. They were cut down in a withering US crossfire.

A second pair of tanks emerged from the tunnel. Another Javelin missile fired, disabling another tank.

"Take out the lead tank!" Merriman shouted.

Jackson was already on it. He directed the next Javelin shot at the tank approaching the second tunnel. They missed, striking one of the APCs. The tank disappeared into the tunnel, followed by the APCs.

"Alpha, this is Bravo CP," Merriman said into the radio. "Be advised, you have one tank and four APCs in the tunnel headed your way. Over."

"Acknowledged, Bravo. We're ready."

Another explosion rocked the Pit as the Javelin team took out another tank. Jackson had timed the explosion so that now two disabled tanks completely blocked the road below.

Merriman felt a surge of hope. This is going to work, he thought.

That's when he heard it.

Wop-wop-wop. The rhythmic beat of helicopter rotors.

A formation of four Chinese Z-10 attack helos rounded the headland from the north. They hovered, their 30mm guns in the chin turrets pouring fire down on the American forces.

Merriman emptied his M-4 magazine on full auto, then hit the deck.

Bullets ricocheted over his head, raining down splinters of rock. It seemed to go on forever but was probably less than fifteen seconds.

The onslaught of bullets stopped, and two explosions followed in quick succession. Merriman popped his head up in time to see a pair of Marine Corps F-35s pass a few hundred feet over his head.

Two of the helos were burning hulks in the ocean, and the other two were bugging out.

He dropped his gaze to the road, and his heart fell. Two more PLA tanks emerged from the tunnel—and they were equipped with flat bulldozer blades on the front of the vehicles. They plowed into the disabled tanks, forcing them off the road.

Highway 9 was clear again.

54

Qingshui Cliffs, Taiwan
7 kilometers north of Hualien

Mission Clock: 8:16:42
Mission Status: Green

After his visit to General Zhang's command post, Gao thought General Ho's CP was a letdown.

It was a first-generation design that did not have the expandable walls, holographic display table, or private office found in General Zhang's state-of-the-art ride. This version was basically a ruggedized office cubicle: a single row of monitors mounted on a troop transport truck. The integrated diesel generator was noisy and made the whole room vibrate. To add to the misery, the air-conditioning unit was broken, so the interior was hot and smelled of diesel fuel.

They'll probably all die of carbon monoxide poisoning, Gao observed from his position in the open doorway. It would serve them right.

To say General Ho was surprised when the injured Lieutenant Colonel Gao arrived at his command post would be kind. *Annoyed* was a better word.

Gao tried to mollify the man. "I'm here only as an observer, sir," he said.

General Ho was not a fool. He knew exactly why Gao was there: to report back to General Zhang. In his politician's mind, Zhang's decision to leave his unit behind in Taipei was a deliberate slight. Now, Zhang was adding insult to the perceived injury to Ho's career.

"I respect General Zhang's wisdom in this matter," Ho replied with a tight smile. "Your experience is greatly valued here, Lieutenant Colonel Gao."

It took about five minutes for the word to circulate among Ho's staff that no one was to cooperate with Gao in the slightest unless they wanted latrine duty for a month.

It didn't matter. Between the suffocating stuffiness of the command post and the overpowering smell of diesel, Gao was more than glad to stay outside. The pain meds were wearing off, and his injuries both ached and itched at the same time. He walked back to his car to retrieve a pair of field glasses.

General Ho had picked a beautiful spot to set up his command post. The clearing on the mountainside overlooked Manbo Beach and gave an unobstructed view of the tunnels to the north. They were safely away from the action here, observers from on high.

Gao breathed deeply of the pine-scented air, trying to clear the sickly-sweet diesel smell from his sinuses. If you ignored the fighter aircraft rocketing down the coast and the occasional explosion, it was a bucolic scene.

At the car, his driver leaped out of the vehicle, but Gao waved him away. His head pounded. He felt flushed and feverish. Gao drank some water, took some pain pills, and ate a protein bar. He took off his uniform tunic in an attempt to cool down.

Only a few hours, Gao thought. That's all it will take. According to the latest update, the PLA had broken through the American defenses on the first tunnel.

"We will overrun the American units blocking the second tunnel within the hour," General Ho announced to Gao. "Then we will deal with that."

He pointed down the valley to Manbo Beach. The area was a beehive of activity as the Americans prepared for the upcoming battle.

It would be a rout, Gao knew.

He raised the binoculars and studied the opposing force. The American forces dug in south of the river, where the wooded mountains ran close to the oceans. It was a defensible position, but the Americans had less than half a division and almost no heavy artillery.

General Ho was bringing down a full division, including heavy artillery from Taipei. Once the PLA was through the second tunnel, the battle was all but over. The timeline for the American defense of Manbo Beach was measured in hours, not days.

It was all going to work out, Gao thought, allowing himself a smug smile.

On the trip to General Ho's command post, Gao had let his insecurities get the better of him. The Americans had discovered some fatal weakness in the Chinese plan to conquer Taiwan, he worried to himself. And Gao's lost tablet had provided the information that would stop the PLA invasion dead in its tracks.

Now, he was glad Zhang had sent him here. He saw the American attack on Hualien for what it was: a last-ditch attempt from a desperate opponent.

No, Gao decided as he walked back up the slope to the command post, today was a great day for the People's Republic of China. A historic day for the People's Liberation Army, a day that Gao would recount to his grandchildren.

When he reached the command post, Gao did not bother to climb the steps and enter. Instead, he sat on the soft green grass and leaned back against a truck tire. He took out his Shandian tablet and sent a text update to General Zhang.

Situation in Hualien under control. General Ho's forces—

A pair of PLA fighters roared overhead, breaking Gao's train of thought. His head ached, and the feverish feeling had returned.

—will control the area by nightfall.

He received an immediate acknowledgment from Zhang and closed down the connection.

Gao leaned his head back against the tire and shut his eyes. I should go to the hospital, he thought. I don't need to be here anymore.

55

A front row seat to Armageddon, Don Riley thought.

His stomach churned acid. He swallowed hard to still a wave of nausea that threatened to overwhelm him.

The video screen at the front of the Situation Room displayed live footage of the *Enterprise* strike force as seen from a Global Hawk overwatch drone.

A blanket of heavy black smoke shrouded the scene. Occasionally, the dark veil thinned and Don was able to catch a glimpse of ships. Flashes of light—explosions, he supposed—lit up the darkness like lightning in a thundercloud. But like a scary movie where you never actually see the dreaded monster, his mind filled in the horrific details.

"Is the strike force still able to fight?" President Serrano asked.

"Unknown at this time, sir," General Nikolaides replied. His face was ashen, and his skin stretched across his sharp features gave him a skeletal look. "As soon as we have an update, we'll pass it on, sir. It's only been a few minutes."

A few minutes, Don thought. That's all the time it took for the attack.

He imagined sailors all across the strike force fighting fires, plugging leaks in hulls, carrying wounded crewmates to safety.

All while he watched on a video screen like it was some war movie. Don saw a hull outline slip into focus and out again like a ghost. This was literally the fog of war.

"Can we at least get a message to them?" Serrano insisted. "Are we in radio contact?"

"We're trying, sir," the Chairman said. "The situation is very fluid. As soon as I have an update, you'll have it, Mr. President."

Serrano turned his attention to the Secretary of Defense. Kathleen Howard looked like she was in shock.

Hell, Don thought, everyone in the room looked like they were in shock.

"What's the status of the attack at Hualien?" Serrano pressed.

"The Army holds the airfield, sir," Howard said, "but our ability to land additional supply planes is limited. Out of six attempts, we've landed three planes. That's not enough."

The briefer running the screen shifted the image to the strip of land known as Manbo Beach. To the north, Chinese forces moved in a column down the coast road, but they were halted at the tunnels. A second column of mobilized infantry was visible winding their way through the hairpin turns of the central mountain range. It was anybody's guess which PLA force would make it to Manbo Beach first.

Don wasn't an expert in Army battlefield tactics, but he knew how to count. The US forces were massively outnumbered, and the clock was ticking.

"We need to get supplies into Hualien," Serrano said. "Get more air support in there."

"Sir, every available aircraft is already there," Howard said. "There's nothing in reserve."

"So that's it, then?" Serrano said.

"Sir, I think we need to discuss next steps," Secretary of State Henry Hahn said in his measured way. "If we approach the Chinese now, we can—"

"Next steps, Henry?" Serrano asked in a tone laced with sarcasm. "Is that code for surrender?"

"Mr. President," Hahn said, "our ability to materially impact the situation on the ground in Taiwan has passed. We are out of options, sir. If you allow a ground battle between the PLA and the United States to occur at Manbo Beach, we could be looking at hundreds or even thousands of casualties from a single—"

"Who said we were out of options, Mr. Secretary?" Serrano asked.

Hahn paused, blinking owlishly behind his glasses. "Sir, if you're talking about tactical nuclear weapons, I strongly advise against that course of action."

Serrano ignored him. Instead, he leaned back in his chair and consulted in a whisper with Chief of Staff Wilkerson.

The room waited. Don saw Howard and Nikolaides exchange worried glances. Serrano turned to National Security Advisor Valentina Flores. "Bring her in, Val. I think it's time."

"Sir," General Nikolaides began, but Flores was already on her feet. She pushed open the door and beckoned to someone waiting in the hallway outside.

Abby Cromwell, CEO of Sentinel Holdings, strode into the White House Situation Room.

She paused to shake the President's hand. Her blond hair hung loose at her shoulders, and she wore a dark two-piece business suit with a stylish blazer that dropped to her knees. Abby moved with her easy grace to the lectern at the front of the room.

"Good afternoon, ladies and gentlemen," Abby began in a confident voice. "My name is Aberdeen Cromwell from Sentinel Holdings." She surveyed the room. When her gaze landed on Don, she smiled at him long enough that others in the room looked his way. Don's cheeks grew warm. "I'm here to brief you on the latest anti-personnel weapon in the Sentinel arsenal."

She flipped her hand at the screen. The battlefield image disappeared, replaced by a video of an outstretched human hand. The picture focused on a black cylinder about the size of Don's thumb. The black object shifted. It sprouted eight appendages, and Don caught the gleam of a camera lens. The device levitated off the hand and took flight.

"This is the C-QDA, an acronym for carbon-based quantum drone assassin," Abby said. "Usually, we call this little guy a Cicada."

Don sank back in his chair.

"This is the state-of-the-art battlefield weapon of our time. The Cicada is strictly used for anti-personnel events and is capable of distinguishing between friend and foe in a live fire situation."

Henry Hahn's face was the color of chalk. "Mr. President, you cannot seriously be considering using this kind of weapon. This could be considered a first-strike weapon, maybe even a WMD."

"I asked for options, Secretary Hahn," Serrano said. "I didn't get any from my normal sources, so I'm making my own." He nodded for Cromwell to proceed.

"Mr. Secretary," Abby said to Hahn. "All I ask is that you listen to what I have to say before you pass any judgment."

Hahn shook his head.

"The Cicada operates on two-factor kill authentication," Abby continued. "Factor one is obvious: the target needs to have a heat signature. We don't want to waste our units on decoys or soldiers that have already been killed."

"What's the second factor?" General Nikolaides said. He sat rigidly in his chair, hands flat on the table.

Instead of answering, Abby changed the screen again. It showed an Army camouflage uniform.

"This is *Xingkong*, or starry sky. The Chinese adopted this camouflage pattern across all the PLA forces—Army, Navy, Air Force, and so on—in 2019. For this exercise, it is a unique identifier to detect and eliminate an enemy on the battlefield."

"Is that what this is to you, Ms. Cromwell?" Howard said. "An exercise? Your plan is to dump a planeload of killer drones on the battlefield and walk away?"

Abby ignored the jibe. "Madam Secretary, I can assure you that we take our responsibility as a US military contractor very seriously. I've worn the uniform and fought for my country. My husband was a Navy SEAL. He gave his life for this country—"

"Your husband was a private military contractor, Ms. Cromwell," Howard interrupted.

"My husband was a patriot!" Abby shot back. "The best that this country had to offer. We started this company together as a way to help the United States do the hard things that no one seems to want to do these days."

Abby stopped, her chest heaving, her face flushed with emotion.

"I apologize, ma'am," she said quietly. "Your question was about safety protocols. We have many. Attacks can be launched from the air or the ground, and they are geographically limited from the point of origin. Each Cicada body has an independent power source that lasts a maximum of four hours, but that time can be preset to expire in as little as a few minutes."

"Can they be recalled?" the Secretary of State asked. "Or reprogrammed?"

"No," Abby replied. "Once launched, each Cicada unit operates until it either completes a kill or runs out of power. The units operate in a mode we call 'cooperative threat engagement,' which means they act as a hive to best accomplish the overall anti-personnel mission."

Don had the surreal feeling that he was listening to an infomercial.

"We can program the Cicada swarm to authenticate on any measurable element: body size or shape, whether or not the target is armed. Really, the possibilities are endless."

"Yes, they are," the Secretary of State said. "Mr. President, I renew my objection to the use of this weapon. If it does everything Ms. Cromwell claims and is one hundred percent successful, we are signing off on a mass killing event, sir."

"A mass killing event, Henry?" Serrano said. "Mass. Killing. Event. What would you call what the Chinese just did to the *Enterprise* strike force, Mr. Secretary? Was that a mass killing event?"

Hahn stood. "Sir, there are rules—"

"Rules?" The President slammed his fist on the table. "Rules? Are you serious? What rules did the Chinese use when they bombed the Naval War College? We are taking every precaution to make sure that this weapon is contained. We are following rules."

Serrano turned back to Cromwell. "What do we need to do in order to execute Project Cicada?"

"The attack profile is already loaded into the missiles on the *Ohio* and the *Michigan*," Abby said. "I would recommend a ten-missile assault radius for the first wave. I also strongly recommend we clear air traffic from the blast zone to minimize any collateral damage during the airburst."

"Very well, thank you, Abby," Serrano said. He turned to the Chairman of the Joint Chiefs.

"General," the President said, "clear the airspace over Manbo Beach. Launch ten missiles equipped with the Cicada weapons systems from the USS *Ohio*. Set Manbo Beach as ground zero."

The room was silent. Don realized he was holding his breath.

Nikolaides was famously never at a loss for words, but in this moment, he opened his mouth, then shut it again. He looked down the table at the Secretary of Defense.

"General," the President said.

The Marine general stood, came to attention.

"Aye-aye, sir."

56

USS *Enterprise* strike force
50 miles east of Taiwan

"Satellite comms are restored, Admiral," the watch officer reported.

In the dim emergency lighting in Battle Watch, the young man was all but lost in the shadows. Since the missile attack, the command center had been reduced to battery-operated devices like the tablet Sharratt held in his hand. He tapped to approve the strike force status report.

"Transmit the SITREP to Washington," Sharratt said.

He took a deep breath. The air smelled of burnt plastic and fried electronics.

It could be worse, he thought. We could *all* be dead.

The *Nimitz* was dying. The aircraft carrier had absorbed three direct hits. She listed fifteen degrees to starboard and was down in the stern. It would be a miracle if she didn't sink in the next hour.

The *Roosevelt* and the *Enterprise* had absorbed one hit each. The *Teddy* had all four catapults fully operational but was making emergency repairs to her flight deck so that she could recover aircraft. She'd be back in the fight within the hour. The *Enterprise* had taken a missile strike forward of the island, taking out the starboard elevator and two catapult systems.

A few meters to the left and the explosion would have taken out the room where Sharratt was standing right now. God favors idiots and small children, he thought.

The escorts in the strike force were a mixed bag of damage. Six ships had been sunk, but there were also three ships that had escaped without any significant damage.

"How're we doing on reconfiguring the strike force, Tom?" Sharratt called.

The first order of business was to get back in the fight, and that meant two things. First, continue air defense for the Hualien landing zone. Second, adjust the escorts around the carriers so they could support mission one.

Until they had the datalink back online, Zachary was manually taking reports from all ships on battle damage and weapons stocks. Ships that had sufficient missile inventories and mobility were repositioned along the threat axis with the PLA. The remainder were moved to picket duty to protect against possible subsurface attacks.

And then there were the ships fighting for their lives. The guided missile cruiser USS *Chosin* had taken two missile hits. She was able to make bare steerageway, and her damage control teams had performed minor miracles keeping her afloat. She would live to fight another day—maybe— but not this day.

"*Enterprise* reports she's ready to answer all bells, sir," the watch officer called out.

"Very well," Sharratt replied. "Get me a status on power for Battle Watch."

Sharratt unhooked a phone receiver and dialed Strike Ops, where he knew CAG was waiting for his call.

"CAG," a voice answered.

"Mongoose, it's Chip."

"Sir." His voice spoke volumes. They didn't know for sure how many pilots the strike force had lost today, but the list was long. CAG knew every pilot by name. He would feel every loss hard.

"You have permission to recommence flight operations."

"Aye-aye, sir." CAG hung up.

The overhead lights clicked on. Sharratt blinked in the sudden brightness.

"The system is coming online, sir," the BattleSpace operator said, donning her VR goggles and manipulator glove. "I'll have an updated table in about two minutes."

Zachary joined him next to the holographic display. The screen glitched, then settled down and started to populate with basic data.

"What's the status of the *Zumwalts*?" Sharratt asked.

The directed-energy weapons mounted on the three *Zumwalt*-class destroyers had performed well beyond expectations in the last engagement. The historians would decide, but in Sharratt's mind, the lasers had made a decisive difference in the battle.

"*Zumwalt* is gone," Zachary said. "Sunk. We're carrying out search and rescue, but...my guess is...all hands lost."

Sharratt nodded, recalling the spectacular explosion.

"The *Mansoor* and the *Johnson* are seaworthy, but the *Mansoor* reports major mechanical problems with the laser. If I'm believing the reports, they melted their power distribution bus. They're rigging a temporary power supply for the laser."

"Anything they need, Tom," Sharratt said. "Anything at all. Give them top priority. They're the one platform we have that doesn't need to reload."

"About that, sir," Zachary said. "Missile inventory is an issue."

Over their heads, Sharratt heard the whining *zip-bang* of the catapult as the first plane was launched off the *Enterprise*. A second later, he heard the reassuring slam of landing gear hitting the flight deck as they recovered their first aircraft.

"Do what you can with what we've got left, Tom."

"Aye, sir."

"Admiral, we're getting video from the overwatch drone," the watch officer called. "I've got eyes on the Chinese fleet."

Sharratt and Zachary turned as one to the flat-screen monitor.

Thick black smoke billowed across the screen.

"What am I supposed to be looking at, Watch Officer?" Sharratt said.

Then the picture shifted, and the smoke was gone.

"Holy shit," Zachary muttered.

The PLA aircraft carrier *Liaoning* was dead in the water with a port list of at least twenty degrees. Sharratt could see at least three different wounds in her gray hull.

"She's not going to make it," Zachary said.

"I agree," Sharratt replied. "Where's the other carrier? The *Shandong*?"

"Coming up on it now, sir."

Sharratt studied the screen anxiously, assessing the damage to the PLA Navy's most advanced aircraft carrier. She had taken at least one hit. Wounded, but definitely still in the fight.

"Make sure CAG sees this," he said to the watch officer without taking his eyes off the screen. "What do you think, Tom?"

"There's bomb damage on the after part of her flight deck, sir," Zachary said. "She'll have a hard time recovering aircraft without major repairs."

Sharratt grunted agreement. The PLA could land planes anywhere on Taiwan or on mainland China, so that was not a huge disadvantage for them.

"She's clearly underway," Zachary continued, "but it looks like she might have taken a torpedo hit here. Possible damage to her screws or rudder?"

"What's the position of the third carrier?" Sharratt asked.

"I've got her on the BattleSpace table, sir," the operator said.

Sharratt turned to study the display. The PLA carrier *Hainan* was at the southern tip of Taiwan.

"All right," Sharratt said, thinking aloud. "We've basically evened the odds for the moment. Meanwhile, those poor Army bastards on Hualien are outnumbered and about to get the snot kicked out of them. Divert all available air resources to pushing back the PLA along the coast road."

"Admiral, we've got a new subsurface contact," the watch officer said. "One of ours."

He pointed to a blue icon for a friendly submarine. Sharratt read the data *USS Ohio (SSGN-726)*. It was within twenty miles of the Taiwanese shoreline, just southeast of Hualien.

"Where the hell did they come from?" Sharratt asked.

"No idea, sir," the operator reported. "They just registered on the system this very moment."

"Admiral!" Sorenson emerged from the top-secret area. "Flash traffic from NMCC. P4, direct from POTUS."

A personal message from the President of the United States?

"Read it to me, Jerry."

"Clear airspace over Hualien. Missile strike imminent."

Sharratt clocked a look at Zachary, who appeared just as stunned as he was.

I can spend my time arguing, Sharratt thought, or I can spend it fighting.

He took down the microphone for the battle network.

"All stations, this is Alpha Bravo actual," Sharratt said. "Clear the airspace over Hualien. I say again, clear the airspace over Hualien immediately."

There was a full second of dead air, then the net exploded with new orders as the principals coordinated their air assets.

Sharratt hooked the receiver and dialed Strike Ops again.

"CAG."

"Mongoose," Sharratt said. "I have new tasking for you." He looked up at the video where the PLA aircraft carrier *Shandong* was in full view.

"Go after that carrier. The *Shandong*," Sharratt ordered. "Sink that son of a bitch."

"Yes, *sir.*"

57

Merriman couldn't believe it. The Pit was a killing zone, but somehow, someone in the Javelin team was still alive. An anti-tank missile streaked down from the hillside and struck one of the bulldozer-tanks. He tried to remember how many more rounds they had for the Javelin, but his brain would not function.

A line of Chinese APCs emerged from the tunnel. They disgorged a full platoon of PLA infantry. Machine gun fire from the US forces on the hillside rained down, but it was a fraction of what it had been only a few moments ago.

It was all over. They were about to be overrun.

Merriman reached his hand back for the radio handset.

Nothing happened.

"Sanchez," he shouted. It felt like his ears were stuffed with cotton.

Nothing.

Merriman turned.

Sergeant Sanchez had taken three 30mm rounds in the chest from the helo attack, nearly severing his body across the torso.

Merriman rolled him over and seized the handset. The radio was dead.

Two more tanks emerged from the tunnel.

Another anti-tank round rocketed down from the hillside and scored a hit on a tank. The PLA infantry turned their fire on the location of the Javelin team.

We're done here, Merriman thought.

He looked across twenty meters of bare rock that separated him from the tree line. Alpha Company was through those trees and over the ridge, maybe half a kilometer away.

He needed to warn Alpha Company what was coming. They were going to need close air support and reinforcements.

He gripped the sides of the rock and launched his body into the open.

His breath came hard and fast. He felt his boots pound into the rocky ridge. He pumped his arms, reaching forward as if he could pull himself through the air.

Little bursts of stone exploded in front of his feet as the PLA forces fired on him. He felt a bullet hit his body armor. He reeled from the impact but stayed on his feet.

Almost there... He crashed into a wall of evergreen branches and sprawled into the dirt.

Keep going, he told himself.

Sprigs of greenery rained down around him as PLA bullets shredded the foliage over his head. His lungs were on fire, but he got to his hands and knees and crawled forward. After a few more meters, he used a tree trunk to pull himself upright. He staggered forward. Running, walking, but always forward.

The ground crested, then sloped down steeply. He dropped onto his ass and half slid, half ran down the hill. He rolled, bounced off rocks and trees, got back to his feet and kept going.

Finally, he burst out of the tree cover. The camouflage netting of the Alpha Company command post was mere meters away.

Merriman lunged into the CP. The expression on Bentley's face told Merriman what he must have looked like.

"Radio," Merriman demanded.

He gripped the microphone. His hand was shaking as he pressed down the transmit button. His breath came in ragged gulps.

"Battalion CP, this is Merriman."

"Go ahead, sir." Turner's voice.

"Bravo Company is overrun. Deploy Charlie Company to reinforce the second tunnel. We need close air support, Sam. We need it right now."

"Roger, CAS required. Stand by."

"How many Javelin rounds do you have?" he asked Bentley.

"Eight left, sir," Bentley replied. "We've got two dead PLA tanks blocking the highway."

"That won't stop them, Chris." Merriman described the PLA efforts to clear disabled vehicles. "Don't stop what you're doing, but we need more firepower. We have to destroy that tunnel."

What was taking Turner so long? Merriman fumed.

"Battalion CP, Merriman, what's the status of our close air support?" Merriman demanded over the radio.

No answer.

"Battalion CP, come in."

"Battalion CP, here, sir." Turner's voice broke. "All air support has been redirected away from Hualien."

"What?" Merriman felt his knees getting soft.

Turner's voice had a tremor in it. "Flash message traffic straight from NMCC, sir. Missile strike inbound. Shelter in place."

---

25 kilometers north of Hualien

Lieutenant Colonel "Pipper" Plechash lined up the reticles in his integrated visor display on the line of armored vehicles queued up on the roadway below him. He pumped the gun trigger and felt a rapid vibration under his feet as the 25mm Gatling gun unleashed a slew of projectiles.

He came out of the dive at 1,200 feet, rolling toward the brilliant blue of the Pacific Ocean before climbing again. His lips peeled back into a grin.

Jesus, that felt good, he thought.

He scanned the tactical display. There was a pair of Chinese J-16 jets tangling with two of Pipper's squadron thirty miles to the east, but most of the action was further south over Hualien proper.

He'd been vectored away from the action because he had only one piece of ordnance left on his bomb rack: a single GBU-32 JDAM stored in his internal bomb bay.

And the gun, of course. When he'd seen the PLA traffic jam on Highway 9, he'd taken the opportunity for some gunnery practice.

It was like a damned parking lot down there. He checked his ammo load and saw he still had another thirty-five rounds in his 220-round magazine. Just enough for another run.

His radio crackled.

"Green One, this is Eagle Eye. You have new tasking. Vector one-eight-zero, buster. Close air support orders incoming."

The AWACS knew he had only one bomb left. If they were sending him in for close air support, things must be pretty ugly down there.

Under the direction of Eagle Eye, it took Pipper all of five minutes to reposition and line up for an attack run. The target was a tunnel on Highway 9 barely a kilometer north of the bridge. He leveled off at five thousand feet, waiting for weapons release by the 1st Battalion spotter.

With precision-guided munitions, close air support was a misnomer. He would release the thousand-pound bomb from a distance, and the GPS guidance system would place it on target.

"Ten seconds," said the spotter. "Clear to release."

"Acknowledged," Pipper responded, his thumb hovering over the bomb release. "Release in five...four...three—"

His visor flashed with a new message.

Weapons hold. Clear the area immediately. Missile strike inbound.

"This is Green One, I have a weapons hold, bug out order."

Pipper cycled his bomb bay doors closed and rolled to the right. On the surface of the ocean below, he saw streaks of white contrails vectoring toward the shore. Cruise missiles.

He said a quick prayer for the grunts on the ground.

6 kilometers north of Hualien, Taiwan

"Take cover!"

Merriman pressed his face into the dirt, clamped his hands over his ears, and opened his mouth. He'd seen what a Tomahawk cruise missile could do, and it was the stuff of nightmares.

His ears rang, his pulse beat like a bass drum. He tasted dirt on his tongue.

Seconds passed. At least it seemed like it. He'd lost all track of time.

A hand gripped his shoulder. Merriman looked up to see Captain Bentley's mouth moving. He held the radio handset.

Merriman pulled his hands away from his ears and shouted his name into the handset.

"It wasn't a cruise missile attack, sir," Turner said. "It was…I don't know what it was, but we're all fine here."

"Stand by." Merriman crawled to the edge of the rocky slope and peered down at the highway. Bentley handed him a set of field glasses, and he focused on the road.

None of the PLA vehicles were moving. He spied two bodies on the pavement.

What the hell was going on?

Merriman got to his feet, his M4 in hand. He gripped the Alpha Company radio operator by the arm. "You're with me." The kid nodded.

Merriman made his way down the wooded slope, keeping under cover but moving as fast as he could. He made it to the edge of the highway, scanning for movement.

The nearest APC was twenty meters away, across open ground. Merriman ran the distance, putting his back against the steel side of the vehicle. The radio operator stayed on his heels.

Merriman snuck a look around the corner. He saw three uniformed bodies sprawled on the roadway. No other signs of movement. He looked back at the tree line and saw that Bentley was there with a three-man fire team in tow. They rushed across the open area to join him. There was no enemy gunfire. Apart from the idling vehicles, it was eerily quiet.

Merriman signaled Bentley to take the left flank while he covered the right. They met at the open rear door of the APC.

"Holy shit," Bentley said. One of the soldiers retched and stepped behind the APC.

The inside of the armored personnel carrier was a bloodbath. Literally, blood pooled on the steel tread plates. There were six bodies inside, all dead, all contorted as if they were trying to escape something. They all had at least one neat entry hole in their uniform with an explosive exit wound.

"Spread out," Merriman ordered. "Cover the tunnel entrance." He held out his hand for the radio and felt the handset hit his palm.

"Battalion CP, Merriman," he said. "What was in those missiles?"

"No idea, sir. We had flash traffic from NMCC of a missile strike. That's all we know." Turner sounded as mystified as Merriman felt.

"Roger," Merriman replied. "We've got a lot of dead PLA soldiers, but we're fine. Send reinforcements forward. We're moving into the first tunnel."

"Roger on reinforcements, CP out."

Merriman joined his team positioned on both sides of the tunnel entrance. It was pitch black inside and still as a tomb. The carcasses of two PLA tanks still blocked the entrance. Five meters inside, a pair of APCs idled, filling the air with the smell of diesel exhaust.

Using hand signals, Merriman moved fire teams into the tunnel from each side. Once they were safely behind the cover of the APC, Merriman lowered his night vision googles. He gave the order to move out.

They did not find a single living PLA soldier. There were bodies everywhere. On the ground, leaning against the concrete wall, inside the vehicles.

"What the hell did this, sir?" Bentley whispered.

"I don't know," Merriman said. And I don't care, he thought.

They jogged down the tunnel, but it was empty. The other entrance was a few hundred meters distant, a semicircle of white light.

"Chris," Merriman said, "clear out two of the Chinese APCs and turn them around."

Five minutes later, the pair of commandeered eight-wheeled vehicles emerged at the other end of the tunnel. Merriman gripped his M4 and hauled his body upright.

"Let's move."

***

Qingshui Cliffs, Taiwan
7 kilometers north of Hualien

The voices inside the command center created an indistinct soundtrack in Gao's head. Now, one voice rose above the others. "General, the US aircraft are leaving the area. They're all headed out to sea."

Gao struggled to surface from sleep. He blinked, shielding his eyes from the afternoon sun. He got to his feet and looked through the binoculars. He counted four PLA war planes and no US aircraft. He swung the field of view out to sea. On the eastern horizon, a thick pall of smoke hung like thunderclouds.

He felt his eyes prick with tears. His chest clenched as a rush of pride overwhelmed him.

The Americans were retreating, leaving their men on the battlefield to surrender.

The PLA had defeated the mighty United States on the field of battle. A monumental day, a historic day—and he had witnessed it with his own eyes. The sun warmed his cheek. A gentle breeze wafted down the mountainside. It was a perfect moment, one that he would treasure forever.

Someone in the command post started to sing the national anthem, and Gao mouthed the words. Tears ran down his cheeks.

Just as he was about to lower the field glasses, a flicker of movement on the horizon caught his attention. He turned the focus wheel with his index finger to sharpen the image.

It looked like a stripe of white rippling across the blue ocean. Then he saw a second one, and a third.

A Tomahawk cruise missile, Gao thought, running close to the water to avoid radar.

"Missile attack!" he shouted, but it was too late.

Already the missiles were climbing to their final "pop-up" attack maneuver. He saw more than just three now, at least six coming from different directions, all converging over the battlefield.

From the ground, pips of white brightness shot into the sky as the PLA missile defense systems activated.

Mere seconds had passed from his first sighting, and Gao watched the attack unfold with a morbid curiosity.

BANG!

One of the missiles exploded in midair.

BANG! BANG! BANG!

More followed in quick succession as the missiles detonated over the battlefield. The explosions were puny, more like fireworks than bombs.

Gao's mind tried to make sense of what he had seen. The PLA missile defense systems had worked! They had destroyed every single enemy missile.

Gao allowed himself to sink back into a sitting position. He laughed to himself. His head dropped back against the truck tire, and he closed his eyes.

It was over. The US had played their last trick and failed spectacularly. He knew he should update General Zhang, but he was exhausted. He deserved a few moments of rest.

He heard a distant droning, like a fly buzzing near his ear. He waved his hand to clear the noise, but it continued. It grew louder.

Bzzzt-SNAP!

Something fell to the ground next to him. Gao opened his eyes to see the guard outside the command post lying facedown, unmoving.

On the back of his uniform was a red splotch the size of a dinner plate.

Gao acted on instinct. He rolled underneath the command post truck, taking cover behind the tire.

"Sniper!" he yelled.

There was no answer from inside the command post.

Gao yelled his warning again with the same result.

He reached out and snatched up the field glasses. He surveyed the tree line, trying to triangulate where the sniper might be hiding. He found nothing.

"General Ho!" he yelled. "Anyone inside, answer me."

The only response was the wind rustling through the tree branches.

On his belly, Gao worked his way to the rear of the truck, behind the stairs. His injured arm was on fire with pain, and he felt blood running down his chin from where he had ripped open his stitches.

The door to the command post was still open. He shouted again and got no answer. Why were they not responding?

Moving as quickly as he could in his injured state, he burst from cover and rushed up the steps.

Gao stopped in the open doorway.

Whatever had done this, it was no sniper.

Every soldier in the command post was dead, most sprawled at their computer screens, each with a blood-soaked hole drilled through the center of their chest. General Ho lay spread-eagled on the floor, eyes still open, a look of surprise on his face.

Gao thought he must be dreaming or high on pain meds. He stumbled back down the stairs and ran down the hill to his car.

The door to the SUV was open. His driver's body was half in, half out of the vehicle. Blood spatter covered the front seat.

Gao's entire body trembled. He was feverish. He was hallucinating. He was trapped in a nightmare.

Movement flashed in his peripheral vision. A gentle buzzing sound filled the air.

In the afternoon sunlight, what looked like a dragonfly hovered a meter from his chest. It zipped away, back down the slope.

The field glasses were still around his neck, and he raised them to his eyes. Down on the highway, outside the tunnels, the PLA trucks had stopped. He could see bodies on the pavement. Chinese soldiers.

A burst of movement inside the tunnel caught his eye. Two Chinese armored personnel carriers emerged, heading north. They maneuvered around a still smoking tank and stopped. Soldiers raced out of the vehicle, taking covering positions across the roadway.

Gao blinked. He was dreaming. They were *American* soldiers.

They moved along the roadway, weapons at the ready. Half of them scaled the rocky cliff face overlooking the highway. The rest piled back into the Chinese APC and continued north.

Using his good arm, Gao gripped his driver by the bloody shirtfront and hauled him away from the car door. Then he got behind the wheel and drove down the mountain.

DAY TEN

58

5 miles south of Mianhua Islet, Taiwan

Janet swam back to consciousness slowly. Her senses turned on one by one.

The fetid smell of damp seawater.

A soft, steady beep, once per second, like a metronome.

The taste of blood in her mouth.

Her head pounded, and she felt like she was falling. She wiped her hand across her face. Her skin was slick and clammy. And she was cold, so cold.

Finally, she opened her eyes.

The submersible sloped downward at a forty-five degree angle. Her body hung slack, held back by the copilot's seat harness. The bow window was dark, but intact, and she could see a line of sand a third of the way up the thick glass where the submersible had crashed into the sea floor.

The cabin was bathed in the sickly red glow of the emergency lights, making everything look shadowy and slightly demonic. The control panel was dead, smashed into a field of shattered glass.

Janet turned her head and gasped. One of the racks had broken free, and Mark was buried under a pile of computer equipment.

"Mark!" she called out.

No answer.

Janet gripped her three-point harness, unclipped the buckle, and half fell out of her chair. She stood on the forward window of the *Manta*. White crystals crunched under her feet. The lithium hydroxide canister they had used for CO_2 removal had ruptured during the explosion.

Janet shivered. The heaters were dead, and the temperature in the *Manta* had dropped at least ten degrees.

"Mark, can you hear me?" she said.

Janet began to move pieces of computer equipment off the unresponsive body of Mark Westlund. She worked carefully, doing her best not to set off an avalanche of damaged equipment on both of them. Everything was slippery, covered in a layer of condensed moisture.

In the dim red glare of the emergency lights, Mark's face looked like it was straight out of a horror movie. He'd been hit on the temple by a sharp corner of a piece of computer equipment. The right side of his face was black with blood and swollen. She felt for a pulse. The skin of his neck was slimy and cold, but his heart was beating strong. Janet let out a sigh of relief as she worked to uncover the rest of his body.

Besides the head wound, Mark's left leg was pinned under a heavy computer case. Janet used her multitool to slit open his pant leg. Although there was no bleeding, the area below the knee was swollen to twice the normal size.

Janet hugged herself against the cold and assessed her situation. The annoying beeping noise was the CO_2 alarm, but with the panels shattered, she did not have access to an actual reading. Still, with the way her head throbbed and the slow pace of her thoughts, she guessed that CO_2 levels were very high.

She took a handkerchief out of her pocket and wiped off Mark's face. He did not stir.

"I'm sorry, Mark."

They were lucky to be alive. When Janet clamped the *Manta* on the Chinese submarine, she'd acted on pure instinct. In the back of her mind, she'd had some idea that if she could surprise the PLA sub, the *Idaho* could get away.

Launching the torpedo? More instinct. A Mark 48 from 1,200 yards was not going to miss the target, no matter what the submarine did. It would all be over in minutes.

Janet recalled detaching from the PLA sub and driving away, but even then she'd known it was too little too late. Time and distance were cruel, and she had not allowed enough of either.

Had the *Idaho* gotten away safely? she wondered. Janet wiped Mark's face again. Was all this worth the price?

"You're babbling," she said out loud. "Stop being a crybaby and take some action."

Talking out loud helped, it turned out.

"Our situation is fucked," Janet continued. "Possibility of rescue is low, but if we stay here, we're dead. Pick your poison: hypothermia or carbon dioxide. Ergo, we have only one option. Emergency escape."

Decision made, Janet worked quickly. She positioned herself under the unconscious Mark and unbuckled his seat belt. He collapsed into her arms.

"Easy, fella," Janet said. "I think we should take this relationship a little slower. At least buy me dinner first."

She gently laid Mark on his back on the incline of the deck. This was going to be harder than she thought. She and Mark were roughly the same size, but he was dead weight. She needed to get him up an incline, into the lockout chamber, and dress him in an environmental suit. From there, physics would take over.

By Navy regulations, the submersible carried one SEIE Mark 10 for each occupant on a mission. The Submarine Escape and Immersion Equipment suit was a combination dry suit and life raft. Janet had trained in the earlier Mark 7 version of the suit exactly once, during submarine school almost seven years ago.

It's like riding a bike, Janet reassured herself as she retrieved a suit and unfolded it next to Mark. It would be easier to dress him out in the main cabin, where she had room to work.

The blaze orange material was rough and smelled of plastic. It was also large enough to fit a professional wrestler with plenty of room to spare. It was relatively easy for Janet to guide Mark's inert body into the suit.

So far, so good. Janet climbed up the sloped deck and opened the lockout chamber, releasing a fresh wave of moist air into the cabin. The chamber was designed to allow four Navy SEALs in full SCUBA gear and combat packs to exit the submersible at once, so there was plenty of room for both of them.

By the time she dragged Mark up the slope and through the chamber hatch, Janet was sweating and dizzy with exhaustion. She opened another SEIE suit and pulled it on. The orange material fit her like a circus tent, but there were Velcro straps on the ankles and wrists to give some shape to the outfit.

The heavy hatch of the lockout chamber hung halfway open, pointed down the pitched deck to the bow window. Normally, the hatch swung easily on balanced hinges, but now she had gravity working against her.

Janet reached down and pulled as hard as she could. Her arms trembled as the mechanism on the hatch neared the catch to hold it in place. She felt something pop in her back as she gave a final tug, and the catch dropped with a soft clink. She spun the wheel to dog the hatch shut.

Janet zipped closed the clear plastic hoods on both suits, then slid along the wall until she worked herself into a standing position in the canted chamber. The space was about four feet square with a steel ladder welded on one wall. The opposite bulkhead was covered with valves and associated gauges to manually flood and depressurize the chamber. Emergency gear such as a foot-long knife and a heavy steel hammer were clipped to the wall.

Janet opened a valve, and a flood of seawater shot in. The din of rushing water was deafening. She felt the coldness travel up her legs and over her waist. The water pressed the rough suit material against her skin as the chamber pressure equalized with the sea outside the *Manta*. Janet cleared her ears every few seconds, but the pressure increased until it felt like someone was poking a needle in her ear.

There was a loud *pop*, and all sound went away. Her eardrums had ruptured.

The water crept over the clear plastic of her face shield and over her head. The cold pressure wrapped around her rib cage like an icy vise, and she struggled to breathe.

Janet watched the gauge that monitored the chamber pressure. When she'd first opened the equalization valve, it had surged, but was now steady at 148 psi.

She hauled Mark upright, and both suits floated to the top of the chamber as if eager to escape. Janet knew she needed to keep a good hold on Mark's suit. When she opened the outer hatch, they would shoot out of the chamber like champagne corks.

Janet spun the wheel to unlock the outer hatch. She grabbed Mark's arm, then released the catch to allow the hatch to open fully.

The heavy steel dome flew open. Janet started to rise, then jerked to stop. Mark's suit shot past her, and he was gone, floating upward.

She twisted in the bulky suit, trying to look down, unable to see in the dim lighting. She grabbed the ladder and used the additional leverage to force her face against the plastic shield and see beneath her.

She was stuck. The ankle strap on her left foot was hung up on the bottom of the ladder. She tried to force her leg down, but the extra material in the bulky suit just absorbed her efforts.

The knife.

Janet felt along the wall behind her for the knife handle. She drew it from the sheath and stabbed down at the ankle strap.

She was shaking from the cold, only able to make out dim shapes in the poor lighting. Janet felt as if her lungs might burst out of her chest, and a wave of panic erupted. She slashed with the knife, again and again.

Then she was free, sucked out of the chamber, spinning, dizzy.

But rising.

59

The Great Hall of the People
Beijing, China

The meeting of the People's Committee for the Reunification of Taiwan did not start on time. The Minister fidgeted in his seat. He had arrived early, as if by sheer force of will he could make time go faster.

The Minister had a private jet waiting to take him to Taiwan to witness the formal end of hostilities. He wore his finest bespoke suit, a dark charcoal gray with a faint white pinstripe. His excellent mood this fine morning convinced him that he should vary his wardrobe beyond his typical black and white. When the pictures were taken at the signing of the Taichung Accord in a few hours, he would stand out in the history books.

"Who is that man on the right?" children would ask. "The one in the gray suit."

"That is Minister Fei Zhen," parents would answer. "It is said he was the grandfather of reunification, the right-hand man to the General Secretary himself. He gave his life in service of the State."

At least the pain was at bay. The new pain medication prescribed to him was nothing short of magical. Instead of feeling foggy and distant, the Minister's thoughts today were clear and sharp. Even though he hardly seemed to sleep anymore, his body felt invigorated, as if he was walking on a cushion of clouds all the time.

The only disappointment in his outlook was the ongoing demonstrations in Tiananmen Square. Despite his best efforts, they had expanded and crossed generational boundaries. As many grandparents were being arrested now as students.

As the arrests grew, a social gesture gained popularity. People began wearing red ribbons around their necks. The exact nature of the symbol was not clear to the Minister. Some reports claimed the red slash meant the Party was cutting the throats of the people, while others said the Party was choking the people, but it was clearly a protest against the Party. It had taken on a certain cachet as well. On his drive to this meeting, the Minister had seen an old woman pushing a janitor's cart pass a thirty-something man in a business suit—both wore red ribbons on their throats.

It was a stupid petty gesture. It would fade when the Chinese economy, bolstered by the added growth from Taiwan, roared back to life. A good economy was the best tonic to boost the people's patriotic love of the Party.

Fei sighed and relaxed in his chair. Although no one spoke to him, the Minister sensed that the other committee members nurtured an air of expectation about today. There were scattered conversations and even a few laughs in these minutes before the meeting started.

They rose as one with the arrival of their leader. As always, the General Secretary's countenance was inscrutable. He settled in his chair and directed his attention at the Vice Chairman of the Central Military Commission.

"Let's have a fleet status report to get us started," he said.

While the Minister felt he deserved a gesture of gratitude from the General Secretary—a simple smile or a nod would have been sufficient—he got nothing.

No matter, the Minister thought. Nothing can ruin this momentous day. The General Secretary knows what I have done.

The Vice Chairman stood and cleared his throat. "It appears the US Navy fleet is operational again. We have witnessed flight operations being conducted from two of the carriers, *Roosevelt* and the *Enterprise*. The carrier USS *Nimitz* is a total loss. The rest of the escort ships around the carriers have suffered serious damage. Their fighting capability is reduced by as much as half, maybe more."

His face was grave. "The Americans have not left the field of battle. Their strike force remains within range of our missiles."

Excellent, thought the Minister, we still have a chance to crush the Americans.

"And our own fleet?" the General Secretary asked quietly. "How have our aircraft carriers fared?"

"The carrier *Liaoning* is heavily damaged, sir. Our admirals recommend that we abandon her at sea. They fear that if we bring her into port, she could sink in the harbor."

The cost of doing business when that business is war, the Minister thought. We have three more aircraft carriers in the shipyards now.

"The carrier *Shandong* went down with all hands after a massive counterattack by the American Navy. The carrier *Hainan* has orders to remain inside the Strait of Taiwan."

The Minister interrupted. "I was not informed we had changed military strategy. The last order from this committee was for the carrier *Hainan* to sail north to engage the Americans. The coalition forces are no threat to us. They will not dare attack Taiwan Province once it is part of China."

The Vice Chairman acted as if Fei had not spoken. "In light of recent developments in the land battle," he said, "the Central Military Commission recommends we pause hostilities to assess our options."

The Minister could scarcely believe what he was hearing. Assess their options? They had the most powerful navy in the history of the world on its knees. One more battle would break the back of the United States Navy, perhaps for an entire generation, and the generals wanted to assess their options?

The Vice Chairman continued in a stronger voice. "The weapon deployed by the Americans in Hualien appears to be a micro drone with the ability to distinguish between friendlies and hostile soldiers on the battlefield. In the opinion of the Committee, the use of this weapon has called into doubt a successful outcome for the entire invasion."

Minister Fei had had enough of this defeatist talk. "The United States deployed a small-scale weapon in a tiny corner of a very large island, and you want to give up the fight? Our generals are only hours away from signing the Taichung Accord. Victory is ours, comrades. Do you not see this?"

"I was not finished with my report, Minister Fei," the Vice Chairman said. "There's been a second attack."

The Vice Chairman took out a Shandian tablet from his inner pocket, unlocked it, and threw a video clip to the large flat-screen at the end of the table.

The Minister's attention was divided between the video and the fact that the Vice Chairman had a Shandian tablet. He had not authorized one of the battle network devices for the man. In fact, besides himself, the only person in the room who was authorized a tablet was the General Secretary. That was deliberate. The Minister had to be able to control the flow of information to his colleagues.

Yet, the Vice Chairman had somehow managed to secure one for himself.

The only person who could have authorized a new user on the Shandian network was the General Secretary. Minister Fei's train of thought was distracted by the video screen.

The scene looked like it was taken from a surveillance camera outside a hotel. A group of four PLA soldiers in uniform stood on a street corner. Civilians passed by them in groups of two and three.

There was no sound on the video, which made what happened next somehow more terrifying. The soldiers crumpled to the ground like puppets with cut strings. A teenaged girl nearby screamed, holding her hands to her face in a silent pantomime of fear.

Blood seeped from the soldiers' bodies onto the sidewalk. A civilian who had been walking behind one of the soldiers when the attack happened also fell. A bright red stain spread across his white T-shirt, and he clutched his shoulder.

"We have video clips like this from all over the city of Kaohsiung in southern Taiwan," the Vice Chairman said. "It clearly shows a weapon that is capable of distinguishing between civilians and military personnel in a multitude of settings. It also demonstrates an aggressor who is willing to use this weapon. We have reason to believe that the Americans will attack the signing ceremony of the Taichung Accord."

He looked back at the Minister. "We had no report from our comrades in the intelligence section that this weapon even existed, much less that it had this level of capability. Furthermore, our assessment of President Serrano's willingness to use every tool at his disposal was flawed from the start.

"For this reason, the Central Military Commission recommends we reassess our options regarding the emergency in Taipei."

"When did this attack happen?" the Minister asked. He felt his breath coming in short, sharp gasps. He tried to focus his mind on this problem, but his thoughts remained scattered.

"Nearly two hours ago," the Vice Chairman said. He took his seat, tapped a cigarette out of a package, and lit it.

The Minister resisted the urge to take out his Shandian tablet and check for updates. An attack of this magnitude would have sent the device into overdrive on alerts.

Maybe my tablet is damaged, he thought, or needs a new battery. Focus, you fool. You already know how to deal with this problem.

He sprang out of his chair.

"The Americans have finally done it, comrades," Fei said. He heard himself speaking as if from a distance. He sounded heated and rushed.

Calm down, he told himself. Make your argument.

"The Americans have used a weapon of mass destruction in Taiwan— not once, but twice! This is a war crime. There is only one possible answer to this atrocity."

The Minister gripped the back of his chair and stared down the table at the assembled committee.

"Tactical nuclear weapons," he said. "Take out what remains of their fleet. Destroy their ground forces. This action will reset the global balance of power for good."

His eyes raked across the members of the People's Committee for the Reunification of Taiwan. He looked for an ally and saw none. His last stop was the General Secretary himself.

"Don't you see, comrades," the Minister said. "This is not a setback. This is a gift."

The General Secretary looked up and nodded slowly. The Minister's heart quivered with anticipation.

But he wasn't looking at the Minister. He was looking past him.

The Minister turned. The door to the room had opened, and two military policemen entered.

The General Secretary stood, which forced the rest of the room to their feet. The scraping of chairs ended, leaving a stony silence.

"Minister Fei," he said. "Thank you for your service."

AFTERMATH

60

The Kremlin
Moscow, Russia

Russian President Vitaly Luchnik considered his options carefully.

In a perfect world, the United States and the People's Republic of China would have destroyed each other on the battlefield of Taiwan, but this was not a perfect world.

Not a bad world, he reasoned, but not perfect. Still, for the first time in a very long while, he had options. Real options.

Luchnik shifted his gaze from the intelligence report on his desk to the man who had delivered the report to him. Vladimir Federov, head of the FSB and his most trusted confidant, shifted in his chair. Federov was many things, but he was not a man who fidgeted.

"You have something to add, Vladimir?" Luchnik asked. "An opinion on the matter?"

"These are the same people who tried to bury you, Mr. President." Fedorov spoke in a soft voice that seemed too high for a man of his size. "It would look like rewarding bad behavior."

"The enemy of my enemy is my friend," Luchnik replied. "Do you not agree in this circumstance?"

"I do not, sir."

Luchnik walked to the tall window overlooking the courtyard. It was already getting dark. In Moscow this time of year, it sometimes seemed like the darkness never ended.

The lights were on in the courtyard below. He watched the breath from the guards freeze in the air like plumes of smoke.

Federov was right, of course. The Chinese had tried to screw him over —and they had very nearly succeeded, too. Ironically, it was the American president who had saved him and averted World War Three. He had misjudged the American. Serrano's fortitude in the fight against the Chinese had been unexpectedly ruthless. If the reports of the drone swarm weapon were accurate, Serrano was not a man to be underestimated.

And yet, Luchnik was considering renewing his fight against the Americans.

New battlefield, he thought. Same battle.

He let his eyes stray to the map of the Russian Federation that took up a whole wall in his office. He had put it there to remind himself of his duty to the *Rodina*, the Motherland.

When the opportunity presents itself, it is my duty to seize it with both hands.

"Set up the call," Luchnik said. "A video call, as soon as possible."

It took nearly an hour to connect Luchnik with the General Secretary of the Chinese Communist Party.

Luchnik studied his counterpart with a careful eye. They had sparred before. Depending on the circumstances, his Chinese opposite was a formidable ally or a brilliant strategic opponent.

But no match for Serrano, Luchnik thought with a sense of smugness.

On that famously inscrutable face, Luchnik detected the subtle signs of stress. A sag in the skin under his eyes, a deepening of the creases around his mouth.

"I should be very angry with you, Mr. General Secretary," Luchnik began. "But today I find myself in a forgiving mood."

"What happened between our two countries over the last year was not sanctioned by me," the Chinese leader replied. "I have dealt with the perpetrator. You should know that."

The gall of the man, thought Luchnik. Impressive.

"But you didn't hesitate to use your advantage when you had it, did you?" Luchnik snapped. "You even asked for my assistance to keep the Americans busy in the North Pacific."

The General Secretary shrugged but had the decency not to smile. "When opportunity knocks, it is my duty to answer the door."

The Chinese leader changed the subject. "Your help with the Americans was greatly appreciated, but I fear the tactical situation has changed for the worse. I have decided to withdraw from the province of Taiwan. For now."

There it was, in plain language.

Luchnik felt a surge of hope. His intelligence was correct, which made the timing of this call nothing short of perfect.

"I would like to purchase something from you, Mr. General Secretary," Luchnik said. "Something of great value."

"I hardly seem to be in a position to bargain," the Chinese leader said. "What can I offer?"

"Time," Luchnik said. "I would like to buy time."

The General Secretary's eyes narrowed. His lips bent in a humorless smile. "Now who is looking to take advantage of the situation?"

"When opportunity knocks," Luchnik said, "it is my duty to answer."

The Chinese man laughed, and Luchnik joined him. He felt a lightness, an inner giddiness that comes when a risky plan coalesces in a single moment.

"Your withdrawal from the island of Taiwan will take time," Luchnik said. "I am sure it is a very complex logistical problem."

"That is true." The General Secretary nodded gravely.

"Perhaps you could extend that withdrawal time," Luchnik said. "Shall we say, thirty days? I would be willing to pay for that."

"And what would be the currency of your payments?"

"Rebuilding is an expensive proposition, sir," Luchnik said, "and your credit in the world is poor. China will be hungry for natural resources. Russia has plenty of oil and gas at preferred pricing for our partners."

The General Secretary shook his head. "Serrano will continue with his damned privateer operations until the last PLA soldier has left Taiwan. I cannot do what you ask."

"Thirty days," Luchnik pressed. "No more. Arm your commercial ships, delay negotiations. You know how quickly the American public loses interest in foreign affairs. Serrano will be under political pressure, and his attention will be elsewhere. Grant me this time. You will not regret it."

The General Secretary looked off screen and nodded curtly before turning back to Luchnik.

"Agreed," he said finally. His shoulders sagged. "What are you going to do with the time you've bought?"

Luchnik smiled, for real this time. "Do you know what happens when opportunity knocks on a locked door?"

"I do not, sir."

"I break down the door."

61

Brilliant sunshine flooded the White House Rose Garden. Although Don had forgotten his overcoat again, he didn't even miss it on this abnormally warm February afternoon. He took his assigned seat in the front row.

Don measured time in hours now, not days. In the thirty hours since the Chinese and the American forces had stopped shooting at each other, the pace of activity had not slackened.

The National Security Advisor had split the NSC into three working groups. The Secretary of State's team opened negotiations with the Chinese over terms to end the hostilities. The Secretary of Defense ran the team dedicated to reinforcing the US military still in the region. Don headed the team that analyzed every trace of intelligence looking for any sign that this latest move by the Chinese was another feint.

Although he had not been back to the Sentinel Holdings site in days, he still received regular reports from Manson Skelly about Operation Lynx. The President insisted that until the PLA had abandoned Taiwan, the privateer operation would continue.

Oddly insistent, Don thought, as if he had a personal stake in the outcome. And maybe he should. Without Sentinel Holdings, the United States would not have stopped the PLA in Taiwan. The privateer operation and Project Cicada were both key pieces of their success, there was no doubt about that.

In his scant free moments, Don looked for any sign of Janet and Mark in the intel reports. Yesterday, he'd spoken with the captain of the USS *Idaho*.

"I'm sorry, Mr. Riley," Lannier said. "My ship was attacked by multiple PLA subs before we arrived at the rendezvous. We barely made it out alive."

"And you've heard nothing from Janet?" Don asked.

"No," Lannier said.

Twelve hours later, the captain called Don back. "There's been a development," he said. "The *Orca*, that's the unmanned submarine drone, has returned."

"Is that bad?" Don said.

Lannier sighed. "It's not good. If the *Orca* loses contact with her control vessel, she goes into a seeker pattern for a set period of time. If there's still no contact, the *Orca* executes an RTB."

"RTB?" Don asked.

"Return to base," Lannier replied. "In this case, the *Orca* was programmed to drive to a safe area clear of contacts and send a message back to SUBPAC. An hour ago, the *Orca* phoned home."

"Can she tell us what happened to the *Manta*?" Don asked.

"We're downloading the logs from the *Orca* now," Lannier said. "As soon as I know something, you'll know it." He hesitated. "There's one other thing."

"What?" Don said.

"The *Orca* is missing a torpedo from her inventory."

Don suddenly felt guilty about enjoying the warm sunshine of a Washington, DC, afternoon. His train of dark thoughts was broken as President Serrano emerged from the West Wing. The assembled crowd surged to their feet, and Don joined them.

Every seat in the Rose Garden was filled, mostly reporters with a few staffers sprinkled in here and there. He spied White House Chief of Staff Irving Wilkerson taking a seat in the last row of chairs.

Serrano had the Secretaries of Defense and State in tow. He strode up to the lectern and opened his leather folio. He smiled and gestured for everyone to sit down.

The President was camera-ready. He was freshly shaved, and it looked to Don like his hair had been trimmed as well. His gaze was bright, and he balanced lightly on the balls of his feet as he waited for quiet.

He won, Don thought, and he wants everyone to know it.

"Since my State of the Union address to Congress was delayed this year due to unfortunate global events"—the line earned him a soft laugh—"I wanted to take this opportunity to address the current state of affairs between the United States and the People's Republic of China.

"This afternoon, I am announcing a formal cessation of hostilities with China. You will all get copies of the press release, but here are the main points." His expression hardened.

"The People's Liberation Army will evacuate the island of Taiwan completely over the course of the next thirty days. To ensure compliance, the United States Navy and our coalition partners will remain in the region. The 101st and 82nd Airborne Divisions as well as the Third Marine Expeditionary Force will serve as security until the Taiwanese military can be reconstituted. Under the leadership of Secretary of State Hahn, we are in active discussions with the Chinese over reparations for their hostile acts against a US ally."

Don noticed Hahn winced at the word *ally*.

Serrano continued: "We expect those reparations to amount to hundreds of billions of dollars, which will be used to offset the cost of this needless conflict. To ensure a speedy conclusion to the negotiations, the privateer effort on Chinese commercial shipping will continue until a final agreement is reached." He closed his leather folio.

"As I said, you will all get the press release. I'm happy to take a few questions."

He called on the reporter from the *New York Times*.

"Mr. President, you mentioned just now that the Chinese were being punished for hostile acts against a US ally. Does this mean that the One China doctrine and the long-standing US policy of strategic ambiguity are over?"

Serrano stepped away from the lectern and indicated Hahn should take the question.

The Secretary of State cleared his throat and leaned into the microphone. "There is no change in our diplomatic relationship with the People's Republic of China. The One China doctrine is still the official policy of the United States."

The reporter wasn't willing to give up. He raised his hand. "Follow-up, sir."

Hahn nodded reluctantly.

"So was the President's use of the word *ally* incorrect, or should we expect the United States to back Taiwanese independence in the future? With all due respect, Mr. Secretary, saying we will all return to the status quo after we just fought a war over Taiwan seems out of synch with reality."

"I stand by my previous comment," Hahn said, his lips pressed in a firm line. "The US will evaluate each diplomatic situation on the individual merits and take action accordingly. The Chinese invaded the sovereign territory of Taiwan, and the President took the action that he felt was appropriate at that time."

Don had to admire the way Hahn tossed the diplomatic word salad, but he got the secretary's meaning: under a different president, we might have had a different reaction.

The reporter tried again, but Hahn stepped away from the microphone to show he was done with that line of questioning.

"Mr. President," asked the next reporter, "can you talk about the use of armed drones in this conflict? We're getting reports from the field that anti-personnel drones were used. Some experts characterize these drones as a weapon of mass destruction. Can you comment on the implications for future warfare?"

Serrano gripped the edges of the lectern.

"War is a messy business," he said. "It's ugly. It's destructive. But sometimes it is necessary. When a new weapon is available that can shorten a conflict, a president is asked to make hard calls about when and how that weapon is used. President Truman made that choice in World War Two. I made that choice in the Taiwan Conflict. What's more, I would do it again."

"Can you talk about the development history of this weapon, sir? We have sources that say that this weapon was not tested by the Department of Defense before it was deployed."

"You need better sources, then," the President said. "Next question."

"Can you talk to us about the privateer operation against Chinese commercial ships? What is the scope of that operation? And how much can the United States hope to recoup in war expenses from that effort?"

"I think someone here can answer that better than I," the President said, surveying the crowd. For a moment, Don thought Serrano was looking at him, but then there was movement behind him.

Abby Cromwell walked up to the lectern. Her hair was twisted into a French braid, and her navy blue sheath screamed DC power broker.

"Good afternoon, my name is Aberdeen Cromwell," she said. "I am the CEO of Sentinel Holdings. My company was awarded a Congressional letter of marque against the People's Republic of China. While the exact details of our operation are classified, the United States government will get a portion of the proceeds from the sale of the captured prizes."

"Our information is that your company has taken hundreds of Chinese ships as prizes," the reporter pressed. "Is that correct?"

Abby offered a plastic smile. "The classification of this operation is determined by the government, not by my company. We operate in accordance with the law."

A reporter called out from the back of the crowd. "What about Cicada?"

Don craned his neck to see a heavyset man with a beard.

"I'm sorry," Abby said, "who are you?"

The man gave his name. Don did not recognize him.

"I have a source that claims the anti-personnel drone swarm used in Taiwan was developed by your company, Ms. Cromwell. Is that true?"

"I'm not at liberty to discuss that, sir," Abby replied.

"Are you planning on using the money from the seized Chinese ships to expand your operations? Develop even more weapons?"

Abby stared the man down. "Sir, I think the President said it best: war is ugly and messy, but sometimes it's also necessary. I would add one thing to that list. Sometimes governments can't handle all of that work themselves. When that happens, Sentinel Holdings is a willing partner. We are patriots, and we are ready to help our country do the right thing in the world."

"So, you're mercenaries?" the man pressed.

"The United States Air Force hires hundreds of contractors to fix their airplanes," Abby replied. "The military uses contractors to build facilities and serve meals and do laundry and all of the other thousand things needed to support a fighting force. We are just one more extension of that supply chain."

The questions moved on, but Don's thoughts did not. He'd witnessed the place that Sentinel Holdings occupied in the national security establishment. If Manson Skelly was to be believed, the company would walk away with hundreds of billions of dollars in profit. How many more projects like Cicada were they developing? How much of that money would end up lobbying Congress for an even larger role in the next conflict?

Most of all, Don worried that Abby was right. National security decisions were messy. Sometimes it was easier to outsource that decision to somebody outside of elected government. Let someone else take out the garbage.

Abby's candid remarks set off a new round of questions, but Serrano took the podium from Abby. "Thank you all for coming this afternoon, ladies and gentlemen, and be sure to watch my State of the Union speech next week." He smiled and waved. "God bless our troops, and the United States of America."

The February sun seemed to have lost its warmth for Don. As he stood, his mobile phone buzzed with an incoming text. It was from Captain Lannier:

We found them.

62

---

60 miles east of Taipei, Taiwan

By order of Rear Admiral Sharratt, all burials at sea in the *Enterprise* strike force were conducted every day at noon local time.

For the first few days after the cessation of hostilities with the Chinese, the entire strike force came to all stop and colors were displayed at half-mast as every ship conducted their own services. On one still day, Sharratt recalled hearing the rifle salute from the guided missile destroyer a thousand yards off the *Enterprise*'s starboard quarter.

But now, more than a week later, only the *Enterprise* conducted noon services. Most of the dead were stored in freezers across the strike force. The bodies would stay there until the ships returned to port, where they would be given a dignified transfer.

But there was a small percentage of sailors who had opted for burial at sea. Although Sharratt didn't remember it, there was a checkbox on some Navy pre-deployment form that let sailors opt for an immediate burial at sea in the event of their death.

According to the legal officer, the practice had grown in popularity since the Battle of Hualien, as the engagement with the PLA was being called in the media. He reported a line of sailors outside of Legal Services every day seeking to change their last will and testament to include immediate burial at sea.

Today there were three flag-draped bodies on the fantail of the *Enterprise*. Sharratt checked his notes. One Catholic, a Muslim, and Protestant. Each faith had their own practices and sacred words, which the Navy was scrupulous about following.

Sharratt had long ago given up on organized religion, but he rather liked the words from the Protestant Book of Common Prayer. He listened as the chaplain said them:

We therefore commit his body to the deep...in sure and certain hope of the resurrection of the body, when the Sea shall give up her dead.

The casket bearers tilted the hinged panels on which the bodies rested. The remains of the sailors slipped out from beneath the flags and dropped to the ocean below.

With the religious portion of the service complete, the military ceremonial machine took over.

The bugler raised his instrument to his lips, and the mournful notes of *Taps* filled the air.

Sharratt felt the familiar tremor of emotion begin in his right hand, which touched the brim of his cover in a salute.

So many dead, he thought, and so young. The index card in his breast pocket gave the details of the three sailors from today's ceremony. None of them had reached their twenty-fifth birthday.

The seven-person rifle team came to attention.

"Firing party," ordered the officer in charge. "Fire three volleys."

The rifles snapped to a precise forty-five-degree angle in perfect unison.

"Ready, aim, fire."

The crack of seven shots rang out over the sound of the bugler.

"Aim, fire!"

Crack!

"Aim, fire!"

Crack!

The rifles remained at the ready until the last notes of *Taps* died away.

"Order arms!"

The rifle team moved as one.

Each flag was folded by the respective casket bearers and presented to Sharratt. He accepted them, placed them on a small table. They would be carefully packaged and sent to the next of kin along with a personal note from the commander of the *Enterprise* strike force.

How many notes had he written already? Sharratt wondered. So many. Too many.

Sharratt breathed a sigh of relief as the ceremony ended. He was anxious to return to the crush of work. Staying busy was a welcome distraction, the only thing that kept him sane.

As the *Enterprise* got underway, the breeze across the flight deck freshened. Sharratt paused to let the brisk wind buffet his face, dry his eyes.

He entered the island of the ship and climbed to the solitude of the flag bridge. Sharratt stripped off his Service Dress Blue jacket and tossed it across the railing of the treadmill. He snatched up a pair of field glasses and focused on the horizon.

A cluster of three ships sprang into view. All three flew the crimson flag of the People's Republic of China. They were salvage ships, hovering over the wreck of the aircraft carrier *Shandong*.

The *Enterprise* strike force had been successful in their attack on the PLA carrier.

Three direct hits with advanced Harpoon missiles, an array of Naval Strike Missiles, and a brace of torpedoes from a *Virginia*-class submarine had finally sent the mighty vessel straight to the ocean bottom with all hands.

How many sailors had died in the two minutes it took for the *Shandong* to sink? he wondered. Three thousand? Four thousand? More?

Sharratt found his brain still had difficulty with that math. He had just buried three sailors at sea. If he conducted the same ceremony every day for three years, he would not account for the number of sailors who had perished on the *Shandong*.

I did what I had to do, he thought. And it was true. Given the same circumstances, Sharratt would issue the same order without hesitation and seek the same result.

His emotions ran just below the surface these days. He was not ashamed of what he'd done, but he wasn't proud of it either.

It was...necessary.

A knock on the door interrupted Sharratt's reverie. He put down the binoculars.

"Come," he called.

Tom Zachary entered carrying a tablet. He wore a broad smile.

"What's up, Tom?" Sharratt said.

Zachary handed him the tablet with the latest message traffic.

"There's a P4 message for you, sir. I think you'll like it."

Sharratt read the message, then reread it.

"Congratulations, sir." Zachary's grin widened.

Sharratt said nothing. He handed the tablet back.

"A second star and a promotion to Seventh Fleet. That's worth celebrating, Admiral," Zachary said. "I have to say, I thought you'd be happier."

Sharratt looked past his chief of staff to an F-35 on final approach. The aircraft disappeared from view below the windowsill, and he heard it contact the flight deck with a solid *thump*. Flight operations still continued day and night. The work never stopped.

Sharratt cracked a smile. "So did I."

63

Beijing, China

Gao inspected himself in the full-length mirror of the waiting room. He'd paid a rush fee to have the Type 07 dress uniform tailored so he could wear it for this appearance.

He smoothed the forest-green material against his stomach and straightened the gold buttons so the insignia all lined up perfectly on his centerline. The field of medals over his left breast now included two Medals of Loyalty and Integrity for both times he had been wounded in battle.

His fingers traced the still-healing scar across his jawline from the American's knife blade. It twisted when he smiled. Gao thought it made him look dangerous.

Finally, he brushed invisible lint from the epaulets of a colonel in the People's Liberation Army. He'd gone into the invasion of Taiwan as a lowly major and emerged from the conflict a full colonel.

He tucked his barracks cap under his right arm and turned to admire himself in profile.

I look good, he thought. Like I was made for this uniform.

There was a knock at the door.

"Come," he called.

Mei Lin, the young enlisted woman who had once served as General Zhang's receptionist, entered. Like him, she was wearing a full dress uniform.

"Colonel," she said with an admiring smile at his new uniform, "they're ready for you."

Gao nodded. "I just need one more moment, please."

As she closed the door behind her, he turned to face the mirror again. This time, he did not see the scars or the medals or the shiny gold-threaded epaulets. He saw only his fear.

"You can do this," he said to his reflection. "You have to do this. There is no other way."

He touched the scar. The puckered skin felt rough under his fingertips.

Here is your Hero of Hualien, he thought. Afraid to face his own reflection.

Another knock at the door. "Sir?" Mei Lin's voice.

He turned from the mirror, snatched open the door, and stepped into the hallway.

The camera crew was waiting and began filming as soon as the door opened. Colonel Gao kept his face stoic, his bearing ramrod straight, his steps measured.

This level of the Great Hall of the People was located below the grand auditorium where the Chinese Communist Party held their massive meetings, but it was no less grand.

The rich red-and-gold carpet muffled his steady footfalls. The white walls were covered in Parisian-style raised panels, studded with brass light fixtures and small paintings of pastoral Chinese landscapes.

The hallway opened to a foyer where there were more people, some in uniform, some in dark suits, but all looking at Gao. He felt a whisper of anticipation ripple through the room at the appearance of the star witness.

He stopped in front of a set of double doors and executed a textbook-perfect right face. His heels clicked together as he stood at attention. Gao's gaze flicked to the guard, and he gave a curt nod. The guards each gripped a door handle. On a soft command, they pulled the doors open.

Gao marched in, head high, shoulders back, every centimeter a loyal warrior of the People's Republic of China.

It was thirteen steps to the seam on the carpeted floor. In rehearsal, he'd been instructed to stop at that point and present himself to the military tribunal.

Gao came to a halt, saluted. His injured right arm twinged with pain, but he kept his face still. "Colonel Gao Yichen, reporting as ordered."

The panel comprised two general officers and one Party official, the Vice Chairman of the Central Military Commission. The man fiddled with an unlit cigarette. "Enter the witness box, Colonel," he said.

As Gao took his seat, he cast a glance at the docket. It was the first time he had seen General Zhang since the invasion.

Zhang also wore his Type 07 dress uniform, but it was not tailored and had not been pressed recently. The general had lost weight, and there were dark circles under his eyes.

His gaze locked with his former subordinate.

Gao had spent sleepless nights wondering what this moment would be like. Would the general look at him with disgust? Accusation? Rage?

Gao did not expect to see the deep sadness that he found in his former mentor's eyes. He looked away.

The questioning was conducted by a PLA major who looked a few years older than Gao. He was lean and hawkish in his appearance and seemed well aware of the camera placement in the room.

"Colonel Gao, please explain your role during the American attack on the city of Hualien."

"General Zhang directed me to monitor the actions at General Ho's command post. We were located on the eastern slope of Mount Nanhua on the Qingshui Cliffs," Gao said. "From this vantage point we were able to assess the American position as well as the PLA advance down the coast from Taipei."

"You were at the front?" the major said in mock surprise. "But you were gravely injured, were you not?"

"That is true," Gao agreed. "I was wounded in action twice in my pursuit of the Taiwanese rebels. Still, I was happy to do my duty for my country. When General Zhang sent me to the front, I did not hesitate."

"And what did you see during the attack by the Americans?"

"The US had no heavy armor and few soldiers. They attempted to stop our advance at the tunnels, but the PLA ground forces broke through. We were on the verge of complete victory." Gao paused. He had rehearsed how to deliver the exact right mixture of empathy and fortitude at this point in his testimony. He cleared his throat and frowned.

"And then what happened?" the major prompted.

"The Americans attacked our forces with a weapon of mass destruction. It was an anti-personnel weapon, some sort of micro drone. Everyone at the command post was killed. I managed to avoid the drones." Gao let his voice break.

"What did you do next?"

I panicked, you fool, Gao thought. But out loud, he said, "My first thought was to warn General Zhang of this new weapon. Our communications were being jammed by the Americans, so I moved away from the front as quickly as possible to reestablish contact with my commanding officer."

The last was a lie, of course, but there were no survivors to prove him wrong.

His mind flashed on the image of his dead driver. Funny, he could not even remember the man's name, but Gao could not forget the exact pattern his blood spatter made across the upholstery of the SUV driver's seat. He recalled pulling the dead man's body out of the car, the frantic ride down the narrow dirt road to the highway, and kilometer after kilometer of dead PLA soldiers.

Bodies everywhere. The roads clogged with abandoned vehicles and sprawling corpses. It had taken him nearly an hour to weave in and out of the idling vehicles. If a body lay in the road, he just drove over it.

And then the carnage ceased, as if someone had drawn an imaginary line in the road. On one side of the line was Armageddon and on the other side, life.

Of course, the soldiers untouched by the American drone attack had abandoned their posts. The road was clear all the way back to Taipei.

"At that point, were you beyond the American electronic jammers?" the major asked.

Gao nodded. In reality, he had kept the accelerator pressed to the floor for kilometers until he tamed his own terror, but that inconvenient fact did not fit with the desired narrative.

"I reported to General Zhang that we had been attacked and there were no survivors," Gao said quietly. "The Americans had broken out of Hualien, and Taipei was at risk. I recommended strongly that he return to Taipei."

"And what did General Zhang do?" the major asked.

"He ignored my report," Gao said in a flat voice.

Out of the corner of his eye, Gao saw the two generals exchange glances.

"What did you do next?" the major pressed. "After General Zhang ignored your first-hand intelligence report from the front?"

"I contacted General Wei in the southern command," Gao replied. "I reported the attack to him."

"And what did General Wei do with this information?"

"Nothing," Gao said. "General Wei was killed in the second attack."

The truth was far worse than that. Gao had been on the phone with Wei when the drone attack happened. The connection had been clear enough that he could hear the *Bzzt-SNAP* of the killing drones. He heard the screams, the panic in the general's voice...then silence.

In that moment, parked on the side of the deserted Highway 9, sitting on the blood from his dead driver, Gao had smiled with relief. Everyone who could connect him with the lost Shandian battle network tablet was dead.

He was free.

"Colonel," the major was saying, "what is your opinion of General Zhang's actions on the battlefield?"

At this point in the script, Gao was supposed to resist the major's question.

"General Zhang was my commanding officer," Gao said.

Across the room, Zhang's eyes narrowed. Gao wondered if the general had figured it out. It had taken several nights for Gao to understand the full meaning behind the public trial of General Zhang.

This public shaming was not the way things were handled in China. In normal times, a person was assigned blame for a failure and the person simply disappeared. There was no public notice, no news stories. History was rewritten in real time. The scapegoat and the failure vanished, never to be spoken of again.

But these were not normal times, Gao came to realize.

The Party was not at fault—the Party was never at fault. Members of the Party had been led astray by rogue elements, people like General Zhang and Minister Fei. The Minister had disappeared a week ago in the normal manner. All trace of his existence had already been scrubbed from the public record.

The invasion of Taiwan had awakened a streak of rebellion in the people of China. Massive demonstrations were taking place in Tiananmen Square. People all over the country wore red ribbons around their necks in protest.

Gao didn't pretend to understand the protestors, but he understood what the men in power were trying to achieve. The Party walked a tightrope. If they cracked down too hard on the demonstrators, they risked disapproval on the world stage at precisely the moment they needed it most. If they acted too gently, they risked their own political future.

A public trial with a public villain was the third way. Convince the people of China and the world that this was all a big mistake, the result of a failure inside the ranks of the People's Liberation Army.

If Zhang was the devil in this play, then Gao was the savior. A handsome, twice-injured war veteran who had warned his commanding officer of the imminent danger. As a direct result of General Zhang's arrogance, thousands of soldiers had perished.

If only there were more brave leaders like Colonel Gao, the story went, the future of the People's Republic of China would be limitless.

The major's voice brought all these thoughts to a screeching halt.

"Colonel?"

Gao's mouth was dry. He didn't think of himself as a liar. The lies had started as tiny seeds, but they had grown into mighty trees that blocked out the sun and thrust him into darkness.

I can end it all here, he thought. Tell the truth. Begin again.

Gao could feel Zhang's eyes boring into the side of his face. He picked up the glass at his right hand. The surface of the water quivered in his grip. He took a swallow.

"Can you repeat the question?" Gao said.

The major stepped closer. He sniffed the air as if smelling Gao's fear and uncertainty. His voice was like ice.

"Twelve thousand eight hundred ninety-two brave soldiers of the People's Liberation Army died on a single day. What is your opinion of General Zhang's actions on the battlefield?"

Gao looked to his former mentor and met his gaze. The scar tissue on his jaw throbbed.

"Reckless and cowardly," Gao said. "He is a disgrace to the uniform."

64

Yokosuka Naval Base, Japan

Navy waterfronts had a smell all their own. Even in Japan. A whiff of diesel, a touch of rotting seaweed, the sharpness of fresh paint. To Janet, it smelled like home.

Her new uniform was uncomfortable. Since returning to Yokosuka, Janet had bought some new clothes to wear until she could reclaim her belongings from the *Idaho*. Although she had washed and ironed them the night before at the Combined Bachelors Quarters, working khakis never fit right until they'd been broken in. The new black uniform shoes pinched her toes.

Janet rubbed at the gooseflesh on her bare forearms. She'd decided against buying a new working jacket, and now she regretted that decision. The overcast sky looked like pooled lead, and a rainy mist shrouded the submarine pier of Yokosuka Naval Base. The precipitation made the stained concrete slick under her feet and amplified the smells of the moored warships.

A forklift piled high with pallets of supplies trundled down the pier, forcing Janet to step to the side. When the forklift passed, she saw the *Idaho*.

The fast attack submarine was moored in the last berth, closest to open water, facing back out to sea. Her sleek black hull emerged from the dark water like a predator.

Janet breathed, and the knot of tension in her chest loosened.

She fought back a wave of emotion. She'd been told multiple times that the *Idaho* had made it out of the East China Sea unscathed, but there was a difference between being told a thing and seeing the thing. Her rational brain chided her for overreacting, but she didn't care.

Pull yourself together, she thought. Get your stuff and get on the plane.

Janet squared her shoulders, marched across the steel brow, and saluted the flag on the stern of the *Idaho*.

"Request permission to come aboard," she said to the petty officer of the deck.

"It's good to see you back, ma'am," Petty Officer Jenkins replied. "We missed you. I'll let the captain know you're here."

Janet started to tell him that wasn't necessary, but she stopped herself. There was no way she was going to get off the boat without talking to Captain Lannier, so she might as well deal with that first.

She descended into the sub through the forward hatch and made her way to the captain's stateroom. The door was open, and Lannier looked up from his desk. Janet could not read his expression.

"Everett, come in," he said. "Have a seat." He shut the door and turned his armchair to face her. In the tiny cabin, their knees were only a few inches apart. The worry lines around Lannier's eyes had deepened since she'd last seen him.

He studied her face. She felt her cheeks grow warm under his scrutiny. "How are you doing, Janet?"

"I'm just back to pick up a few things, sir," she said. "I have to fly back to Pearl tonight. For the inquiry."

"Yeah," Lannier said, "I'm told the Navy doesn't like it when you break their stuff." The joke fell flat, and he scowled. "Sorry, that was in poor taste."

"It's fine, Captain," Janet replied. "I don't mind. I'm not much fun to be around right now, I know. The whole thing is pretty..." Janet searched for the right word and came up empty.

"I understand," Lannier said, then paused. "No, I take that back. I don't understand." He leaned forward, elbows on knees, and his voice took on a new intensity. "Tell me what happened, Everett."

"I'm not supposed to talk about it, sir."

"Fair enough." Lannier leaned back. "You know I've seen the data logs from the *Orca*, right? I've been doing this submarine thing for quite a while, and although I don't have a second-by-second analysis, I have a pretty good idea what happened."

Janet looked past him to a spot on the wall.

"If I'm right," Lannier continued, "then the fact that we're sitting here at all is thanks to you. But for your actions, this ship"—he stamped his foot on the deck—"and every sailor on board would be at the bottom of the East China Sea."

"You make it sound dramatic, sir," Janet said. "It was more...it was more impulse, I think."

"Impulse or instinct?" Lannier asked.

"Honestly, I don't even know anymore." She felt her voice getting shaky.

To her surprise, Lannier reached across and put a hand on her shoulder. "You can talk to me, Janet. I'd like to help, if I can."

Janet took a deep breath, trying to organize the tornado of thoughts in her head.

She gave up and just started to talk. She recounted hearing the underwater telephone communications, how she'd heard the fathometer of the PLA submarine and gone up to investigate.

Her words spilled out. Janet felt like she was talking way too fast, but she couldn't help herself. Lannier watched her, nodding every few seconds.

"It was a *Shang*-class, sir," she said. "The same one that had been tracking us. I'm sure of it."

"They figured out our pattern," Lannier said. "We were driving into a trap."

"I knew there was at least two of them," Janet continued. "I put the *Orca* into a search pattern. I thought if I could get a position on them, I could..." Her voice trailed off. She shrugged. "Then it all went to shit."

"What happened?" Lannier prompted her gently.

"I—we—heard the *Idaho*'s pinger," Janet said, feeling the panic of that moment in the back of her mind. "God, it all happened so fast. The second PLA submarine launched a torpedo at you, and I knew what they were doing. As soon as you returned fire, the *Shang* would have your position and the *Idaho* was dead."

"What did you do, Janet?" Lannier pressed.

"I locked onto the hull of the PLA sub with the docking magnet. I wanted to distract them. Then I lit us both up with active sonar from the *Orca* and..." Janet couldn't go on.

"You launched a torpedo on yourself," Lannier finished.

Janet nodded. She felt her eyes burn with unshed tears.

"It's dumber than it sounds, sir. The *Orca* was only twelve hundred yards away. The torpedo had a lock as soon as it left the tube. I disengaged the *Manta*. I thought if I got far enough away, we could survive the explosion."

"How long were you down there?" Lannier asked quietly.

"I'm not sure," Janet said. "Ten, maybe twelve hours. Long enough for the atmosphere in the *Manta* to turn poisonous. Mark...Mark was in bad shape. It took everything I had to get him out of there."

"How is Captain Westlund doing?" Lannier asked.

"I haven't seen him yet," Janet said. "I'm headed over to the hospital as soon as we're done here. I owe him that much."

"He's alive because of you, Janet," Lannier said. "Every person on board this ship is alive because of you. Remember that."

"I should get going, sir," Janet said. "I have to catch my flight."

Lannier stood and held out his hand.

"I was wrong about you, Everett," Lannier said.

Janet shook his hand. "No, I don't think you were, Captain."

By the time Janet left the pier, the mist had thickened to fog. Cars loomed out of the ghostly white background and disappeared again.

After the close confines of the submarine, she was glad for the anonymity of the weather. Her seabag hung heavily on her shoulder. She'd taken everything she owned off the *Idaho*, not knowing for certain when— or if—she'd be back.

The rumor mill on the *Idaho* had taken sketchy details about the incident with the *Manta* and turned it into a full-blown legend. She smiled, shook hands, and left the boat as soon as possible. None of them asked about Mark.

Janet crossed Halsey Boulevard on her way to the other side of the base. All the streets here were named after famous naval heroes: Halsey, Nimitz, King, Decatur. Once upon a time, she had wanted to be one of them. Now, she wasn't sure what she wanted.

The fog collected on her skin and ran down her cheeks like tears. She walked slowly, dreading the upcoming visit, but all too soon the Yokosuka Naval Hospital took shape in the mist.

The blocky, five-story building was separated from the water's edge by McCormick Street and surrounded by neatly trimmed shrubs and carefully tended grass. The white stucco was gray with moisture.

Janet got Mark's room number from the information desk and rode the elevator up to the fourth floor.

Mark had a private room overlooking the harbor. His door was open, and she could see he was sleeping.

I'll come back later, Janet thought, secretly relieved.

Mark's eyes opened, and he saw her.

The swelling on the side of his face had gone down, leaving multicolored bruises under his skin, especially near the sutures around his temple. The whites of his eyes were blood red.

He pointed at her seabag. "You planning on staying? I know we spent a lot of time in close quarters, but I just feel like it's too soon to talk about moving in together."

Janet forced a smile. "People say I'm an acquired taste."

"I can vouch for that."

Janet entered the room and set down her seabag. "How are you feeling?"

"I'm a little banged up, but I'll be back on my feet before you know it." He grimaced. "Okay, that's a cliché I'm going to have to stop using."

Janet tried to stop herself and failed. Her eyes went to the bottom of his bed. The bedclothes were flat below his right knee.

"Does it hurt?" she blurted out. "I'm sorry. That's a stupid question."

"It's weird," Mark said. "My brain tells me I can still feel my toes, but I know they're not there. The doctor says it's phantom limb syndrome. He says it'll go away, but right now it's really freaking me out."

Janet sat in the chair next to his bed and took his hand.

"I'm so sorry, Mark." She'd promised herself she wouldn't cry, but apparently she'd left her self-control in the fog outside.

"Are you kidding me?" Mark said. "I'm alive because of you. Besides, how often do you get a chance to save a hundred and twenty people in one day? You made the right call, Janet. It was worth it."

Not to me, Janet thought. Not to me.

"Has Don called you yet?" Mark asked.

Janet shook her head.

"He called me this morning," Mark said. "Said I was welcome back as soon as I'm able."

"Are you going back to Emerging Threats?" Janet asked.

Mark looked at the murky gray outside his window. "I think so. I like it there, even though Ramirez is a total pain in the ass."

Janet laughed and wiped her eyes.

"What about you?" Mark asked.

"I'm headed back to Pearl tonight," Janet said. "For the inquiry." She smiled. "Navy doesn't like it when you break their stuff."

Mark laughed. Janet realized she just reused Lannier's joke, and now she was laughing, too.

"You know," Mark said, "they used to talk about you back at ETG like you were Saint Janet. Hell, I was half expecting someone to erect a shrine to you in the break room."

"They haven't set that up yet?" Janet said. "I told them to put it next to the vending machines since that's where I ate most of my meals."

"Don't make me laugh," Mark said. "It hurts."

"Sorry," Janet said.

"I was jealous of you," Mark continued in a serious voice, "but now I see it. They were right. When it came time to make the hard call, you did it. You didn't hesitate. If I'd been in the pilot's seat, I don't think I could've done it."

Janet gripped his hand.

I took the action, she thought, but you paid the price.

65

Minneapolis-St. Paul Airport, Minnesota

Delta flight 1244 touched down on the Minneapolis runway at 5:52 p.m.

Don peered out the window of his economy-class seat at the back of the plane as the rest of the passengers got to their feet and began to open the overhead bins. It was dark outside, and his phone told him the outside temperature was hovering in the mid-twenties Fahrenheit. A few soft flakes sifted down from the dark sky.

The two vodka tonics he'd treated himself to on the flight up from DC had done little to improve his mood and much to amplify his headache.

He waited until the aisles were clear, then retrieved his roller bag and his folded suit jacket from the overhead compartment. The dark suit was the nicest clothing he owned, and he was glad to see the jacket was unwrinkled.

Whatever gesture he was trying to make here, it was important that he look his best.

From the tall windows on the C concourse, Don could see the hangar of the Minnesota Air National Guard where he needed to go. He had time to kill, so he walked slowly up the concourse, avoiding the people-mover walkways, following the signs to taxis.

The guard at the gate for the Minnesota Air National Guard didn't know what to make of Don's CIA identification. Don patiently explained that he needed access to the Air Guard main hangar to meet a plane arriving at nine p.m.

"You're kinda early, sir," the guard said.

"I'll wait in the hangar," Don replied.

"The hangar's open. It'll be cold in there."

"I'll be fine," Don said.

It turned out he didn't have to wait that long after all. A gunmetal gray C-130 arrived less than ten minutes after Don began his vigil in the windswept hangar. He watched the plane park on the tarmac a hundred feet away. The propellers spun to a stop. The side door opened, and stairs extended.

General Nikolaides walked down the stairs.

Don got to his feet as the Chairman of the Joint Chiefs strode into the hangar, followed by six beefy young men sporting precision high-and-tight haircuts. They were all dressed in civilian clothes. Each carried an overnight bag and a hanging bag used for uniforms.

General Nikolaides wore a Dress Blue wool overcoat and snow-white barracks cap used for his most formal uniform set.

Nikolaides pointed to the back of the hangar. "Find a place to set up back there, gentlemen. Be ready to go at ten minutes to nine," he said.

"At 2050, aye, sir," replied the first Marine.

"Riley," Nikolaides said. He peeled off a glove and shook Don's hand.

"Sir," Don replied.

A full minute passed as both men looked at the floor, the ceiling, out the door, and back to the floor. Finally, Don broke the silence.

"What are you doing here, sir?" Don asked.

"I could ask you the same thing, Riley."

True enough, Don thought.

The silence deepened.

"I think I misjudged you, Riley," the general said. "I thought you were a computer geek."

"I *am* a computer geek, sir," Riley returned.

Nikolaides laughed, a hearty belly laugh, and Don felt the tension between them evaporate.

"That's true. You are a helluva geek, but you're more than that. The work you did with the Chinese situation. We were just chasing our tails, and you figured it out. That was damn fine work."

"I appreciate that, General," Don said.

"My friends call me Adam," Nikolaides said.

"Adam, then," Don said.

"I think our working relationship has a short shelf life, Don, but I enjoyed our time together."

"I don't understand."

Nikolaides barked a laugh. "I serve at the pleasure of the President. I don't think my commander in chief and I see the world through the same lens." He sighed. "Probably for the best. To misquote some philosopher whose name I've forgotten, I believe war should be nasty, brutish, and short. But, when necessary, it should be fought by men and women in the service of their country. What we have now is drones fighting drones, and when we can't use drones, we fill in with contractors."

He paused. His tone was not bitter, Don decided, but resigned.

"We're living in a different world, Don," he said. "I can't say if it's better or worse, but I do know one thing: it's not my world. It's not one I understand, and that means it's time for me to move on." Nikolaides laughed, a real laugh this time. "Besides, after our boss finds out I was here, he'll probably fire me on the spot."

Don's response was interrupted by the arrival of two cars. One was a hearse and the second a dark SUV. The rear door to the passenger vehicle opened, and Liz Soroush stepped out.

She wore a long, dark overcoat and a cream-colored silk scarf. Liz hurried across the hangar floor and wrapped Don in a tight hug.

"Don." There was a sad break in her voice that Don recognized. He hugged her back. He felt that same sadness in himself.

She broke the embrace and held him by both hands. Liz studied his face.

"You look like shit, Riley."

Next to him, Nikolaides laughed.

"You look great," Don replied. "Happy."

And she did. Liz's face had thinned with age, and there was a shine of silver in her dark hair, but she was beautiful. She cocked an eyebrow.

"Why are you here?" she asked.

"I came to see you." Don tipped his head at the general. "I don't know about him."

A second woman emerged from the back of the SUV. She was taller than Liz and slim, with chestnut-brown hair drawn back into a French braid. Her brown eyes were dry, but the whites of her eyes were red from recent tears.

Don approached and held out his hand. "Mrs. Lester, my name is Don Riley."

Up close, Don could see in her gaze the sharp pain that comes from the sudden loss of a loved one. He knew that feeling, the way the grief hovered in the background, ready to punch through the façade of control at any moment.

Maureen Lester hugged him. Her thin frame quivered with nervous energy. "I know who you are, Don," she said. "Liz told me all about you. Thank you for coming."

Don released Maureen Lester and turned to introduce the Chairman. Nikolaides extended his hand.

"My name is Adam Nikolaides, ma'am, Chairman of the Joint Chiefs and a proud Marine. I'm here to honor your husband."

Don felt his throat close up. The general had tears in his eyes.

"I don't understand," Maureen said. "I thought Michael's death was a civilian accident."

Nikolaides looked at Don. Don looked at Liz. Just as he opened his mouth to speak, a Gulfstream 650, guided by an Air National Guard ground crew, approached the hangar. The whine of the jet engines filled the frosty air as the sleek aircraft rolled into the hangar. As the engine noise faded, the ground crew chocked the wheels, closed the hangar doors, and departed.

The rear cargo door on the Gulfstream lowered.

"Don," Liz whispered. "Look."

He turned to see the six Marines who had arrived with Nikolaides. The young men, now outfitted in Blue Dress "A" uniforms, stood at parade rest in two ranks of three. In their midnight blue tunics, white gloves, white barracks caps, and blue trousers, they appeared as a perfectly matched unit.

"Adam," Don said, "what's going on?"

"Ma'am," Nikolaides said to Maureen. "These young men are from Marine Barracks Washington, 8th and I, Bravo Company, better known as the Body Bearers. With your permission, they will take care of your husband's remains."

Maureen Lester nodded, unable to speak. At a nod from the general, the Marines marched out of sight around the back of the Gulfstream.

The stairs to the Gulfstream lowered. A young officer dressed in the uniform of a Taiwanese Army captain appeared in the doorway of the plane. Using a cane, he made his way down the steps and toward the small group.

After saluting the general, he went to Maureen.

"Good evening, Mrs. Lester," he said.

"You must be Frank Tsai," she said.

"He spoke of me?" the Taiwanese officer asked.

"Often." Maureen Lester held out her hand. "We never had children, but from the way Michael talked about you, I think he thought of you as a son."

Don saw the man's lip tremble with emotion.

"I am alive today because of your husband," Captain Tsai said. "Gong-gong saved my life twice—"

"Gong-gong?" Maureen asked.

"It means grandfather," Tsai said. "It was his nickname with our unit."

Maureen smiled through her tears. "I bet he hated that."

"He tolerated it," Tsai said.

"Tell me how Michael died," she said.

Tsai looked at Nikolaides, who nodded. He spoke haltingly at first, then found his words. For the first time, Don heard what really happened on Mount Chuyun. Tsai told them how Lester carried Captain Tsai to safety, then used the PLA battle network tablet to draw Chinese forces away from the retreating Taiwanese Shadow Army. He told them of the days spent on

Mount Chuyun searching for Lester and finding his body. He paused, and his face twisted into a scowl.

"My government wishes to keep the existence of the Taiwanese Shadow Army a secret from the Chinese," Tsai said. "They fear the publicity if Gong-gong's true activities were made public."

Maureen's gaze cut to Nikolaides. "Is this true?"

"Yes, ma'am," the general said. "There's been a deal."

"I agreed to stay silent as long as they allowed me to accompany the colonel's body home," Tsai added.

"But all this," Maureen said. "The Marine honor guard."

"That's on me, ma'am," Nikolaides said.

"Thank you," Maureen said, her hands reaching for Tsai and the Chairman. "Thank you both."

"I think we're ready, ma'am," Nikolaides said.

From the rear of the aircraft, Don heard a soft command. Nikolaides came to attention, as did Captain Tsai.

The flag-draped coffin of Colonel Mike Lester, borne by six Marines, came into view. The two officers in uniform saluted. Don and Liz put their hands over their hearts.

In precision slow march, the honor guard conveyed their charge to the open door of the hearse.

Don felt his own heart beat strong under his fingertips. He sensed the swirling emotions in himself and from the people around him.

Sadness...pride...heartbreak...gratitude.

They lived in a wonderful world, but a dangerous one, filled with shifting alliances and threats. A world made less dangerous by the sacrifice of brave people like Colonel Michael Lester.

The door of the hearse closed, a dull thud. The two officers dropped their salutes. Liz's hand found his and squeezed.

Don returned the gesture. He knew she was thinking of Brendan, her husband and Don's friend, who had made the same sacrifice for America. Although Brendan had been gone for years, the feelings felt raw and fresh in this moment.

"These young men will be staying in the area for the funeral, ma'am,"

Nikolaides said. "Unfortunately, I will not be able to attend the ceremony. I'm needed back in Washington." He looked at Don. "We both are."

Maureen nodded. "I understand." She took Captain Tsai's arm and led him to the waiting SUV. "You'll be staying with me, Frank. I insist."

Liz kissed Don on the cheek, then hurried after them. The general walked over to the Marines, leaving Don alone.

The hangar doors opened. The hearse departed, followed by the SUV.

Snow, driven by the wind, swirled across the concrete apron. Don walked toward the open door, pausing where the light from the hangar made a sharp line on the dark ground.

He felt the bite of the cold in his throat. His exhalations smoked in the night air.

Don Riley snapped up the collar of his overcoat, thrust his hands into his pockets, and stepped into the darkness.

ORDER OF BATTLE
Command and Control #3

A conflict in Ukraine threatens to escalate into a global power struggle between the United States and Russia.

When mercenaries attack in eastern Ukraine, the world is thrust into turmoil. Russian President Luchnik is quick to respond, launching a full-scale military invasion to quell this "national emergency" in the former Soviet country.

The United States, reluctant to put boots on the ground in yet another regional conflict, takes a different path. President Serrano hires Sentinel Holdings, a private military contractor, to hold back the Russian threat.

Don Riley, head of the CIA's Emerging Threats Group, sees trouble ahead. The Russian President is hungry for power, and he's got the military might to back up his grand ambitions. The Russian attack in Ukraine is the first move in a much larger campaign that will redraw the map of Europe.

Unfortunately, a war-weary President and his closest advisers decide Riley's input is no longer required. Instead of worrying about his career, Don Riley does what he does best.

Figuring out his enemy's end game. Before it's too late.

Get your copy today at
severnriverbooks.com/series/command-and-control

ACKNOWLEDGMENTS

Writing a book is a solitary event—or in our case, a duet—filled with stops and starts, bouts of energy, and hours of *uh-oh, what do we do now?* when we realize that we've written ourselves into a corner.

Eventually, the writing ends and the real work begins. This second part is a team effort to help us get our story ready for primetime. It's a big team.

Our sincere thanks to the Severn River Publishing crew for all the hard work they've invested in us over the last year. In an industry long on talk and short on execution, the SRP team stands out as true professionals. To Andrew Watts, Amber Hudock, and Catherine Streissguth, we offer a special shout-out, knowing full well that these three are only the tip of a very long spear.

Thanks to developmental editor Randall Klein and copy editor Kate Schomaker for helping us hone our story and our manuscript into the work you read today.

When we start a new book, we are always surprised to find out how much we *don't* know about our chosen subject. To fill in those ~~chasms~~ gaps, we draw on technical experts. Special thanks to Pete Bruns, Cami Bruns, Doug Baden, Mark Canning, and Captain Stephen "Baron" Beck von Peccoz, USN (Ret.). A special acknowledgment to Commander Jim Ronka, USN (Ret.), for his extensive recommendations on the *Counter Strike* manuscript.

Of course, any technical oversights in the story are ours alone.

For the *Command and Control* series, we sometimes use the names of friends as characters. While these are all people we respect and admire, that didn't stop us from torturing them on the page. Thanks to Mike Lester, Captain Chip Sharratt, USNR (Ret.), Lieutenant Colonel Alex Plechash,

USMC (Ret.), Henry Schumacher, Chris Bentley, Doug Baden, and Mike Harder.

To Jennifer Schumacher, David's sister and always willing First Reader, a special note of gratitude for her unwavering support.

Lastly to our families for taking this writing journey with us. Seven years and counting! Melissa, Christine, Cate, and Alex, we love you.

ABOUT THE AUTHORS

David Bruns

David Bruns earned a Bachelor of Science in Honors English from the United States Naval Academy. (That's not a typo. He's probably the only English major you'll ever meet who took multiple semesters of calculus, physics, chemistry, electrical engineering, naval architecture, and weapons systems just so he could read some Shakespeare. It was totally worth it.) Following six years as a US Navy submarine officer, David spent twenty years in the high-tech private sector. A graduate of the prestigious Clarion West Writers Workshop, he is the author of over twenty novels and dozens of short stories. Today, he co-writes contemporary national security thrillers with retired naval intelligence officer, J.R. Olson.

J.R. Olson

J.R. Olson graduated from Annapolis in May of 1990 with a BS in History. He served as a naval intelligence officer, retiring in March of 2011 at the rank of commander. His assignments during his 21-year career included duty aboard aircraft carriers and large deck amphibious ships, participation in numerous operations around the world, to include Iraq, Somalia, Bosnia, and Afghanistan, and service in the U.S. Navy in strategic-level Human Intelligence (HUMINT) collection operations as a CIA-trained case officer. J.R. earned an MA in National Security and Strategic Studies at the U.S. Naval War College in 2004, and in August of 2018 he completed a Master of Public Affairs degree at the Humphrey School at the University of Minnesota. Today, J.R. often serves as a visiting lecturer, teaching national security courses in Carleton College's Department of Political Science, and hosts his radio show, *National Security This Week*, on KYMN Radio in Northfield, Minnesota.

You can find David Bruns and J.R. Olson at
severnriverbooks.com/series/command-and-control